DIARY

of a

HERETIC

A novel by

Ross Stein

Publisher, Copyright, and Additional Information

Diary of a Heretic by Ross Stein published by Gray Area Press

This book is a work of fiction. Names, characters, places, incidents, and dialogue are products of the author's imagination or are used fictitiously and are not to be construed as real. Any resemblance to actual events or locales or persons, living or dead, is entirely coincidental.

ISBN- 9798985716207

rosssteinbooks.com

Cover design and interior design by Rafael Andres

Prologue

*July **, 1935*

Al Valentine had an appointment to keep.

He lay on the bed in his little room at l'Hôtel de Cyprès. Overhead, the chipped blades of a squeaky fan wheeled slow, lazy circles across a cracked plaster ceiling.

Not unlike the hands of a clock, he'd thought to himself when he'd first checked in. A divot in the plaster, no bigger than a thumbnail, lay just outside the radius of the spinning blades. He used this as an hour mark from which to start counting the revolutions, the thing emanating a muted creak once per cycle. It was an unconscious habit, marking the passage of time in such a way. He'd been doing it for years.

Al Valentine knew a little something about time.

The actual clock in the room, an opalescent hemisphere of blue frosted glass adorned with doves, a favorite motif of Lalique, rested upon the mantle over the unlit fireplace. It was an excellent specimen of the Frenchman's superior skills in timepiece design.

The face of that clock read 3:24 a.m. Outside the shuttered window of his room at l'Hôtel de Cyprès, the city of Damascus slept.

❧

But Al Valentine did not sleep. He could not sleep. Not with his appointment to keep. Though the peace of a clear windless night lay over the city like a blanket and the shimmering stars of the vast vault of the heavens continued their slow wheel across the sky, Al's thoughts raced along like the second hand of a stopwatch with monomaniacal precision.

"Through the market gate," he mumbled to himself. "Left at the third junction. Six stairs, right, then four. Fifteen paces from the east wall. Five oh four a.m. precisely."

Al Valentine knew a little something about precision.

He repeated the instructions to himself over and over and over as his eyes turned slow circles in their sockets, locked on the tip of one spinning blade, absently noting the passage of time as it swung lazily past the divot in the plaster—*midnight, noon, midnight, noon, midnight*—while in his fingertips, Al worried a curious object. The desk manager of the hotel had taken special note of it when he'd checked in a week earlier: a remarkably beautiful gold pocket watch emblazoned with fiery rubies and icy sapphires describing the serpentine curves of a snake on its cover. On the reverse, cut diamonds arranged in a fleur-de-lis. This watch, too, like the Lalique on the mantle, now ticked away the hours, minutes, and seconds till his appointment.

Al took a slow breath, then another. With care, he made to calm his nerves by synchronizing his respiration to the repeated squeaks of the fan—*in, squeak, out, squeak, in, squeak...*

But his attempt failed, and his thoughts raced onward.

❧

Back home in Philadelphia, family and friends had thought him mad. What allure could a trip to the Orient at his age possibly hold?

"You're no spring chicken," Dr. Hirsch had told him. "At seventy-five, the stress of an ocean voyage could be fatal. Have you considered the heat? Palestine isn't exactly Pennsylvania. And what about food? I mean, what will you even eat in the desert? Do they even know the definition of kosher?"

"I will eat what they eat," was Al's simple reply.

Kosher or no, it was the fascists Al's nephew Oliver worried most for.

"It's not as if they will just let you through, *Onkel*," he'd said. "Do you even read the papers anymore? Do you have any idea what they're doing to Jews over there?"

"What they do to us now has been done to us before," Al had said, "and will be done again. But where I have to go, they will not stop me. I am just one old man, and, God willing, He will see me through to my destination."

❧

The hour struck four. Time was rapidly becoming of the essence.

Dr. Hirsch had been right. Even at this early hour, the heat was oppressive. Al rose from the bed. His shirt, damp with sweat, clung to his aged frame. He changed it for a fresh one and lifting his spectacles, patted his sticky face with a handkerchief. In the mirror, he straightened his tie. Smoothing out the white wiry hairs of his bushy eyebrows and mustache, he suddenly became trapped in the image of his own reflection. Like a man tracing the lines of a mountain range across the face of a map, his gaze drifted over the wrinkles and crevices of his forehead and the shadowy ravines framing his mouth. His cheeks had sunk and drawn with age, making his nose look bigger. His ears seemed bigger too, and droopier than usual, as he gently tugged at a lobe and let the loose skin slip from his fingertips. Time, as it does with everything, had left its mark on Al Valentine. But his tired face still bore a faint rosiness, and there were still yet remnants of once youthful vitality in the sagging corners of his eyes that surfaced when he smiled.

A smile that had first attracted Zofia.

Drawing back the shutters, Al gazed out over the flat, dusty rooftops of the city still fast asleep under the predawn sky. Random puddles of yellowed light dotted the alleyways below, but the rest was darkness. By the silvery-blue light of a pale waning moon, he could just make out the three towering minarets of the great Umayyad Mosque silhouetted like guardian sentinels against the desert night.

A third-floor room, that's what he'd wanted, so he could keep the mosque in sight day or night. When the manager had suggested a man of Al's advanced years might be infinitely more comfortable with a room on the ground floor, Al said simply he'd been climbing up and down stairs from his home to his watch shop every day for the last forty years. What was another week to one old man?

He could have taken much more luxurious quarters such as to be found at the Biet Oriental or even Palmier Doré, but old-world sensibilities had kept him a man of simple means. The extravagance of a spit-and-polished, gilded hotel room with velvet curtains, buckets of imported champagne, and smartly appointed bellhops waiting at one's beck and call never appealed to Al. The Cypress, with its whitewashed walls and threadbare Anatolian rugs, would suffice. Frugal by nature, he shunned eccentricities. Indulging purely for indulgence sake was to surely invite envy, feed greed, and evoke false pride.

Al Valentine knew a little something about sins.

You see, Al Valentine had been waiting patiently for ten long years to see that very mosque on that very day, that very morning, in fact. His journey across the sea by ship, over hill and mountain and valley by rail, across the sweltering desert to the ancient city, inhabited by man for longer than there had been recorded history, had been all but preordained. No longing to see the sites of antiquity had brought this old man to Damascus. No law pursued him; no malignant past nipped at his heels. He took no refuge from the oppression of some despotic tyrant, nor was he impelled by the will of a higher power, though it could be said his trip was indeed a pilgrimage of sorts.

None of these things had driven Al Valentine from his comfortable workshop in Philadelphia, across the ocean and over two continents, to this humble room lying in the shadow of the great temple to the god of the desert peoples.

Destiny had brought him there. Destiny and a promise.

Al closed the shutters and turned back to the bed. He remarked the enamel face of his watch: 4:05 a.m. Time pressed ever forward. The hour of his appointment was close at hand.

Beside the chiffonier stood the Hartmann steamer trunk he'd purchased in New York. A necessary expenditure for the voyage, it had stayed with him while he crossed the Atlantic by Cunard liner, stopping first in Cornwall, then passing by ferry to Calais, then overland by rail to Paris, Hamburg (with an extra day's layover to pay a visit to the graves of his mother and father), Budapest, and Belgrade. At Athens he caught another ship to Haifa on the western shores of Palestine before finally taking the Al-Hejaz Railway, which skirted the northern shores of the Sea of Galilee, to Damascus.

Al donned his coat and hat. From the top drawer of the open trunk, he retrieved an envelope bulging at its seams with crisp new French francs and a thick, travel-worn brown leather-bound notebook. These he tucked securely in the pockets of his suit, patting both in their place several times as if to reassure himself they'd not been forgotten.

Then he pulled out a third item, a little brass box of curious yet intricate design, and stowed it in his pocket.

Finally, he drew the fine gold and jewel-encrusted watch from his vest pocket and gave the stem a few extra turns for good measure, though, in truth, Al never dared let the thing wind down to a stop, not even for an instant. Not in ten whole years.

Again, he observed the time: 4:10 a.m. Time to leave.

❧

Al shuffled down the three flights of stairs to the lobby. The desk clerk was nowhere to be seen, and the Hotel Cypress's lone night bellhop, a boy of sixteen in wrinkled dishdasha and sandaled feet, slumbered curled up in a high-back wicker chair beside the front desk. No one would witness the old man slipping away.

Old Damascus was a tangle of narrow alleyways, covered bazaars, low stone arches, and gritty dirt lanes rutted from horse carts and sporadic auto traffic. Overhanging *mashrabiya* walled him in at every turn. Walking in the shadows of the buildings, an amalgam of the old, the older, and the very old, the most ancient constructed of just dried mud, the naive tourist might not help but feel all the more the rat blindly fumbling through the labyrinth.

But Al did not feel as such. He'd walked this route before, every day since he'd arrived in the city, sometimes four or five times a day. Twenty-three times in all, just to be prepared.

Al Valentine knew a little something about being prepared.

Thirty-five paces to the double arch, then right at the green awning. Second left after the Nazari garage...

Maneuvering deftly for a man his age, Al navigated this dark morass of lanes and alleys with deliberation and single-minded purpose. Crossing an intersection of two passages, a panting mongrel tied to a post inside a nearby courtyard threatened with a low growl, but the old man moved on unabated. Up above, behind wooden shutters on the second floor of a home, he heard the clanking of plates being laid. Through another window, the crying of an infant echoed down the lane. Damascus was slowly waking up.

Up the stairs, through the gate, straight across Al-Hariqah Square...

Al emerged from this maze of byways in the shadows of the ruins of the Temple of Jupiter, fragments of its towering colonnade the only remaining traces of that place of worship and sacrifice to the ancient thunder god. He paused to look again at his watch: 4:37 a.m. Beyond the ruins loomed the fortresslike western wall of the Umayyad Mosque.

Up the lane, an Arab man dressed in the Western trappings of an impeccably tailored cream-colored suit and crimson fez gingerly approached. Parked behind him was a dirty covered truck, the name *Al-Bega Imports, Haifa,* stenciled in white on the driver's door. Beside the truck, four men in dusty *thawb* and sandals waited, quietly mumbling among themselves.

"*Bonjour*, Monsieur Valentine," he said.

"Mr. Sayid," Al greeted in reply, taking the man's elegantly manicured hand in his own.

"It is good to see you again," Sayid said. "As you can see, we are here at the appointed hour as agreed upon."

"I am grateful," Al said.

Smiling a wide, toothy grin, Sayid turned on his heels and clapped his hands furiously, barking commands in a language foreign to Al's ears, unceremoniously ordering his men to work.

"You did not have any trouble making your way, I trust? Damascus can be a confusing place to one who has not had the pleasure before."

"No, sir, no trouble," Al said. "I see my package is still intact?"

"But of course, monsieur," Sayid assured. "For a client such as yourself, I spared no expense in ensuring your item was handled with the utmost care. Haifa to Damascus direct. As you can see, as promised, I am personally overseeing all arrangements. I have brought four of my strongest men for the job. You might even say your package was *guaranteed by Sayid*. Ha! What do you think of that? I hope you do not mind my taking a liberty with your own bon mot. But you see, after reading it on your calling card, I simply could not help myself."

"Not at all. It's very fitting and should serve you well." Al smiled. "Then there will be no problem moving my item to its appointed place?"

"None at all. Of that, you may rest easy. However, I must admit my contact inside was a bit reluctant initially to agree to such an unusual request. As such, how shall I put this delicately? He demanded of me, let us say, a more *substantial* contribution, which had the unfortunate effect of ever so slightly increasing my expenses. This was *most* unexpected, I can assure you, and I did my utmost to arrange a price that, hopefully, would be equitable to all parties involved. I sincerely hope, monsieur, you do not take offense at my negotiating on your behalf?"

"Money is no issue," Al said as he watched the workers at the rear of the truck. "I am prepared to compensate you for your trouble."

"Excellent! Excellent, Monsieur Valentine. I never harbored any doubt at all you were a man of the utmost discretion in such matters. And now, with that nasty bit of business behind us, if you are ready, my men are ready as well, and we can begin."

Sayid escorted Al up the street, where he could more closely observe the work. A delicate ballet played out, with Sayid's four associates carefully maneuvering a large item out of the truck bed and onto a waiting cart, the operation made more difficult by the unusual dimensions of the cargo in question: a single wooden crate, eight feet by five feet by two feet. Though not an awkward shape, the box proved quite heavy, requiring the men's full strength to support. For his part, Sayid flitted about their robes like a mosquito, whispering commands in Arabic and reassuring Al repeatedly with a wide smile that the utmost care was being taken not to damage the precious cargo within.

The package finally unloaded and secured to the pushcart, the little group set off up the cobbled lane toward the mosque, a funny funerary parade with Sayid in pristine white suit in the vanguard, four peasants bearing a coffin-size crate like pallbearers in the middle, and a lone slouched old man bringing up the rear, the grieving widower.

Al glanced again at his watch: 4:46 a.m.

❧

The Bāb as-Sāʾat, the great western gate, loomed ahead; two enormous doors of bronze framed by blocks of white marble crowned by a half-moon arch of blue and green stained glass. The doors stood unexpectedly closed. Sayid nervously looked at Al, then nervously checked his watch, then smiled a nervous little smile, and laughed a dry, nervous little laugh. His contact, his *well-paid* contact, was late.

"*Pardon*, monsieur," Sayid said to Al, then, turning abruptly, he rapped once on the hard metal doors, paining his knuckles in the process. Garnering no response, he beat heartily on the door several times until the clank of a heavy latch sounded from within, and slowly, one large door pulled open.

There inside stood a bleary-eyed, mustached fellow. Heavy eyelids suggested he'd been rudely roused from a blissful sleep just inside the doorway. He and Sayid exchanged a few curt words, the substance of which Al deduced revolved around the necessity of leaving the pushcart behind. This hiccup didn't matter to Al, who again checked the time. The mu'adhdhin, however, would be calling Damascus to morning prayer in exactly twenty-three minutes. That mattered a great deal.

Sayid clapped his hands vigorously, barking commands to his men. Obediently, they hoisted the cargo upon their shoulders and carefully shuffled their way inside. Under the towering arches of the *riwaq* surrounding the deserted inner courtyard of the mosque, they proceeded until Al signaled they had reached their destination.

The moon hung low, so low as not to be seen for the high walls of the citadel. The sky had lightened to a navy blue with the promise of dawn, and the once numerous stars now numbered but a few dozen.

At Sayid's orders, his men lay open the package with pry bars and claw hammers, taking extreme caution at their foreman's insistence not to damage the goods inside. Al stood a few paces away. He'd taken out the tattered journal he'd brought with him and was reviewing its final pages, intently absorbed in identifying a precise spot along the wall.

"Here," he called to Sayid. "Tell them to put it here."

Sayid clapped his hands. His men finished clearing the last of the loose straw from inside the crate to reveal its single item of content: a large antique mirror situated in an ornate, gilded frame of the rococo style. The glass itself stood taller than a man, nearly seven feet high and almost four feet wide, when they raised it upright.

"*Kun hadhiraan!*" he insisted, commanding his men to take care. "*Kun hadhiraan albalha'.*"

Al identified the spot against the wall where the mirror was to be placed. The work complete, Sayid dismissed his men, who collected their tools and filed rapidly out of the courtyard.

"It would seem, monsieur, our business is now concluded," Sayid said. "With your permission, I will take my leave as well."

"Of course," Al replied and, procuring from his pocket the envelope filled with francs, gave it to Sayid. "Your payment, as agreed upon. You will find a sufficient bonus included as well. It should more than compensate you for your extra expenses and any inconveniences. I thank you for your service."

Sayid smiled, tucked the money discreetly into his breast pocket, bowed humbly, bid Al au revoir, and took his leave.

At the western gate, his bleary-eyed associate followed Sayid out, pulling the door shut behind them, leaving the old man alone in the great, wide space of the courtyard.

Al noted the time: 5:03 am. Time to begin.

❧

All was quiet. Al removed his hat, approached the mirror, and gazed into his reflection.

Ten years, he thought. *So many hours, minutes, and seconds.*

Time is a funny thing. Al had learned as much from years of watchmaking. At times fleeting, at others abundant, it seemed to move slower or faster, crawling now at a snail's pace, now whizzing past like a bullet. One man's second was another man's eternity. Time was measured, weighed, and valued. Time was money. Time was ever present. It had always existed. It simply was, is, and always will be. It marched ever forward.

But there was still a little time remaining.

Ten years I have waited, he thought to himself. To be more precise, as Al was wont to do, it had been exactly ten years, five months, three weeks, four days, twenty-one hours, sixteen minutes, and seven seconds... eight seconds... nine seconds...

Al Valentine knew a little something about time. And he knew there were still fifty-one seconds more to wait.

Inside the Madhanat al-Arus, the minaret of the bride jutting above the northern wall, the mu'adhdhin began his slow climb up the spiral stairs to the tower's balcony, while below, Al removed from his pocket the box he'd taken from his trunk in the hotel.

It was a beautiful case of carved brass, no bigger than the watch Al carried in his vest, its surface inlaid with an intricate gearwork mechanism of cogs, springs, levers, and tiny gemstones. A masterwork of skill and craftsmanship, the thing had no discernable lid, no hinges or clasps where it might be opened. An impenetrable safe for priceless cargo. Only three small holes, nearly invisible to the untrained eye, hinted at a method for entry by key.

That key, a simple miniature clock key, had hung from a chain around his neck for the last ten years. Removing it now, Al carefully inserted the key into one hole, then the next, then the third, winding the box in an order and number of turns known only to him, which set the sophisticated gearworks below the surface in motion. A faint ticking commenced from within the depths of the box, a delicate dance of balance wheels, mainsprings, ratchet wheels, and escapements, all synchronizing their movements, building to a crescendo of whirring clicks and ticks until all the nerves in his body began to tingle and his every muscle tensed. His old heart thumped violently against his ribs. Finally, the ticking ceased with a muted, almost benign, click, and one side of the little case flicked open, precisely fifteen seconds from the last turn of the key.

Inside the box lay a compartment lined in green velvet. Within this compartment lay a folded piece of cloth no bigger than a thumbnail, bluish gray, and stained with a single crimson spot.

The mu'adhdhin's call pierced the sky, dancing across the dusty rooftops and echoing through the cloistered passages of Damascus, shaking the ancient bones of the city to life once again.

"Allahu 'akbar, Allahu 'akbar. Ashhadu an la ilaha illa-Allah."

Al checked his watch: 5:04 a.m. Time was up.

Taking the tiny swatch of cloth from the box, he stepped forward and, like an artist dabbing the final drop of paint on his masterpiece, pressed it gently to the surface of the glass.

The rising sun breached the crest of the great courtyard's eastern wall, casting a wave of pure, bright light against the shimmering face of the mirror. In his trembling fingers, Al still gripped the bloodied swatch of gray cloth. Before him, the image of his reflection undulated and distorted like ripples across the surface of a still lake disturbed by the first falling drop of rain. He watched himself break apart into a thousand ribbons caroming against each other, against the wood of the frame that held the mirror fast against the cold stone of the great mosque's western wall.

But soon, the waves subsided, and the image of himself coalesced. He could see the wrinkles creasing his old face once again and, behind him, the columned feet of the Qubbat al-Khazna, the octagonal Dome of the Treasury standing on its eight stone pillars. Beyond that, the open expanse of the courtyard and the far eastern wall of the mosque. Al stood motionless, fixing his eyes intently upon the reflection.

It came at first as a near-imperceptible dimming over his left shoulder. A momentary bending of the light. Something invisible to the eye yet so vaguely solid, its presence blocking out just one, perhaps two, of the sun's rays.

But slowly, this bending progressed, refracting more rays until the faint outline of a form took shape: the form of a man. Al watched this phenomenon in the mirror's reflection with wide-eyed wonder. His heart stirred to a flurry of excitement as the shape began walking toward him from within the mirror.

- PART I -

Chapter I

December 4, 1925

On Time with Valentine. That's how the little sign read.

It stood propped up between a mahogany and brass 1903 Ingraham mantle clock and an unusually squat, and quite heavy, black marble camelback Gilbert shelf model in the display window of the shopfront for all passing by to see. Scrawled neatly in a woman's flowing script, on a simple white placard adorned at the corners with hand-drawn filigree, it was a familiar sight on the Row.

Behind this display window lay a cramped showroom of clocks, stocked chockablock with Thomas tambours and bronze Ansonia figurine models—some adorned with grinning cherubim, others playing host to frolicking maidens. Beyond these stood shelves of cheap brass carriage clocks in various states of disrepair. The walls played host to the cuckoos, the regulators, and the schoolhouse clocks, each passing the hours with the hypnotic swaying of their pendulums. Exhibited atop a display case was an elegant Badische four-hundred-day anniversary clock under a thin bell of glass, guaranteed to run a full year on one winding, while underneath, inside the case, rows of Ball, Waltham, Hamilton (men's and women's), and Rockford custom-made watches lay on green and white felt cloth: green to accentuate the gleam of the gold pieces, white to complement the silver models. Like wooden Beefeaters, two grandfather clocks, a majestic Luman Watson tall case in tasteful cherry, and a Chippendale mahogany Ellis and Clark dating from 1807 stood solemn watch.

And past this horologic hoard of tickers, timekeepers, chronikers, and chronometers, at a cluttered workbench near the rear storage room, amid piles of empty clock cases, disused movements, and piles of small screwdrivers, hammers, cogs, and levers, sat the owner hard at his craft.

To say Al Valentine kept his nose to the grindstone would be an ill use of the metaphor. In fact, he more often kept his nose to the gemstone, setting tiny ruby and sapphire bearings upon which so much time depended. To say Al worked *hard* would also be doing an injustice to his profession. On the contrary, he always worked patiently, delicately, some might even say piously, at the craft he'd come to love and respect over fifty years spent at his workbench.

❧

The dinner hour rapidly approached. Outside the shop, foot traffic on the Row had all but ceased. The sun hung low in the sky and twilight was not far off. Shabbat would begin soon, and Oliver had not yet returned. But there was little cause for concern. His nephew's increasing tardiness of late, while disheartening, was nothing new. Al had thought his apprentice responsible enough to take on the task of hand delivering specialty repairs to his more respectable customers. It was an extra service no other shop on the Row could boast but his, and it continued to garner respect and repeat business. However, Oliver's lateness aroused his nagging suspicions that the boy's time was being occupied less by work and more by that other pursuit often guilty of ensnaring young men, namely young women.

Al lay aside these suspicions for the moment and returned his attention to the work at hand, putting the finishing touches on a Waltham Riverside 1906 with a sticky mainspring. It wasn't uncommon to spend hours, even whole days, tuning and retuning a movement until it fell into rhythmic perfection. In moments like this when he was alone, he could sit back in his chair and just watch the graceful fluid movement of a job well done. With a few twists of the stem, a veritable ballet of motion, all choreographed by him, commenced for his pleasure alone: a glorious dance of perfectly timed assembles and pirouettes performed with masterful precision on a stage no bigger than a half-dollar.

He closed his work-worn eyes and listened to the music of the escapement keeping time for this mechanical wonder. After a lifetime listening to ticktocks and clicks, his ear had become acutely attuned to the rhythm, the pitch, and the tempo. The slightest deviation from the music never failed to escape his notice. His uncle Gerhort used to call this music, the rapid ticking of metal on metal, the "heartbeat of time." Listening to it gave him infinite pleasure. With this piece, Al knew he had finally achieved nothing short of orchestral perfection.

A dozen pieces in the showroom chimed four o'clock. It was getting time to close shop when the front door swung open with a great flourish and in swept a portly gentleman, gray of hair, in a black Inverness cape and wide-brimmed oil-cloth hat set off with a quail feather. He carried a cane topped with an ivory hound's head and took the long, dramatic steps of an actor on the stage, surveying the shop with a skeptical gaze.

"Can I help you, sir?" Al said.

"Croft," the man replied, not deigning to look at the shopkeeper.

"I'm sorry?"

"My name. James Croft, impresario," he said, old money dripping from his puffy Bostonian lips. Al cringed at every *r* juicily rolling off his tongue. "I'm told this house of horology is one of the finest in this city."

"This I cannot say is false," Al said. "Who was it referred you to me?"

"You're a German," Croft said with some surprise, taken aback by Al's accent, the ancestral remnants of which remained an inescapable holdover from his childhood.

"I was born there, yes."

"A warrior people," Croft dismissed absently, perusing the clocks on display, thoroughly ignoring Al's presence. "Not known to be trustworthy. But renowned for their philosophy."

"I wouldn't know of such things."

Al lingered behind the display case while the strange, rude, and wholly piggish Croft poked and prodded at his stock. The blowhard's shallow disdain was lost on Al, whose calm and genial nature was rarely affected by the insensitivity of others. Time spent concerning oneself with the little inequities of life was, in his opinion, almost always time wasted. And Al Valentine knew a little something about time.

Seemingly satisfied he'd come to the right place, Croft produced a beautiful Hamilton hunter case watch, its cover adorned with an etched cartouche bearing the initials *JC* in the center and an elegant carved laurel wreath surrounding a second cartouche on the reverse inscribed with the motto *tempus edax rerum*.

"Time, devourer of all things," Croft said. "From Ovid. Even Helen, daughter of Menelaus, whose beauty loosed a thousand ships to besiege the great citadel of Troy, could not evade its ravages. I assume you've not read the *Metamorphoses*?"

"This is the story of the man who turned into a bug?" Al said. "I know this story." Croft recoiled with indignant horror.

"There are no bugs in the Metamorphoses, sir. Only the highest degree of wit and erudition. Though Daphne does become a tree and Hecuba a German shepherd. But that is neither here nor there. But no *bugs*, I can assure you."

"Why a German shepherd?"

"Well, maybe not a German shepherd, per se," Croft conceded. "But a mongrel nonetheless. She'd been driven mad with grief and began barking at her captors like a dog, so the gods turned her into one."

"Such a terrible fate," Al said.

"Well, when one loses all hope... Speaking of which, are you able to do anything with this? I'm attending a production of *Hamlet* at the Merriam this coming Thursday evening and must have it. It is, after all, John Barrymore, you know."

"What is wrong with it?"

"How the devil should I know?" Croft said. "It simply won't run. You're the expert. You're supposed to sniff out the issue and resolve it. Remember, it must be finished for Thursday, so I will return no later than Wednesday morning next."

"This won't be a problem," Al said. "I'll get started right away. After all, we can't have you barking like a dog in the aisles."

Croft saw no humor in Al's joke, and, snatching up his cane, he strode to the door before turning back with bravado.

"Until Wednesday, then. I trust the sign in your window is not only for show. If it is, I can assure you teeth will indeed be bared when I return. Good evening."

With that, Croft flung open the door and swept out with another flourish. After the self-styled patron of the arts had gone, Al turned over the Hamilton in his fingers, pondering the curious gentleman's words.

Turning into a dog for grief, he thought. *Who could imagine such a strange thing?*

❧

When he was twelve years old in Hamburg, Al had witnessed a man mugged and nearly beaten to death. Running errands for his uncle, he'd come upon three men in a scuffle on the banks of the Zollkanal in the shadow of an ally near the church of Saint Catherine. He knew nothing of what the dust up was about, only that two of the men were clearly in league against the third. One of the bandits grabbed at his coat while the other struck him repeatedly about the back and head with a wooden cudgel until the man, an older, well-dressed gentleman, succumbed to the blows and collapsed in a heap. Secreted from view, Al could only watch the terrible scene unfold. Lying in the wet dirt, the old man moaned pathetically while his attackers rifled through his clothing, seizing for themselves a purse and watch before running off. The whole affair lasted but a few seconds.

When it was over, the young Al's first thought had been to flee. A sudden feeling horrified him. Having watched the scene play out, had his presence not in some way made him complicit in the crime? Bearing witness to a man's suffering and not interceding gave him over to tremendous gloom, and an inescapable sense of shame accompanied him all the way back to his uncle Gerhort's shop.

Later that day, Al would recount the story to his uncle. Contrary to what he'd expected, the elder watchmaker declared his nephew's actions a mitzvah.

"But I did nothing to help him," Al said.

"Didn't you?" Gerhort replied. "You stayed by his side until others arrived to help. And you told the soldiers what you saw."

"I couldn't stop them."

"What do you think you might have done, hmm? *Diese männer hatten böses in ihrem herzen.* In the face of vicious men whose hearts are filled with such malice, would you have raised your hands to them the same way they did? How would this be more right than what they had done? It is but for God to revenge, and revenge he will. But for you, sometimes the best way to stand against such things is not with your fist but with your heart."

"But I did nothing because I was afraid."

"And God will not reproach you for your fears. Had you stepped in, you might have suffered the same fate as that unfortunate man. That you stayed with him, comforted him, means much. You didn't abandon him in his time of need. This is compassion. And compassion for suffering is what separates a good man from an evil one. A man without love in his heart is lost. Turning our grief into compassion, not being consumed by it, is just one expression of a man's loyalty to both himself and to God. Remember this."

❧

Al did remember, and his life, and peace of mind, had been all the better for it.

But it did nothing to change the fact that Oliver had still not returned. The boy finally arrived, moments before sunset, and hurriedly hung his hat and coat beside his worktable.

"Back later than usual," Al remarked as the young man made a show of straightening his bench. His nephew's capacity for clutter amazed Al. Despite his disorganization, though, Oliver showed a remarkable aptitude for the craft of watchmaking. He'd make a first-rate clockmaker in time, if he could just keep his priorities in order.

"Sorry, Uncle."

"Third time this week."

"I got caught up talking with Mrs. Felsheim. You know how she can be."

"I do," Al said. "And what did you two talk about?"

"Nothing in particular. You know, the usual things."

"No, I don't. What does a young man like you and an *oma* like Gloria Felsheim have to talk about for so long that made you almost late for Shabbat?"

"Well, she asked after you, of course, and Aunt Zofia. Then we got to talking about other things."

"Other things? What other things?"

"You know, other things."

Al looked up from his work, peering over the rim of his spectacles with a familiar inquisitiveness that never failed to stymie even the most accomplished fibbers.

"Well, there was..." Oliver stammered. "She was asking about..."

"It all sounds quite interesting. So, tell me, who is she?"

"She?"

"The girl," Al said, laying aside his tools.

"What girl?"

"The girl you've been meeting while you should be here working," he said. "Or while you should be taking pieces to my customers like I ask you to." Oliver lowered his eyes. Al placed an arm over his shoulder. "I don't need to tell you how important our customers are in this business."

"No, Uncle."

"And this business will probably someday be your business, so please, for both our sakes, try to remember this?"

"Yes, Uncle."

Though twenty, Oliver still seemed a boy in need of fatherly guidance. He was just five when Isaac passed on, leaving Zofia's sister, Maja, "Fat Maja," as Al secretly liked to call her, to raise her three sons alone. Al wasted no time stepping in, taking the youngest under his wing.

"Good," Al said, leading his nephew to his chair and sitting him down. "Now, tell me about her. Do I know her?"

Ollie's face lit up with joy. Indeed, he'd been bursting at the seams to tell anyone, any soul about her.

"Sie ist das schönste Mädchen auf der ganzen welt."

"In the whole of the world? Apparently, she must be as beautiful as you say, if she should cause you to so neglect your duties as of late."

"She has the deepest brown eyes you've ever seen," Oliver went on. "Like the bonbons in Goldbaum's window. And her smile. It could drive away the rain on a cloudy day and bring back the sunshine. Her hair shines like a raven's wing."

"So does this angel from heaven have a name?"

"Ruth."

"Ruth," Al mused. "A pretty name. Mrs. Felsheim has a granddaughter I think with that same name. I met her once before, Asher Lehmann's girl. But that was many years ago now. Wait? Ruth Lehmann?"

Oliver smiled.

"No. Ruth Lehmann, as in Lehmann's Jewelers on Rittenhouse Square? Little Ruthie Lehmann?"

Oliver laughed. "She's not so little anymore, Uncle."

"But how?" Al said, flabbergasted. "How long has this been going on? Where?"

"It's only been a few months. We meet here and there, usually with friends. Ruth didn't want her parents to know. They think she's still too young to be talking to boys. And I didn't say anything because I thought you'd be upset with me."

"What would make you think that?"

"Because Asher is the competition. Well, one of them anyway. I thought you'd think I was, I don't know, betraying you in some way."

"Don't be ridiculous," Al said. "I don't feel betrayed. Surprised, yes."

"Then you don't mind?"

"What's to mind? Who am I to keep a young man from seeing the girl he loves? But you know it's not me you should be worrying about."

"I'll tell Mother. Just not right now."

"I was speaking of Asher Lehmann," Al said. "That man could win an award for *sturheit* if they gave away such things. You've got to be careful."

"And please don't say anything to Aunt Zofia," Oliver pleaded. "We were waiting for the right time. Ruth was going to ask to have me over for Sunday supper. I think Mrs. Lehmann already suspects something."

"She probably dislikes secrets as much as I do."

"We're planning to tell her we're in love," Oliver said proudly. "We've even talked about getting married."

"*Mein Gott*," Al said. "Married? You are barely twenty! And Ruth Lehmann is just...I don't even know."

"She's nineteen," Oliver said.

"And far too young to marry."

"You married Aunt Zofia when you were just twenty-two."

"That was different," Al said.

"How so?"

But Al's mind had drifted for a moment, lost in the memory of *his* first love. He'd no particularly compelling answer for his nephew. Reason failed him now as much as it had then.

Chapter II

Albrecht Wallenstein was born in 1860 in the village of Kaiseraschern on the banks of the Elbe River in the Grand Duchy of Mecklenburg-Schwerin.

His father, a cobbler named Fredrich, died when Albrecht was eight, leaving him and his mother, Alma, to eke out an existence on her earnings as a charwoman, a pittance hardly enough for two.

The decision was swift and without discussion. Little Albrecht would be unceremoniously shipped downriver to Hamburg to apprentice under Fredrich's elder brother, Gerhort. Once destined to follow, quite literally, in the footsteps of his father in the shoemaking business, Albrecht would instead learn the trade of the watchmaker.

Gerhort Wallenstein at that time ran a decent business in clocks and watches in a small shop a stone's throw from the Rathausmarkt. Thin of hair and of slight build, tight-pursed, with a skeptical, reserved air, Gerhort was a man obsessed with his craft, possessing an almost religious devotion to precision and a zealot's fascination with time. The isolated nature of his work suited him to a T, so the sudden appearance of a child on his doorstep proved an unwelcome distraction. Sparing what few coins he could, Gerhort enrolled Albrecht in a local *Grundschule* as a way to keep the boy out of his hair. But after two years, when his frugal nature demanded Albrecht stop wasting his time in school and finally learn a trade, he made the decision to teach his nephew the art of horology.

"You may never be a wealthy man," Gerhort would say to his new apprentice. "But if you are dedicated to what you do and make those who come to you for help certain they have done right by coming to you and no one else, then you can make for yourself a full life. Time is something everyone needs and never has enough of," he would joke, "and that is why they are willing to pay dearly for keeping it in their pockets with them so they will know exactly how much of it they have got left."

It was under Gerhort's tutelage that Albrecht came to develop a great respect for both time and precision.

"Dependability," he went on, "like the slow swing of the pendulum. Watch as it oscillates back and forth, to and fro, rushing and ebbing like the ocean tides. Steadiness, reliability, these are the qualities that make up a good man. Your father had these qualities. And so will you. Your father shod men's feet so they might walk through time. You will help them keep it so they know when theirs has run out."

Albrecht learned all his uncle could instruct on making a living through the business of springs, cogs, and crystals in an apprenticeship lasting six years. His natural aptitude for the craft surprised Gerhort, and through steady encouragement, Albrecht soon mastered many of the techniques employed. In addition to repairing pieces, he aided his uncle in running the shop, arranging deliveries, and keeping the books. This, in turn, gave Gerhort more free time to indulge his real passion, that of timepiece design and manufacture. With a flair for the extravagant and impeccable attention to detail, handcrafted Wallenstein watches soon became sought-after items, and the name synonymous with both elegance and quality throughout the city of Hamburg. The shop grew and flourished.

Years passed, and a growing desire to expand his horizons increasingly began to occupy Albrecht's thoughts. Enjoying his work was one thing, but apprenticeship was not a profession, and he wished to have a shop of his own in America, where so many of his countrymen were proclaiming a new land of opportunity.

In 1876, at the age of sixteen, he told his uncle of his wish to seek his fortune across the sea.

"There is a man I know," Gerhort said. "Yankel Hartenstein, though these days he's calling himself Jacob Hart. This he thinks makes his name sound less Jewish. Why he should want to do this, I do not know. He lives in America now, making watches. I knew him from when we were boys. Your father too. Abel moved the family many years ago. I will write to him. Perhaps he can help you if you are set on going."

By early summer the following year, young Albrecht once again found himself standing at an unfamiliar doorstep, this time of Jacob Hart's watch shop on Sansom Street in Philadelphia.

Hart's Horologic occupied the first floor of a three-story Georgian row house once home to a wealthy family with roots dating back to before the revolution. Abandoned in the late 1850s like many others on the block as Philadelphia's aristocracy began their slow migration to the city's west side,

Hart bought it cheap after the Civil War and took up residence on the upper floor, proudly hanging his sign above the front bay window.

Others quickly followed suit. Over the years, the block between Seventh and Eighth Streets would become home to countless jewelers and gemstone merchants, engravers, tinkers, and appraisers, eventually acquiring the nickname Jeweler's Row, a moniker it retains to this day.

The day of Albrecht's arrival, the Row hummed with activity. Cigar-smoking gentlemen in frock coats and silk top hats with ladies of demure and regal bearing hanging on their arms, their parasols extended to shield delicate complexions from the summer sun, perambulated the streets around the shop with the carefreeness of wealthy folk of leisure. Under the shade trees of Washington Square, a group of children gathered to watch a funny little gentleman mount a wooden velocipede and pedal clumsy figure eights around two gas lampposts. The clomping hoof falls of horses drawing hansoms over the cobbled lane sounded in his ears as Albrecht made his way from the waterfront to Jacob's door—a door propped open to the street to welcome one and all who would peruse the horological paraphernalia on display within.

"You will have to change your name," Jacob told him at their first meeting. "Albrecht Wallenstein is too much of a mouthful for most people. If you're going to get into business here, you'll need something that rolls easier off the tongue, something less Old World, less Jewish. If we put our heads together, no doubt we will come up with something suitable."

And so, in the early summer of 1877, Albert Valentine was born.

For three years, Al worked as Jacob's assistant, living in a small storage room at the back of the shop. The quarters were cramped, but his cot soft, and the corner woodstove kept things cozy in winter. A narrow staircase communicated with the floors above, and a doorway led out to the alley behind the building so Al could come and go as he pleased. For hours, he and Jacob toiled at the business of watchmaking, and Deutsche was their common tongue. When the workday was done, he lay in bed by the light of an oil lamp reading *Tom Sawyer*, Robert Louis Stevenson, and the stories of Edgar Allen Poe to improve his English. On Saturdays, he attended shul. Sundays were his own.

On those days, he put on his suit and joined the crowds promenading the waterfront or the park. Sometimes, if he were feeling homesick for the old country, he would venture farther south to the markets and boardinghouses overflowing with newly arrived immigrant families. Listening to the familiar chatter of German, Italian, Polish, and Dutch as people filed past him on the pavement or catching a whiff of fresh *Roggenmischbrot* or *flaczki* boiling in a street-side pot brought a comforting sense of peace and belonging.

On one of these excursions, on a breezy May morning, his eye caught a most wondrous vision: a moon-faced girl in a simple green skirt and white apron. She stood by a cart of turnips haggling for price with a portly hawker, a woven basket slung over her arm. Al stopped across the lane and instantly became enamored of her natural, provincial beauty. A braided tail of golden-brown locks trailed down between her shoulders from under a babushka patterned with red blossoms tied about her chin, while the singsong manner she employed when speaking with the locals drew the attention of all around her.

She passed from stall to stall, greeting every merchant with an infectious smile they could not but help returning in kind. Al remarked her eyes most vividly: big eyes, bright and happy, round as tea saucers and brown like smoky quartz. When she balked at the price of beets, they flashed with indignation. When she laughed, they positively beamed.

Al followed her the length of the market and back, up and down both sides of the street, before he finally mustered the courage to say hello.

"Sie ist das schönste Mädchen auf der ganzen welt," he told Jacob, dancing about the shop on his tiptoes upon his return. "She's from Katowice, and I tell you today, I'm going to marry her."

Jacob laughed. "They say Silesians have the most beautiful daughters in all the empire."

"I cannot disagree."

"What is this angel called?"

Al's eyes shined. His face lit with joy.

"Zofia."

❧

The courtship was short, and the new love between them strong. By September, they wed. As his gift to his apprentice, and by way of blessing their union, Jacob drew up papers to make Al a junior partner in the business. The increase in income, combined with a little savings, allowed the young couple to take rooms a few blocks from the shop. When Jacob Hart would die some ten years later at the age of sixty-one, Al would take full possession of the business and he and Zofia would move into the apartments above the store, where they would keep house the rest of their days.

Theirs had been a life filled with peace and happiness, but not one without its scars.

Zofia was a good woman—a loving and devoted wife, thoughtful and caring, who would have made an excellent mother had it been Nature's plan. But the stillborn birth of her only son, Henry, when she was just twenty-two would serve as an impenetrable doorway to motherhood. To be sure, they tried and tried again, but all had been for naught. She could bear no child.

Now sixty-three, the time for miracles had long since passed. Mothers should not be made to bury their babies, and though Al never lost faith that God had seen fit to make their lives full and joyful, secretly, Zofia had. But she never resented her husband for keeping true to his faith, the rock upon which stood his belief that all things should happen for a reason, whether or not God had a hand in it. Instead, she'd devoted almost all of her energies into ensuring both she and Al enjoyed their roles as doting *tante* and *onkel* to her sister Maja's three boys, Nathan, Arthur, and, of course, the youngest, Oliver.

Incidentally, it was Zofia's inspiration that created Al's now-famous bon mot. In 1903, she put the sign in the front window proclaiming, *On Time with Valentine since 1887*, and the name Valentine had remained both respected and appreciated as a mark of quality and dependability on the Row for nearly forty years.

❧

"How so, Uncle?" Oliver said again.

Now Al found himself in the same predicament he could only assume old Jacob Hart had. This young man, his promising apprentice, standing before him overflowing with joy at the prospect of taking for himself a most beautiful bride, yet practically just a boy. Al had hoped Oliver's time spent in the shop, learning the craft and trade, was preparing him to slip into the shoes of ownership when the time came. Both of Maja's older boys were already enjoying the fruits of their labors, with Nathan head of his department in the city housing office and Arthur a junior manager in finance. They'd no interest in the watchmaking business. Oliver was really the only hope the shop had of carrying on after Al was gone. This, God willing, was still a way off, but at sixty-five, how many more years could he reasonably count on before it would be time to finally put down his tools for good? Perhaps he ought to follow in his own benefactor's footsteps and make an offering of partnership to the boy now as a way to help ensure his and Ruth's financial future?

"You should not rush into anything," Al said. "Young or old marriage is a big step. For your aunt Zofia and me, it wasn't so easy at first. And we had Jacob's help."

"We're only talking about it, Uncle," Oliver said. "Nothing has been written in stone. All I'm asking is you promise not to say anything to Mother or Aunt Zofia."

"I don't like such secrecy," Al said, wringing his aged hands defiantly, in the end agreeing to remain silent. "We'll talk more about this later."

Chapter III

Later never came. Only a few days after his Sunday dinner with the Lehmanns, Oliver boldly proposed to Ruth, and she gleefully accepted. Soon, the young man would need to begin providing for his new family.

Worry for his nephew's future kept Al awake many nights. His apprenticeship moved along at a comfortable pace, and he'd already acquitted himself a competent craftsman, but the youth of the day was not the same as the youth of Al's day. Competence and speed never stood fitting substitutes for craftsmanship or tradition. The world was moving forward, and like all young men, Oliver wished to move with it. Therein lie the paradox of age. When a man is young, his eyes forever look toward tomorrow; when old, his gaze never leaves today.

Al had locked up for the night and sent Oliver home. Outside, a cold January wind blew, and the crisp, damp smell of impending snowfall hung in the air. Only the light from the lamp on Al's worktable gave any indication life still breathed in the shop. Seeking to melt away the stresses of the day, he buried himself in his work.

At seven o'clock, the light padding of Zofia's footsteps coming down the stairs drew Al's ear. The sound heralded the coming of another indictment. Yet again, he's missed his supper.

In years past, he'd thought nothing of skipping meals or even sleep for the sake of his trade. In truth, it was never a question of thinking nothing about it, rather a question of not thinking about it at all. When immersed in his work, Al, ironically, always lost track of time. Food, like time, was a constant and would always be there when he needed or wanted it. Why the necessity of allocating a specific period for taking it? Neither hunger nor fatigue concerned him much, and age had neither slowed down his mind nor tired out his limbs. He even kept the cot and mattress he'd slept on all those years in the storage room, for the nights when he worked well into the wee hours of the morning.

Increasingly, though, Zofia had taken to protesting her husband's long days sacrificed to his work. She would descend the stairs bearing lukewarm food, guilt, and wifely chastisement meant to slowly wear him down.

"*Mój Boże.* How can it be you live in a world surrounded by all these clocks and yet you still cannot remember your supper is at five thirty?"

Her small frame shuffled out of the darkness carrying a bowl of broth and a cup of coffee. She placed them on the table's edge and put aside his tools. It was her small offensive in a constant battle to get Al to slow down.

"I don't have time to eat soup," Al said, regarding the bowl. "Work does not finish itself. Mr. Carter will be back for his Welby in the morning."

"Soup now, work later," Zofia said, plucking the tweezers from her husband's fingers. "This can wait. You are too old to be skipping meals."

"And you are too beautiful to be serving soup to an old man like me," he said, placing a kiss on her forehead. The years had treated Zofia well. True, she moved slower, and a gradual curving of her spine gave her already diminutive frame a gentle stoop, but her eyes remained as big platters and brown as dark chocolate, though now they lived behind a pair of silver spectacles. Despite it all, Al thought her as beautiful now as the day he'd first seen her in the street all those years ago. But while he constantly worried for her health, she fretted over the hours he whiled away keeping time for other people, often to the neglect his own.

"Pssht. I won't bring it to you anymore if you don't start eating it."

"That sign in the window is more than just words, you know," he said. "The Boulle with the cracked enamel still needs done."

"Ollie can do it in the morning. You take too much on yourself. You need to let him do more."

"He has enough to worry about," Al said.

"If you do not take a break and eat now and then, you will be dead. Then he will have much more to worry about. So please, Albie, eat."

Her wisdom won out, and reluctantly, Al set aside his work. Zofia pulled a stool up to the bench as Al tore a piece of bread roll and dipped it in the steaming broth—barley soup with potatoes and a few chunks of tender beef, a Zofia classic.

"It looks like the soup is eating you," she said, seeing Al absorbed in thought. "I know that look. You're worried. What is it?"

"I just wonder if he's ready for the responsibility."

"Ollie?"

Al nodded. "A new wife coming. Children certainly. This place has always done well, but it has always just been the two of us, and what have we ever really needed? But to support a whole family? I don't know if it will be enough."

"Why don't you—"

At that moment, a tremendous crash, like a cannon shot, rocked the quiet of the shop. Zofia screamed and sent Al's heart racing in his chest. The spoon tumbled from his fingers, splashing soup down his shirtfront.

The impact startled them both to their feet. Al rushed toward the back of the shop, to the origin of the commotion. Zofia shuffled after, clutching at his shirtsleeve, her wide saucer eyes peering warily over his shoulder. They stopped just inside the entrance to the storage room, finding the source of their fright.

The rear door of the shop had burst in, by the force of a body crashing against it. Brisk night air raced through the open doorway, filling the room with an icy chill. Heavy flakes of wet snow blew in, accumulating on the back of a man slumped across the threshold; he lay motionless facedown on the floor, one soot-smeared cheek pressed against the cold linoleum.

"Bóg w niebie," Zofia said. "Is he dead?"

Who could say? Tattered clothes and a threadbare overcoat obscured the body within its folds, making it impossible to see if he was breathing. Al wanted to take a step forward, but Zofia's viselike grip held him fast to his spot. What if this man was the victim of some heinous villain lurking just outside in the alley waiting to spring upon them? What if the man himself were the villain, and his playing dead a ruse to lure them closer so he could surprise and rob, or perhaps even murder, them? Zofia fairly swooned from panic, such were the thoughts swirling in her head.

Al leaned forward, craning his neck for a closer look, but dared not leave the relative safety of the entranceway.

His clothes bore the signs of months, if not years, of neglect. Great tangled mats of black hair hung to his shoulders, and a filthy gnarled beard of impressive length caked with dust and mud knotted about his ears, chin, and neck. He described a man marooned, shipwrecked on some distant shoreline at the farthest point from humanity. But for all his dishevelment, Al noted the man's face, though drawn and cadaverous, held a distinctly youthful, if not vital, aspect, one at complete odds with the rest of his putrid state. He could be no more than twenty-five or twenty-six years old.

"Maybe we should phone the police?" Zofia said. "I will phone for the police."

But before she could move, life suddenly rushed back into the intruder's body. Animated as if with a great surge of electricity, the man jolted upright, struggling to get to his feet but slipping repeatedly on his muddied shoes, floundered like a fish flopping on the deck of a ship. After several seconds, he'd only managed to sit semi-upright, his bulk slumped awkwardly against the doorframe. He panted heavily. Two bluish-green eyes darted wildly in their sockets. Despite the bitter cold pouring in through the open doorway, beads of sweat dotted his brow and cheeks, and flecks of white spittle foamed at the corners of his mouth. An overwhelming stench wafted from his unwashed body. Tremors shook his hands, and their fingers danced erratically as if tickling the keys of an invisible piano. A flood of words streamed from his lips like so much water from a burst dam.

"I call, but still no answer... no answer... no return... no forgiveness... It burns and swells, but still no answers, no closer to the answer... Reflections only, reflections of my, reflections... What can it mean? It is not here. C'est une autre fin, une autre fin sur un chemin sans fin. The light persists yet still hidden by the dark... hidden, lost, forgotten. The lies... les mensonges que nous disons. The key to erasing the stain. The balm, the reason, the secret. Tell me!"

A torrent of spittle flew from his lips as he screamed, the furious, hoarse scream of a man at the end of his tether. He bellowed them with rancor, as if standing upon the precipice of a great abyss at the very edge of the universe, and shouted them into the vacant void of nothingness beyond. His whole being convulsed with rage. Zofia gasped in fright.

"He's possessed," she whispered. "A dybbuk!"

The man's eyes fixed their stare upon Zofia: a wild, piercing gaze freezing her to her marrow.

"*Masz rację, Babcia. Diabeł stoi przed tobą.*" He laughed hysterically.

"My God," she cried, nearly fainting. "He does have the devil in him!"

Al didn't know what to do. He watched, speechless, as the wild man's tempestuous stare fell from Zofia only to settle forlornly in the middle distance, a vacant and hopeless resignation shrouding his face, concealing his madness behind a mask of abrupt lucidity.

"*Pulvis et umbra sumus,*" he mumbled wearily as if recalling a distant memory before his head lolled heavily on its shoulders and his body slumped to the floor once again with a final dull thud. He stirred no more.

Al and Zofia remained transfixed for some minutes. The room became colder still for the night air drifting in through the open door. Silence returned, save for the ticking of the clocks and the thumping of their hearts in their chests. Only when sure the man was long into unconsciousness did Al venture to examine him closer.

A noble, almost lordly, quality graced the man's features. Angular cheeks and slim nose leant him a distinctly handsome profile, and his ragged beard marked a strong jawline. Jet-black hair, heavy brows, and a slightly olive complexion suggested a Mediterranean origin. Looking at the face in this calm state, a memory flashed in Al's mind. It was the vague image of a well-heeled man, impeccably dressed, one he couldn't place, but also one he couldn't help feeling he'd seen before.

"But he is too young," Al mumbled to himself. "Much too young."

Something shiny in the man's vest pocket caught Al's eye. He bent down and lifted it in his fingertips, the broken fob end of a braided gold chain. He gave it a gentle tug and teased out a pocket watch. Holding it up to his face, he thought for certain his old eyes deceived him.

The thing was incredibly beautiful. He'd not seen any before rivaling its style. Crafted by the hands of a master of the trade and possessing a supreme elegance not to be found in the banal creations of the New World artisans, it was, in a word, a masterpiece. Made entirely of gold, the unusual image of a serpent, its body made of finely cut rubies and garnets entwined around a pillar of blue sapphire adorned the cover. The reverse, equally as remarkable, had been etched all over with a damask pattern of floral sprigs and held a stylized fleur-de-lis done completely in shimmering diamonds.

Al hurried back to his bench. With the flat of a small knife, he gently prized off the back of the case, revealing the sterling-silver barrel bridge covering the movement. It bore the maker's name etched in a familiar script—*Gerhort Wallenstein*—and below that, the ancient quote of Horace so recently uttered by the mysterious interloper, now playing upon Al's lips as he read them soundlessly.

Pulvis et umbra sumus. We are but dust and shadow.

The path memories take from their storage in the deepest recesses of the human brain to the place where they become conscious recollections within the greater framework of experience, complete with taste, smell, sight, and sound one can easily recognize and verbalize, is rarely a straight one. Oftentimes, this path is not unlike the one taken by a bolt of lightning jutting down from the sky. When examined with the naked eye, connection occurs between heaven and earth in a literal flash, beginning at one point and, almost by magic, arriving at the other instantaneously. But capture the same effect on film, and one can easily see the jagged course traversed, the sudden bends, the crooks and splits, the false starts, the doubling back, and the sinewy branches leading off to terminal ends.

Such was the path a memory was at that very moment taking from the depths of Al's brain to the surface of his waking mind, where he would put it into words once all the disjointed pictures floating about in his head took order and organized clearly for him the crucial elements of where, when, and, most importantly, who. When they finally came into focus, the result remained doggedly confusing, mystifyingly improbable, and downright baffling.

"*Mein Gott*," he said. "I know this man."

"You most certainly do not," Zofia insisted.

"I do," Al said again, not quite believing it himself, yet somehow knowing it to be so. "I know I do. Help me to bring him inside."

Chapter IV

It was in the summer of 1894 when Al had received the letter from his uncle. Business for the old German was prospering, it read, burgeoning, even. Orders for custom pieces came in all the time, so rapidly that old Gerhort had been forced to expand his enterprise. He'd uprooted, moving from the little two-room workshop on the Rathausstrasse to a new, larger space on the Poststrasse. He needed the extra room to accommodate the five additional staff he'd taken on to assist with completing all the orders. It came with a beautiful new front display room where he proudly showcased his examples of some of the finest watchwork in all of Hamburg. Al could practically see the old man's face beaming with pride as he read, and it warmed his heart.

But all of this was secondary, of course, to the real reason he'd chosen to write. Gerhort wished to relate to his nephew a much more momentous item. Eagerly, Al read, noting the giddiness with which the old watchmaker described his most recent commission, one he was sure would be his unequivocal masterpiece:

I was approached by a most peculiar fellow recently. A young Parisian. You know the type I speak of. Haughty, debonair, and self-important. *Blut so blau wie lapis.* Walking about as if he owned the whole of the world. And for the finery of his attire, you would think he did. Not in a long time had I seen such clothing on a man, but it can hardly be denied Paris is where such people sprout up like so many blades of grass. The French have always been a people of royalty, even though their last king is long dead.

This young Frenchman wanted me to make for him a watch. But not just any watch. The most beautiful, most elaborate, and most whimsical creation I have made to date. He spared no expense, demanding the piece be made of nothing less than solid gold, and gave instructions for a lilie made entirely of diamonds and a snake of rubies to be emblazoned on the case. I told him what such a piece would cost. He only scoffed at the amount, muttering some strange phrase he wanted etched inside it. Money is of no concern for such a man. Ah, to be as fortunate...

The letter went on to say it had taken Gerhort two months to complete. When it was done, the young patrician thought nothing of paying a small fortune for it without so much as batting an eyelash.

⁂

And now, in the dim light of his shop, Al held in his hand the very same piece Gerhort described with such pride in his letter. This couldn't possibly be the same man from the letter too, could it?

With Zofia's help, he maneuvered the body inside and shut out the cold winter evening. They dragged him off the floor and heaved him onto the old cot, stripping his overcoat and shoes and laying a blanket over his emaciated frame. Al stoked the corner stove to restore some warmth to the room.

"He's not eaten in days probably," Zofia said as she leaned over the man's sunken chest and bony neck. In the slumber of oblivion, the once raving-mad face assumed a more peaceful expression. He looked to her less a man possessed by the devil and more a corpse in repose. She'd all but forgotten her recent bout of terror and was now imminently curious about how he and her husband could possibly have any association.

Al took the man's ragged overcoat and hung it on a nail. It stank of moldy wine and the fetid odor of the gutter. A thickish book, bound in leather, bulged from one of the pockets. Thumbing through the edge of the pages, he found it to be a handwritten journal, perhaps a diary of some kind.

"What have you got there?" Zofia said.

"Nothing," Al said, quickly stuffing the book back in its pocket.

"He's dead asleep," she said, still bent over the body. "Stinks like an old *dzik* too."

"Whiskey," Al noted. "It's soaked into his clothes."

"Why did you bring this man into our home?" she said, turning to him. "How can you say you know him?"

"Because of this," Al said, producing the watch and broken chain. He showed Zofia his uncle's mark etched into the barrel bridge. She regarded the detail curiously, but it failed to jog any memories.

"Don't you remember? *He* brought this in," he said, the memory beginning to come into focus. "It was Christmas, I think. Yes! It was just after Christmas the year Ollie was born."

Al said it triumphantly. He remembered it well now, recalling it all for her in minute detail. It was 1903, the ten-year anniversary of Jacob Hart's passing. The winter had been unseasonably mild, and the day stuck in his mind because, the same morning, he'd read a most remarkable item in the newspaper about two brothers in North Carolina and their amazing flying machine. Everyone who'd come in talked about it, about how air travel was sure to supplant the horse and carriage much faster than Henry Ford's noisy automobiles ever would. Al listened to all their bluster with reserved incredulity. There was no way you'd convince him to take his own two feet off the ground and fly around in the air like some crazy bird, sir. No way, no how.

Al sat at his bench, working with delicate care to seat a new sapphire bearing in a Hampden railway special, when the bell over the front door chimed and in stepped a most unusual young gentleman.

His gait bore the hallmark of royalty. Like a *comté* or duke or prince of the Old World, he carried his head high and his aquiline nose slightly higher. Peering down upon the world through pale-blue-green eyes, he regarded the dirty commonness of it all with reserved disdain and not the least bit interest in its troubles or its offerings.

Tailored to an exceptional fit, every article of the suit adorning his impressive physique spoke of the highest quality; only the finest materials and the most attentive hands had dressed him from the soles of his patent leather shoes to the crown of his silk top hat. Al imagined his a higher plane, one filled with palace dining and meals consisting of only the choicest morsels, the finest champagnes. His carriage was surely pulled by a team of ivory white stallions, his days packed with hunting outings and garden parties. When he spoke, the whole room listened. Men applauded his wit; women blushed as his lips pressed their offered hands. Kings and presidents alike had turned to him for counsel, and willingly, he'd offered it. He'd summered in Yalta, or Corsica, or Valparaiso, and slumbered the winters away high in the Alps, his bed piled with silk sheets and furs beside a roaring hearth; the icy chill at the top of the world nowhere to be felt under an immense pile of wealth.

Al saw all this and more as he watched his customer casually take in the sights of the shop with muted disdain. The man's bearing exuded it like a fragrance. The air around him bore the odor of money and power. One can easily tell when one is in the presence of such a person. Over the years, they'd come and gone on the Row, strutting like so many prideful peacocks.

He spoke with a thick French accent and that affected air so many of his countrymen employ, making them simultaneously admired for their worldliness and despised for the contempt dripping from their every word.

"I have this trinket," he'd told Al, his English as conceited as his French. "A silly thing, really, but it has stopped, and I don't quite know what to do with it."

He pulled from the pocket of his silk vest a watch of unimaginable beauty and craftsmanship. Al recognized it as his uncle's work immediately, fairly snatching the thing from his hand. It was the very watch Gerhort had spoken of in his letter nearly ten years before.

"To be honest, I'm not even sure I want the thing anymore," he said. "But one can't go around without a watch, I suppose. Can you do anything with it?"

Al turned the golden bejeweled thing over in his fingers, admiring the detail of the etching, the uniformity of the stones, the perfection of the assembly. It was far more stunning in person than Gerhort's rather casual description of it had been.

"How did you come by such a thing?" Al said.

"I purchased it some years ago from a shop," the man said absently. "I don't recall where. Is it important where it comes from?"

"It was Hamburg where this was made," Al said.

"Possibly," he replied. "I travel to so many places. I can't be expected to remember every detail of every one of my trips. Can you fix it or not?"

"It may take some time."

"No matter," the man replied. "I'll be staying on here for a while longer. I'm having a new residence built in your Fairmount Park. A charming place, it does quite put me in the mind of the forest at Meudon. For now, I'm at the Saint James. You can call on me there when the work is complete. Spare no expense. I must have a watch, after all."

The young gentleman produced an ivory-colored calling card from his overcoat, placed it gingerly on the display case, and left. Al lifted the card to his nose. It smelled of lilac. The name on it read *Etienne Allard*.

❧

But that was twenty-two years ago. Al puzzled over the body slumbering on the bed, worrying the jewel-encrusted watch in his hand. Silently, he tried to reconcile the image of the dapper gentleman from his memories against the pile of human wreckage lying before him. If the two men weren't one in the same, then the physical resemblance was remarkable.

"What are we going to do?" Zofia said. "He can't stay here. We must make him go away."

"Why?" Al said.

"Because he might be dangerous."

"In his condition, I think the only one he could hurt is himself. Look," Al said, seeing a trickle of blood emerge from under the man's hairline. "Go, boil some water and bring the iodine."

"Albie," Zofia pleaded meekly.

"What harm can he do in such a deep sleep?" Al said. "I will not turn out a man into the cold in such a condition. It would be a *sünde*. I'll get some cloth. We'll clean him up a little and bandage his head while he sleeps. And then…"

"And then you phone for the police?"

"We'll see."

Together they compiled a meager kit of first aid, tending to the open wound on his head, and another found on the back of his left hand. When these were sufficiently cleaned and wrapped, Al decided it best to give him a thorough looking over.

Stripping the unconscious man of his shirt and pants, they found the rest of his body to be in a terrible state. Among the mass of hair half concealing his face and shoulders, a long, jagged scar extended from just behind his left ear down the side of his neck, terminating below his collar bone. Like a living record of wrack and ruin, little of the man's flesh remained untouched by some past horror. A road map of scars crisscrossed his chest and back, some quite fresh, others long since healed. He'd been shot at least twice before, in the back, no less, and stabbed multiple times, the most severe evidence being a nearly seven-inch gash starting above his right hip that snaked around to his spine, roughly following the contour of the bone—an injury so deep and jagged that, by all rights, it should have killed him outright.

"What is this, now?" Zofia said, examining two small parallel divots in the skin above his right ankle.

"I don't know," Al said, peering over his glasses. "A snakebite?"

"Albie? What kind of man is this that should be so broken?"

Al remained silent, studying the history of the man's horrors.

"He can't be such a good man, I think, to have been through so much pain. He is a criminal, maybe? A robber, or even a murderer."

"He did not look like this when I met him," Al said.

"*If*," Zofia said, exasperation straining her words. "*If* you met him. If this is even the same man you think you remember, which we know it cannot be."

"But the watch?"

"This is proof of nothing," she said, snatching the thing from Al's hand. "I heard you before. You remember the watch more than the man. Maybe this is the same watch, but might it be that this is not the same man? Maybe he stole it. Maybe he killed the man who bought it to get it for himself. You saw this man once, maybe twenty years ago? And you think *this* is the same man? How can that be? Albie, find reason."

"I do not want to discuss this anymore." Al waved her off, tired of struggling against her logic. It didn't matter whether or not she agreed with him. He knew this was *that* same man. The more he thought back to the day, the more he recalled about the piece, the more everything came back into focus: the elegant mannerisms, the perfumed coiffure beneath the top hat, the air of devil-may-care. Al had felt he was in the presence of grandeur not of the ordinary variety. More importantly, he believed that something had brought Mr. Allard into his shop bearing his uncle's work that day. Perhaps it was fate, or even a hand more powerful at work, but Al refused to believe their paths should have crossed for now the second time, separated as it were by nearly two decades, wholly by chance. Though that grandeur now lay torn, tattered, and broken, he could not escape the certainty that the image from his memory and the body before him were one and the same. *He knew it.* Even if Zofia did not.

"I'll stay with him," Al said. It was nearly ten o'clock. "If he wakes, he can leave if he wants. If not, then in the morning."

"Are you certain this is the best thing?"

"No," he said. "But it is the right thing, I think. And that is the better of the two."

Al went upstairs and retrieved a spare shirt and pair of trousers. They would not fit his guest too well, but they would do better than the rags he'd come in with. He brought the clothes downstairs and left them in a small, neat pile on the chair beside the sleeping man's bed before settling back at his workbench.

It was some time before Al managed to calm Zofia's rattled nerves and coax her back upstairs to bed. When she'd finally gone, he turned his attention to busying himself with a little tinkering at his bench but found he could not focus. Like a cogwheel missing a tooth, its absence disrupting the harmony of the whole mechanism, a sudden lingering doubt cast an unwelcome shadow over his certainty, bringing his unshakable thought train to a grinding halt.

He laid down his tools and, for a time, looked on the figure resting tranquilly in the bed. Warmth had returned to the storeroom, and the snow that had followed the vagabond intruder through the door had all but melted and dried up. All was quiet once more.

A sudden groan from his guest roused Al from his chair. All he had to defend himself with was a two-ounce tack hammer. What could such a thing do to a body that had seen so much horror? Cautiously, Al approached, brandishing the hammer like a sword before him. To his relief, the body only twitched in its sleep, threatened groggily to awaken, then settled back again into oblivion.

Returning to his bench, Al caught sight once more of the book peeking out from the pocket of the overcoat hanging by the door. He'd already felt a rush of shame for intruding on its privacy earlier, but now the white edges of those same pages, shining like a beacon against the inky-black cloth of the coat, drew forth an insatiable curiosity.

Might it be within those pages there lay some clue as to his identity? Wouldn't it be neglectful on his part, seeing as how he'd taken the trouble to care for him this far, if he were to not at least attempt to learn something more about the poor man's state and what might have brought him to it?

With the tips of his fingers, Al cautiously extracted the book from the coat pocket and shuffled noiselessly back to his workbench. Running his finger along the spine, he noted the thickness of it—as thick as the Chumash he kept on the nightstand. *That* book held the Law. It held God's own words given to his people. What could a man write of his own mind that could fill so many pages? But even more so, if this were indeed the patrician from his memory, what could make one once so high fall so low?

His inquisitiveness getting the better of him, Al gently lifted the cover and began reading.

Chapter V

It is with a heavy heart and a conscience tormented with immeasurable guilt that I have decided to put pen to paper and endeavor to catalog the trial of my wretched life. Let this diary, this confession of a lifetime lived in the shadow of vice and sin, serve as a warning to all who may fall into the trap of viewing its pages. For damnation surely follows sin, and just as the setting sun, whose fading majesty I have observed from every corner of the globe, is swallowed up by the serpent of the night, so, too, will my soul, which once shone so brightly, be forever swallowed by eternal darkness. This I know for a certainty. Voltaire once asked whether confession did more good than evil. I do not have an answer for this, nor hope to ever discover one. Hope is no longer a fruit that I care to taste, for it is bitter and bears rotted flesh.

My name is Etienne Allard, and I was born in Marseille, on a bright May morning, in the year of our Lord 1870. Though I remember them vividly, the details of my very early childhood are immaterial to my purpose. It will suffice to say children born of privileged homes often fill their days with careless amusements and wonder seeking. And mine was one such home. Situated on a hill overlooking the sea in the Vauban district, in the shadow of la Garde where now stands the great basilica, it was an estate set unto itself. I recall its parlor and great hall playing host to many a gathering of the local *haute bourgeoisie* in its day.

My father, Jean Allard, a cunning and intelligent man with no small measure of charisma, made his fortune at twenty after founding the Compagnie Générale Méditerranéen et de la Côte d'Ivoire in 1860 with just two small ships. Employing questionable business practices and a lion's ferocity for stomping out competitors, in short order, he acquired three more, expanding his small operation running cargo along the Mediterranean coast into a full-scale enterprise conducting regular ferries between Marseille, Assini, and Grand-Bassam—sending out settlers and speculators, bringing back palm oil and cocoa. Within a few years, the Compagnie amassed a capital of nearly twelve million francs, expanding to a fleet of ten cargo ships and four steamers all running scheduled routes to Algiers, Tripoli, Athens, and numerous ports along the Levant.

It was from my father I would receive my first introduction to the perplexing and devious animal that is man. His study overlooked the gardens and described a veritable temple to the gods of commerce; cabinets displayed artifacts of exotic stone and wood from the dark continent, while the walls hung with the skins of beasts slain of the savage wilds. No sooner had I taken my first steps than he had me sit in a corner armchair and silently observe him run his empire from behind a massive oak-and-marble desk.

"Read a man as you would a book," he would instruct. Only after the endless parade of subordinates and sycophants had ceased for the day would he deign to address me directly. "Every man's face tells a story. It doesn't matter what language it's written in either. You just have to know how to read. You *can* read, can't you?"

But at the age of three, I could not.

My formal education did not begin until my fourth year, when my father deemed it necessary I be groomed in his image. He wished me well positioned to succeed him when the time arose, and hired a battery of tutors for the purpose, the best his money could buy.

There was arithmetic and reading and penmanship. There was history and grammar. Daily instruction on piano and violin by an oily-haired Teuton named Haberlin was followed by Latin with M. Martin, then Italian and English with M. Faure. Further on there were the Greeks, Dickens, Gogol, Milton, and the humanities, which proved increasingly at odds with my ecclesiastical studies. Religion, specifically the doctrine of the Catholic church, was delivered at my mother's behest through regular visits by a certain Abbé Frère. Middle-aged, pasty-faced, and balding, he eagerly relished the opportunity to visit our home to instruct me in the ways of heaven and hell, if only to seize upon the opportunity to be nearer my mother, upon whom he bestowed unnatural attentions obvious to even my youthful eyes.

Beautiful yet reserved, and some years Jean's junior, Aline had been raised a Maronite Catholic in Ottoman Lebanon. It was there where he'd found her. Entranced by her Levantine exoticism, or more likely her servile nature, Jean's attentions enticed Aline's father, who was anxious to see his eldest daughter married. His promise to take her back with him to Marseille in luxury and wealth, and with no small sum delivered to her father in exchange, sealed the arrangement. A businessman through and through, Jean's marriage was nothing more than a bill of sale—a contract for a new piece of equipment, with terms negotiated and all the proper requisitions signed.

But my mother was out of her element in the social circles of Marseilles. More trophy than wife, the men entering Aline's sphere found themselves captivated by beauty only to be repelled by her unwavering piety and intractable devotion to God. If my father was a slave to his business, then my mother was enslaved by her faith. Truly, her place was in a convent, not by my father's side, and I know not how it was fate had brought them together, so clearly mismatched as they were in the stuff from which they'd been made.

Her days were her own to fill. A small army of servants artfully kept the house in order, so what time Aline didn't spend looking beautiful and acquiescent by my father's side as he made the social rounds, she spent alone, either in her rooms or in the private chapel Jean had built for her in our garden. There she whiled away the hours in solitude and reflection, an anchorite under her own roof.

If my mother took little interest in her marriage or home, she took even less in the raising of her only son. My presence seemed only a constant reminder of her general melancholy. It is why my fondest childhood memories concern not my mother but rather our family's chief servant, a Rumanian girl named Lipa. Barely twenty when she arrived on our doorstep looking for work, quick-witted, and a quicker study, who hid more intelligence than she let on, she soon earned the trust of my parents and found herself the favorite of the household. I'd just turned five.

With my father absorbed in the tedium of running his empire, and my mother's increasing isolation, the responsibility of my caregiving fell to her. When I wanted food, it was Lipa who fed me. When I played a trick, it was she who laughed. When I fell, it was she who tended to my bruises and wounded pride.

Early adolescence brought with it burgeoning self-discoveries. When not at study, my time was increasingly filled with more competitive pursuits. To not put too fine a point on it, I'd developed a singular penchant for games of chance—rounds of teetotum or draughts among friends or with servants. Card games I liked the best. Lipa taught me le Pouilleux and Triomphe, while Alphonse, my father's driver, taught me Bassette and Bouillotte, the latter of which eventually became my game of choice. Though only twelve, I found myself sneaking off with Alphonse to clandestine games with chauffeurs, merchants, and others in some of Marseille's less-than-noble establishments.

By the time I'd reached my fifteenth birthday, my father's edict that I "learn to read" had borne fruit. I had learned to read, and read well, both books and men. The hours spent in his study watching him work, observing his trade with the singular goal of learning to read a man—his hopes, his fears, his desires, his strengths, and his weaknesses—proved more effective than he could have possibly foreseen. I had a perspicacity for the subtle, often finding that when I concentrated, I could instinctively sense what others were feeling or thinking. If the seeds had been sown in my father's study, then they truly blossomed around the card table. Every man's face did, indeed, tell a story if you knew how to read it. And I excelled in observing the unconscious, involuntary movements of others, what they refer to in gambling circles as the tell—a faint falter in breathing, a quickening of the pulse, a nearly imperceptible deflection of the iris. Things easily missed by the casual observer were plain as day to my eye. Detecting them became a study in and of itself, and I found the practice both fascinating and educational beyond measure.

Accompanying this insatiable curiosity for the human condition and all its quirks and nuances, I soon discovered I had also been endowed with the tremendous, almost preternatural gift of good luck. Countless times, through simple observation and only a modicum of cunning, I successfully brought off all manner of trickery and deceit among not only my closest compatriots—for how simple really are the minds of children—but also the adults who congregated about me. My machinations did not escape the attention of Alphonse, and together, fleecing the local merchantmen became a particularly enjoyable pastime.

Gaming aside, I often exploited this gift to increasing success with the female sex, for concurrent with my flowering intellectual talents came the realization, despite all her faults, that my mother's beauty had contributed in no small measure to my developing into a young man of notable attractiveness. I was tall for my age, standing almost a head higher than my closest peer. My hair grew full, wavy, and black like the wings of a crow. A heavy brow, a gift from my Levantine ancestry, lent my gaze gravity, and a strong jaw gave balance to a somewhat drawn face. Women visiting our parlor often discreetly commented to my mother, sometimes describing my carriage as almost statuesque. To these whispered praises, I would take nonchalant actions, preening as it were for them, to earn further attentions. I worked diligently, perfecting my poise and posture, as I performed routine tasks such as raising a cup to my lips or standing at the window, gazing upon the garden so as to give the impression of being in deep philosophical reflection. As I approached manhood, it was not lost on me that being an object of women's baser desires was a goal worthy of attaining. I used my skills honed at the gaming tables to observe their gazes, ascertaining the perfect moments to strike a pose, pout my lips, or arch my brow so as to elicit the maximum amorous desires. Later, a particularly splendid endowment would prove to be of great utility in the boudoirs of the continent and further afield, though, at the time, I had no foreknowledge of this.

Mere grist for the mill that was to come, these flirtations laid the foundation for my downfall. I have come to learn all men are possessing of a single sin. Mine was and always has been vanity. A prideful child I was, and I prideful man I was becoming. Everyone entering my circle became potential targets upon which to test the mettle of my skills—adversaries to be humbled by my intellect and unnatural good fortune.

I blame my father for this, as many men who reflect on the injustices they have suffered are wont to do, though I live with the full knowledge every injustice wrought upon my head was of my own doing. His, too, was the sin of pride, pride that made him believe, despite my education and all he taught me about the illicit nature of men, he could conceal from me his own inner demons. But, in time, I could read him as expertly as I could any man. And I saw in his actions and heard in his words his own sin.

To be sure, I never *witnessed* his adulterous acts. But it was easy to see the many women he'd had over the years. In my youngest days, I could not perceive the forces both tearing and coalescing the fabric of my family. My mother's beauty was undeniable, but for Jean, she was merely another item in his collection of chattels acquired in his travels. Steadfast in his work, yet prone to distraction, and weak in the face of temptation, it would be from my father, and not all those books and tutors, that I would learn the caprices of man. By the time I had reached my eighteenth birthday, I had become only too aware of his deceit. As I have said, my father was a man of great intellect and cunning—an imposing figure whose personality dominated lesser men. And where they would shrink from his overpowering presence, women would inevitably surrender to it. But when his charisma was at its strongest, his willpower was at its weakest. I had learned to read men well, as he'd instructed. But perhaps he'd not intended me to open the pages of his own life?

I cannot in good conscience continue my story without first admitting, though I could not understand his motives for dishonoring my mother, that I loved my father. And though I could neither understand why she tolerated his infidelities nor why she chose to stay with him despite them, I loved her just as much, but respected her little. In fact, you could say I indeed laid blame for his behavior as much upon her shoulders as his, lost as she was in her piety in the hunt for virtue in a man clearly lacking it. It could be equally said, quite convincingly, I might add, this view was sorely misplaced, and the fault was Jean's and his alone. Today, with so many years passed, I cannot but agree. My father, for all the charms that allowed him to lord over his vast empire like a king and impose his will upon all who came within his orbit, was at his core a wretched, sinful man.

And like father, like son.

However, I feel I am getting ahead of myself, and so shall leave my childhood behind.

By my eighteenth year, having learned all I could from my tutors, and with Lipa in tears at my departure, I left Marseille to commence my studies within the venerable walls of the Sorbonne. It was the year of our Lord 1888.

❧

Paris. What words can I say about such a glorious city not already spoken a thousand times before and that will not be spoken a thousand times hence? I am no poet, and my words do scant justice to that place renowned for its magic, its merriment, and its intrigue. That right is reserved for men more gifted of tongue than I.

I arrived in the city under crisp autumn skies. With generous funds provided by my father in my pocket, I took rooms on the second floor of a stately old home overlooking rue du Cardinal Lemoine, a mere stone's throw from the university.

The concierge, a singularly plump, gray-haired, jovial old Parisian named Madame Crespi, welcomed me and my coin warmly. Puttering about the place with a penguin's gait, she kept the house in general order, regaling her lodgers with endless tales of her life in Paris. Widowed several years prior, and with both her children dead as well, Madame Crespi, or Angelique, as she once confided in me, had witnessed the procession when the remains of Napoleon returned from Saint Helena, seen the wonders of Exposition Universelle in 1855, and survived both the Prussian siege and, of course, the Commune. Many a night in those early days, I willingly entertained her stories at the communal dinner table. She cooked marvelously, filling the air with the rich aromas of andouillette, ragouts, salmon, pike, and poulet.

The house on rue du Cardinal Lemoine had five floors, not including a wine cellar and pantry. Angelique kept her own small room on the first-floor rear, near the kitchen, while my rooms, three in all, occupied a full half of the second floor. A handful of students resided on the third and fourth floors, while the garret, I was told politely by Angelique, remained off-limits to her lodgers.

"Those are Monsieur Albin's quarters, and he prefers his privacy," was all she said on the matter.

I thought little of it, and after she showed me my rooms, I assumed the task of settling in. No sooner had the sound of her footsteps faded than a knock at my door interrupted my operation. Standing in the hallway was a young student. He introduced himself as Dumont.

"So, you're the new fellow?" he said cheerily, his hand brazenly outstretched in welcome. "I saw you arrive earlier. My rooms are upstairs from yours."

"A pleasure," I replied, introducing myself. "Is there something I can do for you?"

"Do? Oh, nothing. I just wished to greet you. I do it with all of the new lodgers." A gold pince-nez balanced on the bridge of his nose, and an ill-fitted suit hugged his thin frame. It was the standard outfit of a poorly funded student. A pallor lay in his face, the result of some underlying malady, most likely. He remained standing in the doorway, expectantly silent.

"Yes, well," I said. "I do have a bit of unpacking still to do, so..."

"I could assist if you like," he said happily. "I couldn't help notice you had quite a baggage train."

"*Mon Dieu*, Paul," said a handsome young man casually descending the stairs. "Enough with the ridiculous pretexts. Ask the fellow to invite us in." Gliding past us both, he made his entrance into my rooms with the familiarity of a man entering his own boudoir. He stood tall and lean, carrying himself with the air of a chevalier from the days of the old monarchies. Well groomed, of delicate features, and dressed in fine fashion, he casually surveyed the room before spinning on well-shined heels and extending a neatly manicured hand.

"*Enchanté*. Matthieu Vallaton," he said by way of formal introduction. "I see you've made the acquaintance of the good doctor Dumont."

"Aspiring," Dumont hastily interjected.

"Don't be modest, my friend. Modesty is for the feminine. You are not a doctor in degree and title *yet*, this is true, but you must never think of yourself as anything less. A doctor you wish to be, so a doctor you shall be. There's no time like the present to start wearing it. Don't you agree?"

Vallaton turned to me for confirmation and paused, as though we two were actors on a stage and mine was the next line in the scene.

"Well, a man's worth is no greater than the worth of his ambitions," I offered.

"There you have it," Vallaton said, putting the matter to rest. "I see our new housemate is not without an education. Citing Marcus Aurelius this early in the day is dangerous stuff."

"You know the *Meditations*?"

"I have meditated on them from time to time, yes. But too much rumination is not good for the spirit, and I do find the Stoics so prosaic." He stood before my bookshelf perusing the spines. "I myself go in for much simpler thinkers. The Cyrenaics, for example."

"I'm not familiar," I said.

"Hedonists," Dumont chimed in with a smirk.

"Libertines!" Vallaton corrected.

"He goes on about them quite a lot. If you get to know him well enough, he'll try to convert you."

"And I'll succeed too," Vallaton said triumphantly. "And I can foresee the challenge continuing in your case, Doctor. But for our friend here... What is your name again?"

"Etienne," I said. "For the first time."

"Right." Vallaton resumed without breaking stride. "But our friend Etienne here is clearly a man of taste. One need only to see his Voltaire to see that. Baudelaire, Zola, Diderot, Rabelais, ah, here he is." He lifted a thick volume of Montaigne's *Essais* from a half-unpacked trunk and began leafing through. "So, you're going in for belle lettres? Dumont here thought for sure you were pursuing a medical. Even put money on it."

"Sorry to disappoint you," I said to my timid new friend. "If I'm to be perfectly honest, I don't really know what I'm in for."

"That's of little importance," Vallaton said, snapping the book shut, his face beaming with satisfaction. "What is of the utmost importance is I've won! Pay up, *ami*, a wager is a wager."

Dumont produced a *sou* from his pocket and surrendered it to Vallaton's proffered hand.

"*Et voilà!*" he said. "Now, let us dispense with the pleasantries, and allow me to dispense my good fortune upon the two of you. Dumont, fetch your hat and be so good as to bring mine as well. Etienne, you can see to your things later. Come, my friends, 'tis almost evening and Paris awaits! There is much to see and more to discuss. We shall move this fine introduction to a more suitable venue. I shall supply the funds for our excursion, so, as such, the institution shall be one of my choosing, say Le Veau Noir? Objections? No? *Allons-y!*"

❧

Gritty and smelling faintly of musk and urine, The Black Calf, an obscure watering hole on the southern edge of Montmartre, did not present itself the type of establishment I imagined a fellow like Vallaton to haunt. His crisp tie, silk topper, and pristine gloves stood out among the rabble like a diamond embedded in a pile of manure. Along the way, he told us he preferred the spot for its proximity to the brothels and even once heard Toulouse-Lautrec was rumored to pop in from time to time before beginning a night of debauchery.

Drunkards slumped at filthy tables, while whores loitered in the shadows waiting to ply their trade. Paris was full of brightly lit, gilded, gay cafés lining the boulevards I thought would be much more suited to Vallaton's character. But it was precisely those types of places that repelled him.

"I abhor the salon," he said, calling for wine. It was brought in a chipped carafe by a poxy old woman. "The saloon is much more to my liking. Here, there is life at its most raw. The parlor of the aristocrat is a venue where fantasy is created, discussed, painted, even philosophized. But here, here in the dust, is where it is realized. Look there!"

He trained his gaze across the room, at a harlot lazing in a corner. Her head lolled precariously atop her neck, and the ruffles of her dress shamelessly exposed her limp, bruised legs. Tousled curls spilled over her shoulders and face. Her eyes were as vacant as a corpse.

"Magnificent, isn't she," remarked Vallaton.

"Opium," noted Dumont. "It's rampant in this area."

"See how more alive it makes her, how much more raw? This is her natural state, is it not? Given over to the freedom the drug grants her, she abandons the mere posture of the harlot and becomes the authentic slut. How much more desirable in this state is she than when she is not? Does it not increase her wantonness?"

"I question the term 'desirable' in this context," Dumont said.

"Dare you, then?" Vallaton said. "Have you forgotten the wisdom of Saint-Ange so soon? 'Women's destiny is to be wanton, like the bitch, the she-wolf; she must belong to all who claim her.' The tincture simply enhances what is already there, innate in her. The effect is intoxicating, and I haven't even partaken of it myself. She is remarkable." Then, steeling himself with a gulp of wine, he rose. "I'm going to invite her to join us."

"Are you mad?" Dumont said, reaching to seize Vallaton's arm. But he was too late. In a flash, our friend had marched across the room and sat himself beside her.

"Is he always like this?"

"No," Dumont said. "He's been getting bolder by the day. It's a fool's errand to try to stop him. He's fascinated by all things low."

"Who is this Saint-Ange? I've not heard his name before."

"A woman," he corrected. "A role in a play he's taken to reading to me as of late. It's all he thinks about, this new philosophy of his. I've known him for several months now. We arrived at Madame Crespi's at nearly the same time, you know. I think it might be some sort of psychosis."

We watched Vallaton for a moment, rapt by the spectacle. A broad smile graced his face. He eagerly chatted up the girl, who drifted hazily between conversation and unconsciousness—one moment cognizant of his presence; the next, oblivious to it. Vallaton, for his part, carried on gaily apropos of these fluctuations. He seemed content to merely hear himself speak.

"He'll go on like that for a while," Dumont said. "Then he'll disappear with her, I suppose. And it will be on my franc."

"The cost of another wager?" I ventured. Dumont smiled.

"He's not got much of his own—money, I mean. At least, I think he doesn't. There must be some, since he's never wanted for clothes or the trappings of the gentleman. He's just damned lucky is all."

"Perhaps you're just poor at wagers."

"*Touché*. Tell me, how have you come to Paris?"

"By way of Marseille."

"I myself am from Orléans. I plan to return to when I've achieved my degree. You've probably taken notice of my condition. It's the reason I've chosen to go in for medicine. That and my father."

"He is a doctor?"

"After a fashion. He's a pastor. Wants nothing more than to see me enter the church. I respect his position, but..."

"But what good is healing the spirit if the body wherein it resides fails to stay in proper order?"

"Precisely," he agreed.

"I cannot argue," I said. "My father, too, would see me follow in his footsteps, as it were."

"And you don't wish to?"

"God no!" I said. "Forgive the blasphemy."

"I'd hardly call it that," he said. "And what of your rooms? Do you find them to your liking?"

"Indeed. Madame Crespi is most hospitable. And it would seem I won't be at a loss for company."

We raised glasses and drank to our health and new companionship.

"And to divergence," he added, draining his wine. "May our father's wishes remain their own."

"Speaking of company," I said, remembering Angelique's odd prohibition about the garret, "what do you know of this Monsieur Albin?"

"The hermit in the attic? Not much. She gives strict instructions not to disturb him."

"Perhaps he is her lover?" I ventured in good humor.

"I doubt that. Her prisoner, more likely. In all the time I've lived there, which hasn't been long, mind you, I've not seen him leave his rooms, not even once. He does not come out, and no one goes in, save for her, and then only to deliver his meal twice a day and retrieve his linens once a week. Beyond this, I know nothing more about it."

"A strange arrangement," I noted. "How long has he lived up there?"

"A decade? A century? Who's to know? She is reluctant to speak about it. I don't press."

Just then, Vallaton returned with the whore from the corner table in tow.

"Gentlemen, *quelle chance*! It's quite comical. I was just relating the amusing adventures of Encolpius and Quartilla to my lovely new acquaintance Michette, and she was telling me about a wonderful abode in the rue de Douai where her associates ply their time-worn trade. Quite a coincidence, don't you think? We are, after all, three travelers on an escapade. Now, for the players. I shall take the role of Encolpius, of course, while, Etienne, you shall assume the guise of Ascyltus, and, Dumont, the part of Giton. Fear not, though, Michette has assured me it is not *we* who shall be buggered, unless, of course, either of you gentlemen fancy that sort of thing? Paul, we've only known each other for a brief time, and, Etienne, we've just met, but don't fret, for as Seneca famously said, 'I suspend judgment.'"

"Pah!" Dumont uttered in disgust. "The mere suggestion."

"Then it is agreed. We shall settle our bill and escort Michette to her lodgings."

Vallaton wheeled on his heels and retreated, leaving the still half-conscious Michette swaying like a reed beside the table and myself and Dumont quite speechless.

❦

Outside, Vallaton took Michette's arm under his, ambling ahead like a man out for an evening promenade with his wife. Passersby took note of the absurd pair, but being so close to the Place Pigalle, it was perhaps not so unusual as I had first perceived. Dumont and I fell a few steps behind, dragging along like sounding lines cast off the side of a ship. We kept our voices low and our eyes locked to the pavement.

"Where is he taking us, do you suppose?" I said. Dumont's eyes darted nervously about.

Twilight had settled over the city, a pastel palette of pink and blue skies. The electric streetlamps lining the boulevard de Clichy flickered to life, but in the recessed doorways, porticos, and alleyways of Montmartre, an inky darkness had already nestled in for the night.

"What's troubling you?" I said of my companion.

"It's nothing," he replied.

"Nonsense. You've been worrying your fob since we've left the tavern. Something you should know about me if we're to be friends: little details never escape my attention. Besides, it's written on your face. You're clearly vexed."

"It's just…" he started, then stopped. "It's nothing, really. Quite silly, actually."

"Most things usually are," I said.

"Those are your Stoics speaking again. Making molehills out of mountains."

"It gets me by," I said. "Come, out with it. Perhaps I can help."

"Well," he began tentatively, "back in Orléans, you see, much of my time was filled almost exclusively with academic pursuits. I'd not had many friends."

"I understand," I said.

"Then yours was a childhood of similar experience?" he said, hope rising in his voice.

"Most likely, yes," I said, trying to sound reassuring.

"And perhaps you, too, were restricted by your studies? To such an extent, that is, that they left little room for other more 'recreational' pursuits?"

"On the contrary, I had ample time to devote myself to such distractions."

"Oh?" He deflated slightly.

"Yes," I said. "Though I've never been one to favor physical sport, I did master many games of chance."

"You miss my meaning, I think. I was referring to recreations of a more *indelicate* nature."

In truth, I had not missed his meaning at all, but raising the subject of my own virginity would, I felt, in no way serve to further the conversation nor ease his anxiousness at the impending event. The fact was, though I was an extremely handsome boy and had many admirers, I'd never actually *been* with a woman.

"I've never been with a woman," Dumont said, unwittingly coming to my rescue.

"What's that?" Vallaton called back over his shoulder. "Fear not, my sweet Giton. I assure you there are no tortures awaiting you would not wish upon your own person. Recall the teachings of our great Marquis, and all shall be right. Ah, we have reached the temple of Priapus!"

We'd stepped through a green wooden door under a brick archway, turning off the rue de Douai into a narrow passage sandwiched between the high, damp walls of two apartments where the lights of the boulevard did not creep. No number marked this entrance, but I've no doubt were I to return to Paris tomorrow, I could find the place with the same ease I might find my way to my own bedroom.

The path ahead terminated in a shadowed courtyard. Mechanically, Michette turned us off the passageway through a door into one of the houses. It could only have been sheer muscle memory that guided her steps through the fog of opium enshrouding her brain.

The door led to a cramped foyer at the foot of a wooden staircase. In a parlor to our left sat four girls: three crowded on a squat, threadbare settee, the fourth brazenly astride a backward chair, her thighs parted wide, a bent cigarette depending between her fingertips. They ignored us. An aging grotesque whore, shamelessly painted, appeared and marched straight up to Michette.

"Where have you been?" she said. "You were supposed to be back an hour ago."

"I've brought them," Michette said, gesturing lazily to the three of us.

The old whore eyed us suspiciously.

"Quartilla emerges," Vallaton whispered conspiratorially before returning his attention to the matter at hand. "Bonsoir, mademoiselle," he said, doffing his hat. "We three are weary travelers on the road from Campania on our way to visit delights in the house of Trimalchio when the maelstrom of the boulevards caused us to seek refuge. Fortunately, we encountered the lovely Michette, who ably led us into the graces of your Providence. My friends and I seek rest from the road and the companionship offered by your house."

The madame looked unimpressed, but when Vallaton produced his purse, her mood noticeably improved. She smiled, revealing her few remaining teeth, and barked into the parlor.

"On your feet! We have guests."

Quartilla's command stirred the languid girls to life. Cigarettes were extinguished, hair was fluffed, bloomers straightened. In a flash, a hefty redhead with fleshy bosoms spilling over her bustier fairly enveloped Dumont. Snaking a plump arm over his shoulder, she playfully plucked off his spectacles and casually used her bulk to coax his small frame up the stairs.

"Ma-Matthieu," he stammered in nervous terror as he was led away looking like a man for the gallows.

"Enjoy, sweet Giton, and forget not the lessons of the great master, our beloved Marquis. Though I'd avoid *riding Saint George* this round. She's enough for two."

"Monsieur will choose," the madame said to me as I watched a pair of meaty thighs chase the young doctor up out of sight.

"Yes, by all means, choose," Vallaton concurred. "Though it appears Dumont has unwittingly narrowed the field for you, and I'm afraid *I* must speak for the fair Michette. Still, there yet remain three delectable options. I'll leave you to it."

And ending there, Vallaton took Michette under the arm and guided her up the stairs, a query on his lips echoing from the turn on the landing.

"Tell me, my dear, are you familiar with the remarkable adventures of *Thérèse Philosophe*?"

"Monsieur sees something he desires?" Quartilla asked, bringing my attention back to the parlor. "Perhaps Sidonie is to your liking?"

Buxom and unrefined, Sidonie stepped forward. Dark eyes, thin lips, and a tapered jaw lent her face a mysterious Far Eastern quality. It was she who'd sat unabashedly straddling the chair, crudely displaying her sex for one and all. Beside her waited another, equally voluptuous and equally indifferent, but Sidonie stood the fairer of the two. Then I caught sight of a slender girl trying to conceal herself behind them.

No rot had yet claimed her teeth, no scars had yet sullied her porcelain arms. She was small, fragile, and looked to be no older than myself. A faint patch of freckles spread across her nose, and her pale-green eyes bore a gaze of muted fear.

"Ah, Ingrid, then?" the old whore said. "She is new to my house, arrived this very morning, and as yet has not known a man, of this, I can assure you, as I have inspected her myself. She came to me from a poor family who could not care for her, cast her out to the street when she was only a child. Such a sad turn for such a pretty girl, *non*? For this unique pleasure, Monsieur will have to pay more, much more. But if you do not wish it, no doubt Sidonie or Mirielle can accommodate you."

Without thought, I willingly agreed to her price. I'd more than enough to finance my own pursuits. Nevertheless,

I dared not disturb the charade and permitted Vallaton the victory to his ego.

"Then she is yours. Ingrid, *bougez petit oiseau.* Are you deaf? Go with the monsieur. He does not wish to wait all night."

My own nervousness did little to reassure her. Ingrid remained anxiously rooted to the spot. Finally, the painted fool seized her gruffly by the arm and ushered her out of the parlor.

"The monsieur will kindly wait a moment," she said in passing and led Ingrid up the stairs. A door slammed overhead. Sidonie and Mirielle listlessly returned to the settee and lit fresh cigarettes. A moment later, the old trollop glided down the stairs wearing a spurious grin.

"Pardon. Ingrid needed time to prepare for monsieur. You understand how young girls can sometimes be, *non*? But she is quite ready now."

❧

I made to knock on the door but realized the gesture utterly foolish. The cold brass of the knob rattled in my hand as I entered. Ingrid was waiting inside. She sat on the edge of the bed, a forlorn expression upon her pale face, her eyes lowered to her hands folded in her small lap, like a child at prayer. She could not bring her eyes to meet mine.

I looked about the dreary room. Not much bigger than a monk's cell and spartanly appointed: a three-legged stool; a threadbare Turkish rug; a dressing table atop which rested a hairbrush, a bottle of scented water, and a dented tin of talc. The musty air smelled faintly of mold. There was no window.

"*Bonsoir*," I said, my back glued to the door. She did not move. I clumsily removed my hat but, finding no place to hang it in that wretched room, stood worrying it in my fingers like a fool. She would neither speak nor look at me. She only raised a delicate finger to indicate a nail protruding from the chipped plaster.

"Do you sleep here?" I said. "I mean… no. What I mean is, is this your room here? Is this where you stay?

"*Oui*," she replied mutely.

"Where are your things?" I gestured to the empty space. "Surely, this can't be all you have?"

"*Oui*," she said. "All I have."

Silence reigned. I hung my things and sat on the crooked stool. Neither of us quite knew what to do. After a time, muffled giggles and muted grunts of libidinous pleasures penetrated the walls. I wondered which of my compatriots it might have been. Ingrid merely shifted uneasily, her stockinged feet barely touching the floor, not an ounce of the erotic about her. I suddenly felt ashamed and filthy.

"Perhaps this was a mistake," I said, getting up. "I think perhaps I should go. Yes, that would be best." I made for my hat and coat.

"No," she said, jumping to her feet. "Please do not go."

"No, I think it better if I just—"

"You cannot go. If madame learns you were not pleased with me, she will not allow me to stay. Madame says all must earn their keep in her home."

"This is not a home," I said.

"It is my home," she replied. "I have no other."

"Look, I can give you some money. You can tell madame whatever you like. I won't say anything. Tell her I was rough. Make something up. Tell her I fell asleep. I don't know."

"But you heard her before. She knows I am *une vierge*. She will demand to see for herself, and she will know."

"I don't think I can do this," I said.

"Monsieur does not want me?" She was panicked, verging on tears.

"It's not that," I stammered, getting lost in her imploring gaze. "Of course, I do. I don't know. I'm just not sure this is right for either of us."

She sank back onto the bed. I sat beside her.

"Madame spoke the truth when she said I've not been with a man before. One came last night and wanted me. I was so afraid. He looked so brutish, and Sidonie said she knew him and that he was a rough sort and that I should not be able to bear it, but I must if I were to stay. I begged Madame to not make me do it, and she relented. She said I was sick with a fever and not right for him. He took Claudine instead. She will not be so kind to me again. I must earn if I want to remain here. I've nowhere to go. Please, monsieur, the first man I am to have cannot be a brute like him."

"I don't know."

"You are a kind sort, *non?* You talk to me. Men, when they come to a place like this, do not come to talk. I think this makes you a gentleman. And for my first, I think a gentleman should have me. Will you have me?"

She placed a small hand on my leg. Her touch emanated warmth and sent a rush of pity that filled my heart as one might feel seeing an orphaned doe in the wild. I felt an overwhelming urge to secret her away from the ravages she would suffer at the hands of the vile men to come. But just as quickly, a growing urge to seize her in my arms usurped these thoughts—to overwhelm her, feel her flesh pressed to mine, and obliterate her fears. If a gentleman was what she needed, then a gentleman I would be for her.

I became lost in the simple plight of that girl and took her there in that stale room amid the musky odor of the filthy mattress and damp walls. At first, she lay still, an artless youth reeling from the emotions clashing within her. I saw in her face first fear, then pain, and finally peace as her body yielded to mine, enfolding me in a blissful animal passion I'd not known before. I wished it to last forever, but it was over all too soon.

୫

Later when I told Vallaton I'd given the girl a small pile of francs to keep for herself out of pity for her state, he laughed, thinking me a complete fool.

"Ah, the provincial mind is so wonderfully naive. Do not concern yourself with the welfare of these girls," he said. He, Dumont, and I were lunching in a café near Les Halles a few weeks after our dalliance in the rue de Douai. Since then, we'd made several more forays into the various houses of ill repute to be found on offer in Montmartre. "I'd hardly think the fair Ingrid was indeed intact despite what she and the old trollop would have you believe. No doubt a story they cooked up to beggar sympathy from the uninitiated like yourself. You know, tug at their heartstrings and they'll pony up a few extra francs. But no matter, lesson learned, eh?"

Still, I said, I couldn't help feeling some tinge of remorse for having taken advantage, regardless of what her true situation might have been.

"Why feel guilt at all?" he said. "Do you feel any guilt when you hire a coach or bring your clothing to a laundress? You are merely purchasing a service they have chosen to provide. The harlot is no different. In fact, I would argue their service to society is unquestionably greater and their moral character beyond reproach."

"You don't seriously believe that?" Dumont said.

"And why should I not? The prostitute is the ultimate expression of feminine freedom. Once she casts off the burdensome chains of religion and shame—chains I might add forced upon her, as they are upon us all, by a society encumbered by baseless morals—she is a slave no longer. The harlot represents the ideal woman. She is free to bare her soul and body without remorse, as Nature intended. And we are free to partake of her, without fussing over propriety or concern for her cares. If she wants us, she accepts us. If she doesn't, she rejects us. Either way, the decision is freely hers to choose. Other women, those from polite society, have surrendered this choice in favor of securing a suitable matrimonial match, also a burdensome shackle imposed by a skewed sense of imposed morals. Prostitution destroys these bindings. It is how all of the charming sex should be, really."

"You'd have all women become whores?" I said.

"'Whore' is such a vulgar word," Vallaton said, sipping a café au lait. "I do so enjoy it. But, my dear Etienne, as in all things, moderation. There are degrees of turpitude, and the prostitute, like all objets d'art, is subject to interpretation. Applying the term 'whore' to them all unnecessarily, and I might say unfairly, generalizes their individual accomplishments and talents. After all, some women, like pebbles, sink to the very bottom, while others, like cream"—and here he gestured to his frothy demitasse—"will rise to the top."

"And which is your Michette?" Dumont said. Vallaton had sought the girl out several more times since that first night.

"Ah, she," he said, finding himself momentarily lost for words. A greedy smile played upon his lips. "A stone of the heaviest kind. When under the influence of her demon, there is little she won't do."

✦

From that first evening in the rue de Douai, we became an inseparable trio. Our days were filled with study, our afternoons with lectures on the essence of man's existence, his literary accomplishments, and his endless pursuit of both temporary happiness and infinite sorrow. To be sure, there were exams to sit for, treatise to compose, and many an hour spent in the early-morning gloom of my rented library reading by dying candlelight the works of some obscure Latin text. But, to me, studying always manifested itself to be more a formality than an actual enterprise.

Which is not to say I did not apply myself. It remained necessary to my character to quench my insatiable curiosity whenever possible. Study became my religion, though a short-lived conversion it was. I excelled in rhetoric and immersed myself in all manner of philosophy, finding the Latin and Greek I'd mastered in my youth to be most formidable debate weapons, but I found theology especially a complete bore. Uninspired, fraught with contradictions and contrivances devised solely to deflect skepticism brought on itself by painfully obvious logical deficiencies, religion was, for me, a subject of utter disdain.

I'd no love for the church or its teachings. As I reflect now, this revulsion for all things ecclesiastical surely had its roots in the piety of my mother and her self-imposed monastic reclusiveness. More devoted to God than her own son, her deference deprived me of her love. Though Abbé Frère had worked diligently to instill in me a view to righteousness, filling my adolescent head with passages from Aquinas and others of his ilk, I could thankfully boast none of it had stuck, and proudly wore my contrarian nature regarding all things ecclesiastical like a badge of honor, if only ever in the private company of my companions.

In Vallaton, I'd found a brother—one who shared this same loathing for the church but whose own seeds of discontent were sown more deeply than mine.

He'd once confided in me his grandmother had conducted a clandestine affair with a monseigneur, and her daughter, his mother, was the product of that vile coupling. He painted the picture of the innocent young penitent falling victim to the influence of a powerful, hypocritical man. Of course, the holy father denied even knowing the woman, and while he retained his office, she was forced to leave her village in disgrace. I don't know if what he spoke was the truth or a lie he'd told himself through so much repetition it had become his truth, but, for him, it stood undeniable proof of the corruptibility of the cloth and the falsehood of their doctrine. In consequence, he took pleasure at every opportunity to ridicule God and His institutions.

Equally undeniable was the increasing influence Vallaton's carefree demeanor exerted over me, which led to some magnificent, if not entirely horrifying, truths about myself I shudder to recall. I know my most egregious sin to be pride, but as I reflect today, I take none in the actions of my youth and the lengths they drove me to. For as the apostle Paul wrote, "Let nothing be done through strife or vainglory; but in lowliness of mind let each esteem other better than themselves." Sadly, I learned this lesson only too late.

To augment my formal studies, Vallaton took to giving me other reading assignments. From his own personal collection came the works of Laclos, Wilmot, de Viau, Crébillon fils, de Kock, and Rétif. Later, on the occasion of my nineteenth birthday, he presented me a copy of de Sade's *La philosophie dans le boudoir,* boldly proclaiming it my new Bible. The dialogue, by turns both titillating and revolting, put into words sensual delights and perversities I'd not thought possible. I lay awake all night reading it, and when I was through, nearly faint from exhaustion, I found my body drained of its essence but my eyes opened to a new, exhilarating world of potential pleasures.

"It's almost ritual for him," Dumont confided in me one afternoon while we walked on the rue Daguerre. "He read its contents to me in one night not long after we'd met. It was an intriguing spectacle. I'd not seen anyone so overcome with frenzy. I worry for him. I truly mean that, from a purely clinical standpoint. The duality in his nature frightens me at times."

I have come to understand that like a defining sin, all men are also possessed of this duality, this schism, of character in one form or extreme to another.

Though by all outward indications, a distinguished young man of fine quality and demeanor, Vallaton harbored a second, more reckless self, which pursued heavy drink, games of chance, and women of desperate means. His mind was not fractured, not in the medical sense at least. On the contrary, Vallaton maintained a constant grip on his character, almost to the point of obsession. Everything about his mien was carefully measured and honed to a fine perfection. His duality came not from mania, but rather from what I can only describe as a sort of shadow he kept hidden, both from himself and the rest of the world, one that dwelled in the recesses of his deepest consciousness.

This shadow, this "other self," Vallaton wrestled with had as its source a philosophy of rebellion against the moral conventions of civilized society. In this insurrection, he played the part of a spy embedded deep behind enemy lines. By day, he existed as the perfect specimen, the epitome of the high-society gentleman: studious, manicured, proper. But by night, he devolved and allowed a more primeval sensibility to control him that craved to throw in the face of society everything it held dear.

His appetite for the depraved was as insatiable as it was magnetic, and all too rapidly, I had become drawn into the vortex of his Cyprian doctrine. But whereas for my intellectual education Vallaton ably supplied a nearly unending stream of written works on the subject of libertinage, my physical education required a completely separate set of tutors. These I would have to seek out on my own.

I recall one such teacher, if only to provide a sample of the lowliness to which I sank in those early days.

One evening saw me venture out alone into the night in search of my pleasure. I wandered the lanes on the edge of the Place Clichy for several hours when a familiar face drew my attention.

"Monsieur is in search of someone?" she said. "Perhaps I am that someone?"

It was the painted face of Sidonie. A dirty blue frock hung from her shoulders. Her stockings were torn at both knees, and she smelled of onions and wine. Her hair was messily pinned about her head. She'd lost a tooth since last we'd met.

"I do not believe so," I said, stepping on, but she hastily insinuated herself in my path.

"Am I not young enough for Monsieur? You prefer a child, like the little slut Ingrid, then? What does a child know, huh? What can she teach you? Whereas, a woman like me, I can teach you plenty."

Not knowing why, I let her guide me into a passageway off the avenue. Once out of view, she seized my hand, roughly thrusting it under her dress between her bare, cold legs.

"You see? You can have this how you like. Buy me some wine and bread. Let me eat, then you can have me. I have a room not far."

"I know your rooms," I said.

"Not there," she said. "Georgette kicked me out, the bitch. But I have new rooms close by. Some bread and wine first, that is all I ask."

"You don't want money?"

"No one will serve a whore in this neighborhood," she said, spitting. "I am always turned away. What good is money to me if I cannot buy food? Buy me my dinner, and you can fuck me all you want."

I agreed and she led on. Along the way, we stopped at a boulangerie, and I bought a baguette and a half liter of burgundy. In her room—just a cubicle in a ramshackle basement with a rusty bed—she tossed the baguette aside for later. The wine, she downed in quick, greedy gulps from a filthy glass.

"I remember you," she said, hiking up the folds of her dress, revealing a shapely thigh. "You did not want me before, but you do now, yes? Tell me, did you enjoy the petite *la putain* Ingrid? Did she have legs like mine, or were they like sticks? The legs of a child are so hard and bony, don't you think? And what of these?"

She lifted her two weighty breasts to my face. Where Ingrid had been ever the mere girl, Sidonie was much more so the woman.

She clicked her tongue. "A pity one so young should find herself in such a state. I was once like her. Young and inexperienced. She has much to learn, in time."

Sidonie brought her face close to mine. The reek of wine wafted through my nostrils. Again, she brought my hand to her sex.

"Perhaps you want more than a child now, yes?" she whispered, her foulness intoxicating me. "Come have your way with a woman as you should. I'll do whatever you like. Would you like me like a dog? You can use my ass, if you wish? I know many men who say it is much more pleasurable to be inside a woman's ass than in her cunt. I will give it to you. Maybe you would like to whip me? I was once whipped by a fruit merchant until tears of joy streamed down my thighs and soaked the mattress through to the floor. Have you never seen a woman come and spill her fuck like a man does?"

A sudden impulse to beat her, to press her, to flog her, seized me. She grunted all manner of vileness while I forced myself upon her, around her, inside her. I pursued my pleasures with voluptuous abandon. She gave me instruction, caused me to penetrate her over and over, and when that wasn't enough, she begged me to force the neck of the wine bottle in her rectum while she took me in her mouth. I spilled my fuck inside her over and over in great convulsions, leaving me awash in a sea of ecstasy, guilt, and shame. I'd felt pleasures I'd never known possible, torn the veil on my decency, and revealed myself for who I truly was. The corruption of Sidonie's body mingled with the corruption of my soul and brought forth a new man in me, one whose existence could be neither explained nor denied.

From that time forward, physical pleasure took on new, exciting, and terrifying forms. No longer satisfied with pedantic amours, I strove to achieve ever-increasing heights of sensual satisfaction, and this, I confess now within these pages, was merely the beginning of a descent that would carry my soul to depths of profligacy I would have never imagined.

Chapter VI

The journal sat on the table, its pages bookmarked with a length of loose watch chain. Al lay slumped over it, a bent arm tucked under his head for a pillow. His spectacles, still hooked over one ear, hung precariously askew his wrinkled nose. He snored loudly.

This was how Zofia discovered her husband when she came bearing his morning cup of tea. Gently, she nudged him awake.

"You got rid of him, then?" she said.

Al pulled his head up, squinted, and righted his glasses. He saw the empty cot. The clothes on the chair were gone, as was the overcoat.

"He must have left in the night," Al said.

Zofia puttered about the front room, stirring up dust motes as she drew back the curtains. The light of a bright, crisp morning flooded the showroom. Across the street, Katz busied himself laying out rings and necklaces in his display window. A truck lumbered noisily over the cobbles. The Row was waking up. Zofia moved about the store methodically, examining the shelves and walls, scanning the display case, opening the register.

"What are you doing?" Al said.

"Have you opened the safe?"

"He didn't steal anything."

"He might have stolen something," she said.

"He might have also beat me to death in my sleep, but he didn't do that either."

"Where is the watch?"

Al glanced about his table and padded his pockets. His uncle's watch was gone.

"What is that?" Zofia said, noting the journal on the table.

"It's nothing," Al said. "I found it last night." He took the thing and pushed it to the corner of the bench.

"Might he come back for it?"

"I don't think so."

"But if it's his?"

"Don't worry. I don't think it's too important," Al lied. "If it were, he would have taken it with the watch. Besides, he was probably in too much of a hurry to notice he'd forgotten it."

Al spent the rest of the morning stirred to distraction. He tried to work but found himself unable to focus on even the simplest tasks, his thoughts hopelessly preoccupied with the events of the previous evening. Even Oliver took notice. For hours, his uncle barely spoke two words. The details of Etienne's story both intrigued and unnerved him. So much so that, after lunch, Al did something he'd never done in his nearly forty years in business. He left the shop early to take a walk.

The air was unseasonably mild and the park at Washington Square almost deserted. Sidestepping piles of muddy snow and semi-frozen puddles, Al meandered a slow, circuitous route around the patchy green, his hands tucked in his pockets, his thoughts clouded by doubt.

The incredulous tale could hardly be believed. Even if Al were to give himself over to it fully—that the Etienne Allard of his memory was the same Etienne Allard he encountered the night before—he would have to be at least fifty-five years old, and that was simply an impossibility at complete odds with the reality of the man. A complexion such as his, no matter how disheveled, could hardly be mistaken for otherwise. Even the best of men, past their middle age, could never appear so young. Not even on the stage had Al seen it pulled off so convincingly.

And what of the watch? It was not so far-fetched to believe such a thing could pass from hand to hand. Yes, it had been almost thirty years, and it was improbable, yet not wholly impossible, that he should see it again. But if that were so, then it could just as easily have passed into the possession of the man he met last night. Zofia was right. Finding it in his own hands again was indeed proof of nothing.

And yet, he could not so readily dismiss what he had seen. Even if the watch had made such an unlikely journey, this did nothing to explain the presence of the diary, so personal a thing, it could only belong to he who had written it. If it, like the watch, wasn't his either, why keep it?

Al's feet carried him aimlessly out of the park and several blocks away, so preoccupied with his thoughts that he only came around when he'd found himself passing the granite steps of the First National Bank. The memory of Gerhort's masterpiece held so recently in his hands put him in a mood of sudden nostalgia.

Inside, the must of ink and old papers filled the lobby air. A fastidious clerk in square spectacles welcomed him from behind the barred window at the counter. Al requested access to his safe-deposit box.

He was told to wait while the bank manager was fetched. Obediently taking a seat on a bench near the entrance, his hat in his hands, Al waited, and disappeared. Few people tend to take notice of an old man on a bench. He quickly becomes just another part of the scenery.

Sitting there, quietly observing the comings and goings of people buzzing around him, he recalled a line he'd read in the journal: "All men are possessing of a particular sin." It was a strange notion the Frenchman had, that the entirety of a person's life should be judged in this way. He wondered what had brought Etienne to such a narrow conclusion.

To his left, a corpulent clerk with a napkin tucked into his collar sat in a side office munching greedily on a sandwich of tomato and bacon dripping with thick mayonnaise. He slurped loudly from a mug of hot black coffee. Across the room, a handsome junior manager leaned casually on the edge of a desk, laughing and making eyes with a secretary. At the teller's window, a well-heeled gentleman nonchalantly counted out more than five hundred dollars in cash on the counter, while those standing behind him in line craned their necks curiously to catch a glimpse of real wealth on display.

To pass the time, Al made a game of cataloguing each sin he witnessed. All around him was lust, greed, envy, and gluttony. He could not help but think it strange. But can any man be said to sin for following what comes naturally to him? What young man doesn't feel lust in his loins during his lifetime? And who can be blamed for wishing they made just a little bit more than the next man?

These questions would remain unanswered, for just then, the bank manager arrived to escort him to the vault. After his box was retrieved, Al was led to an anteroom to attend to his business in privacy.

Box number 96. An unusual but not extraordinary coincidence it should bear the same number as the year of Gerhort's death, 1896. Nor that it was the same year Al took out the box. Nonetheless, these coincidences served only to feed the feeling of nostalgia growing within Al ever since the night before, when he'd discovered the name *Wallenstein* etched inside the Frenchman's watch.

Rarely these days did Al think of the old country and his youth. But long-forgotten memories sometimes resurfaced. Often, these were mere fleeting sensations, like the heady odor of Old English wafting from his uncle's pipe. Other times, an innocuous image, like the crack in the plaster above Gerhort's tool bench that eerily resembled the crooked, meandering path of the Danube, popped into his mind. But most rare of all was a memory of the old country coming hand in hand with the very object of its source.

The day the telegram arrived from Hamburg informing Al of Gerhort's death had been an ordinary one. There was little to be done. His uncle had engaged a solicitor to help put his affairs in order. The business would go on; the name Wallenstein would still be found on pocket watches for many years to come. Two months later, a man entered the shop, introduced himself politely as Deilman, the self-same solicitor hired by Gerhort, and deposited with Al a small parcel per the instructions in his uncle's will. After Deilman took his leave, Al opened the bundle to find it contained a few unsent correspondence, a handful of photographs, including a daguerreotype of his late father, Friedrich, and one additional item.

He'd seen it only once before, when he was ten years old. Gerhort showed it to him one night not long after Al began his apprenticeship. Its exact origins remained hazy. His uncle would only say it had come to him from his own father, but how *he* had come to acquire it remained a mystery. The ceremony with which Gerhort revealed it to him, and the reverence the old man seemed to hold for it, had remained with Al his whole life.

But at the time, to Al's inexperienced eyes, it appeared nothing more than an inconsequential trinket: a sphere of brass, plated in gold, no bigger than a chicken egg. Intricately engraved with a floral pattern of interwoven vines, evenly spaced, teardrop-shaped perforations, forming a sort of rudimentary latticework pattern pierced the top half. A simple pin-and-knuckle hinge along one side bisected its equator, allowing the top hemisphere to open like a box, revealing the treasure inside: a clock face of pure gold. A single hand counted off the hours one through twelve etched in Roman numerals around the face. There was no minute hand, for there were no minute hashes. It could, at best, only tell the time by the approximate hour. On its base, a tripod of three small, curled gold feet stopped the thing from rolling away when put down. An eyelet secured at the top gave purchase for a chain to be fed through, presumably so it could be worn around the neck or wrist like a piece of jewelry. It was a feat of remarkable craftsmanship and, in a word, beautiful.

"What is it, *Onkel*?" Al asked when the old watchmaker lifted it from its little wooden box.

"A piece of our heritage," Gerhort replied. "Made by the skilled hands of our own people."

"Is it valuable?"

"Beyond measure. It is very old. Three, maybe four, of these remain in the whole of the world," he said, holding it up to the lamplight, peering at its gleaming surface over the spectacles dangling at the end of his thick Teutonic nose. "Once, these were only owned by kings and emperors. But this one is ours."

"If it's valuable, mightn't we sell it?" Al said.

"I would not dream to do so in a thousand years," Gerhort said, chastising the boy for his impetuous suggestion. "This was made by the father of our industry. Would you give away something so important for something so trivial as a few pieces of gold?"

Shamed by his uncle's reprimand, he said he wouldn't had he known how important the thing actually was.

"Value comes in many forms," Gerhort said. "A thing can have monetary value, or it can have value in its essence. The simple fact it exists gives it meaning beyond what men could possibly pay for it. This is not an artifact from history; it is history itself. One cannot just buy and sell history. This has passed through time, possibly by the will of God himself, and made its way to us. It is ours to preserve and care for until God deems it necessary to have it pass through us to someone else. Sell it? I would sooner sell my own soul to *der Teufel*."

But such extremes would not be necessary. Gerhort packed *das kleines ei*, or the little egg, as he called it, back into its wooden box and hid it safely away in the recesses of the workshop. That was 1870. Al wouldn't see it again for twenty-six years. When that same wooden box arrived at his door, the sole item of his familial legacy from the old country, he'd taken no chances to secure its safety. He promptly walked to the First National Bank and deposited it in a safe box, which he'd maintained ever since.

Al lifted the steel lid of box 96 and took out the wooden carton seated within. He plucked a layer of cotton cloth stuffed inside and removed the petite treasure nestled in its folds. It had been some years since he'd last looked at the egg, and it was even smaller than he remembered, brittle almost, like a stiff breeze might carry it right off the table and send it crashing to the floor. Carefully, with the tip of his finger, he unhooked the clasp holding the two halves together and lifted the lid, revealing the gold face still gleaming as brilliantly as the day it had been made. It hadn't run in ages, even when it was in Gerhort's possession, and Al dared not try to unseat the movement for fear of damaging the exquisite workmanship and the priceless four-hundred-year-old mechanism within.

Curiosity always got the better of Al when he saw the thing, and he longed to know its secrets. He knew it now to be a rare specimen, probably made in Bavaria or Middle Franconia, and maybe the very last of its kind. There was little history beyond what Gerhort had told him about it, which was practically nothing. Inside the smooth dome of the lid, an area had been etched, possibly with a previous owner's name, but this had been scratched away a long time ago. The only thing Al knew for certain was, beyond its sentimental value, it undoubtedly held a significant financial one.

"Might my own sin be greed?" he thought to himself as he contemplated it. Certainly, selling the egg would be a boon. He could pass on a fortune to Oliver and his soon-to-be new bride while still keeping a tidy sum for himself and

Zofia in their twilight years. There would even be enough for his other nephews and Fat Maja.

But Al loved his work too much to surrender to retirement. And his own tale of hard work tugged at his conscience every time he thought of taking the easy way out. Wouldn't giving away money with abandon, even to his own family, be just replacing greed with sloth? How would he be teaching Oliver anything about responsibility if the boy never had to work another day in his life?

Staring at the egg, Al let his mind wander. What use was there in puzzling over such matters? He wasn't going to sell it at any cost. Perhaps one day he would pass it on to Oliver and let the boy choose for himself whether he saw value in its substance or its speculative worth. For now, he simply wrapped it back up in its cotton blanket, seated it in its wooden box, and returned it to the vault.

❧

He walked the streets for hours, not returning home until after dark. The air, so refreshingly mild during the day, had turned brisk once again as evening approached. Toward dusk, a layer of grayish clouds rolled across the sky, threatening another night of snowfall. The falling temperatures quickened Al's step, and by the time he'd arrived back at the shop, the cold had crept into his old bones once again.

The apartment above the store where he and Zofia had lived for decades was a model of frugality: one bedroom, a cramped sitting room-cum-dining room, and a small kitchen with a door leading to stairs communicating with the storeroom of the shop below.

Al caught a whiff of cabbage and fish in the air—another dinner he'd missed for the second night in a row. He knew he might be in for it this time. At least in the past when he'd missed supper, it could be blamed on work. Tonight, there was no excuse.

Zofia sat in the dim sitting room, her hands occupied with darning socks beneath the light of her lamp, the warbling voice of Caruso floating quietly from the Victor phonograph on the sideboard. Al tried to act relaxed, as if his unexplained absence were nothing at all out of the ordinary. He told himself coming up the stairs, she'd have not been worried. He was wrong.

"*Tutaj jesteś!*" she said, tossing aside her knitting. "My God, where have you been all this time?"

"Just walking," Al said.

"My husband works," she said. "That's what he does. My husband does not 'just walk.' He does not leave his work. Where did you go?"

"Nowhere special. Everything is all right."

"But this is not like you to go off by yourself. This is because of last night. Because of that *szaleniec*."

"Maybe," Al said. "I don't know." Hours of walking had failed to ease his mind. Questions still filled his head and turned over like so many dumplings in a pot of boiling soup.

"It is making you sick, I think. We should have phoned for the police. I knew it was wrong to let him stay. Promise me, Albie, if he comes back here, you will call for the police. For me, you will do this?"

Al promised. He took her in his arms and hugged her small body to his.

"But you are chilled," she said. "What were you thinking going out into the cold?"

"I haven't caught my death yet."

"Come," Zofia said, leading him into the kitchen. "I made some *kapuśniak*. It's still hot. We eat now, we forget about the madman, and you tell me where you have been."

❧

Later that night, Al found sleep difficult. Unsettling dreams kept his mind turning, giving him over to fitful bouts of anxious rest that saw him stirred awake several times. By three a.m., he deemed the whole enterprise of sleep hopeless and quietly slunk out of bed.

Making sure not to disturb Zofia, he padded softly down the hall to the kitchen, carefully opened the door, and crept downstairs to the storeroom, stepping lightly to avoid any sound. It was nearly freezing, and though he had his robe, he regretted not taking his coat to keep warm. But he dared not risk going back for fear of waking Zofia. Why had he gone downstairs in the middle of the night? It was a conversation he simply did not wish to have.

He switched on the lamp and stopped short. There on the stool beside the cot lay the shirt and trousers he'd put out the night before. Neatly folded, they'd been returned in the exact spot from which they'd been taken. A handwritten note, folded in half, stuck out from the trouser pocket. It read simply: *Avec une sincère gratitude.* So, the madman had come back, after all.

Al looked about with a start but found no one there but himself; the only other set of eyes in the place his own, reflected in a small mirror hung on the wall beside his bench. Knowing if Zofia learned their raving intruder had indeed returned, she'd be thrown into another panic, Al hastily tucked the note back into the trouser pocket and then shoved the lot under the bed, concealing the pile of clothes behind a box of old tools.

Instinctively, to calm his nerves, he began to tinker. He took up the 1905 Elgin silver hunter case he'd left unfinished before leaving that morning, but it was no use. As unfocused awake as he had been asleep, Al could not stop thinking about Etienne's unusual story. He felt his thoughts drifting back to the journal; the written history of a man seemingly out of place in time.

He knew the book lay in the top drawer of the bench. He'd hastily secreted it there to hide it from prying eyes. Now he felt wracked with guilt for ever opening it. Confession or no, a man's thoughts were his own unless he *chose* to reveal them, and Etienne had certainly not done so. But could his questions ever hope to be answered without learning more?

Reluctantly, with no little sense of shame, he pulled the book from the drawer and began again.

Chapter VII

I continued to pay regular call to Sidonie. The flowering of my carnal desires coincided with a new appreciation for art and beauty heretofore unknown to me. Prodigious study of form became my mind's chief occupation, the marriage of the objectively physical and subjectively sensual. Ordinary objects and everyday occurrences took on a new definition. The smooth curvature of a violin's lower bout described the curves of the female hips and buttocks, the fleshy bloom of a tulip, the folds of her pulpy sex. The pungent aroma of sweat, once offensive and undesirable, now recalled the tangy odor of a whore's breath when seized by the convulsions of her *petite mort.*

With Sidonie, the animal woman had taken on a new essence. No longer a mere tool to be handled, she became more an instrument to be played. With deft hands, she could be made to play any tune I commanded.

Dumont revolted at the comparison.

"An instrument is also a tool, isn't it?" he inquired once while we sat in his rooms.

"To be sure," I replied. "But there is a uniqueness that sets it apart from the others. To each its purpose. You can see the difference between the blacksmith's hammer and the surgeon's cutting blade, a tool you yourself strive to master, can't you? Aren't the inner workings of the human corpus not unlike those of, say, the piano? Lift the lid or peel back the skin, and what do you find? You see bones and vein and sinew; I see struts and strings and pins. But are they not one in the same in function and purpose? Misalign any one item, and the whole construction falls out of tune. As with your patient, so it is with woman. We are both musicians of the body, you and I, striving to align the internal works to achieve a pleasurable harmony. Once you've learned the melody, the rest is simply a matter of practice. But I think I find my hours of rehearsal a bit more enjoyable than yours."

"There is much more to what I'm trying to do." Dumont coughed, hurt by this oversimplification. He drew a handkerchief to stifle his wheeze. Stress always incensed his condition. A weakness of his respiration, he once told me. "There is no tune to be mastered. A patient, like a piece of music, is unique and must be treated as such. You do an injustice to all of humanity, females in particular, if you believe there is a universal key to bringing them to heel simply through physical pleasures."

"Matthieu disagrees," I said.

"I'm not surprised. He's often blinded by his own inconstancy. You'd do well to avoid becoming ensnared in the same trap. He calls those women free, but make no mistake, they are slaves. And slavery, even to one's own passions, is bondage nonetheless, and not the natural state of man."

In recent weeks, Dumont's studies occupied nearly all his time, and he spent noticeably less with Vallaton. A distance had grown between them, brought on, no doubt, by a fundamental divergence of philosophies. More and more, he found Vallaton's doctrine repugnant. I believe he'd suffered a private crisis of moral conscience and had been atoning for his recent behavior by rededicating himself anew to his studies. He'd begun going to church again too, though he would not openly admit it to me.

I thought to question his subjugation to God as replacing one form of bondage for another but held my tongue for fear of aggravating his condition. If shackling myself to a cause was my lot, then to be chained to pleasure was a surrender I made without reservation.

Despite our difference of opinion, our friendship remained intact, though increasingly libertine desires drew me further and further from my academic pursuits, something Dumont took no hesitation chastising me for time and again. I never faulted my friend for his overly cautionary nature and dutifully maintained I would heed his warnings.

❦

With the arrival of spring, Vallaton and I sought out new ways to appease a growing appetite for the voluptuous life. Ambling the botanical gardens one afternoon, our heads filled with the aroma of rebirth after the long chill of winter and brought forth a stirring for new conquests of the soul.

"It is marvelous to be French," he said while casually eyeing a pair of debutantes reading beneath a shade tree. The stimulating titter of coquettish giggles filled our ears as we passed. Further on, two old gentlemen on a bench engaged in a bout of draughts, intently studying the board like *maréchaux* surveying a battlefield. The sight seemed to spark inspiration in him.

"I feel like gambling," he said. "Have you any money?"

"A little," I demurred.

Vallaton knew well my penchant for gaming. By the middle of my first year in Paris, there were few secrets between us anymore, a stark comparison to my friendship with Dumont, whose increasing prudishness had become a bit of a bore.

The first time we'd visited a gaming room, I'd astounded my friend and confounded everyone at the table with my preternatural command of the cards. Adolescent years spent perfecting the art of reading faces brought me swift and decisive victories at the Brelan tables. But civility reigned in the houses of Clichy, and the stakes remained surprisingly small, especially when in noble company. Sadly, individuals of class and reserve rarely abandon themselves to impulsive propositions. For more exquisite hazard, I had to venture further afield, to the frayed edges of Parisian civilization, to the domain of the opium eaters, the pimps, and the outcasts.

"The addict is a strange fellow," Dumont once told me. "The force compelling him is almost supernatural. The ultimate slave"—a word he'd taken to using more and more in my presence—"his free will is abandoned to the drug, and all sensibilities, all inhibitions, cast off. Of a singular mind, with near superhuman focus, he will disregard all rational thought in pursuit of the assuagement of the pain of his separation from that which he believes, only *believes*, can cure him of said pain. In this way, you might say the addict is a slave not to the drug, nor to the pain he seeks to alleviate, but to himself alone. There is nothing he will not do to fulfill the lust for his next dose: forfeit his possessions, surrender his freedom, even kill." I listened attentively, and thanked God such pain did not afflict me.

I found these sorts, the lowest of the low, the ones will-ing to wager the most, taking the most delectable pleasure in wringing from them the last drops of their good sense and worldly possessions.

Once, in a sordid tavern on the outskirts of Saint-Ouen while playing Bouillotte, my good fortune saw the ruin of a wholesale merchant calling himself Saloman. Time and again, he challenged me only to walk away with his pockets turned out. This went on for several days, the sums he lost to my hands substantial, until finally, the greedy sot turned up no longer. Vallaton said he'd heard the man hanged himself. I could never confirm if this were true, and at first blush, the thought horrified me. It wasn't until sometime later, when my libertinage had passed its budding stage and assumed its full bloom, that I came to understand, and ultimately relish, the delight such control over the destiny of another could provide.

At the conclusion of my first year of studies, I returned home to Marseille at the written request of my father. I was nei-ther eager to leave Paris nor see my family, but my mother had taken ill, and he felt my presence might lift her spirits. I traveled south in early July, intent on staying no more than a month.

Lipa greeted me upon my arrival. Though it had only been a year, my former caregiver looked to have aged ten or more. Strands of white prematurely streaked her once dark hair, and her strong Slavic cheeks had plumped ruddy and full, like the flesh of a peach. Only thirty-four, she already re-sembled a woman in a much later stage of life. In my absence, she'd wed our gardener, a fellow called Hugo, and had two months earlier given birth to a daughter.

"A beautiful child," I remarked upon seeing the baby. The comment was no frivolous observation. The child's face held the promise of beauty to come.

"We called her Yelena," she said with a tinge of sadness. "After your mother."

The girl lay in her bassinet pleasantly awestruck by the new world around her, glimpsing it all through a pair of bright-brown eyes.

"It is strange," Lipa said. "She is my own, yet I feel I have already raised one child to adulthood. Now I will begin again."

I made no reply.

"I'm sorry," she said, realizing how I might take her meaning, "I didn't mean to imply that your mother..."

"It's all right," I said. "How is she?"

"Not well. Difficulties persist. Your father is thinking of taking her away from here for a time. Taking her back to her people."

"What is it that's wrong?"

Since I'd left, Lipa's duties as chief servant had shifted from caring for me to caring for my mother. Too consumed himself in his own affairs, my father failed to notice his wife being consumed by her own inner demon. Physicians were consulted, tests performed, recommendations made to visit the mountains and take the waters, but physically, she presented no symptoms of sickness other than a nameless malaise that plagued her spirit.

"A weakening in her soul," was all Lipa could say. "It is as if she is simply surrendering. She's always been fragile, your mother—not meant for the strain this life has put on her."

"I want to see her," I said.

"Later, I think. She's just come back from her chapel. It's always at its worst then."

I took my leave of Lipa and her child and went to consult my father in his study. I'd hoped to find him alone but was dismayed when it was not he who'd greeted me but his secretary.

A weaselly sort, parasitic and pandering, Michel Bloch had been my father's clerk since the early days of the Compagnie and a fixture of his study as much as the skins hanging from the walls. A crafty Jew, part advisor, part aide-de-camp, he was rarely far from Jean's side. A blind man could see he'd positioned himself as the natural successor to lead the enterprise and viewed me as nothing more than the sole obstacle barring his way to this end.

"The young Etienne makes his triumphant return," Bloch said, crossing the room to greet me, a tactic he often employed to prevent me from disturbing my father at his work. He was an ugly man, tall and wiry, with a thin, scraggly beard. His punctilious demeanor lent his character an air of the artificial. Everything, from his mincing gait to the measure of his smile, felt practiced and false. It had always been this way. I felt squeamish taking his hand.

"How go your studies?"

"Well," I replied curtly.

"And what of life in Paris? I myself have not been in some time. What's the agenda for the youth of the Sorbonne today, eh? Filling young heads with Marxist rubbish, are they? You'd do well to stay clear of that nonsense. Stick with Turgot or Quesnay."

"Actually, I find Diderot more to my liking," I said.

"And what is his position on Bastiat's broken window, then?"

"Don't encourage him," my father said, though, in truth, I did not know for which of us his reprimand was meant. He did not deign to raise his eyes from his work. "Though I'd hardly categorize belle lettres a worthwhile endeavor. Is that where my money goes?"

The Mediterranean sun cast a broad wall of light across the room. Like a king behind his portcullis, my father sat in the shadow beyond this blinding sheet swimming with dust motes. Stepping through, I felt its intense warmth upon the side of my face, as well as the calculating eyes of Bloch on the back of my neck.

"Sometimes," I said. "Other times, it brings me great joy to spend it with reckless abandon."

"So I see," he said, regarding the smartness of my suit. "Have you seen your mother yet?"

"She's unavailable at the moment. Lipa says she's been taking to her chapel with more frequency than usual. A sudden renewal of her fervor?"

"Obsession is more like it," he said. "We'll be sailing to Tyre in a few months."

"Lipa mentioned."

"Good girl. Loyal too. That's important at times like these."

"I should say so. If not for her, it would seem Mother would have practically no one at all."

He didn't bother hiding his annoyance.

"It's by her own choice she's brought this about," he said. "It's petulance, plain and simple. I've always made sure she doesn't want for anything. You think this languor she's fallen into as of late is a result of some coldness on my part?"

"It has never been 'of late.' It has always been. What makes it any different now?"

"I don't know. She doesn't speak much to me anymore."

"Did she ever?"

"There was a time," he said, his ire rising.

We fell silent.

"Why wait to go?" I said. "Why not leave sooner?"

"The business places great demand on your father," Bloch said, making his presence known again. "There is much that requires his attention if he's to take leave. Meetings, correspondence..."

"And you are not capable of dealing with these things yourself?"

"It would be folly on your father's part if he did not take the matter in hand personally."

"So then the folly *would* be in leaving things in your hands alone?" I replied cavalierly.

"Enough," my father, said returning to his work. "I have to tend to them personally. I have responsibilities to the company." The minute purse of his lips and sudden contracting of his iris betrayed him. The lie on his face was clear as day.

"Tell me, Father, do you receive all family like clients, or am I the only one to have the privilege?"

"You've caught me at a bad time," he said. "I've work to do. Go and find your mother if you can. She'll be pleased to see you. Perhaps *your* presence will raise her spirits, though I highly doubt it."

He abruptly returned to his figures as way of my dismissal. As I left, he inquired how long I'd intended to stay, but I did not answer.

⁂

I thought of nothing but returning to Paris.

My presence in the house did initially seem to please my mother, but nonetheless, she would not be diverted from her routine. There was the odd exchange, but much of her days were filled with an endless cycle of practiced devotions and lengthy periods of a type of waking catatonia. Her monastic rituals had taken a severe turn. The upper floors bore less the atmosphere of a home and more of a cloister. Silently, she moved from room to room, her eyes perpetually lowered. When she did deign to look at me or speak to me, it was as if she were doing so across a great distance. I felt myself not her son but a simple visitor in her home, a morbidity that made my stay nearly unbearable.

Mercifully, an unexpected letter from Dumont briefly revived my spirits. I'd not heard a word from Vallaton since I'd left, which made the letter all the more welcome. It seemed he'd been unwittingly pulled into a bit of intrigue he was only too eager to relate.

Dearest Etienne,

I hope this missive finds you in good health among the comforts of your family home and the affections of your loved ones. I trust your journey south was a pleasant one, and I sincerely hope you can find time to relax and take a respite from your Parisian distractions.

I myself have been having quite an adventure of my own. It's the oddest thing. A sort of mystery has been laid before me, and though I have my ongoing studies to consider, I must admit an entirely new diversion has been occupying nearly all my time as of late. I can barely contain my enthusiasm and felt perhaps you might be entertained by my findings as well.

About two weeks ago, as I was preparing to go out for the evening, I was startled by a terrible crash of glass on the landing and a desperate cry of pain. I raced to the hall to find Madame Crespi collapsed in a heap on the floor having slipped and taken a fall down several stairs. (Don't worry, it was not too bad. A few bruises and scrapes. She was quite shaken, however, but is already well on the road to recovery). She'd been on her way to deliver an evening meal to that bizarre M. Albin up in the garret when it happened, and the tray of food was destroyed. I thought it strange at the time, but as I helped her back to her room, all she could think of was how the old hermit would not be getting his meal.

The following morning, after the doctor had tended to her, Madame Crespi called for me and asked if *I* wouldn't mind bringing the recluse his meals, as she was still rattled from her accident. I was apprehensive, but she pleaded with me. Someone must tend to him because he was incapable of tending to himself. I was, at first, reluctant, but I, of course, relented. After all, what kind of doctor could I ever hope to be if I refused to aid a poor invalid?

She gave me strict instructions; I was to bring his tray to the door and knock six times. She was very keen on it being six knocks, no more, no less, after which I was to open the door (he would not let me in), place the tray on the bedside stand, and then leave. Under no circumstances was I to look around the room, comment on its state or the state of its occupant, or speak directly to him at any time. Suffice it to say, I was more than intrigued by the curious nature of this direction, and up the stairs I went.

I did as she asked, knocked six times, and then tried to enter. The handle turned easily enough in my hand, but it was an effort to push the door in. When I finally got it open, I saw why.

It took a few seconds for my eyes to adjust to the dimness. Though there are a few small dormer windows up there, they are caked and crusted with years of grime and permit little natural light to invade the space. And what a space! Books, everywhere books. There must be more than a thousand volumes crammed into that decrepit attic. They were everywhere, stacks from floor to ceiling, some two or three rows deep. What space was not occupied by these tomes was taken up by a wretched straw mattress bed, a dusty iron stove, and a faded Georgian writing desk. This is where I first spotted the hunched figure of the literary anchorite huddled over an ancient volume, his nose mere centimeters from the text.

I'd half expected to see the wizened face of a wrinkled old man, for it was the only vision of a man I could conjure who would live in such a place. An old friar or abbot in dusty tunic. But to the contrary, he's young. Not as young as you or I, mind you, but he does not appear to be much past his middle age.

He was deep in contemplation, mumbling frantically to himself. I knew I was on the precipice of overstaying my welcome but found I could not take my eyes from the scene. Suddenly, he jerked from his studies and I thought took notice of me lingering in the doorway. He didn't look up but merely sensed my presence as if he'd felt a disturbance in the air around him, then he returned to his strange mumblings. But there is the aura of madness about him. The room is like a cell in an asylum. I cannot lie when I say the minute gesture of his sudden pause sent a shudder through my very soul, and I cannot say how Madame Crespi has kept going in there for all of these years. It's terribly odd. One gets the sense the place is under the shadow of some kind of shroud. I placed the tray of food on the bedside table as instructed and left as quietly as I could.

I continued this service for Madame Crespi for several more days until she recovered enough to resume the odious duty herself. But fate intervened and put a stop to both our torments. Albin died, quietly, but quite suddenly, just two days ago.

I inquired about kin, and learning she believed he had none, as he'd had no visitors in the nearly seven years he'd lived in her house, I immediately inquired what she planned to do with his library, and was ecstatic when she permitted me to go through at my leisure and take what I wished, claiming a learned student such as myself had more use for dusty old books than she.

I tell you, Etienne, the trove that strange man had accumulated defies belief. There are volumes in his collection spanning nearly four centuries, maybe more: texts bound in fine maroquin, codex in at least two dozen languages, diaries, illuminated manuscripts, a folio of scrolls the museums of Europe could only dream of owning. I've only just begun to catalog everything, a task that will no doubt take months to complete.

You can see for yourself the sheer magnitude of this undertaking when you get back. I hope your curiosity might be as equally piqued as mine and you would be willing to assist me in going through it all. We can discuss it further when you return.

Yours sincerely,

Paul

❧

On the last evening before my departure, I took dinner with my father in the main dining room, a space usually reserved for parties or large gatherings. My father had taken to eating there alone with regularity while my mother ate in her rooms, where she preferred spartan meals in her own company.

If Jean were the king lording over his realm from behind his desk by day, he was evermore the emperor without a court at the dining table by night. Solitary, but far from contemplative, he ate with meticulous precision, undisturbed by his solitude.

But with my presence came the rare opportunity to give vent to his royal vexations. It began between the fish course and the lamb.

"You know," he said, "Bloch was right. You'd do better to focus your studies on the practical, not the esoteric. The metaphysical mind brings little to the table that can serve a nation. These idle studies will produce nothing of value for you. A terrible waste of time and money."

"Socrates said the only good was knowledge and the only evil ignorance."

"Frivolous nonsense," he said. "Philosophy is the occupation of the sluggard."

"And management the occupation of the dullard," I waxed poetically. "Really, Father, for a man as worldly as yourself, I expected more appreciation from you."

"Travels haven't made me worldly. They've made me wealthy. And you'd do well to remember where the source of your wealth comes from," he snapped, jabbing the end of his fork at me. "It was your Voltaire who said work staves off boredom, vice, and need. Don't look so astonished. Yours is not some immaculate insight. Think you're the only one who's ever read philosophy? But most of us took it for what it was, the overinflated babble of inactive men. Only, in this case, he happened to be right. I am an important man. And the Compagnie must endure."

"And it shall endure," I said. "In the more-than-capable hands of Bloch. Why are you not satisfied with that?"

"The Jew will have his share," he spat with animus that took me aback. I saw, perhaps for the first time, he'd no love for Bloch either, but viewed him as an effective tool to be utilized in the name of prosperity. Like my mother, just another piece of chattel. "But he'll not have more. You will take my place, and the sooner you reconcile yourself to it, the better. I'll not have him seizing your legacy, nor will I have you discard it so childishly."

And on and on. There were threats, rebukes, and censure on both sides. There is neither need nor purpose in telling the tale further. By the time the cheese was brought, I'd lost my will to argue. In the end, I relented, in the name of futility, and tacitly agreed to consider his position, though it was obvious I was lying.

I departed the following morning. Lipa was there to see me off, my father too. Like all our interactions, the parting was brief and officious. My mother chose to remain in her rooms, watching my leaving from a second-floor window like a sort of haunting phantom. As the carriage rolled down the house drive on its way to the station, I could not help but take a breath of relief that soon I would once again be far from the troubles of that house of woe.

It would be the last time I would ever see my mother and father.

My return to Paris in that late summer found Vallaton entertaining his whimsies with a certain Madame Janvier, a married woman with whom he'd become acquainted in my absence. It was due to this distraction and no other, he claimed, he'd neglected to write while I was away.

He lounged on the settee while conferring upon me the more sordid details of their assignations.

"She's a woman of shifting passions," he mused. "Inflamed with desire one moment, melancholy the next. As mercurial as the breeze. The only way to tell which way it is blowing on any given day is by judging her feet."

"How is that?" I said.

"She has quite small feet," he said. "And that unusual condition whereby her middle toe is longer than the others. Dumont would know what to call it. Anyway, how is the doctor these days? I haven't seen much of him around as of late."

"I wouldn't know either," I said. "Spends most of his time at the college or locked in his rooms with the books he seized from the garret."

In truth, I'd yet to spend any real time with Dumont since my return several weeks earlier. We did while away a few evenings looking through the collection of the hermit's horde, which Paul had relocated to his own rooms, but while his interest continued to be piqued, I soon grew weary of the endeavor. I found the manner of Albin's death to be eminently more curious, but Paul had dismissed it as a simple apoplexy and said there was little to discuss. He was by far more intrigued by the stacks of papers the man had left behind, but really, it was just a mess of dusty, old books, after all.

"Pity to waste so much time on such useless pursuits," Vallaton reflected before returning to the topic of his lover's feet. "Anyway, they provide no end of trouble for her, always causing discomfort. She's accumulated a multifarious collection of shoes and slippers from the four corners of the earth. Every time I visit, she's wearing a different pair. And I've come to discover she coordinates their color with her mood. If it's green, she's feeling pensive and preoccupied. Pink, and she's sad, but only if it's a Friday. Any other day, she's contemplative. Blue, and she gives herself to me before I'm practically in the door."

"Sounds a trifle to keep it all straight."

He went on to dissect other body parts and their respective coverings in a similar fashion, his sensuality piqued by the opposition of emotions with the textures, colors, and cut of her clothing and jewelry. After a time, I'd begun to develop an image of a woman of regal bearing and a penchant for taking younger lovers into her bed whenever the fancy struck her. He said there were others before him, and there would be others after him. There was most probably another who occupied her bed when he was not there as well.

"And what of her husband?" I said.

"An official, and as ignorant as the day he was born. A bureaucrat in the ministry of urban planning or some such nonsense. A perfectly boring man, to tell the truth, but quite wealthy. Family money, of course. Keeps magnificent apartments in Passy when he's in the city, but there's a larger estate near Vaux-le-Vicomte I hear is quite impressive. Eugénie only admits me to the apartments, you see."

"And he suspects nothing?"

"Sadly, yes. I find it a bit of a disappointment, if I'm to be honest. To be sure, the clandestine element of our rendez-vous gives rise to an intense felicity, but I can't help believing its effects would be magnified a hundredfold if there were even the slightest danger the fool would discover us. As it is, his work is all-consuming and there is no chance of this. The spice of danger is missing from the recipe, and it makes the dish rather bland."

"Then why carry on the affair? Find some other fare to whet your appetite. Besides, I thought you abhorred the parlors of the upper crust?"

"Oh, I do." He sighed. "There are many others. Eugénie is not the only whore in my retinue, just the most elegant. She showers me with gifts every time we meet. It's my finer nature, I think. She's a respectful woman, and so I play the respectful lover. It's all quite proper, even in the boudoir. She's organizing a séance soon. An unusual penchant she has. I can give you details later. But come and see for yourself. I'll make your introductions. You might find yourself to her liking as well. And who knows, it might be a welcome change from that Clichy whore you've been busying yourself with."

The mention of Sidonie instantly set my mind aflutter with visions of lascivious activity.

Before my trip south, I'd made regular visits to her subterranean hovel. My carnal delights had expanded at an exponential rate, demanding ever more rigorous explorations, and with my steady supply of food and francs, Sidonie was only too willing to find new and grotesque ways to debase herself for my amusement.

Wishing to resume our acquaintance after several weeks apart, I sought her out the very night of my return but, alas, found her cubicle deserted. I inquired in several brothels but turned up nothing. No one knew or had seen a girl of her description. I began to lose hope. Like so many street harlots on their own, plying their trade for scraps of moldy bread, staving off the reaper and God knows who else every night, I could not but conclude she'd no doubt met a miserable and lonely end.

But it transpired late one rainy evening fate would grant me one final encounter. Walking along the edge of the ramshackle hovels of Le Maquis in the shadow of the butte Montmartre, after having spent an evening in the arms of a bewitching Algerian girl possessing remarkable agility and frightfully ferocious climaxes, I spotted the huddled figure of my dear Sidonie taking shelter from the drizzle in a dimly lit portico.

I made to cross the lane, but my route was intercepted by a dark figure in oily bib overalls and a tweed hat. This ruffian, perhaps a machinist or stevedore, judging by his rough garb, reached her first and struck up a conversation. I ducked back into the shadows and observed the exchange.

I could not hear the substance of his proposition, but clearly, Sidonie wanted no part of it. He proffered coins, but she refused. He looked about the avenue, his face obscured by the darkness. The street was deserted but for we three. He returned the coins to his pocket and produced in their place a small phial of liquid, the appearance of which gave her over to a sort of withering hopelessness. Like a thief, she made to seize the bottle from his hand. The brute yanked it back out of reach, but not out of sight. There was a standoff and a curt negotiation.

I followed some distance behind, concealing myself in the shadows. They turned a corner, then another, and for a moment, I thought I'd lost them in the labyrinth of low houses, broken fences, and clapboard shacks that make up the slum of Le Maquis, when their huddled figures emerged crossing a dusty yard beneath the gnarled branches of a dying linden tree. They crossed a dry culvert by way of a rough plank bridge and entered a decrepit shack standing on a foundation of crumbling limestone.

The light drizzle increased to a steady rain, concealing my footsteps. I hid around the back crouched in the mud between a mess of tall weeds and a row of pickets, watching through the broken slats of the shutters as the macabre scene unfolded.

Sidonie, soaked to the bone, hugged her arms, shifting impatiently as he beat the wet from his coat and lit the lamp. But this discomfort ceased with the reappearance of the phial. Impulsively, she lunged for it, but he caught her in his strong arms. In the lamplight, I got a full look at him; calloused hands and broad shoulders spoke to the rough life of a tradesman. Weasel-faced and whiskered, he described a bulbous rat in human form. She struggled to get free of him, wincing in pain as he clutched her arms in his paw-like hands. Through the rain, I heard her hoarsely exclaim the name Gaspare and beg to be given what she'd been promised, but he remained unmoved not the least for her writhing. He held her fast until she went limp, sagged to the floor, and wept, her tears evincing a stirring in my loins.

The rain fell harder. Squatting in the mud, I watched this Gaspare pass her the bottle, in his own time. Greedily, she tore out the cork and downed the draught in two or three gulps, her exposed neck convulsing rhythmically as she drank it down. Her breast swelled as the tincture coursed warmly down her throat and the empty phial spilled from her fingers. Already, the ingested potion was taking the desired effect. Soon, Sidonie looked to be far away, her eyes heavy, her head swooning, her mind adrift on the waves of an invisible sea.

She sat on the floor like a child, propped up on one arm, gently rocking. With her temporarily sedated, this Gaspare removed his coat and hat, slumped down in a tattered chair, and lit a cigarette. Through squinted eyes and the haze of acrid smoke, he dully observed Sidonie in her luscious reverie, studying her as one might contemplate a sculpture in bronze. For that is what she had become, an object to be admired—curious, perhaps even beautiful in a way, but intrinsically one devoid of purpose. Like a piece of art, her meaning came only from what others saw in her.

I had mused upon this subject from time to time, noting the vacuity of a person such as Sidonie, one who is simultaneously existent and nonexistent. I'd come to view prostitutes not as human per se, but rather like holes in the otherwise homogenous cloth of humanity—a shadowy form where a person should have been, but instead where one only found an abyss of space, the absence of a person, a void without meaning. This non-purpose, in turn, itself gave purpose. For it was only when someone so low as Sidonie could be reduced to a vapid impression in time, a blank canvas, so to speak, that I could truly appreciate the beauty in the sensual process whereby I created my own pleasure, at the exclusion of all other concerns. Sex had become for me by then a purely artistic process, my own depravity being the creative muse.

Which is why viewing the scene as I was, from the outside, gave the entire affair a new and wholly voluptuous delectability, like the feeling one might get watching a great artist at work.

Stubbing out his cigarette, Gaspare picked her up and tossed her on the bed. She giggled as if in a dream as he brusquely jerked her dress from her shoulders, causing her large, loose breasts to spill out. He tugged the folds of cloth aside, exposing her ample thighs. The master was preparing his canvas. All that remained was to ready the instrument.

And what an impressive and frightful instrument it was. Perhaps three inches short of a full foot, Gaspare's member looked a menacing sight, and for a brief moment, I felt the slightest pity for poor Sidonie, who would surely be rent from such a cudgel. But there was hardly time for pity, for the artist was impatient and set to his task with cruel vigor.

Pulling her near, he thrust himself into her in one violent push, wrenching from her throat a bestial cry. This only encouraged the brute, his face unmoved by his work, to intensify the force of his attack. Sidonie lay limp under the assault, her will to fight blunted by the drug. When she did try to free herself, he seized her in his paws, pinning her down.

Not content with riving her in the usual fashion, he proceeded to sunder her ass with the full extent of his weapon. With his great bulk pressing down upon her with abandon, Sidonie's face became entangled within the folds of the ragged bedsheets, but he cared not a bit for her desperation. She could but grunt and wriggle helplessly about as he spat all form of vileness into her ears until, after several minutes more, she ceased to resist at all.

When it was over, Gaspare returned to his chair and lit a cigarette. Sidonie's damp, kneaded body lay sprawled across the mattress. He kicked her limp leg, but she did not stir. He tugged on her torn dress, but she remained still. There was blood on the mattress, and blood on his member. There was the steady patter of rain on the roof. But there was no longer breath in the pitiful Sidonie.

I remained transfixed upon the sight of her lifeless body, and found a strangled pain burning in my chest, as if my lungs sought to burst. It seemed I'd been holding my breath through the whole gruesome ordeal and could only now experience the release of expectation that had been building inside me.

Later, I would relate this experience to Vallaton, who would dismiss the affair, assuring me I was in no way complicit in the crime.

"That girl had been dead long before you met her," he said. "Where there might have been a soul there was only an empty carapace. Gaspare did not take a life. There was none to take in the first place. It was, of course, the great Marquis, speaking via Dolmancé, you recall, who lights the way," he said, quoting, "'it is only by exploring and enlarging the sphere of his tastes and whims, it is only by sacrificing everything to the senses' pleasure that this individual, who never asked to be cast into this universe of woe, that this poor creature who goes under the name of Man, may be able to sow a smattering of roses atop the thorny path of life.'"

It was easy for him to dispense with pity or remorse. For the libertine, mourning, much like forgiveness and repentance, was a foreign idea better left to those still chaining themselves to the anachronistic teachings of the Judeo-Christian penitents. Instead, he applauded my discovery, vowing to experience it for himself at the first opportunity.

For my part, this first exposure to the marriage of death and the sensual would remain with me, serving to whet my appetites for more intense horrors yet to come.

❧

It was no more than a week later when Vallaton came to me with happy news. I was to accompany him to a small party being hosted by the Lady Janvier on the Tuesday next.

"There's to be a gathering," he said excitedly. "The husband is at the estate. He always stays away from these things. Thinks it's all a bunch of bosh and poppycock. He's right, of course. Pure rubbish and foolery. But Eugénie takes it seriously enough. She's mad about the occult. Even has an advisor in these things. Calls himself Brother Faustus, do you believe it? The gall. A drunkard and a charlatan of the first order, but admittedly entertaining in a *voix de ville* sort of way. About a month ago, I was present when he summoned the spirit of Ravaillac."

"What did the regicide have to say for himself?"

"Sadly, not much," he said. "Research is not one of Brother Faustus's stronger suits. But it's really more about the majesty of the affair that gets Eugénie excited."

It had not been easy for Vallaton to secure my place, he told me. Normally, this Brother Faustus exerted a sort of royal privilege, limiting these gatherings to only those whom he could properly vet, for spiritual "alignment," he'd called it, lest his communion with the spirits of the dead be disturbed. It had been a trial for Vallaton just to convince Eugénie to persuade Faustus to admit him in the first place.

"Everyone wears black," he told me. "Even the servants and footmen are instructed as such. She had uniforms made for them specifically for such occasions. It's all very Black Mass. The thought of being so close to 'the other side,' as it were, puts quite a fire in her loins, and that is, of course, where I come in, and where you could too, if you like. To tell the truth, I've grown a bit bored with her. It's not at all bad, just a little too routine for me. My oats seek to be sown upon greener pastures and all that."

❧

Shortly before midnight, we rode by coach over the Seine to the rue de Passy. The driver deposited us before the imposing entranceway to a block of apartments. As we disembarked, a dour-faced doorman clad in a black satin robe greeted us solemnly at the door and noiselessly escorted us through the house to the second-floor salon.

The room had been well prepared for an occult gathering: walls painted in the darkest hues of blue and green, windows concealed behind latched shutters and heavy curtains, green marble tiles framing the fireplace and doors. Brass sconces in the figures of coiled serpents hung from the walls; candles emerging from their upturned maws bathed the room in fiery yellow light. At the center of the room stood a circular table of carved ebony wood inlaid with mother-of-pearl surrounded by a dozen chairs. Incense fumed from a silver bowl above the mantle. The odor of sandalwood filled the air.

Guests milled about chatting quietly in small groups, among them the corpulent and scraggily bearded Brother Faustus. Reeking of camphor and freely partaking of the wine on offer, he stood by the central table surrounded by ears eager to hear his thoughts on what lies in wait for us on the other side. In a far corner, the staid yet alluring Madame Janvier held court, incuriously observing her guests.

She wore a dress of black velvet set off by fringes of glittering silver crepe. A somber gaze and expressionless lips suggested to me a woman in search of new amusement.

Our eyes met, and I knew from that moment we would have each other. Though twice my age, the fluidity of her graceful motions, the ebb and heave of her breast, betrayed a youthful concupiscence lurking just beneath the skin, the embodiment of a more mature carnal desire. For as Balzac said, beauty and talent cannot be found in the child, only the promise of the woman she is to become. I saw in her eyes that promise fulfilled, realizing then I'd merely been sullying my pallet with the rough and unrefined fare of the bordello, cleansing it for the purer delights to come.

Our arrival signaled a quorum. Brother Faustus began making his preparations at the center table with great ceremony. This included the stretching of a silken cloth of deep scarlet over the tabletop. Upon this cloth, which had several unusual symbols and rune signs stitched in gold about it in concentric circles and which he took great reverence to arrange, he placed a silver tray of votives set in the form of a pentagram. He produced a dagger and laid out a handful of smooth pebbles in the shape of a triangle. Then he lit the candles with solemnity while the enraptured guests looked on, asking all manner of questions regarding the import of the various accouterment.

Having witnessed this ridiculous ritual before, Vallaton took the opportunity to discreetly make my acquaintance to Eugénie. The headiness of her jasmine perfume set my mind ablaze with desire. We exchanged formal pleasantries while Vallaton took leave to mingle among the others.

"Matthieu speaks of you often," I said. "He'd not mentioned how you came to meet."

"Does that matter?" she said, her voice serene as a calm sea.

"I suppose not."

"I meet many men, and they meet me. The young and the ambitious. It's a consequence of being a bureaucrat's wife. Where Rene is, they always are."

For a moment, she returned her attentions to the assemblage gathering round the table.

"But not now," I noted. "Your husband does not entertain the mysteries of the arcane?"

"He prefers his own pursuits."

"A pity he does not share in your fascination. Though his absence would suggest an anomaly in the pattern. I am a young and ambitious man, and yet he is nowhere to be found. It would seem his distaste is as much a result of the dark arts as it is of fate. Perhaps it was the will of the spirits that brought me here tonight, after all. Tell me, what is your attraction to the supernatural? What does it *arouse* in you?"

The word hit its mark. The breath held a pause, the pulse quickened along the jugular vein, the skin along the clavicle quivered imperceptibly. All signs of resistance to an urge. Her self-control impressed me. She turned her dispassionate eyes to mine.

"You have come here seeking someone, have you not?"

"I have," I replied.

"It is someone you are long in missing?"

"To speak the truth, I'm not sure we'd ever met before. But I cannot help feeling a force at work I cannot explain willing me to be near her. If she is missing, I know that I must find her, to connect her spirit with mine that we might know a shared bliss we cannot realize apart."

Faustus methodically extinguished all the candles about the room save for those burning on the table. The reflection of the small flames shimmering in the dark pools of Eugénie's irises. The fire lent her gaze the wild ferocity of a cat on the hunt.

"The hour approaches," Faustus said solemnly, breaking the spell ensnaring us.

We took our seats at the table. I passed behind, gently dragging my fingertips against the small of her back. She did not recoil.

"Join hands to form an impenetrable circle," Faustus commanded. "So whatever spirits should come, of light or of dark, shall not be permitted to escape."

Eugénie sat beside me, and I wrapped her hand in mine. I felt her rapid pulse, the rhythmic throb of blood coursing through her fingertips against my skin. The other guests locked hands, and the strange ritual commenced.

Faustus began by leading the group in a chant of Sumerian babble and druidic nonsense, which he instructed us to repeat over and over again, with our eyes closed tightly, of course, while he read aloud an incantation from a small book he'd produced from the sleeve of his robe.

Gather the living under midnight's moon,
With amber flame and souls attuned.
We call upon those passed on,
That they may show us 'ere come the dawn.
With knowledge gained from this world,
We await our minds unfurled.
To speak with spirits of the other side,
And know our fates and what betides,

Beyond our sight, our senses mortal,
Come forth, spirits, we open the portal!
Eugénie tightened her grip as she repeated the chant, the steady beat of her pulse falling in time with mine. Faustus renewed his efforts, his stentorian basso breaching the darkness.

"Into this circle be welcome. Fear not the light. Make your presence known to us who seek the wisdom of the spirit world. Is there someone there? Can you hear our words? Make your presence known."

Suddenly, a dull thud jolted the table. Someone gasped. Eugénie jerked my hand. Her pulse raced; a pocket of hot, moist air formed between our palms. It was intoxicating.

Another knock, sickening and raw, like the violent cracking of a joint reverberated under the table.

"Keep your eyes shut!" Faustus commanded, his voice wracked with strain. "Keep chanting. I feel the approach of a spirit!"

A new, strange odor reached my nostrils, more acrid and honeyed than the incense still fuming from the mantle.

"Who summons me?" Faustus menaced, his voice low and croaky. "Open your eyes, damn you, and look upon the face of the dead."

Faustus loomed over the table, smoldering beneath the folds of his robe. Wisps of blue-gray smoke emanating from under his collar formed a rich cloud about his head, partially obscuring his fixed, wild stare. I concede it was a most splendid effect.

Eugénie and the others tensed with terror at the billowing apparition. Across the circle, even Vallaton looked mildly impressed. Clearly, Faustus had chosen this occasion to pull out all the stops.

"Who are you?" a guest said tremulously.

"My name," Faustus said, pausing to maximize the dramatic impact, "is Sunukkuhkau."

"What kind of name is that?" someone whispered.

"My people waged war when the white man named English came to our homeland. I and my brothers aligned with the white man named France to fight them."

"He means Guerre de la Conquête," another murmured. "He was *there*."

"Why are you here?"

"I was summoned by the father of all spirits. The Great Eagle bore me on his wings to this spot."

"Where were you born?"

"I was born… on a hillside. I cannot remember where."

"How did you die? Were you killed in battle?"

"In battle, yes," Faustus said, as if having forgotten. "I fell in battle with the white man named English. I felt the blow of his musket against my skull, and the pierce of his bayonet as it split my bowels." He gripped his abdomen and tore at his robes, his hands searching for a wound.

"What have you come to tell us?"

Questions started coming rapid fire. People wanted specifics, details. Was he at Montreal when it fell? How many British had he killed? What was his tribe? What did his name mean? Did he scalp white men? Faustus moaned and swooned under the onslaught. His eyes rolled, and he collapsed into his chair, his head sagging in a stupor. All fell silent. The smoke emanating from his collar billowed for some time, and the mountebank lay still for several moments.

"Is that all?" Vallaton said. "Isn't there anyone else in there? Someone chattier like Charlotte Corday or maybe Montesquieu?"

"Silence!" Faustus shouted, leaping once again to his feet. "Who interrupts my repose? Is it not enough I hand you the Jew as you ask, but must I declare it publicly as well? I refuse, I am innocent of the blood of this just person." With practiced theatricality, he dipped his hands in an invisible basin and began scrubbing them.

"Pontius Pilate," someone exclaimed. "It can't be."

"Why did you relent?" another said. "Why did you not set him free?"

"What did he say to you? You heard the words from his own mouth. Tell us what he said."

It went on for more than an hour. Over and over, Faustus channeled the spirits of everyone from Nero to Catherine the Great. Eugénie remained rapt throughout the performance, her hand never leaving mine, even when the others broke the circle. By the end, she'd dug her fingernails into my palm deep enough to draw blood. The skin of her arms and neck turned to gooseflesh. I could all but feel it tingling with electricity. The display had put her in a heightened erotic state, filling her with a nameless passion—the theatrics, the smoke, the smells, the beating of chests and tearing of the flesh. It was all grist for her aphrodisiacal mill. I could barely contain my anticipation of having her.

Eventually, it ended. Faustus collapsed in his chair a final time and announced the spirits would not return. The gathering slowly dispersed. Vallaton bid the hostess good evening, affecting a light kiss to the back of her hand, all the while, his eyes smiling in acknowledgment at me as he dutifully relinquished the field. Soon, only Eugénie and I remained.

I reclined on the bergère while Eugénie stood across the room by the mantle. For a few moments, neither of us spoke. We were as two combatants before a duel. There would be an exchange of formalities before our passions would ignite our actions.

"I trust what we witnessed tonight amazed you as much as it did me," she said, launching the first volley. "Never before has Faustus been able to conjure spirits so vital and raw."

"Of that, I've no doubt," I replied. "I must admit the smoke adds a touch of the magical to the experience, though it's a wonder he didn't set his beard alight."

Eugénie suppressed a chuckle. A wry smile broke at the corner of her mouth.

"Then it's as I suspected. You don't really believe."

"My guests do," she said, twirling a stick of unburnt incense between her fingertips. "Their amazement and their fright add something to it as well. Would High Mass said in Notre-Dame have the same effect were it recited, say, in a sheep pen or a café in Clignancourt?"

"Of course not."

"Why do you suppose that is?"

I feigned ignorance.

"Because without the spectacle the weight of the words would be lost in the open air," she said. "But beneath the soaring vaults and prying eyes of all those saints and martyrs, one can't help but be enraptured in the experience. Feeling like God himself is watching, listening to their thoughts, seeing into their hearts, brings them closer to their spiritual natures. What I'm doing here is no different. The fantasy brings transcendence, doesn't it? I merely seek methods to explore new ways to encourage that transcendence."

"And these theatrics accomplish this?"

"In a way. The suspension of belief is a type of surrender, is it not? A giving over of yourself to another so they may carry you to another plane of experience you could not hope to achieve by yourself. The more real the suspension, the deeper the surrender."

She'd worked her way casually around the room, pausing to feel the fabric of the curtains, to caress the sinuous curves of the golden serpents adorning the walls. Eventually, she stopped before me.

"I suspect you, too, have a desire for this same transcendence," she said.

⚕

We moved to the bedroom. Entertaining Eugénie's penchant for theatrics, I sought to enhance our pleasures and give full vent to her desire for surrender. I became as an actor on the stage, devising a scene of violence and sensuality to bring forth her fear, anticipation, rage, and shame, all with the goal of breaking the shackles of her deepest inhibitions.

I lashed her to the bed and took my belt to her bare body. She cried out in ecstasy, begging me to whip her without mercy. Twice, she cried out that she might die, but still, I did not relent. Her spirit transported, her teeth and nails digging deep into my flesh, she became as a wild animal, coarse and violent. In time, after hours of torture, we fucked savagely, brutally, and together crossed a boundary within ourselves neither knew existed.

When it was over, she lay on the divan, her naked body loosely concealed in a wrap of bedsheet. Perspiration dotted her breast, glistening like frost in the moonlight. One of her legs hung garishly to the floor. I reclined at her feet gazing into her exposed sex.

"If it were nature's intent for us to be covered, then we would have been born clothed," I said, tugging gently at the sheet covering her belly.

"You exhaust me," she said, playfully kicking me. "How is it someone so young should know how to bring pleasure to a woman of maturity."

"A woman of maturity?" I said. "You mean a woman of beauty. You are as young and as radiant as a child of sixteen."

"I've known men twice your age and more who could not make me feel as you did tonight. They bring lust, they bring love, some have even knelt at my feet in worship, but all have only cared for their own desires. They sate their longings as if it were an itch to scratch, and when they are done scratching, there is little else. But you are different. You could sense my desire, even before I could. You read my body and soul as you would a book. It made me feel safe, and terrified. Together it gave me over to something new. Though restrained, I felt..."

"Free?"

"I have never known such freedom as you have shown me this night."

I pulled her down to the floor beside me and ran my hands over every part of her marble-like skin, exploring every curve and crevice with my fingertips.

"You may do with me what you wish," she said, her breath moist and heaving in my ear.

Never had I felt such power over another person. With the common whore, submission is purchased, lending an artificiality to the experience. But knowing someone submits themselves to you, offers you their very soul completely free of obligation, that is where the true awareness of the supremely sensual lies.

The uniquely piquant flavor of our amours gave continual rise to our mutual sensual satisfaction as we plumbed the depths of our newfound desires.

Sex, for me, became a study in textures, smells, and tastes. From the mercer came an education in silk, muslin, and satin. In the shops of the rue des Jeuneurs, running my fingers over green taffeta or scarlet crêpe, creamy charmeuse or crushed velvet, gave rise to wonder at how Eugénie's eyes might look blindfolded by them, my mind veritably rent asunder by the exquisite choice between binding her wrists in Egyptian or Italian cotton. At the tanner, I ran hides across my arms and neck to feel the quality of the grain, pressed swatches to my nostrils to inhale deeply the musky odor of the animal, knowing the same raw smell of nature would fill the air of the bedroom and send her into raptures of bliss when I used strips of the stuff against her bare flesh. I had whips and crops commissioned from only the finest suppliers, their pommels bejeweled in tanzanite, opal, or pearl.

To bring pleasure to her olfactory senses, I paid visits to a curio shop of a Chinaman who supplied me with various concoctions of incense and oils that, when burned, evinced the heady aromas reminiscent of the mystical buddhas and dragon worshippers of the Far East—odors describing supernatural, otherworldly places. When inhaled, the smoke from these sent Eugénie into a state of trance from which it might take hours for her to emerge, during which time she remained almost immune to physical pain.

My libertinage gained its full blossom in the arms of Eugénie, who fed my desires with both her body as well as her mind. When I was with her, I thought nothing of my duties to friends or family; when away from her, my thoughts wavered between extremes of boredom and mania. My studies suffered, as I spent less time in the lecture hall and more nights pursuing only those activities bringing me the most joy and sensual satisfaction.

❧

This sloughing off of responsibilities did not go unnoticed by Dumont, who reprimanded my increasing intellectual slothfulness, placing the blame squarely on Vallaton's shoulders.

"How is this my fault?" Vallaton said, taken aback by the mere suggestion he should be held in any way responsible for the actions of another. "I say, Dumont, you have become quite the bore as of late. You've been taking the fun out of everything. If the man wants to indulge his delectations with this fine woman, who are you or I to protest?"

We walked along the Champ de Mars one afternoon, admiring the magnificence of Gustave Eiffel's great iron skeleton, whose completion was nearly at hand. The Exposition Universelle would be commencing in a few months. On the eve of that grand event, I would receive news that would alter the course of my life forever, but just then, petty arguments were the order of the day as Dumont and Vallaton battled over my soul like an old married couple. Playing the role of the puritanical mother, he fired volley upon volley at Vallaton, whose pagan idealism deftly deflected every blow.

"I'm telling you this as a friend," Dumont said. "Your behavior is not becoming a man of your qualities.

"And what qualities are those, Doctor?" Vallaton said. "Shall we take them in turn? Let us begin with our dear friend's heart, that noblest of organs. Is it corrupted by his actions because he chooses to bring joy to another soul while losing none of his own in the process? Why, I would argue that is at the very essence of selflessness. Were we not engendered by Nature herself to live lives whereby we seek the highest good for ourselves?"

"You obscure the issue by oversimplifying it," Dumont said.

"On the contrary, as your Isaiah says, I am merely 'being a light for the Gentiles.' It is light, the light of truth that blinds you, my friend. Our baser nature rules and commands us. The only immorality would be to disregard such inclinations. No, the pleasures of the flesh are not to be ignored. It's a higher calling indeed that drives a man to cast aside the pedestrian mores of shame and decency, those tepid concoctions of the Christian moralist, and embrace his natural desires."

"I'm not arguing your actions are in any way immoral," Dumont said to me, ignoring Vallaton for the moment, whose own discourse had been cut short by the pleasing distraction of two young ladies passing by.

"And what of his charity?" Vallaton resumed as the girls disappeared from sight. "Has our dear Etienne not, on countless occasions, taken every opportunity to share his kindness with the two of us? How many dinners, how many visits to the theater, has he deigned to show his magnanimity to our two poor souls by funding our recreations? You speak of a lack of qualities. I show him gratitude by supporting his endeavors, while you lecture him on his perceived inequities."

"That's not what I'm saying at all," Dumont protested, then rounding back to me. "I am grateful for your generosity, but I don't care for or ask for your money. It's your friendship I value. Which is why I'm concerned. You're changing, and not for the better I fear."

"And I am grateful for your concern," I said. "But I assure you it is completely unwarranted. Eugénie is merely a vehicle to transport my desires. She is a distraction, nothing more."

"You play her for a fool, then," Dumont said.

"Hardly," I countered. "We both know what we're doing cannot last. It shouldn't either."

"You see?" Vallaton said triumphantly. "You see before you a man confused and corrupted, whereas I see a man with full clarity of vision. The woman is merely a distraction, as all of them are, mind you. Pleasing to the eyes, voluptuous in their emotions, and ultimately slaves to their own wantonness, woman is a hobby to be indulged when the fancy strikes us, disregarded when it bores us. Well said, Etienne. You are indeed becoming the man of letters you so seek to be, encapsulating all I've said in a single word, 'distraction.' Astonishing."

Visibly incensed, Dumont became mute with frustration. I quickly seized the opportunity to change the subject.

"How goes your work archiving Albin's library?" I said.

"*Mon Dieu*," Vallaton exclaimed. "Not this again. Are you still wasting your time with this nonsense?"

"It goes well," Dumont said, happy the conversation turned. "I am astounded by the collection of works he amassed. Though I believe I am making some headway."

Despite Vallaton's disinterest, Dumont proceeded to relate some of the more outlandish details of Albin's unusual and depressing existence. He'd found among the hundreds of volumes accumulated a journal of sorts, written in the poor lunatic's own hand, outlining a most fantastic history.

"He had a great love of music and claims to have personally met both Haydn and Chopin. And he writes with amazing detail about his travels, going so far as to say he lived for a period in la Haute-Louisiane before it was sold to the Americans."

"Fanciful rubbish," Vallaton dismissed. "Really, Doctor, I hardly thought one of such a logical bent as yourself would go in for mere irrational ravings."

"I admit the literary value is questionable. But the mystery is far more intriguing. It has a pathology well worth investigating."

"The mystery?" I said.

"The man was on an obsessive quest," Dumont said. "He was *looking* for something."

Chapter VIII

Etienne did not return, and Zofia was all the happier because of it. The Frenchman's abrupt intrusion into their lives, while not forgotten, had begun to take on the character of something from a distant past, a memory to be laughed at rather than frightened of.

Al hadn't picked up the journal in several weeks, and he felt all more at ease for the abstention. The book shed little if any light on the mystery of the man, appearing more a massive aggrandizement of the author's own inflated ego and less the confession he claimed it to be. Despite this, he couldn't help, at times, but to reflect that his own fortune, when compared to Etienne's, was the better of the two.

Al had always held to the line that the true measure of a man lay not in his actions but in the manner in which he conducted affairs of the heart and mind. The reprobate Monsieur Allard clearly fell outside this camp. For all his amorous pursuits, his gambling, and his carousing, his was a vapid life, bereft of any meaning or purpose.

His friend the young student doctor, however, saw things for how they really were. If it were man's nature to be debauched, as the impious and inconstant Vallaton insisted it was, then how could he explain the existence of someone like Dumont, a man who'd tasted the pleasures of libertinage, yet chose to turn aside from them? And what madness could cause a man to hold to a doctrine of acceptance at the suffering of another?

The recounting of Sidonie's death disturbed Al most of all. It was the logical conclusion for the woman, such as she was, but still a fate undeserved, made even more so by the inescapable fact Etienne had done nothing to prevent it. If anything, he'd certainly sped the poor girl along to her unfortunate end. Al felt an innate sense of culpability in Etienne's crime, like he, too, stood dumb witness to the horror playing out in the miserable shack, much as he had when he was a boy in Hamburg, paralyzed with fear and unable to help someone in clear need of rescue. Etienne's ignorance of his own guilt was cowardly at best, despicable at worst. That he'd been talked out of it so easily by the puerile tongue of Vallaton made his stomach churn all the more. Here was a man who saw value in nothing. He'd begun to develop a hostility for the Frenchman, having opened this window into his life Al now felt unable to ignore.

The book remained packed away beneath a pile of oily rags and a box of disused parts in the bottom drawer of his workbench. Out of sight, out of mind. But despite the visceral effects of its narrative, for a reason he could not define, Al could not bring himself to throw it away. The unusual story held a sort of morbid fascination for him, one since he'd begun reading it, he could neither embrace nor dismiss. He'd sensed a bad end for the Frenchman, one that, in *his* case, might not be as undeserved as his unfortunate concubine's. But whatever distracting thoughts Al conjured regarding Etienne's tale would be pushed aside in the early days of February.

Master and apprentice toiled noiselessly side by side engrossed in their work. He'd given Oliver a challenge: an 1887 Ansonia recently brought in after being damaged in a fire. It was to be a test of the boy's technical and aesthetic abilities, one of many Al had been arranging as of late.

Zofia had gone out early to market and did not return until almost midday. When she did, Al was alarmed at what he saw. The old woman's wind had nearly gone. Leaning against the display counter for support, she could barely stand, her strength all but dried up.

"I just need to sit," she breathed. "Just to sit a minute and I'll be all right."

Al helped her to the cot in the storeroom while Oliver fetched a cup of tea. A fit of coughing seized her. Her whole body contracted in frightful spasms. It was sometime before she regained her bearings.

"Go and bring Dr. Hirsch," Al instructed Oliver.

"There's no need," she said, regaining her breath. "Really, it's nothing. I was walking, and then suddenly I felt so sleepy. But it's all right. I think I just want to lie down. Help me up, Albie."

Never had she felt so small and fragile in his arms before. Leaving Oliver to tend the shop, he took her upstairs to bed. The night was restless. He brought tea with honey and hot mushroom broth. Her fits of coughing increased. The following day brought no relief. By evening, the dry breath normally filling her lungs had turned to a wet, labored wheeze. The doctor was summoned. The diagnosis: pneumonia.

"She should really be moved," Dr. Hirsch told Al as they stood in the sitting room discussing things while Zofia slept.

"Is it that serious?"

"She needs a course of antiserum to be started right away. Vitamin A as well. A hospital is the best place for her. There's little we can do if she remains here."

"How long will she have to stay?"

"It's hard to say. She's not a young woman anymore, and treatment could be expensive. But if we're going to move her, it needs to be today. I don't think I need to tell *you* how important time is here."

"If you think it's best. I only want for her to get better."

"If we move quickly, she stands chance of recovery. I'll make the arrangements."

In the end, Al could only numbly concede.

❧

That evening, an ambulance conveyed Zofia to the Jewish Hospital, and for the next three days, Al remained by her bedside. Despite treatment, by degrees, her condition worsened, first through a debilitating cough, then by the ravages of pyrexia. When her fever-addled brain made her forget her own husband's face, Al wept. On the morning of the fourth day, when she slipped into an unconsciousness from which she would not stir, he was taken aside and told to believe the end to be near.

Al carried himself outside into the cold air. He could no longer bear the sight of Zofia's comatose body. He could no longer bear the overwhelming helplessness—that, for all being done, there was nothing that could be done. He wandered the snow-covered grounds bent under the weight of a crushing grief. Before the hospital's entrance stood a little stone shul. He went inside but found it empty. Seating himself on a bench before the Ark, Al closed his eyes and let a flood of memory wash over him.

He drifted back to the day they'd met. The sound of her voice, soft and melodious, like the warble of a dove on a spring morning, filled his ears. From the moment he first heard it, he knew it to be the most wondrous sound in the whole of the world—that he must hear it every day lest he never be happy again.

He remembered their wedding day, and the garland of pale-pink peony adorning her veil.

His nostrils filled with the odors of her cooking, the sweet scent of her *Napoleonka*, wafting down the stairs from the kitchen, flooding the shop with aromatic delights of sugar and buttercream. She would give them away to the customers, but she always kept some aside for just the two of them. These special ones, sometimes drizzled with melted chocolate, they would share in the kitchen together when work was done and the sun had set.

And he remembered the day they lost their first and only child, born cold before his precious soul ever saw the light of day.

Alone with his anguish, trapped with his thoughts, his fears, his consternation, and his regrets—as men often are when confronted with the looming shadow of death— Al felt the walls of his faith begin to crumble around him. Doubt weighed heavily upon his soul, an inescapable feeling of betrayal. Doubt that for all his devotion to his beliefs, in the end, he would not be made to endure the sorrow of her loss—that, selfishly, it would be him to leave first, not her.

There were still too many years ahead for Zofia to be taken from him now. And as men are also wont to do when faced with such circumstances, a desire to reverse their stations, to sacrifice his life for hers and trade on the currency of his faith, surfaced from within the depths of his spirit.

A sudden chill draped its icy fingers down the back of his collar, coursing over his bones like a flood at the thought. Could it be so easy, to offer his own soul in exchange for hers? To sin against his faith and surrender to the darkness? At that moment, he would have agreed willingly. The words bubbled on his lips. He felt he need only set them free.

"At such times as these," said a voice, breaking the silence, "the desperation strangling a man's heart might bring his mind to ruinous calamity of nerve and spirit."

Al recognized it immediately. In the open doorway of the sanctuary stood the Frenchman.

"Giving voice to this desperation is not something I recommend."

The young man's appearance had greatly improved since their last encounter. Gone were the tangled beard and threadbare clothes. No longer sunken and cadaverous, his cheeks flushed with radiance and youth, and his once emaciated frame stood strong, full, and upright, filling the doorway with its stately presence.

Al said nothing and turned his mind back to its thoughts.

"I wished to thank you for your kindness," Etienne said.

"You already did," Al replied. "I found the note you left."

"Yes," Etienne said awkwardly. "So it would seem."

Al fell silent again, leaving Etienne holding his proverbial hat in his hand. For a moment, the Frenchman, too, reserved his thoughts.

"I am sorry to learn of your wife's illness," he said at length. "I stopped by your shop to thank you in person. Your son told me I would find you here." Then, hesitating: "I also wished to apologize for having no doubt given you both quite a scare."

"My nephew," Al said.

"What?"

"Oliver is my nephew, not my son."

"I see," Etienne said. "Still, he seems a capable lad. I wish I could tell you there was a reason I sought out your shop that night, but truth be told, I don't have one. I wasn't myself just then, as you might have surmised. It felt like I'd been wandering for years. I'd lost something, you see, or at least I thought I had. Somehow, I recalled this strange little tinker shop, I couldn't remember where I'd seen it. London, Algiers maybe. Anyway, I got it in my head to go there, and my feet..." He trailed off. "It's all quite confusing sometimes." The conversation was in no way progressing as he'd hoped. He turned, thinking it best to leave the old man to his grief. "Well, I'll just..."

"I do not think it was to thank me that you came," Al said, his eyes lowered to the floor. "Nor do I think it was to apologize, though the former is welcome, and the latter accepted. And if you are truly sorry for my Zofia, then you will do me the kindness to sit and pray with me."

Etienne cast his eyes about the small empty chamber of the sanctuary but did not enter.

"Something is the matter?" Al said. "Something weighs on your conscience?"

"I'm afraid I'm ignorant of the practices of this house," Etienne said, "and of the language used."

"If you believe God will hear your voice, then what matter the language you speak to Him in?"

Etienne hesitated and seemed to steel himself as if he were preparing to step over the edge of a precipice. A tremor twitched across his brow that was only arrested with considerable effort on his part. Taking slow, deliberate steps, he crossed the room and sat on the bench beside Al.

"Do you believe in God?" Al said.

A sudden gloom cast a shadow over the Frenchman's face.

"You look as though you expect the ceiling to come down on you."

"It's long since I've been to church," Etienne said.

"I've been going to temple since I was a little boy. Every Shabbat, like clockwork. I go to the shul, and I sit, and I pray, and I speak to God."

"And does He listen?"

Al fixed his eyes in the middle distance.

"I believe the ears of God might be too big to hear the echo of just one man's voice."

"Yet you still try to be heard?"

"I do."

Etienne reflected on this paradox.

"Call out for aid, knowing no one is listening?" he said, speaking more to himself. "In other circumstances, one might mistake prayer for a cry of anguish and this place more a kind of hell than a house of God. It's the very nature of hell to beg mercy and be rebuffed by dumb silence. You ask if I believe. I would ask why you would worship one who chooses to torture you so."

"If you are here to speak ill of my faith, then you don't come as a friend," Al said.

Etienne apologized.

"You ask if I believe? You might say my relationship with God has always been a bit strained."

"Hell is relative, I think," Al said quietly. "For you, it is the place you describe, where prayers go unanswered. But for me, it is enough to know there is someone listening, even if He chooses not to respond. Our faith does not allow for the separation of His love such as others would believe. We will all be with Him, in time. If this is Zofia's time, then it is her time. We will be reunited someday. Of that, I am certain. Her suffering will pass. As will mine. But knowing this does not make it any easier. I would give all I have that she would come back to me. I'm not ready for her to go. Not yet."

"You've been together a long time?" Etienne said.

"What is time to two people in love as long as we have been in love? If you had asked me a few days ago, I would have said, *Yes, a very long time.* Now? Now it feels like we only just met."

"I've known men to bargain with their faith before," Etienne said. "It rarely ends as one hopes. I tell you this as a friend."

"What else can I do?" Al said. "I have nothing more to offer."

Etienne's placid eyes betrayed an inner turmoil Al could not quite identify. It appeared as though the Frenchman were straining against a great weight lying upon him, and it was only through tremendous effort that he resisted the crushing force of it. Sitting side by side, they presented an unusual pair: the hunched, wiry-haired old man, his worn overcoat nearly dragging on the ground, and the dapper young gentleman at his side. But for their accents, one might have easily mistaken them for father and son.

"Why did you come back?" Al said.

"I told you," Etienne said, "I wanted to thank you. It has been a long time since anyone has done me a good turn. I'm not deserving of it."

Al dismissed this comment with more stoic silence. It would be improper, he thought, to inquire as to what had brought Etienne to the state he'd found him in that night, and so, he let it pass.

"That is why you came back the first time," he said. "Why do you now return? Not to inquire about my wife. You could not have known. So why, then?"

Etienne remained quiet.

"I think you are looking for something. Something you think you may have misplaced? A book, maybe?"

"Then you do have it?" Etienne said, sounding hopeful.

"No," Al said. "I did have it. Not anymore, though. I threw it away."

Etienne shrunk; his spirits momentarily deflated, he sought to hide his disappointment behind a lie.

"No matter," he said. "It's probably for the best the thing be forgotten."

"I don't think you believe that."

"What I believe is immaterial," Etienne said. "It always has been. The book was nothing more than a compendium of narcissistic drivel. The ramblings of a self-absorbed mind. What other type of man writes his autobiography if not one who believes himself to be the center of everything? Frankly, that man I came to learn a long time ago was not someone I should have ever wished to be."

"You are too young to be talking in this way," Al said. "Young men should be thinking about the future, not reflecting on the past. That is a practice for old men like me."

"I've been told I've an old soul," Etienne said.

"Still, you look too young to be carrying around so much regret." It was impossible not to see. Al examined his companion's still boyish face. How could it be that he had not changed since that first meeting so long ago?

"Appearances, as is well known, can be and usually are deceiving."

"You are not the man you appear to be?" Al said.

"Can any man say he isn't? I've no soul at all, old, young, or otherwise."

"I don't think you believe that either."

"Don't I?" Etienne said. "Once, maybe, but now?"

"All men have a soul," Al said. "To not have one would make you nothing more than a golem. You say you sought me out to thank me? I say that's your soul commanding you to do so. You say you are sorry for my wife's sickness? That is your soul feeling my pain."

"You make it sound quite logical."

"But, beyond this, what kind of soul you have, and what you choose to do with it, is entirely of your own making. This, I firmly believe."

Etienne contemplated this briefly but seemed to dismiss the old man's argument. Al began to sense not very much affected his mind at all. In fact, considering the young man more closely, he began to feel he was looking less at a person and more a statue come to life. From the lines of his angular face to the vacancy looming behind his blue-green eyes, to the coldness he exuded—a distance in his demeanor, barely perceptible, but palpable, nonetheless. Al struggled to give name to this feeling of joylessness, but could only manage to describe it, poorly, he thought, as a sort of bleakness of spirit. The man existed in a sort of middle space, being both distinctly there and *not there* at the same time. This feeling he failed to give name to, but the uneasiness it caused him had a definite name. *Separate.* This man was separate in some way, from himself, from the rest of humanity perhaps, and the apartness, though unseen, did not pass unnoticed.

"How is it that you come to be here?" Al said, turning to look the Frenchman firmly in the eyes for the first time.

"I told you," Etienne said, "I stopped by your store."

"That is not what I mean. You know of what I speak. How is it you come to be here? You would not fault me for thinking it impossible."

"Many things are possible," Etienne said, somewhat discomfited by Al's question, the strain within him surfacing as subtle fractures in his composure: a pulsing vein below his hairline, a thickening of his jaw from clenched teeth within. He described a man in a great deal of pain. Al pressed his attack.

"A young man does not appear in my shop once, then again twenty-two years later not having aged a single day. That is not possible. He doesn't carry a watch made by my uncle thirty-one years ago and claim he bought it himself. That is not possible. He doesn't tell the world he is fifty-five years old when he is clearly not so. He could not believe these things to be true himself unless..."

Al stopped himself, not wanting to say something he would regret.

"Unless he is a madman," Etienne said flatly. "But that would make you as much so, if you were to believe such fantastic things."

"I am not mad," Al said.

"Nor am I. Nevertheless, here we sit. And against your own better judgment, you do believe, don't you?"

Etienne put a hand into his coat pocket and produced Gerhort's watch, the broken chain entwined in his fingers. He held it up, watching it slowly twist back and forth before his eyes, both men mesmerized by its beauty.

"It was meant as a gift to an old friend. A young doctor I once had the pleasure of briefly knowing. I was very fond of him."

"What happened?" Al said.

"What usually does. People grow apart. What starts out as differences of opinion become differences of character. Before you know it, the person you thought you knew like a brother is more a stranger than you ever realized."

Al spied the Frenchman blink away the glisten of a tear at the corner of his eye. He placed the watch in Al's hand.

"Trust, Monsieur Valentine," he said. "Trust is the foundation of all friendships. For a long time, it was the very basis of my own faith. But I was too arrogant to see faith is blind, that it can exist in total darkness, whereas trust needs the light of day if it is to be granted. Truth, like trust, requires a light to be shed upon it to make it real. You ask how I came to be here. I believe you know the answer. You have already taken a look inside my journal. I also have faith that, despite what you say, you did not destroy it. Read it, if you must, but I do wish it returned."

"And what will I learn if I do?"

Etienne said nothing but stood to go.

"What was it you said to me earlier?" Al said. "'Desperation leads to ruin of spirit?' What does this mean?"

At the threshold, Etienne pushed open the doors, letting in the rush of cold again that filled Al's coat and chilled him to the marrow. It was the cold of the grave, he thought, the cold of the abyss pushing out the warmth of life from his veins. There the Frenchman stopped and turned back to speak.

"A desperate man will go to great lengths to preserve that which he treasures most in life, will he not? But the folly of irrational endeavor is revealed only when he learns his treasure is nothing more than the reflection of his own vanity, thin as paper and devoid of substance. Only then does he see the error of misplaced faith for what it truly is. But by then, it is too late. Turn your eyes from desperation, my friend, lest the eyes of desperation cast their icy gaze upon you."

Al wished to ask more, but already Etienne had turned and walked away into the February mist, his figure vanishing behind the heavy wooden doors of the sanctuary slowly shutting behind him. When they had closed, and the warmth returned to his body, Al felt the pull of a lingering thought, that somehow the Frenchman's appearance had rescued him from some grievous yet imperceptible danger.

Hours became days. Days became weeks. Zofia's condition remained unchanged.

Al refused to work, giving over the running of the shop to Oliver. It was to the credit of his tutelage the young man performed admirably in his new role. Word spread quickly down the Row. Customers and competitors alike sent cards and paid visit to Al at Zofia's bedside. Concerned wives baked day and night, filling Al's larder with kishka, pierogi, kugel, blintzes, tzimmes, rouladen, and latkes till it had nearly burst.

Sleep eluded him. Coming back to the dark, empty apartment each evening, he became only too aware of her absence and the hollow it left behind. The place was no longer home without her, just a collection of furniture and knickknacks devoid of essence. Zofia's presence imbued the place with life and light. Without her, there remained only the fossilized residue of a once bright happiness.

At night, he waited, the cushion of his armchair gradually sinking beneath his weight as he counted the hours, minutes, and seconds until morning, until he could return to the hospital and resume his vigil. Time, once his love and passion, became a dreaded enemy, his jailer and his torturer. Each tick of the clock a reminder of his time with Zofia slipping away—each vacant, soundless space between the click of the gears a silent home for yet another regret.

Guilt assailed his heart, while self-recriminations pricked at the fabric of his soul. How much time had they lost together to his work? How many trips put off? How might he have been a better husband to her?

❧

Oliver, seeing his uncle withering away, urged a distraction. Mightn't he try to work again, just for a little while, to clear his head?

It had been weeks since Al put tool to hand or even gave the shop a second thought. He'd felt a return to routine would be like a betrayal, that distraction in any form, even one so familiar, was somehow akin to letting her go. But what to do to quell this misery and loneliness consuming his heart? Should it continue much longer, would he go barking mad like the woman from those stories the impresario Croft spoke of?

The hour struck ten. Desperately seeking some semblance of peace, Al went to his workbench to tinker. He found a piece Oliver had left unfinished and, picking up his tools, gave himself over to the detail of the work, lifting the fog of woe, if only briefly.

And yet, in the midst of distraction, he could not keep his thoughts from drifting back once again to the Frenchman. Their conversation in the temple had greatly unsettled him. If he found no answers by reading the journal, then he'd found only more questions when speaking to its author.

"Calamitous ruin." The words haunted Al. Teetering on the very edge of his belief, looking into the abyss of doubt he had been pulled from the precipice by a most unusual avenging angel. God was not one to intervene, so, if not by His hand, how had Providence placed this man in his path at so fortuitous a moment? He could not but feel the Frenchman had rescued him somehow. But from what had he been saved?

Al knew the book to be near at hand. Like the still-beating heart hidden beneath the floorboards from a Poe story he'd once read long ago, it lay buried in the bowels of the bench. Since entering his life, both book and man had become an unavoidable presence, willingly drawing Al closer to their mystery, entwining their destinies with his own.

He eyed the closed drawer, a line of contempt drawn across his face. He detested himself his own hesitance. The decision had already been made. If there were still answers to be found, he would have no choice but to seek them out within those nefarious pages.

Putting down his tools, he lifted the thing out from under the pile of rags and disused parts and began once again to read.

Chapter IX

The season wore on. With time came the end of my affair with Eugénie. Our rendezvous grew less frequent, and to my eyes, more mundane. The caprice of my desires blew my passions in new directions. There were other Eugénies to be sought out. As Vallaton was wont to point out, the libertine is not one to confine his lusts to just one man or one woman. His passions are to be shared with as many as possible. He must give vent to his cupidity at every turn.

The passing of Eugénie out of my life in the early spring of 1889 would coincide with another passing, one of much greater portent.

Word reached me via telegram that the SS *Île de la Réunion*, the vessel my mother and father had taken to the Levant, had disappeared in the Tyrrhenian Sea off the coast of Sardinia and was presumed lost. At the earliest convenience, I returned to Marseille.

Lipa had sunk into an inconsolable state, her heart simply broken by the loss of my mother. The absence of my father gave her license to speak words kept chained inside for years.

"She had such a brittle soul," Lipa said. "But she had a kindness not found in most these days. She pined for her home often, you know. She was horrified by your father's godlessness, and the spiritual anarchy she thought infected his soul and the society he kept. She feared beyond everything you would become like him, callous and unkind, but she lacked the strength to truly confront him. But I know he wasn't without his own faith. He just chose to express it in a different way."

"My father worshipped power and wealth, nothing more," I said. "He could see no farther than his next contract. But I cannot fault him for that, nor can I abjure him for lacking belief in spiritual nonsense. It is the only point upon which we might have actually agreed. I do pity my mother having suffered him all these years, though."

Taken aback, Lipa reprimanded my insolence, saying she would pray I remember to honor my father and all he had done to provide for me. I, in turn, reassured her I was indeed eternally grateful for the lessons he had instilled in my youth, that they had served me very well. As for my mother, I admitted I hardly knew her.

Numerous city and Compagnie officials, including the mayor of Marseille himself, paid visit to our home in the days following the news of their deaths. Jean Allard was, after all, a vital patron. Each offered words of consolation and praise for my family's contributions not only to the city but the Republic, all the while secretly scheming how to work my succession to my father's seat to their own personal benefit.

It all led up to interminable meetings with lawyers, representatives, clerks, and accountants—their presence as mites creeping over my flesh, their words an endless cacophony of arguments, concessions, reconciliations, strife within the labor force, assets, seizures, liabilities, insurance. The atmosphere was stifling.

In a twist of irony, my savior came in the most unlikely form of Jacob Bloch. Knowing the distaste I held for my father's intentions, he was more than eager to hold the door open for my escape.

After the last of the lawyers had gone, I sent for him and awaited his arrival in my father's study. The room, once the nexus of his empire, had become nothing more than a museum of his trinkets and a mausoleum to his dreams. The musky odor of old wood was suffocating. I pushed open a window to take in fresher air. Cursing, I swore to leave the place as soon as possible and never return.

I told Bloch six o'clock, and he arrived promptly at the appointed hour, his face betraying no hint of surprise at his summoning. For him, this was a moment years in the making. He entered with practiced solemnness, stepping with slow, heavy footsteps, one might even say they were reverent, and took the chair before my father's desk as he had done every day for years.

"That is your place now," he said, indicating my father's empty chair behind the great walnut desk. I remained by the window and lit a cigarette.

"You know that's not to be," I said.

"It is what your father wanted."

"My father was a determined man. He often got what he wanted, didn't he?"

"Always."

I gazed out the window toward the calm sea. The smell of the salt air faded. The vast blue-green mass of water stretched desperately to the horizon. I thought of Jean, sitting behind that desk commanding his empire, fleets of ships tugging to and fro across the great watery expanse now crushing his lifeless body to the floor of its frigid depths. Of all the years he'd spent in this room, how much of life had he missed amassing his fortunes? Had he no other dreams?

"This business was his life," I said. "Not mine."

"What he did, he did for the benefit of his family, you and your mother. This house, this life, your schooling, all of it with a singular aim. To have a legacy, something to outlive him. Even outlive you. He heard the name Allard live on the lips of men for decades, maybe even centuries."

"A fool's dream, for a foolish man."

"Don't!" he said with a sudden flash of chafe. "You may not wish to carry on what he began, but you will not speak of him this way. Your father commanded respect from all who knew him, even you."

The uncharacteristic outburst gave him pause. Bloch the underling, Bloch the unappreciated, bristled just beneath the surface like a wild dog. The closeness of his reward challenging his reserve, he resumed a demeanor of quietude.

"You know why I summoned you?" I said.

"Yes."

"This business is to be concluded with haste."

"It will be handled," he said with phlegm. "But there is much to be settled. Papers will have to be drawn up. There are many things to put in order."

"If you want to have it, then you will do what you must," I said. "They're reading his will tomorrow. I'll be returning to Paris on Friday. You can have everything conveyed to me there."

"What of the house?" he said.

"I don't know. I haven't reached a decision yet. In the meantime, the staff can attend to it. You will have to make other arrangements for your offices."

"Very well," he said, getting up. "You're to be a very wealthy man in short order. What do you intend to do?"

"That is no concern of yours."

"Indeed. Then if the matter is settled, I take my leave. As I said, there is much to be done. But I almost forgot. There is one more thing."

He produced an envelope from his coat pocket and laid it on the desk. Scrawled across the front was my name, in the hand of my mother.

"She gave this to me before they departed and asked that I deliver it should any tragedy befall her on her journey. Poor woman. She had a good soul, your mother did."

Bloch took his leave. I remained for several minutes staring at the envelope. It looked a tiny thing against the broad surface of the desk. It was as she had been in this house, a trifle set against the grandeur of my father's import. Returning to the open window, I broke the seal and read by the dying light of the bright southern sun.

My Son,

If this letter has reached you, then you know me to be dead. And unless your father has decided to conceal the truth or tell you otherwise, it was by my own hand that my life was ended.

Know firstly, my choice is my own and is made freely. The thought of death has pursued me for some time, its shadow casting a pall everywhere I go, over all I do. I have come to welcome its presence, its seed planted within me gradually blossoming into a flower of tranquility. For so long, my path has been clouded, my prayers unanswered, my future obscured by both fear and disgust. God remains silent. He gives no council.

You ask why I should take my own life? It is for that very reason. God has turned his back on me; I am left in turmoil, lost in a darkness surrounding my soul, through which I cannot find my way. At first, I thought my faith merely tested, but now I know I am forgotten.

For years, I have known nothing but unhappiness, unable to find solace in even the simplest of pursuits. My days are filled with remorse, regret, and an undying ambition to purge my spirit of all reminders of the world that brings only pain. I find no comfort in prayer and no hope for better in the next life.

Still, you ask why? How can a melancholy so bleak invade my soul? Surely, there is a way to return brightness to my mind and drive out these mad thoughts? There is not. And if you must continue your search for a reason, a source of blame for my unfortunate state, then I shall tell you all that it might illuminate your way.

You know me as Aline Allard, but I was born Alheena. I do not know my family name. When I was but a child of five or six, my father sold me to a nomadic merchant who took me as his servant, for I was too young to be taken as a bride. I stayed with this trader, a disgusting oaf called Fawzi, for the next four years. We traveled far and wide across the sultan's empire, from Ankara to Acre, bringing cotton, olives, and cereal, anything that could be traded. Fawzi saw profit in everything that came into his hands, even me. At Tarābulus al-Sham, he sold me to the proprietor of a *bayt daeara*, where I stayed for many years. It was there your father found me.

All you may know of my history is a lie. I was not born the daughter of wealthy parents, and I was not married off to your father in a ceremony of happiness and blessings. I was a common whore, purchased by your father in a common business transaction. He bought my freedom as easily as he would buy a horse or a new carriage and took me back with him as his new bride.

I asked him to build me a sanctuary. At times, a priest would visit the house in Tarābulus al-Sham. My owner, a Greek, allowed him to preach to the girls sometimes, and it was in his words where my faith was born. He spoke of Mary, the mother of God, and of the sufferings of her son. He told us we were God's children, that we were not forgotten. I didn't believe him. I couldn't believe God had allowed me to suffer such a fate as I had, that he could suffer a prostitute to live on his earth. Then your father came and delivered me from my enslavement, and I believed it the work of God. From then on, I dedicated myself to Him and did my best to honor your father as a dutiful and faithful wife in accordance with His teachings.

In the beginning, I do believe your father thought he loved me, but as years went on, I knew whatever affection he may have had for me was fleeting, and I became for him another artifact for his collection, a beautiful gem he could display to the world, and then set aside. He took lovers when he grew tired of me. It was a failing of his character. I had borne him a son and had no further use. I became nothing more than another servant, chief among them, but a servant nonetheless. My faith began to waver.

As years drew on, I withdrew further into my faith, asking God why he had delivered me from one enslavement into another. But again, he did not answer.

Quietly, I sought aid from your spiritual tutor, Abbe Frére. A lecherous man with a wanton gaze, he gave only devious counsel, betraying my devotions to satisfy his own gross prurience. In the end, I would not suffer his caresses in exchange for guidance, and he, too, turned his back on me.

You ask why I did not take my life then, when God and his counselors ignored my pleas? It was because of you, my son. I saw in you a purpose, a child to be saved from following in your father's footsteps. I redoubled my efforts in this vein, returning day after day to my cloister to pray you would not become what he wished you to, that you would turn your back on him as he had on me. When last you returned home, I thought my prayers answered. The words spoken against your father were proof of my success. I rejoiced in this good fortune and realized the end of my work had arrived. I resolved then to take my life, as a means of escaping my solitude and further punishing your father. It matters little to me what becomes of my soul. What purpose is there for a soul if God himself does not care for it?

In a few weeks, your father and I will be making our journey back to the land of my birth. He has been told it would be beneficial for me, but he cares little for my well-being. Perhaps he intends to find for himself a new, younger bride with which to replace me. It is the practice of inconstant men such as he, and it brings my heart some small measure of comfort to know it is not the type of man you will become.

It is on this journey I intend to throw myself into the sea. I am sorry if this causes you pain. Know what I do is as much for your sake as my own. Perhaps God will be more kind to you than He has been to me.

Your mother,

Alheena

My mother's missive put me in a disturbed state that brought forth a hatred for my late father that had hitherto lain dormant. This seed, sown long ago, now bore fruit, and made concrete my decision to blight his memory from my existence.

I established a doctrine whereby all my future actions would be taken with a keen eye to offending any sensibilities he may have had.

The first act of this new rebellion included withdrawing myself from my studies completely. Time at study was time wasted. Where lay beauty, ardor, or passion in the auditorium? I would seek them out myself.

Dumont thought me a complete fool. But Vallaton applauded my integrity and perspicacity, calling my decision the single most important step a libertine could take.

"Destruction of institutions is the core of all revolution," he said. "The fetters of conformity and established conventions are the purview of weak-minded men who cling to them as if drowning in a sea of hopeless indecision. Let no one tell you otherwise: it is the strong man, the libertine, who struts boldly forward, with clarity of vision, amid the ruins of social convention. What need have we of institutionalized education? Like institutionalized religion, it serves only to mold and form us into mindless slaves to doctrine long since passed its freshness. Institutions look only backward for inspiration, while the libertine looks only forward. You know, your actions inspire me yet again, my friend. It would be of the utmost crassness were I to allow you to embark on this new journey of discovery alone. I, too, will embrace destiny as you have, and together, we will bite from this proverbial apple of forbidden knowledge!"

A month after my meeting with Bloch, I signed papers selling my concerns of the Compagnie Générale Méditerranéen et de la Côte d'Ivoire. This settlement combined with the remainder of the legacy provided me in my father's will—increased substantially by the death of my mother as well—left me with a sizable fortune upon which I sought to draw indefinitely.

To fully enjoy all the comforts of the voluptuous life, I found an exquisite *maison* in the Faubourg Saint-Germain, an urban marvel miraculously well intact from a period dating before the *Monarchie de juillet*. I purchased it with unabashed glee and engaged a small army of tradesmen to restore the structure to its former glory. Painters, decorators, and carpenters—all handsomely funded—worked nonstop for months making the place ready for my arrival.

The arrangement of each room sought to provoke a sensual transcendence, evincing thoughts and emotions both subtle and intense, pleasurable and horrific.

A savage jungle scene filled the foyer. Columns carved to resemble the trunks of baobab trees and pots of elephant, molasses, and coolatai grass surrounded one upon entering. A mural depicting a lush canopy covered the walls, while the stuffed carcasses of leopards, chimpanzees, and a river boar stared on glassily, ready to pounce.

The parlor revived the rococo style of Louis XV with garish hues and sinewy rocaille vines climbing the walls and furniture like so many invasive weeds in a garden. Rugs brought in from Aubusson covered the parquetry, and panels of green damask silk lined the walls. The bare pink rumps of Boucher's *Louise O'Murphy* and *Odalisque 1745* hung over the mantle recalled a wholly quainter time of voluptuous enlightenment and aristocratic poise.

The dining room resembled a medieval tavern replete with heavy wood paneling and a floor of broad slate stone. An elk's head hung above the open hearth, and a grand tapestry depicting Aesop's The Old Man and Death spanned the wall behind the head of a table with seating for more than twenty.

For bacchanalian revelries, I'd had the ballroom transformed into a Roman atrium complete with Doric columns and a travertine fountain at its center large enough to accommodate three or four bathers. Under a fresco of a rich evening sky, guests could recline on plush cushions of velvet, listen to the rippling waters, and savor bottles of wine and victuals laid out on long tables of white Carrara marble.

Beyond this lay a smoking room, a library, and, of course, a gaming room. Room after room, each ornamented in a unique, exotic flavor and resplendent in its sensual glory. But the most exquisite delights I'd held in reservation for my own bedchamber.

For its inspiration, I drew upon the infernal image of the Hellmouth from *The Hours of Catherine of Cleves*. The shocking contrast of the yawning, bloody maw against the shaggy, atramentous face of the beast bears an uncanny resemblance to a gaping pudendum complete with a glistening oversized clitoris. Undeniably erotic and a wholly depraved, it stands a spectacular failure by the Church to paint woman as the root of all sin. I applauded their effort and endeavored to magnify its effects tenfold.

To satisfy the sensual appetites and evoke the Hellmouth in all its fiery glory, the walls of the boudoir were coated in a sooty charcoal black, while arched recesses lined in red velvet gouged the inkiness like drops of blood. In these carved spaces hung prints by Bosch, Memling, and Bruegel the Elder. The bed, a hulking hand-carved canopy made to resemble the peaked roof of a cathedral, stood among this macabre museum, framed by two of my favorite works by Doré.

In the first, *Andromeda*, the titular Grecian princess is about to be devoured whole by the serpentine Cetus, his frothy maw and amphibian forked tongue lapping at her toes. Chained to the rocks, the look of horror upon her face is betrayed by a pair of erect nipples, revealing the undeniably arousing anticipation of the encounter, the foaming waves a vivid metaphor for the stirring in her moistened loins.

The second, *Paolo and Francesca da Rimini*, depicts the doomed lovers in a fleeting embrace while the shadowy silhouettes of Dante and Virgil look on. Standing larger than life, at least much larger than their interlocutors, the tragic figures, swathed in a flowing, almost majestic blue shroud representing the buffeting winds of lust eternally harassing them, bare twin wounds—a piercing through their hearts where the spited cuckhold Gianciotto's rapier forever joined them. One immediately imagines the lovers sweating and heaving oblivious in their carnal embrace when discovered, and the shimmering blade running through Paolo's back, not ceasing until the point emerges through Francesca's on the other side. Left there skewered through like so many quail on a spit, they died in each other's arms, their hearts rent, their gazes locked upon each other. It is left to the imagination if either, or both, achieved their climax at the exact moment of penetration and death. I'd always liked to think this was so.

To complete the effect, a grand hearth nearly the height of a man framed in rough-hewn Nero Marquina marble blocks tore forth from the wall, a dark, confused mass of stone broken by elongated bricks of pure-white Carrara tapered into sharpened teeth. The blazing effect being, when lit, the horrific resemblance to the fiery fanged maw of the Hellmouth itself.

Vallaton and I embarked on a program of corruption, seeking out pure souls whom we might convert to our cause. While the chaste were in no short supply, a surprising, and sometimes frightening, number of contrapositive souls roamed the parlors and salons of Paris looking to escape the trappings of spiritual morality or societal constrictions. These would form the greater part of my circle. Like a star whose revolving mass draws in all the bodies orbiting it, so did I become the gravitational center of this circle, providing light and spectacle for all to worship and enjoy.

Vallaton appointed himself minister of propaganda and wasted no time spreading word quick as a virus across Paris of the establishment of a new palace of Priapus. Using funds drawn on an account I established for him, he spent his days flitting to and fro, paying visit to the wealthy and the notorious. Telling stories and churning rumors became his chief occupation.

"There is a certain Monsieur Travere who has expressed to me a desire to meet you," he said one day.

"And how does this concern me?" I said.

"It would be to your benefit. He's quite wealthy and, like you, has a penchant for games of chance. Loses more in a night than most make in ten years. I mentioned in passing our affiliation, and he practically leapt at the opportunity to face off with l'Hérétique."

"Who?"

"You, of course. Don't look so surprised. I told you about it some time ago."

"My memory seems to be failing me," I said, certain he'd not.

"I'm sure of it. But no matter, it's a minor detail, but brilliant, nonetheless. I knew no one would respond to the name Allard. Known as it may be in Marseille, it bears scant weight in the northern reaches. All great men have gone through life with a moniker as their banner, my friend. History doesn't remember Attila, it remembers the Scourge of God. Jeanne d'Arc? *Non*! La Pucelle. And there is no end to it for nobility. The Lionheart, the Good, the Terrible, the Mad, the Red, the Blue, and every other color you can conjure. The nom de guerre brings power, and infamy. It inspires courage, instills fear. But either way, it brings respect. It also, coincidentally, lends an air of mystery to oneself, which was ultimately my aim. I have been planting seeds all over this great city, and, in time, they will germinate and bring forth a bounty to your door. As we speak, your name is being bandied about in the salon, whispered at the opera, overheard in conversation in the galleries. There are women, young and old, blushing at the mere mention of it and men puffing their chests to try their skill against yours. They are practically lining up to meet you, to experience firsthand what I have told them about your legendary fêtes. And, believe me, the things I have told them are the stuff of legend. It is but for us to make it real."

"But," I interrupted. "There have been no fêtes."

"I daresay we are behind in that game," he said. "A problem we must remedy forthwith."

"And," I ventured. "The Heretic?"

"I admit it wasn't exactly planned that way. I needed something enigmatic but with a touch of romance if you were to be a convincing patron for me. Something to really solidify you as a man of consequence. Then it occurred to me. Who better to understand consequence than an apostate?"

We began in earnest. Here, for a sampling, a mere hint of the flavors I added to the stew of my depravity.

The idea was simplicity itself: To stage an affair representative of the power of the human over the divine, to expose the corruptibility of the so-called incorruptible. For the libertine, nothing brings more incomparable joy than the marriage of the carnal and the blasphemous.

The Banquet of Chestnuts, the infamous bacchanal of beastly delights organized by Cardinal Cesare Borgia of that nefarious family, emerged as the theme. Vallaton leapt at the notion of donning the papal robes of Rodrigo Borgia, but I claimed the right to play Pope Alexander VI for myself. My home, my rules. After all, who better to showcase the impracticality of God than one of his most offensive, sinful, and lust-filled representatives here on earth? Vallaton would have to content himself in the role of my duplicitous son and *condottiero* Cesare, and the task of engaging the requisite fifty prostitutes for the entertainment of the partygoers fell to him.

Paying court to the brothels of Montmartre day and night, he worked tirelessly, acquiring assurances from no less than a dozen houses that their *filles de joie*, and indeed a few willing gentlemen, would be made available in return for ample compensation.

By the evening of October 30, exactly 390 years to the day of the notorious feast, the stage had been set.

Nudes from Soudan français, their skin smooth like burnished leather, drifted languidly about the room, bearing upon their shoulders an endless train of victuals; Belons from Brittany, braised lamb shanks, pot-au-feu, veal tongue, turtle soup, coq au vin, Dover sole meunière, andouillette, beef tenderloin, foie gras, eggplants, apples, pears, turnips, radishes, grapes, and, of course, piles upon piles of chestnuts sated the gluttonous bellies of my guests, while palates basted in a continuous flood of Burgundy, Bordeaux, and imported ales from Bavaria, Württemberg, and Hanover.

Tables lined the atrium enclosing a central arena, where the floor played host to dozens of naked writhing whores—some lazing about the fountain, others soaking in it—who sang, lolled, danced, drank, or otherwise satisfied each other carnally, both by natural and artificial means, for our viewing pleasure. Those not engaged thusly took to games, giggling like excited children as they ferried loads of chestnuts to and fro about the room—balanced between their bosoms, stuffed between their ass cheeks, tucked behind their balls—

dropping their cargo on plates, in glasses of wine, in hands, in hats, in shoes. More than one displayed a remarkable talent for inserting several of the morsels inside themselves—then straddling the tables—depositing them one by one into waiting mouths like so many coins in a well. A lottery of sorts was improvised whereby three or four nuts having been etched with numbers were inserted into the readied orifice of a certain lady of ample means. With glee, she proceeded to shake, squeeze, and twist, giving them a good shuffle. Wagers were laid as to the order in which they'd emerge. I invoked my privilege as both pope and host and personally drew the results; the winner of this human raffle receiving the woman, or man, of their choosing, each to their own desire.

A musical quartet played for our entertainment but was soon drowned out by the cacophony of laughter and choruses of bawdy shanties and lyrical excess. Artists sketched the scenes of amusement, but found the effort challenging, what with all the random fucking going on. Soon, the party spilled out of the atrium, and revelry of the most unabashed kind spread to every room of the house.

Word circulated of an extemporaneous reenactment of the Rape of Lucrece taking place in the parlor. A Rubenesque beauty, auburn curls tousled and falling about, played the role of the unfortunate noblewoman being set upon by a tall, hairy, and remarkably well-endowed Sextus Tarquinius. Naked and recumbent upon the divan, roused from her false sleep, Lucrece put up surprisingly weak resistance while Tarquin showed noteworthy stamina and fortitude. When it was over and the Etruscan lay spent at her feet, rather than run to her suicide, the rotund Lucrece offered up as many encore performances as there were actors in the room willing to try their hand at impromptu theater.

In the dining room, someone erected a makeshift *chevalet*, which was being put to vigorous use as merrymakers queued up to take turns buggering each other over its back. The waiting line ran clear through the apartments. Other industrious revelers took to escorting my servers in turn to the foyer to enjoy a native fuck among the thickets of grass dotting the African plain.

At the head of it all, before a floor-to-ceiling mosaic of Botticelli's *Primavera*, I sat lord and commander over the chaotic profligacy, a fur-lined mozzetta of red velvet over my shoulders and a white zucchetto atop my head. As Cesare, Vallaton had acquired a striking blue doublet, matching breeches, and copper codpiece, though, after a few hours, he'd discarded the breeches and took to gallantly roaming the corridors *sans* pants, exercising his amorous whims as the fancy took him.

Toward dawn of the second day, it was over. Pockets of life breathed here and there, and as I wandered the halls, the muffled grunts of the yet still virile resounded rhythmically behind many a closed door, the cadence of coition braying and spurting like so many trumpets and oboes of an orchestra tuning up for performance.

Many had gone home. Some ran away. Yet others had to be carried, their vitality drained from a surfeit of fucking. Broken chestnut shells strewed the floor, finding their way into every crack and crevice, human or otherwise. The musicians had long abandoned their posts, as had the chefs and most of my footmen. Those who'd fled in horror would be replaced. Those who'd stayed rewarded themselves with still willing harlots in the closets and pantries. I found an unconscious Vallaton recumbent upon the billiard table, his codpiece dangling from a nearby sconce. I left him to his blissful slumber.

❦

Balls followed banquets, each more depraved than the last. Soon it would be nearly impossible for me to go out of an evening and not be recognized, so pervasive had the stories become.

There he is. Do you know why they call him the Heretic? But he's quite young, isn't he? They say he hosts Roman orgies in his house. But why the name? Surely, no one worships the devil anymore. Is there anything more passé than the occult? How can you say so? You've been to the Cabaret du Néant, haven't you? They come from miles around for it. It's nothing compared to the Cabaret de L'Enfer. But does he really sleep in a coffin? He looks too young to have such a fortune. I heard he made a pact with Lucifer. Don't be ridiculous, it's probably old money. Still, he's quite handsome. But why do they call him the Heretic? How does one get invited anyway?

I cannot deny the pleasure of this mythos surrounding me. Vanity, as I have said, is my greatest sin. The whispers served only to feed my ego and the monster it had developed into. Actions speaking louder than words, I plunged headlong into the role of modern-day Dionysus, arranging all manner of bacchanalia to stimulate the senses, appease wanton appetites, and fulfil the latent fantasies of the ever-emerging circle of followers orbiting me. *Panem et circenses.*

❦

Three years passed in this fashion. Immersed in the persona of l'Hérétique, I reposed in the lap of opulence, drinking deeply from the ambrosial cup of the gods of old.

When the rumors and whispers began to spread beyond the confines of Paris, I left the city with Vallaton at my side and traveled abroad, sparing no expense.

En route to Rome, we visited Florence to tour the Uffizi and enjoy firsthand the magnificent *Venus of Urbino*. At Vienna, we heard Strauss the Younger with his orchestra and danced an evening of waltzes with the handsome daughters of a minor official attached to the emperor. We took the waters in Budapest and rested a month behind the high stone walls of a hilltop castle deep in the Carpathians. In Hamburg, I spent an exorbitant sum on the commission of an exquisite handmade pocket watch from a local jeweler of no small repute. The case was to have the Staff of Asclepius, the historic symbol of the healer, emblazoned in gemstones upon its front and a lily of diamonds on its reverse. I intended it a gift for Dumont upon his receiving his doctorate, as much a congratulatory token as a peace offering. We'd fallen out some time before, our troubles beginning shortly after I'd left the Sorbonne. His discomfort with my affairs gave him over to bouts of melancholy. He rarely came to my home anymore, instead insisting we meet either in his rooms—he still lodged on the rue du Cardinal Lemoine—or in a café. I felt Vallaton only too relieved to see him fading from my thoughts.

The whole affair had come to a head nearly a year before, in November of 1893 when Dumont came to me in uncharacteristic good spirits. A flush filled his usually pallid face as he told me joyously he'd fallen positively in love. Her name was Caroline, and she'd seized his heart with all the force of a steel trap.

"She's a glorious one," he said, describing all the qualifying features of this glory: the deftness of her mind, the breadth of her knowledge, and a stubborn will not seen among many women of the day.

"She reads. Wollstonecraft, Rousseau, Saint-Simon. What do you think of that? And she's of a completely independent bent," he said, the pride swelling within him. "She supports the movement, of course."

"What movement?" I said.

"What movement? *The* movement. Suffrage. Good God, don't you read the papers?"

"Not really. The trivialities of the day are so trivial."

"I fear for you," he said. "Consider what you're sacrificing. You've the whole world ahead of you. There's more to life than all this superficial materialism."

"And where is this 'more' to be found?" I said. "In settling down? My God man, you are so young. Cut yourself off from all other possibilities, and you might as well drown yourself in the Seine. What pleasure can be gained by anchoring yourself to just one person? That is the primary difference between us. You resist the flow of your natural urges; I let them carry me where they may."

"I worry one day they may carry you down a path from which you'll not be able to return."

"Your concerns are, as always, appreciated but unwarranted," I said. "I know you've not come to lecture. You've come because a girl has struck your fancy so much so, you're undoubtedly going to tell me a dreadful and horrific thought has already invaded your mind. If you've come here for a blessing, I'm afraid you won't get one. But nonetheless, I'll not let a dear friend commit himself to a life of boredom and indentured servitude without at least having the pleasure of meeting this intellectual succubus who has so enchanted you."

Dumont hesitated at first, but then capitulated, and I arranged for dinner the following Tuesday at La Tour d'Argent.

We dined on wine and pressed duck and sipped our coffee over a plate of daintily crafted *religieuse*. A petite figure with reddish-brown hair, a slightly upturned nose, and a flat chest, this Caroline presented herself with grace and charm. She conversed politely, ate sparingly, and drank even less.

Dumont displayed an uncharacteristic jocundity and ease that I'd scarcely seen in him before. His usual timid reserve had been usurped by a genuine sense of joy. In her presence, he laughed easier and smiled more broadly.

Over the meal, he eagerly related the story of how they'd met.

"It was at a bookshop," he said. "I'd been puzzling out a troubling detail, a trifle, really. Something I'd read among Albin's notes about the Inquisition. He'd become positively obsessed with a fellow named de Huerca, a fairly influential man and confidant of Torquemada toward the end of his life. A full quarter of Albin's scribblings concern him and his time in the Aragon region of Spain, but aside from what he'd written, I could find little else about the man. Anyway, I thought I'd pop down to the rue de Rivoli and see if one of the bookshops might have something I could use. I tried several stands but came up empty. And just when I'd decided to call it a day, I see a *librarie* sign over an obscure green door across from the Tour Saint-Jacques. So, I think, why not? And what do I find but this pearl tending the stacks."

"It's my father's store," Caroline said. "He's a bit ill, so I help him from time to time. Paul was so shy. He only talked to my father, who, sadly, couldn't help him. But the next day, he came back, this time looking for something else."

"I went back every day for two weeks," Dumont resumed. "Trying to work up my nerve. Each day, I came on a new pretext, and each day, Raymond, that's her father, got more annoyed with me. He must have thought me the dumbest medical student in Paris for my questions. But I suspected Caroline knew. Eventually, she interceded, we got to talking, and, well, here we are. It's funny, in a way, you could say that strange hermit was the one who brought us together in the end. A wondrous thing fate can be."

"Charming," I said. "And I see the fair lady was receptive to your unorthodox approach at courtship."

"His bashfulness was adorable," she said. "But once he stopped fumbling over his words, I felt he had a sensitive soul."

"I suppose one needs such a thing if one is to become a physician," Dumont said.

His comment gave me pause.

"I disagree," I said. "I would think it better to be hardened, inured as it were to the harsh realities you'll be facing in the wards. A soul, especially a caring and sensitive one, might prove quite a hindrance."

"I don't follow," Caroline said. "How can caring about the suffering of others be a bad thing?"

"Well, futility is a hard taskmaster."

"Futility?"

"Yes. I'm not suggesting your endeavors won't be honorable. On the contrary, I applaud your nobility. I certainly couldn't will myself to battle fate day after day, knowing, in the end, I'll lose all the same. But surely, you see?"

"I don't understand," Caroline said. "Alleviating suffering is never futile. Healing the sick is never futile. Mending the broken is never futile."

"These are challenges to nature," I said. "And though we can challenge nature, we cannot conquer her. It is in our nature to become ill, to suffer, and to die. Life is, after all, a terminal condition, is it not? Prolonging nature's course, while admirable, is ultimately pointless."

"Perhaps this isn't the best place for this discussion," Dumont said. "I think what Caroline means to say is—"

"You think it's God's intention for us to suffer?" she said.

"I'm not speaking of God," I said. "I said nature."

"There is a difference?"

"Did I forget to tell you my friend is an atheist?" Dumont said.

"That's horrible," she said. "But not surprising. Paul mentioned you had some unorthodox approaches to courtship yourself."

"I do not court," I said.

"No, you only presume to hold it apparently," she replied.

"Comely and witty, I see why Paul finds you so desirable. Be careful, Paul, this rose has thorns. She's quick to draw blood. Not a quality favored in most physicians, or their wives, for that matter. Tell me, dear, what role does God play, if not to bring about disease, violence, war? Why does he cause children to die in infancy? Why does he drive the murderer to violence, the rapist to rape? These are wretched acts society would hold as most heinous. But aren't they committed under God's watchful eyes? If they are permitted by Him, why not by us? Why should the laws of men countermand what God abides?"

Caroline's interrogative gaze remained unmoved by my argument.

"Those are acts of madmen who've lost their reason. It's not man's nature to do evil, but it's his freedom to choose to do so, and he must accept the consequences. As you are a libertine, I would think this freedom would be one you embrace. But make no mistake. God punishes, he does not permit."

"A sad catechism," I said. "Piety would have us surrender the commission of such acts to free will, the choice to defy God, so he and the saints can take pleasure in viewing the eternal damnation of the sinners. This would make him the ultimate libertine, wouldn't it? What I choose to do is the same, though free will plays no part in my decisions. Remove God from the equation, and what have you left but a man and his penchants. Remove God from the equation, and you remove the notion of evil altogether and usurp it with something far more respectable and desirable."

"And what is that?"

"Sensuality. And there is no more supremely satisfying act than the one that offends the religious sensibilities. To throw in the face of their beliefs the pleasure of the unbeliever is the ultimate show of libertinage. You'd do well to discard your God, my dear. I did long ago, and it has brought me nothing but freedom."

"A flimsy license built on a foundation of self-deceit," Caroline said. "You're too blind to see the circle of your own poor reason. How can you derive satisfaction from acting in defiance of something you yourself claim not to believe in? If there is no God, why seek to offend him, if not because in your heart you *do* believe? In that case, your pleasure is merely childish impudence. A son defying the will of his father."

"The only impudence I see here is from a girl who has forgotten her place," I said, my patience wearing thin.

Dumont, who'd been quiet until then, and who, it turned out, was full of surprises, flashed eyes sharp as daggers.

"That's enough," he said. "You'll not speak to Caroline this way."

"It's all right," Caroline said, rising from her chair. "I've met men of his ilk before. Ones who think a woman has a place. They're of a dying breed. But if I've any place, it is definitely not here. Thank you, Etienne, for an enlightening conversation."

Dumont look at me disdainfully and followed her out. That had been almost a year before. It was the last time we'd spoken.

❧

It was in Hamburg I first took notice of a change in my accounts. A wired communication from Société Générale showed my once vast fortune dwindling with rapidity, a decline I attributed to several failed investitures and not to the impetuousness of unbridled spending. But while God may lie, money does not. After three years of undisciplined excess, only a fraction of what I once possessed remained.

I still maintained my family home in Marseille, which hung around my neck like a very expensive albatross. The upkeep of property required retaining servants. Servants required pay, and property required taxes. There was also my home in Paris, a regular box at the Palais Garnier, horses stabled at the Hippodrome de Vincennes, holdings in two mines in Australia, and at least a dozen other ventures of which I'd not the faintest idea how much I'd given to and what, if any returns, I'd seen. There were also Vallaton's expenses. Never short of whimsies, he'd made an industry of spending my money. It had ultimately been his idea to take a tour of the continent in the first place.

In Hamburg too, I'd taken notice of a subtle change in my friend's behavior, a curious leveling of his mien. One might even call it a cooling of sorts—a tempering of his passions. It started as we left Vienna. On our final day in the city, a time usually gay and filled with anticipated pleasures of our next destination, his comportment became morose and, dare I say, bordered on disconsolate.

I found him in his rooms at the hotel, at the desk finishing his correspondence. He'd not dressed and wore the countenance of a man burdened by an unseen trouble. I told him as much, but he dismissed my concerns out of hand.

"You make an excellent rake but a poor liar," I said. "Come on, out with it."

"It's nothing," he said. "Just feeling a bit under the weather. Probably exhaustion."

"Nonsense. I've known you to pass days without sleep or drink, or have you forgotten that dalliance in Fontenay with that Durivage woman and her niece? Speak up, man, else I'll have no recourse but to send for one of those horrid Viennese brain doctors everyone is always prattling on about to probe your 'zexuality.' What's troubling you?"

"I tell you I'm fine," he said, shaking off his gloom, becoming a flurry of activity. His correspondence shut away in the drawer, he milled about the room gathering his toilet.

"What shall it be this evening, then?" he said, dressing in the mirror. "They're performing Shubert at the Musikverein. Or there's always the Staatsoper…"

Despite the quick return to his usual self, Vallaton's eclectic behaviors only increased as our journey wore on. Joviality that once carried him for days at a time was replaced by a mercurial turn. I'd find him, apropos of nothing, lost in his own thoughts, distracted in open company, even outright bored at times. Frequently, he sought solitary respite from our activities, and on at least two separate occasions, in Brno, it was, I observed him politely, yet nonetheless definitively, rebuff the advances of the beautiful, young second cousin of a Polish princess.

Contrarily, at other times, he sprang from his funk, practically over the moon with joy. I began to have concerns a medical condition might be the cause of these tidal fluctuations. At Leipzig, I consulted a physician about *lues*, thinking his behavior might be symptomatic of the pox, but the man would make no diagnosis without seeing Vallaton personally. I'd even contemplated writing to Dumont for his considerations but thought better of it. In the end, vacillating between speaking up and remaining silent, I chose the latter.

❧

I'd intentions of returning to Paris in the midsummer after stopping a few weeks in Brussels, but while still in Hamburg, Vallaton expressed other plans.

We'd dined in a restaurant along the Elbe and afterward took the evening air on the promenade of the Jungfernstieg. Families strolled the waterfront avenue, and young lovers watched the last rays of sunset dance across the shimmering waters of Lake Binnenalster. It was an idyllic scene disturbed only by Vallaton's pensiveness. He'd been distracted all day. After walking several minutes, he finally broke counsel with himself.

"I'll not be coming back to Paris with you," he said. His eyes squinted against the glow of the setting sun.

I'd sensed something like this might be coming, yet the anticipation of impending strife made it no easier to accept. I affected a calm air, as if I'd known all along of his plan. Employing the tactic might throw him off his guard and give him over to revealing something he wished to conceal. It worked.

"I'm returning to Vienna," he continued. "I made a connection there, of sorts."

We'd stopped along a low balustrade to admire the lake.

"You remember Herr Reisinger?"

"That stolid little deputy from the trade ministry?" I said. "I remember dancing with his daughter Lena. Rigid girl, like dragging a mannequin about the floor. Big ears. Wretched nostrils as well, much too long."

"Yes, well, him," Vallaton interrupted.

"What's he offering you? *Mon Dieu*! You're not actually thinking of going to work for him? You're not thinking of actually going *to* work?"

"Of course not," he said. "I'm not going back to see him."

"Then with whom did you make this connection? The crown prince?"

"His daughter."

"The crown prince has a daughter?"

"No," Vallaton said, his voice registering annoyance. "Reisinger's daughter."

"Lena?" I said, baffled. "What on earth has gotten into you? The girl is like a walking tree."

"Not Lena," he said, rounding to face me. "Anja."

The name stirred a memory. Anja was Reisinger's younger daughter, a girl of nineteen or twenty, neither exceptionally beautiful nor memorably radiant—slight of build, with a high, broad forehead and squared, Teutonic jaw. Wholly unremarkable. I'd forgotten her completely.

The look in Vallaton's eye conjured a hollow dread not felt since Dumont had come to tell me of Caroline. His face became serene, as if saying her name out loud had released the tension of a rope stretching inside him. We'd left Vienna nearly eight months before, and I'd not given the girl a second thought. But Vallaton had done nothing but that since their parting.

"I don't understand," I said, still not comprehending the gravity of his demeanor. "You danced with the girl, nothing more. Why would you want to go back there?"

"It was more than a dance," he said. "We talked all evening. I don't know what it was about her, but I felt quite at ease just being with her. She talked of her family, I talked of mine, what little I could remember without shame. We laughed at the odd innuendo, she told me about her love of art and the theater. She'd never been to Paris. I told her about Gautier and Racine. She's read Zola and Molière."

"And because she knows *Tartuffe*, you want to traipse all the way back to Vienna just to fuck her?"

"Don't be so crass," he said, clearly offended.

"What has come over you? You're not seriously telling me you have feelings for this girl? Matthieu Vallaton, the greatest libertine I know, who once brought a whore to orgasm with the long end of a crucifix while she was dressed as the Virgin Mary? Who once—"

"Stop, please," he said, turning aside. "I'm not proud of some of the things I've done."

"Some of the things?" I said. "You should be proud of all you've done. You're a master of your craft. You taught me everything I know. Together have we not experienced the most amazing sensualities life has to offer? Are you telling me it was all meaningless for you? I can't believe it."

"I love her," he said. A finality hung in his words. The look on his face spoke of a man who'd reached not only a decision but a turning point. The glowing sun had passed beneath the rooftops and the crowd around us thinned as people returned to their homes. Soon, there was but the two of us. Vallaton, the totality of his crime laid bare in three simple words, looked out upon the dark-green waters and made confession.

"I don't know how, or why, but I fell in love with this girl. She's beautiful and charming and intelligent. I've not felt this before. She returns to my thoughts over and again. I cannot explain it, nor can I deny it. Ever since that first night, all I've thought about is being near her again. This trip, these miles I've put between us, I can't bear them anymore. I have to go back to her, to make her mine."

"Listen to yourself," I said. "It's like you've lost your mind. You love orgies and whores and torturing others for your own pleasures."

"Juvenile pursuits. Years wasted vetting out youthful indiscretions. Rendezvous without meaning, without passion. I realize now what I've been doing can't be right. Anja's words have made me see that."

He reached into his breast pocket and passed me a folded paper. It was a letter in a woman's hand.

"We've been corresponding for months," he said as I read. "In secret, of course. I tell you, each new letter brings me joy I'd not thought possible. And with each week passing while I await the next, I've known only sadness. I see her words on the paper, and I hear her voice speak them in my head. It's as if she were in the room with me. I tell her how much I miss her, how I wish I could return to her. She tells me to be patient, that we will be reunited if it is fated for us. But I'll not wait for fate any longer. I'm going back. My heart tells me I must go back."

I felt ill. This giant, this monument to debauchery, whose licentious nature knew no bounds and who had committed acts both remarkable and unspeakable, had been brought low by love. I simply could not believe it. I refused to accept it and gave vent to my vitriol.

"Love is an illusion, you taught me that. The heart is the seat of frailty. It's the mind that guides us. Don't you remember those words? What you feel for this girl, it's not love. It's a passion, to be sure, but love? You're no more capable of love than I am. You cannot be anything other than you are, just like a river will never reverse its flow. To give up your lustful nature and remain true to one woman alone for the rest of your days? Impossible. I cannot dream you capable of such fortitude. This feeling you have for Anja is a passing fancy, nothing more. If she knew you like I do, she'd see you're unable to love her."

"It's more than that," he said. "I've her told much about me, what I've done. She doesn't care. She says I've been scared, living behind a façade to hide my true self, and I believe she's right. I'm ready for something more than myself, don't you understand? Don't you feel there is more to our existence than just the endless chase?"

Disgust filled me.

"You led me down this path," I said. "We walk this road together, and you want to turn your back on everything we've done. Do you think you can just erase your past and start anew with this girl? You're mad. People do not change. Whores will always be whores. Believers will always be fools. And you will always be a libertine. But go, if you must. Go to your Viennese whore and make her your wife. Make yourself a boring little life. I'll not surrender myself to such absurdity."

Night had fallen, and the gas lamps cast islands of pale-yellow light on the cobblestones. I'd said all I could without surrendering my composure. Turning my back on Vallaton, I left him standing there overlooking the bank of the lake.

The next day, I traveled on to Brussels, alone.

In the early days of fall, I returned to Paris. I sought to pay visit to Dumont and present the watch, but arriving at the rue du Cardinal Lemoine, I found him gone. Angelique had passed away the year before, and the house had fallen into the possession of a distant cousin who'd promptly sold the property on. The new owner said the young doctor had moved on some time ago, but he didn't know where.

With both Dumont and Vallaton gone, I'd not a friend in the whole of the city. Their absence left a void that drove me to gloom. I retired to my home neither entertaining nor venturing out for several weeks. My servants observed me only peripherally. I kept counsel with myself alone, taking my meals in solitude.

Depriving myself of the pleasures of women and drink, I'd committed to a sort of fast, scorching my desires with a cleansing melancholy. Word continued to come to me of my strained finances. Seething at the news, my ire turned to Vallaton as the prime mover of my ruin. To stave off the inevitable, I let go of most of the house staff and sold several pieces of artwork.

I began proceedings to have my family's home in Marseille sold as soon as possible. A buyer soon emerged with an offer substantially less than the value of the property, but I accepted without hesitation, needing the money to maintain my house in Paris. In the end, I sold the estate for barely more than half its actual worth.

Shortly after the conclusion of the sale, the following letter arrived:

M. Allard,

By now you have undoubtedly received the money from the sale of your home in Marseille and have moved your interests on to other endeavors. I am saddened to learn the place I have called home for so many years will no longer welcome me. A representative of the new owner arrived last week to relieve much of the staff, and renovations have already begun. He has an eye toward eliminating all traces of your family's legacy. All the artifacts of your father's study have been carted away, and your mother's chapel demolished. Removing old and familiar faces seems just one more step in this process.

That my beloved Lipa has not lived to bear witness to this stripping of history is my only consolation. She is gone just these four months, but I know had not the grippe taken her, the events of the past few weeks may surely have. I turn my worry now to our daughter, Elena. I pray I may find new work and a new home for us.

I write to you, sir, to find it in your heart to perhaps provide hope for us, an uneducated man and a motherless child. Work in Marseille is scarce, and though I know I can find pay for my skills, there is little hope I will be able to find adequate education for my daughter under such unfortunate circumstances. She is deserving of more than I can provide.

I can only pray Lipa's devotions to you and your mother helps guide your wisdom and compassion. I implore you to see your way to helping us.
Regards,
Hugo Jubert

The Dickensian platitudes disgusted me. I cared not a fig for the fate of the house or its contents, the last relics of a long-distant past, and I'd barely enough to keep my own affairs afloat let alone provide for a child. The thought alone was absurd.

Scribbling off a curt reply, I suggested the fellow redouble his efforts to find work and, failing that, to send his daughter off to a convent so as to unburden himself of the responsibility of her.

❧

The new reserve of currency reinvigorated my energies and raised me from the doldrums of isolation. I sought to break the monotony by hosting a soiree and sent out invitations across the city to boldly announce l'Hérétique had returned from his sojourn abroad and welcomed any and all who would come to drink of his wine, eat of his table, and pit their skills against him in any game of chance, no limit too high.

It was fate's cruel trick that after a year's absence, my notoriety should dry up with my money and the fickle nature of society to abandon its sacred cows. In the end, only a handful of revelers turned out to welcome me back and relive past excesses. The whole affair felt but a pale and tawdry shadow of former glories.

The humiliation of such cheek was almost too much to bear, and again, I withdrew into solitude, only to be drawn out a second time by the arrival of a mysterious invitation, hand delivered by a dour, broad-faced Slav. Formal almost to a fault and written on exquisite silk parchment dyed the pale purple of lilac, it read simply:

> It is with great hope and anticipation of acceptance that the one known as l'Hérétique will kindly be a guest at my table tomorrow for an evening of music, revelry, and chance. I have heard tale of his skill at cards and wish nothing more than the honor of testing my mettle against his own.
> With great affection,
> M. D. Kazakov

Beneath a flourished signature read an address for a chateau in Rueil. Turning the fine linen paper over in my fingers, I detected the faint smell of the flower that had lent its color to the page. Clearly, this Kazakov had some degree of taste, and I accepted the offer, sending his man off with my thanks and instruction to inform his master as such. As soon as he'd departed, I sniffed the edge of the paper again, my mind churning at the prospect of such a potentially lucrative opportunity.

❧

Watching listlessly as the scenery passed my coach window, I turned the invitation card over in my fingers, entertaining my curiosity of this Kazakov, and a familiar image took shape in my mind. I'd met several Russians in my recent travels— all stolid champions of the Romanovs, clothed in regimental uniforms gleaming with medals, each one with its own story. Grim-faced, decrepit, and smoking profusely, they spoke but few words, and those only in praise of the tsar or the glory of conquest. To the Russian, cards are a serious affair, though he loses often, most times more than he can afford, but always with grace. This Kazakov would be no different. I'd already started planning how to spend my winnings when we turned from the main road and up a broad drive lined with poplar trees, at the top of which stood Kazakov's home.

Not as magnificent as Fontainebleau, but much grander in style and composition than the Château de Malmaison, onetime home of the empress Joséphine, I puzzled over how the presence of such a beautiful home so near to Paris could have escaped my attention.

A footman awaited my arrival before the main entrance. He took my invitation with a subtle bow before silently enjoining me to enter.

Structured after the palatial style, the house was laid out as a large rectangle formed by a series of connecting rooms surrounding a central courtyard and garden. I was led through several of these, each more garishly decorated than the last. There was an opulent salon, the walls hung with rich tapestry and works of the old masters. A cursory glance showed them to be originals of unquestionable value. This led on to a formal receiving room, spartanly appointed save for an ornate gilded throne on a raised platform upon which, no doubt, the master of the house held funny court. We passed a trophy room, the walls frescoed with hunting scenes of all four seasons. Bears, tigers, bucks, foxes, hawks, falcons, and crocodiles, frozen in time and all their ferocity stood mounted about the perimeter, claws and talons and teeth bared in proud defiance of their miserable defeat at the hands of the rifle that felled them. Beyond this gruesome menagerie lay more sitting rooms, parlors, receiving rooms, and studies, each one more majestic than the previous.

We proceeded to the next wing, where a growing clamor of music and laughter met my ears. Undeterred, my guide led unwaveringly on as the cacophony of screams and caterwauling built to a chaotic crescendo. I took note of the ghastly strains of a violin being tortured.

We stopped before a set of doors at the end of the passage. The footman gestured for me to remain outside while he slipped behind them. Intrigued, I leaned close to spy on the proceedings when, from within the room, a harsh, sonorous voice boomed above the din.

"What? Who? Of course, show him, show him in, you *blovant*!"

The footman stolidly returned and led me inside.

Like a blast from an open coal furnace, the wave of heat filling this dining hall took me aback. Fifty guests, or maybe a hundred, I could not tell for their mass, packed the room around the length of a great table piled high with a feast of terrific proportions.

Upon the table itself lay nudes in repose, men and women alike, their living flesh serving as platters. One gorged himself on wine straight from the bottle while feeding waiting mouths with bunches of grapes dangling from his toes. Another knelt writhing on all fours, her breasts jiggling with delight, while a swarthy-looking fellow in a green frock coat devoured a mountain of soft meringue packed between the cheeks of her ass. Beside the hearth, a violinist, the source of the appalling noise I'd heard earlier, struggled through a Glinka sonata while having his manhood pleasured by the mouth of a stout, fleshy whore, her plump arms wrapped securely around his hips preventing his escape. Try as he might, he could not break free. It mattered not anyway. No one was listening.

At the head of this gluttonous orgy sat Kazakov, suffocating with his face buried betwixt the splayed buttocks of a blonde-haired nymph. He struggled to get free, but she held his head fast, making as if to drown him in the crevice of her ass. Standing beside his master, the footman formally announced my arrival.

"Yes, yes, sit," he mumbled in reply, the rumble of his voice sending his plate into convulsive giggles. "Eat. Eat."

A moment later, he emerged with a great gasp of air, red and panting, his cheeks dripping with bits of half-chewed olive.

Perhaps forty years of age, sweaty and rotund, a toothy gash of a smile slashed across his face amid a forest of a thick, unkempt beard. He stared out from lustrous coal-black eyes. A fez teetered atop his mat of bushy black hair, threatening to topple at any moment. He laughed a great bellowing laugh that shook the pillars of the house.

Two buxom ladies in valet coats and nothing else tended his wine. Wheezing with laughter, he coughed and spat, rolling his great mass like a man seized with fits. He cast bones picked clean of their meat across the room, spilled wine on the floor, and farted loudly. He was as a lunatic escaped from his cage.

I was given a seat at the right hand of this mad Caesar. As if from the thin air, a plate was thrust in front of me and no fewer than four glasses of wine poured.

"You got my invitation, I see," he said, his voice booming. "I was beginning to fear you'd not come. I hope you don't mind we started without you." Then, rolling his eyes and shouting over his shoulder: "Damn it, Mashka! Will you finish him already? My ears bleed, woman!"

Behind us, the tortured violinist's bow raced to a wobbly crescendo as Mashka's red curls tossed in the violent rhythm of her redoubled efforts. With a final squeal of the strings, it was over. As he slumped into an empty chair, the instrument fell from his hands and bounced across the floor. Mashka wiped her mouth, rose, and curtsied like a schoolgirl. All rejoiced and vigorously applauded her performance.

"Get him some wine," Kazakov commanded. "Five minutes respite, no more, then I will hear some Mozart. And if you do not capture his essence, I will have her suck you all the way through Concerto no. 5."

"That's no punishment," someone protested.

"Through his ass?" another questioned.

"A job for Phillipe, perhaps," Mashka said, pointing to the fellow still gorging on the pile of meringue from his lady's backside.

"Perhaps if we stick a grape up his ass, Mashka can suck it out through his cock!" Kazakov roared with delight, the tears streaming down his ruddy cheeks. "What do think, Monsieur Allard? Shall we lay a wager?"

"I think I'll stake one hundred against," I said.

"Against what?" someone shouted. "That we can't get a grape up his ass or that she can't get it out?"

"Wager or no, I'd still like to see her try," Kazakov said. "What say you, Mashka? Up for seconds?"

Mashka, her tousled curls falling about her shoulders and pendulous breasts, plucked a grape from the table and examined it casually in her fingertips.

"Too small," she said, her tone as icy as the Volga in January. Seizing a ripe plum, she smiled. "This is better. Bring him."

But the violinist was already off. Tearing through the doorway, he ran screaming from the room. They all fell into convulsions. Mashka shrugged, took a juicy bite of the fruit, and tossed the rest over her shoulder.

"You Parisians," Kazakov said. "No balls. Now who will play the music? I want music, damn it. Tolya, sing something for us."

A profoundly drunk man rose and steadied himself at the end of the table. With one hand on the back of his chair, and the other across his heart, he inhaled deeply. Solemnly, he closed his eyes. All fell silent. The room dripped with anticipation. Suddenly, his mouth opened, bringing forth a belch of such verve and pitch even the ribald Kazakov was struck dumb at its might. It had form and mass and seemed to rise from the very pit of the young man's bowels. That took it all. They bore him aloft on their shoulders and paraded him around the room laughing like hyenas. Kazakov looked on drunk with mirth.

"You have come on a good night," he shouted over the din. "They are in good cheer."

"I find it difficult to believe there is ever an evening here without it," I said.

"My home here is a modest one," he said. "More of a country cottage. My dacha in Petersburg, *that* is another affair. There they really behave like animals."

"You make your home in Russia?"

"I make my home wherever it pleases me. But I came to my Paris home so I might meet you. The great Yeretik is a man of some renown. Word first reached me in Bern. They said your gatherings are quite notable affairs. I wished to see for myself, but alas, you were no longer hosting."

"I regret to disappoint you."

"No matter," he said with a wave of his fat, hairy hand. "It is your skill I am most interested in anyway. You will do me the honor of indulging me?"

"What kind of guest would I be if I declined such an invitation?"

"Splendid!" he cried. "But first, eat, eat! Drink! Fill his plate and his gullet so that he might share in my *gula*," Kazakov commanded.

Mounds of food were piled before me, overfilling my plate, spilling onto the floor. Wine from every region of the continent poured out in torrents, some I'd never sampled, others I never knew existed.

"Every man is possessed of one great sin, you know?" he said conspiratorially. "To not know your own is a most dangerous and tragic thing."

❧

We retired from the dining room after midnight, leaving the rest of the party going on its wild and merry way. Remarkably steady on his feet for the voluminous quantity of drink he'd consumed, Kazakov led me on a tour of the house, pointing out rare artifacts, antiques, and magnificent works of art. In the library, he proudly displayed dozens of illuminated manuscripts and a collection of volumes far surpassing those of the odd phantom of Madame Crespi's attic.

"These are just a portion of my library," he said, fingering the spines. "Books are a passion. I seek only the most perfect, the ones that contain the most secrets."

"Quite a few rare gems," I noted, identifying an ancient sixteenth-century Spanish text on fine vellum, a manual from the days of the Inquisition, nestled among dozens of volumes of Iberian origin. "Though I doubt you'll find many secrets here. Spain holds some interest for you?"

"A passing fancy. Beautiful country. Beautiful women. Bad food. Come. The others will join us soon. A drink while we wait?"

Walking on, we entered an elegant drawing room done in Imperial style. Four empty chairs surrounded a pedestal card table. Hung above the hearth was the framed portrait of a beautiful but sad girl in peasant garb. Kazakov poured cognac at a side table while I admired the picture.

"Who is she?" I said.

"Gohar," he said, handing me a glass. "I was a younger man then. And a thinner one too."

"You knew her?"

He gazed into the girl's doleful blue eyes.

"She was for me my only true happiness."

"What happened?"

"What always happens? We came from different worlds," he said, downing his glass. "*Takovazhizn.*"

Presently, we were joined by two other guests: Polachev, a gaunt, lanky Russian in pince-nez and pencil mustache, and Merson, whom I recognized from the dining table as the connoisseur of meringue in the green frock coat.

"Have your fill at dinner?" he said.

"Quite," I said.

"You know, a lot can be gleaned about a man from the amount of food he eats at the expense of his host."

"Indeed," I concurred. "And even more from the manner in which he indulges his portion."

"You refer to my choice of platter." He laughed. "It was a simple one. Mashka, as you saw, was otherwise preoccupied. Perhaps you judge my fancy ungentlemanly?"

"On the contrary. A predilection is merely a facet of one's character. Not its definition."

"*L'homme est un bijou*," Polachev said. "He can be viewed from many angles."

"Man is a worm," Kazakov said, his gaze still fixed on the portrait above the mantle. "He has but one face, and like the worm, you cannot tell his face from his ass. Sin is what defines a man at his heart. Don't you agree?"

"Only for the man who believes his actions can be sinful," I said. "Trespass implies limitations. If one holds to a doctrine of no boundaries, transgression is categorically impossible."

"Spoken like a bona fide heretic." Kazakov laughed. "How can one offend God if one does not believe in God?"

"Precisely."

"Ah, but can you be so sure? Can you know for certain God is indeed not?" he said.

"To tell the truth, I do not concern myself with such matters," Polachev interjected. "The question itself is absurd."

"And that is why your sin is *lenost*," Kazakov noted. Then he turned his attentions back to me. "Sloth," he clarified. "But you see, Monsieur Allard, a man can know his sin, indulge in it, even, and still believe as I do. Polachev does, though he won't admit it. He relishes his sloth. By admitting he does not care for our discussion, he shines a light upon it. I know my appetites, and I sate them. God watches, and he disapproves. That is why He thinks I will not be welcome in His home. At least, not yet."

A wide, unsettling grin played across his lips as he poured himself another drink.

"Are we to talk or are we to play?" Merson said.

"Of course, of course," Kazakov said, barking loudly for cards and tokens. Presently, we took our seats at the table.

"You are familiar with the American game of poker?" he said.

I said I was. It was being played here and there in some Parisian dens, and like all other diversions, I excelled at it, owing to my perceptive talents.

"America is a great land," he said as his servant divided chips among the table. "I have been across it many times. In the West, especially, there was much to remind me of my native Sakartvelo."

"Have you ever been back?" I asked of his home.

"Not for many years," he said, once again regarding the eyes of the peasant girl. "Monsieur l'Hérétique will play to his reputation, I trust? A man who does not believe in boundaries will see no obstacle to making this game most enjoyable. Shall we begin at two hundred francs?"

Play began in earnest. Tempering greed with wisdom, I surrendered several winning hands early in favor of drawing in Merson and Polachev, whose unconscious actions betrayed them. Merson particularly presented little challenge, his changes in breathing perceptible to even the most unpracticed ear. A flare of his nostrils informed me of the strength of his hand. In four consecutive deals, he'd cast aside nearly three thousand francs. Polachev, too, lost with impunity. Lighting his cigarettes in a long meerschaum holder, he affected no mood as hand after hand fell against him.

Kazakov, however, proved an unusual challenge. If my ability to read faces was preternatural, his ability to conceal his emotions was supernatural. Mercurial to a practiced fault, crescendos of jocularity vanished behind icy calculation.

One moment, his laughter filled the room; the next, his face seized with steely intensity.

"The Russian capacity for stoicism is impressive," Merson quipped after taking Polachev for another thousand.

"I once knew a general who lost his horse and his entire estate at the roulette table in Baden-Baden," Polachev said. "Turn after turn, he kept losing, thousands and thousands. He never said one word, just kept betting. A crowd gathered to watch the spectacle. I was there, of course, just as astonished as the rest. Money flowing away like a river. When it was over, I heard he went home, put on his uniform, and shot himself."

"Maybe he had a wish to die a poor man," Merson said. "Enter the world with nothing, leave it with nothing, one of those fools said."

"Timoti," Kazakov noted. "He may have been right. Perhaps this is what I will do when it is time for me to die."

"Seems honorable, in a way," Merson said. "Paul said money is the root of evil."

"Pavel spoke of the *love* of money," Kazakov corrected. "Love is the evil to be avoided. But who among us cannot love? I love food. But I do not love money. What about you, Monsieur Allard? What does a *yeretik* love?"

Kazakov's gaze set upon me over the tops of his cards. I was holding four sevens, a strong hand.

"I do not hold to a principle of love," I said. "Love requires permanence. The fleeting nature of pleasure demands its constant pursuit. A thing's value comes not in holding it but in using it, experiencing it, then disposing of it in favor of something new."

"So disposed," Polachev said. "It's easy to see how God does not find a home within you. The permanence of eternity might be a bit much for you to bear."

"The most extreme joy is to be found in the defiance of such foolish notions," I said. "I've as much use for God as he would have for me. If his glory is dependent on my love, then let it be he who worships *me*."

A gleam sparked in Kazakov's eye.

"I know now what your sin is," he said with a smile.

"And will you enlighten me?"

He said nothing, only laid down his hand. Four queens.

Kazakov swept his great arm across the table, collecting the pot. Five thousand francs. Merson clicked his tongue in disgust.

"The Lord gave, and the Lord has taken away," he said, his piles of tokens vanished. "Time to retire."

"It's only money," Polachev said. "You've still your health."

"And meringue." Kazakov laughed.

Merson poured another drink and retired to observe the game from the sofa. Two hands later, Polachev, too, would fall.

"Perhaps another drink before we begin again?" Kazakov said. "You need something to keep your spirits up?" The hour was late. I sensed in his tone a subtly sinister mien. "Now that it is just the two of us, might you stand for a real challenge?"

"What do you suggest?" I said.

Kazakov shifted his great bulk to his feet and called for his footmen. Presently, a servant arrived bearing a tray with a dusty bottle of wine and fresh glasses. The master poured two fingers of the pungent red liquor for himself and two for me.

"This wine was bottled in the village of Tvishi in 1717," he said. "It is the village where I was born."

"How did you come to own such a rare vintage?" I said.

He brushed my query aside, downing his glass in one violent gulp.

"My sin. Even rarity cannot sate my excess. Once I've had the taste, I cannot stop myself. Desire is what drives me. It is much the same with you, I think."

"My sin, as you call it, is not gluttony," I said.

"No," Kazakov said, pouring out another glass. "Yours is the sin of pride, Monsieur Allard. I've known the type. Men like you are all cut from the same cloth. And yet, I sensed there was something different at work. The others, they have no imagination, no creative identity, no sin. But with you, I knew there was something you were after more than mere money. All your wild parties, your gambling, your women, all your talk of seeking infinite pleasures, it is all a façade, is it not? These are not the endeavors of a man seeking something, they are the endeavors of a man running from something, am I correct?"

Kazakov glared at me over the rim of the glass.

"The hour is late," I said.

"What is time for men like us?" he said. "I have heard many rumors of the great Yeretik, but none said he was one to retire early. I ask one final game, a true test of fortitude, not these childish distractions. Everything I have against everything of yours. What say you?"

Their curiosity piqued, Polachev and Merson returned to the table. I'd already lost a considerable sum, more than I could afford. Nearly everything I'd worked to replace.

"That is not..." I began.

"Tempting?" he said. "Your sin against mine. I indulge my sin, Monsieur Allard. I take what I want when I want, and so do you. I have taken nearly everything from you tonight; only your pride remains. I wager it will not let you leave here without revenging itself upon me. I give you a chance to redeem yourself."

His grin grew wide and wet, an insolent smirk that cut me to the quick. In the face of it, defiance swelled in my chest. I would accept the challenge, regain my losses, and crush the impudent Cossack all in one blow.

Merson rubbed his hands greedily. Polachev clenched his meerschaum stem between his teeth and looked down over his hawkish nose.

"I will deal," Merson said, taking up the cards. "So as to be fair."

"Perhaps the gentlemen should sign an agreement first?" Polachev suggested.

"To the devil with your agreements," Kazakov grumbled. "I am an honorable man."

"As am I," I said. "My word is good enough."

"But to clarify the conditions—"

"There is no need," Kazakov said. "The wager is understood. One hand. If he wins, the money is his. If I win, everything is mine. Agreed?"

"Agreed," I said, my indignation rising like vomit in my throat.

Polachev begged off. Merson shuffled the cards. I'd heard the tune countless times before. Like the beating of a pigeon's wings as it takes flight, the raspy flap of shuffled cards had become part of nature itself.

Kazakov trained his stern, intimidating gaze upon me. I measured my breathing to the cadence of the shuffle, a technique I'd picked up as a child. I listened for my own heart-beat, timed my breaths to the beat, like rolling waves on a moving sea while Kazakov's labored breaths, deliberate and forceful, expelled through thick, wide nostrils described a lo-comotive at slow start.

Finally, the deal commenced. Kazakov made no move to raise his cards, nor I mine. It was a game of brinksmanship. Neither of us wanted to make the first move, to reveal any-thing to the other. It might have gone on all night, but, at last, he smiled and swiped up his hand. But not until I'd first collected mine.

All was silent save for the crackling fire.

"Cards, gentlemen?" Merson said. Kazakov puzzled over his hand, a useless scheme he'd employed to suggest a poor draw. His breathing all but ceased, a strategy he'd also em-ployed throughout the night. His great lungs, once filled, could remain still for several minutes in a feat of superhuman endurance. His dark eyes betrayed no secrets, his pressed lips broached no sign of quavering.

"Two," he said in a low and measured voice.

I called for only one card, drawing a queen of diamonds. That made three and two eights.

"I wish to make this more interesting," Kazakov said un-expectedly. "Are you game for a raise?"

"What do you propose?" I said.

"This house," he said, gesturing around in a wide sweep of his great arms. "All of it. Everything and everyone in it. Against your Paris home, and everything and everyone in it."

"That is preposterous," Polachev cried.

"Agreed," I said hastily, pride coming between me and my rational self.

"And your carriages," he demanded. "And your horses. All of it."

"Done," I said, losing my senses.

Thinking only of the humiliation I would inflict upon the great Russian buffoon for his impudence, I lay out my hand on the table.

Dumont had once said how the addict was a slave to his will. He abandons all to the drug, even rational thought, and in this way, he becomes a slave to himself. Even Hobbes said appetite was a lust of the mind. But I say pride is a lust of the heart, and therefore stronger and more devastating than any appetite.

Kazakov lay down his hand, a neat, practiced curve of white rectangles describing the delicate folds of a lady's fan, a vicious grin cutting across his face. Dread gripped at my throat like a man drowning in a flood, clutching at the branch that keeps him being swept away by the rushing torrent.

Four nines.

Chapter X

Al plodded up the stairs. He took them one at a time. The going was slow, each step a marathon.

Nearing exhaustion, he reached the top and paused. A nurse offered help, but he kindly waved her away. She knew Al from his daily visits. It was just part of the routine they'd created for themselves. She would ask; he would politely refuse. After a moment, he started down the long hall to the women's ward but stopped short of entering at the door. Off to one side, a small crowd surrounded Zofia's bedside.

There was Fat Maja, a pudgy, gray-haired woman of sixty, with her red babushka knotted tightly under her chin. She sat in a chair, an open tin of flaky *kolaczki* in her lap. Oliver, her youngest and most adored *dobry wypadek*, her happy accident, as she often called him, stood behind his mother. His brothers were with him, and their wives and children too.

They'd come when they'd heard the happy news. Zofia had beaten back the darkness and found her way home from her deep sleep, the light returned to her big, smiling eyes. She'd been gone nearly a month.

Al stood apart from this happy congregation, watching from the doorway. He could hear little of what was said, but the cheer on their faces and the ease of their smiles required no sound to discern. He contented himself to stay away. He wanted them to have their time with Zofia. Soon, they would go back to their lives, and when they did, his new time with her would begin.

Eventually, a nurse arrived and the party dispersed. As they left, Al pulled Nathan aside, placing a hand on his nephew's arm.

"I wondered if I might ask a favor of you?" Al took a folded paper from his pocket and placed it in Nathan's hand. "I would like it if you could look into something for me."

Zofia observed this brief exchange from her bed, though, from across the room, she could hear nothing of what was said. The ward grew quiet after the shuffling of feet died away.

"You look exhausted," Zofia said as Al eased himself into the chair recently vacated by his corpulent sister-in-law. The warmth still clinging to the seat made him instantly sleepy. He felt if he could just close his eyes for five minutes, take a quick catnap, everything would be restored to its proper order. Their roles now reversed, it was she who was alert and healthy, while, sagging in the chair, Al described a man gone to seed.

"When was the last time you slept?"

"Many days. Too many to remember. I wanted to be here when you woke up."

She looked at him tenderly.

"You haven't been eating."

"How could I eat?" he said. "I thought I'd lost you forever."

He turned his hat over in his hand. He couldn't look at her.

"What is it?"

"I feel ashamed." The remorse in his voice forcing the words to halt in his throat. "I was so angry."

Zofia said nothing. She could see the defeat in the deep lines of his brow.

"Angry with me?"

"Angry with God," he said. "I thought if I could just give something, He might send you back to me. But I didn't have anything to give. What had I to give? I could only ask what I could do to make Him give you back."

She reached out, placing her small hand on his arm. A tear welled at the corner of his eye.

"And when He did not answer, I became angry with you. I feel so ashamed. I thought if God was not taking you, then it was you who chose to go. And I got mad with you. Forgive me, I got so mad with you."

He broke down in tears.

"Albie," she said. "How could you think such a thing? You know I could not leave you."

"I know," he said. "That's why I'm sorry."

"You don't have to be. I know why you feel this way."

"How can you know?"

She hesitated, unsure she should open a wound so long closed.

"Henry," she said.

Their stillborn son. The name left her lips, and the memory of him came rushing back from a place Al fought so hard to bury in the past. The image of his lifeless boy materialized before him. So small and fragile, like a bisque doll. He weighed so little. *Like holding a cloud.* It was the first time either had said his name since the dreadful morning of his birth.

"I asked God to take me in his place," she said. "I hated Him for so long. I thought, how can this be? How can I live while my child dies? Who could do such a thing, take a child from his mother before he'd even a chance to cry for the first time? I felt like everything was taken from me. I wanted to die. I wanted to die, and I wanted him to live."

"You felt betrayed."

"I felt robbed," she said. "When the doctor said there could be no more children, it was like falling down a deep hole and I could not reach the bottom. To spend my whole life thinking if I believed what I was told to believe, everything would be right—that I would be rewarded with children and a family to love. But it was not right. For so many years, I blamed myself. Sometimes, I even blamed you. I don't know why."

"Because the helplessness brings with it the doubt," Al said. "This is what I felt."

Across the room, another young-looking family gathered at the bedside of a frail old woman. Al noticed her only obliquely when she'd been wheeled in a few days before. A middle-aged man, probably her son, sat on the edge of the bed, while his wife and their little girl stood apart. The old woman's husband had probably died some time before. Al surmised the son was all that was left, since no one had come to visit her except for the young man and his wife.

"She's in a bad way," Al said quietly. "I don't think it will be too much longer."

"I do not like to be surrounded by so much death and sadness. When can we go home, Albie?"

"Soon," he said, patting her hand.

A week later, Nathan came to see Al at the shop. The old man eagerly looked up from his reading and came to the counter.

"It's the damnedest thing, Uncle," Nathan said. "And it took some doing, but I think I have what you're looking for. What have you got there?" Nathan remarked on the curious book Al was stuffing back into the drawer of his bench.

"It's nothing," Al said. "Just trying to finish something I started a while ago. But what have you found?"

Nathan opened his briefcase and pulled out a small stack of documents.

"It's quite a mystery," he said, laying out the pages. "There are few, if any, records of the sale of any land to a man by the name you gave going back before 1900. The only item I was able to locate was this," he said, taking up a yellowed register page. Al skimmed over the paper indicating columns by name, date, plots of land each labeled by letter and number with a list of acreage.

"This shows a list of properties dating back as far as 1823," Nathan resumed. "The last estate built in the park on the scale you were thinking of was well before that—1789. Summerville, though they call it Strawberry Mansion today. There have been additions and renovations: Laurel Hill in 1846, Chamounix in 1853, and a few others, but that's all."

"Is it possible records might have been lost?" Al said.

"That's unlikely. Besides, even if a new home like the one you suggested were built, surely, it wouldn't have gone unnoticed by the general public. Which got me thinking. What if it wasn't Fairmount Park at all? What if it were somewhere else and your friend had been mistaken about the name?"

"That is possible," Al said. "He isn't really one to be concerned with details, I think."

"Well, I am. Comes with the territory. I made some inquiries and found this."

He handed a document to Al. It was a land purchase agreement for thirty-seven acres of undeveloped woodland near Mill Creek, northwest of the city, in Gladwyne. It was dated 1897.

"Construction on a home just north of Rolling Hill began shortly after the purchase. Beyond that, there is very little. But have a look at the name on the deed."

There, toward the bottom of the page in a flourished signature, read the unmistakable name.

"So, he bought the land," Al said.

"At tremendous cost. Nearly a hundred and fifty dollars an acre."

"What about the house?"

"It's out there, but one can't get to it easily. What's more, there is even less information about it than the land sale. No one can recall much about its construction. All I could find was it took almost four years to finish, and everything, every brick and beam, must have been paid for in cash. There are no records of bank transactions, mortgage agreements, anything. It's almost as if the entire thing happened in complete secrecy nearly out of thin air."

"What about tax records? There must be something more than this?"

"Nothing I can locate. Your friend must be a very wealthy man, Uncle, with some pretty powerful connections. How did you come to know him?"

But Al's mind was already drifting far from their conversation.

"Have you got the address?"

Chapter XI

"It would seem your famous luck has abandoned you," Kazakov said. "Do not be sad. You played well, but it was not me who beat you."

My whole being contracted. Trapped between fury and terror, memory of what followed remains a haze of disjointed images: a trembling hand, a broken wineglass, an upturned table, a flurry of playing cards falling like snow. A drawn pistol? And sounds. Invectives, vile and base. The tremor of the fat Russian's laughter. A single centime shoved hastily in my pocket.

"An obol for the heretic," Kazakov said. "His fare for the boatman. Take him to his home. Let him sleep one final night in his own bed, then to the devil."

Two footmen brusquely dragged me through the halls screaming like a madman. I raged in protest; the villain had cheated me, my drink had been tainted, his two cronies conspirators against me. I demanded recompense, refused to pay a single centime. The more I struggled, the weaker I felt, their iron grip like a vise. At the front door, I made a final push to break free and run back inside, but one of them struck me sharply on the back of the neck, bringing me to heel. I passed into unconsciousness.

I came to as the carriage jolted to a halt before my home. I got out on unsteady legs and staggered wearily up the stairs to my bedroom.

Room after room stood dark and empty. Where were the cries of delight once filling their open spaces? Where the heady aromas of wine and repast? Where the sights of naked flesh and the taste of wanton passions?

I relit the fire in the great Hellmouth hearth and collapsed into a chair, watching the flames rise, stewing in my anger.

In moments of extreme despair, when the fire of one's soul begins to dim, the flower of desperation unfurls its petals. In these moments, a man truly dreams, forsakes his nature, forgets all that guides him, and turns his mind to thoughts weird and fantastic. In this darkest hour, some men call upon God for guidance, forgiveness, and salvation.

I am no such man.

Instead, my animosity glowing like the white-hot embers boiling on the tongue of my great Hellmouth, I begged for vengeance. Pity of the worst kind, pity of the self, enveloped me; my temples throbbing, my pride shattered by the laughter of Kazakov bouncing through my skull, I trembled with impotent rage. The gold coin, my obol, as he'd called it, hung heavy in my pocket like a cannonball. My last *cent sou*. The final nail in the coffin of my utter ruin. I crushed the thing in my trembling fist.

My mind turned to ludicrous perplexations of infernal visitations. I saw Kazakov broken and destitute, begging in the streets, blind, deaf, and mute. I saw the traitorous Vallaton clutching the lifeless body of his Viennese whore to his breast, dead by her own hands. There was Bloch, like my father, drown at the bottom of the sea, and the self-righteous Dumont too, buried beneath his books while the vexatious Caroline weeps helplessly as he withers away in dull isolation. And even the rapist and drug pusher Gaspare. He, too, expired, wheezing with my hands wrapped around his throat.

There was the lot: friends, enemies, and family. I saw myself a king over them all, a judge of their crimes, and a swift executioner.

"To hell with them all!" I cried, hurling the coin into the hearth.

Blazing heat choked the room. I opened a window to let in the cold and collapsed once again into the chair. Though the hour late and the night long, dawn signaled no sign of approach. The December air made no headway against the oppressive heat of the boudoir.

Suddenly, there entered a most strange and unwelcome apparition through the open window; a blue-eyed jackdaw, perched on bony legs and ebony talons, its oily bluish-black wings gleaming like mother-of-pearl, alighted on the sill and fixed its icy, inquisitive stare upon me.

"What do you see here, eh?" I said. "Thieving jackdaw, I've nothing left to pilfer for your nest. I've already sent my last cent to the devil. And you can go there just as well. Singe your avaricious wings in the flames if you seek your prize."

The bird cocked its head curiously as if it both heard and understood. Emitting a piercing cry, a ghastly *tchyak*, the thing took to wing, wheeling great circles overhead. I leapt from my chair and gave chase. It landed again, this time upon the broiling andiron. Undisturbed by the crackling flames, it danced on its skeletal feet, hopping round to face the fire, and to my utter amazement, jumped straight down into the center of the inferno. Remarkably, its feathers remained unsinged by the flames as it sifted through the white-hot embers and emerged triumphant with the smoldering coin gripped between its osseous beak! But not wanting to have its prize stolen, it hopped straight back into the fire and disappeared.

I rushed to the hearth and made to rescue the damned thing, but the flames burst forth in a great blast, sending me retreating to the chair. Like an ebbing tide, the conflagration rapidly receded, and where it had once flared and threatened to engulf the room, there in its place stood a man.

Thin of build and tan-skinned like a Persian, his angular face was split by a long, hooked nose. Deep leathery creases framed his mouth, turned down at the corners in a perpetual frown. His scalp was bald, smooth, and shiny. Pale-blue-gray eyes perched beneath a dark, flat brow; their color perfectly matched those of the rapacious daw. He stood with a slight hunch, leaning casually on a crooked ebony cane. Between gloved fingers, he held a smoldering coin.

Thinking my eyes deceiving me, I shut them tight against this new apparition.

"I am going mad," I said. "This is madness, pure and simple. Why can't I have died instead?"

I opened my eyes, hoping this vision impossibly born from the fire had vanished from the room and I might believe my mind had not thoroughly split in half. But there he stood unmoved, with a wretched beaked nose and those dreadful slate eyes. Though the fire still burned, the intense heat that before filled the room vanished, replaced by a chill colder than the waters at the bottom of the sea.

"Death does not become one of such high standing." He spoke in perfect French, his voice calm and measured. "Nor could we hold equitable congress if your mind were splintered. It would be improper to begin if you are not of an even mien."

"Who are you?" I said, first quavering, then recanting. "No, this is madness. You are not here at all. I'm speaking to no one but myself."

"Hardly the truth," he said. "I am the reality that stands before you, flesh and blood, of a sort. I assure you I am no conjuration of your mind, which, I remind you, is not fractured in any way. I am who you believe me to be, and I came from where you believe me to have come. Belief is a most powerful force. It drags minds to foolish depths and drives nations to war. But allow me to correct a slight error in your flattery. I am not He whom you believe me to be, but I am one who once stood with Him and who stands with Him still. May I sit?"

"Your polite manner belies your truer nature," I said. "If what you say is so, you don't need my permission to do anything."

"Rightly so," he said with an oddly warm smile. "But there is no reason why some decorum shouldn't be maintained. Besides, it isn't right I should stand while you remain seated. It is, after all, I who come as your servant, not the other way around."

Resting his cane against the arm of a chair, he seated himself opposite me. Though his manner was gentlemanly, his closeness repelled me.

"I have no need of a servant such as you," I said. "And besides, what servant dresses in finer clothes than his master? Your suit is of a quality surpassing anything I have ever owned."

"The trappings of wealth," he said. "I admit I've developed a penchant for fine tailoring. Call it a vice. Nevertheless, I am here to serve. Would you have me return to my former state? Are dry feathers and dusty crow's feet more to your liking? I must warn you, conversation with a bird can be a quite one-sided affair."

"So, you are both man and beast as well?"

"I am many things to many people, many names in many languages. Like you, I indulge my whimsies at my will. Though, if I am to be honest, the daw is my most natural avatar."

"You choose forms like I choose wines?"

"I choose forms like you choose women," he said. "To the task, so the tool. Has that not been your credo?"

"You mock me as well," I said with rancor. "You make a poor servant indeed."

"My sincerest apologies," he said, bowing humbly. "My aim is nothing of the sort. I often forget myself. Call it an absence of restraint. As a merchant, excess is my stock in trade. My kind is not known to possess much moderation."

"Your kind?"

"Demons."

"Enough of this jabber," I said. "Your presence is nothing more than the result of stress working upon my mind. A figment of my imagination, granted more real than any before, but incorporeal still, and utterly false nonetheless."

"And yet we converse," he said. "Truly your madness is manifold if you're capable of carrying on a conversation with such a flagrant apparition of your own delirium. But if, as you say, this spirit is here only by your will, why not send me away? Why carry on this charade? Indeed, you have other matters more pressing to attend to. Packing perhaps? I understand you're vacating this house."

"You mock me again. Now I know you to be a creation of my own design. A manifestation of my shame."

"Shall I fetch a doctor?"

"I'd rather you fetched me a drink," I said. "If you truly are my servant, then bring me something to calm my nerves. Even if both you and the drink are figments of my imagination, I'd just as soon imagine myself drown in alcohol if it's all the same to you."

My phantasmal guest bowed, a flourished and practiced maneuver, and swiftly left the room. A moment later, he returned carrying a bottle of claret and two glasses.

"You know your servants have all gone? I had a devil of a time finding the kitchen. This house is dark as a tomb."

He uncorked the bottle and poured two glasses, passing one to me.

"No need to let this breathe," he said. "It's quite an old vintage. Where did you come by it?"

"You mean to say you don't know? I thought you to have knowledge of everything."

"I freely admit I possess many talents, but omniscience is not among them," he said, reseating himself and sipping from his glass. "This is one of your most magnificent achievements. The Egyptians had it all wrong. The Gods had nothing to do with it." Then, staring deeply into the glass, he waxed poetic:

Hearest thou not the echoing Sabbath sound?
The hope that whispers in my trembling breast?
Thy elbows on the table! gaze around;

Glorify me with joy and be at rest.

"Well dressed and well read," I said. "A devil who recites Baudelaire? I don't know whether to be impressed or offended. Tell me, do they have theater in hell? Poetry? Do your hoary caverns sing with the lyrics of Byron or La Fontaine? If one listens closely enough, can you hear the cries of Tartuffe as he's dragged away to prison?"

"I think this time it is you who mocks me," he said, smiling. "No matter. We've plenty of time to discuss whatever you like. Though, come morning, you are expected to vacate these premises, if I'm not mistaken. So perhaps we shouldn't take *too* long to conclude our business."

"You say you lack omniscience, yet you know quite a bit about my situation," I said, annoyed.

He acceded with a nod.

"Then you should also know it was my last cent I cast into the fire, so if you've come to sell me something, I've nothing left to buy with, unless I can offer you the shirt off my back, which, as you can see, is in a sorry state."

"I wouldn't presume to offend your vanity with such an irreverent suggestion," he said. "Yours is a pride long lived and imbued with strength. To expose you to ridicule after all you've suffered would be tantamount to sacrilege. And that is something I take quite seriously, as I know you do as well. The Orgy of Chestnuts? An impressive feat! Impiety is a subject of great enthusiasm for you, and I can tell you your theories are not misplaced, save for one small detail, of which I am most assuredly living proof. Though living is a relative term. *Ego daemonium, ergo sum.* My presence puts your denial of God out to pasture. But that should be no great cause for concern. There is God, and then there is *not* God. I simply represent the latter faction. All other discussion as to which or whose God is irrelevant. It's strictly a quagmire of human creation. But I have not come to debate theology. I have come to treat."

He'd put down his wine and pinned me with his beady irises. A crisp chill forced its way through the open window, reinvigorating the cold already settled on my bones. I poured another glass of wine and downed it in two swift gulps, hoping it would warm me. It didn't.

"Every so often," he went on, "a soul burns with a sin so bright as to draw the eyes of hell upon it. It's a lie the church tells people, you know, that everyone who sins will go to hell. What rot! If that were so, then heaven would be as desolate as this house and hell would be bursting at the seams. In truth, God forgives much. Hell is reserved for only those whose sins surpass the ordinary, whose blasphemies resound like a clarion call. Yours sounded thusly, which is what brought me, your humble servant, to you. And as your servant, I bring to you an arrangement that I believe you will find most satisfying."

"I made no such request," I said. "I did not ask you here."

"Didn't you? Do you not wish to see the authors of your sorrows brought to heel? Would you deny the retribution your pride demands?"

He stood up and approached the hearth. Silhouetted against the fire, his great gray coat hung over hunched, rounded shoulders tapering around two spindly legs protruding down like sticks from beneath the hem. His round, bald head bent over the flames as he pecked at the embers with the butt of his cane, his entire form describing a huge bird.

"I'll ask now, but only once," he said, his attentions still on the fire. "If you accept my terms, then you will know your vengeance and much more. It's that simple. If you refuse, I shall go and not return. But this I can leave with you, for payment not earned is payment not received."

Drawing my centime from his pocket, he placed it on the mantle.

"An honest devil? That breaks with tradition," I said. "Suppose I choose to bargain with you. What is it you propose?"

Turning back from the fire, he seated himself once again.

"The agreement is simplicity itself. Reciprocal, of course. Seventy years of uninterrupted bliss, the freedom to indulge your senses, sate your every whim, taste every pleasure. Go anywhere you please, possess anything, or anyone, you so desire. Expand your genius to encompass vices or virtues as you see fit. Death will turn aside for you. Remain as youthful as you are today, your body ravaged by neither sickness nor nature's decay."

"An enticing offer," I said. "But what good are time and freedom to a poor man?"

"If it's money you are concerned with, worry not. Hell's coffers are open to you. Your accounts will be replenished and shall never deplete again until the term of this agreement reaches its natural end, or you fail to fulfill your requirements."

"And what are my obligations in this overly generous arrangement? Am I to round up infant sacrifices or perform a Black Mass at every full moon?"

"You are an amusing fellow," he said. "But no, quite wrong. The terms, like the agreement, are simplicity itself. Seven sins, seventy years. A *décennie* for each sin, no less. You will find one soul whose vice outshines its virtue, and you will deliver it to us. More if you please, but that is your affair.

I require but the one. The manner in which you choose to do so I leave entirely to your discretion. I'm not picky. Itching to explore the sensation of taking a life with your own hands? Or perhaps you'd prefer to coax your target to madness and suicide? Drive the glutton to deadly excess, ruin the penurious financier, expose the adulteress to her cuckhold and let nature take its course. Let whimsy be your guide. In this fashion, our designs will proceed. Bring us seven worthy examples, and you will have your seventy years. Fail, and our agreement is nullified forthwith. And, of course, all transactions are to be held in the utmost secrecy."

"This is a funny business deal," I said. "You rattle off terms like so many items on a manifest. And all I surrender for my troubles is my soul."

"You could remain here," he said, gesturing about the room with the sweep of his arm. "But dawn approaches, and time is running short. Your soul in exchange, yes. But what use has it been to you until now? A small fee for what I bring to the table."

"You forget, sir, my father was a merchant like you. I've enough sense and reading to see, as enticing as this all is, there must be a caveat in this transaction you've not yet brought to light. Some inexplicable clause that is to be the lynchpin of my downfall. I agree to your terms, and then in a week or a month, I find myself imprisoned by the authorities and spend my seventy years in a cell."

"Impossible," he said. "No secular arm will exercise authority over your actions. The only cells you'll find yourself in will be those of your own making. And what is so easily made can be unmade just as easily. Besides, these thoughts never troubled you before, so why start worrying about them now?"

"And I will see my enemies crushed?" I said. "You will see to it?"

"What pleasure would there be in my acting on your behalf? Crush them yourself, you'll possess ample means, their suffering restricted only by the limits of your own imagination. Their fate is of no concern to me. But every decade, a new sin for a new soul. This you must perform. The order is yours to choose, though you could do better than to start with pride. I believe you'll be hard-pressed to find a soul as venal as your own."

"And money?"

"A bottomless well of wealth to do with as you please. Fill your heart and home with legions of admirers. Just not this one, though. You lost it fair and square, and if we are to contract, then we must both hold true to a sense of honor. Settle your debts that you may forget them forever. Besides, it's but a trifle, this place. The pleasures you have already experienced have but scratched the surface of your potential. Treat with me, and you will see truly there are no boundaries you cannot breach."

"Then, under these terms, I accept your offer," I said.

"Excellent!" he said, springing to his feet. "There is but one last detail. A minor element almost not worth mentioning."

"I knew it," I said. "You've deceived me already."

"Hardly," he said, feigning insult. "I always honor my agreements. This article concerns the small matter of a deposit. Like any transaction of this magnitude, a withholding on credit is to be expected."

He retrieved the coin from the mantle, eyeing it covetously, and placed it in my palm. With his hand, he enclosed mine, muttering an incantation of some sort, its language completely alien to my ears. In all my years of travel hence, I have never heard it spoken again.

I felt within my chest a sudden rising warmth. It began at the pit of my bowels and journeyed up my spine, down my arms, and into my hand. The coin became like a broiling ember, and I struggled vainly to escape his viselike grasp, but to no avail. He held firm with superhuman strength and kept to his conjuring. The agony stirring within sapping me of my will, I felt on the verge of collapse when he abruptly released me, my body limply falling back into the chair. Opening my fist, I found no burns, no signs of blistered skin, no scars.

As if it had passed straight through my flesh into his, he now held the coin in his own hand. I watched it glow momentarily with residual white heat, then slowly cool to orange, then to red, then to the familiar patina of brass, its fading color mirroring the feeling of warmth slowly evaporating from my body. I felt a sudden, intangible sense of loss as he tucked it swiftly away in the pocket of his vest, as if suffering a momentary fugue, like I'd forgotten my very identity. Then, taking up his cane, he performed that ridiculous flourished genuflection one final time and, with surprising abruptness, turned to leave.

"Our business is concluded, sir," he said. "Life and good health to you."

"Wait," I said. "Before you go, I have one final request."

"My dear sir, the hour of parlay has passed. Morning approaches. It is getting late."

"But you are my servant," I said, thinking to outwit him. "If I am your master in this arrangement, then it is incumbent upon your station to honor my request."

The fiend puzzled over this a moment, his beady eyes darting thoughtfully in their sockets, then seated himself once again in the chair.

"I wish to see my place of future abode," I said. "Take me there that I might see for myself what I have purchased with my soul."

"You are a bold one," he said with a sinister smile. "Though I must admit a request such as this is highly unusual and all but unprecedented."

"Then you will not honor your word to be at my bidding?"

"Never has a word of untruth passed my lips," he said with a seriousness that sent a shudder rippling through my very being.

He bid me follow him to the wall beside the bed where there stood an oversized gilded mirror in the Louis XVI style. Here, he paused to admire the gleam of the shimmering gold trim.

"Truly, your vanity is sumptuous," he said. "Beautiful craftsmanship. Shall we?"

Confused, I glanced toward the hearth from which he'd made his entrance.

"'The shape now haunting your sight is only a wraith, a reflection consisting of nothing,'" He said, quoting Ovid. Then, without hesitation or reserve, he placed a gloved hand on my shoulder. "Shall we? There is just the—"

But here, the journal ended, its final pages torn out, lost to time and history.

Chapter XII

The taxi dropped Al at an entrance gate. A low rock wall ran for some distance along the road in both directions. Two towering stone pillars stood at either side of the long drive leading from the lane far into the surrounding wood. Atop each, encased in glass, the cast-iron figure of a phoenix with wings unfurled rising from the flames. But there were no flames to be seen this day, and the birds, with their wings outspread, looked frozen and lifeless in their glass cages. The illusion of rebirth dead.

The iron gate hung ajar, rusting on its hinges. Recent rains left the path pocked with puddles, their muddy surfaces reflecting the flat slate-colored sky. Al started up the drive, stepping carefully to avoid them as best he could.

He walked through the woods for some time, and he thought he might never reach his destination. But gradually, the drive widened, and behind the thicket loomed the house.

Its architecture recalled the best of the Old World, a long-forgotten example of Châteauesque styling. Leadlight windows cut into the walls. Ornate dormers and richly carved pilasters ringed the roof. Al counted six stone chimneys jutting from its blue slate peak. Towering spires of iron reached toward the sky capped with long spears bent on piercing the heavens.

A low cloud of ashen mist trapped by the surrounding trees hung about the house. Nary a sound disturbed the air save the huffing of Al's own labored breath and the odd chirp of a goldfinch stubbornly waiting out the winter.

The closer he came, the more the luster of the house's grandeur dissipated with the fog. Everywhere, signs of decay crept about the edges. Several of the windows were knocked through. Grotesque ivies strangled the stonework. Leeching water rived deep crevices in the mortar. A great octagonal fountain stood dry and cold: its centerpiece, a naked youth armed with a sword towering over a seething lion, frozen in time. Gangrenous green mold wrapped the statuary like veiny monstrous fingers. The gardens rotted from neglect.

Zofia begged him not to go in search of trouble, pleaded with him that evil men should be left to their own collapse. Even when he'd told her how Etienne had plucked his own soul from the very precipice of the doubt that might have caused his own faltering, her objection did not waver.

But Al could not let it go so easily.

The heavy arched doors of the main entrance stood sheltered beneath a columned portico. Armored with bulky iron fittings, like sentries standing watch, the doors dwarfed Al. Decorum dictated he knock, but he felt this a futile gesture given the inert atmosphere settled over the place. Half-heartedly, he gave one of the doors a push, then the other. Neither budged. He would find another way inside.

He sought out a servant's entrance and came upon several possibilities: a squat red door tucked behind a hedgerow, another cut into the stonework beneath a balustrade overlooking the sloping acreage behind the house. All were locked tight. At last, he spied an impressive iron-and-glass conservatory jutting out in the direction of the gardens, and there, an open door.

He called out a cautious hello into the darkened recesses at the end of the passage. No reply came. He called again. It was, he conceded, a ridiculous effort. The house was so huge, it was unlikely he'd be heard even had he shouted at the top of his lungs. Steeling himself, he stepped inside.

The thought he might meet some unknown horror, perhaps even the devil himself, had not entered Al's mind. Firm in the knowledge Etienne was not a man subject to the laws governing the rest of humanity, that he'd indeed surrendered his humanity to circumvent those very laws, brought scant comfort. It remained unclear if he considered Al friend or foe. The fickle nature of such a man would seem to place either at the mercy of his inconstant whims.

He passed a gallery of sorts. Pale rectangles of varying size along the walls described the placement of artwork long since removed. Beyond this, he found a sitting room adorned with rich dark wainscoting and coffered ceiling done in shades of green and gold. Al pressed his hand against the cushion of an elegant Victorian settee, drawing his finger through a considerable layer of dust. A large mirror once hung above the mantle lay smashed to pieces, its shards still strewn about the floor. He kept walking.

Room after room, each more desolate and gloomier than the last. A billiard room, a trophy room, a smoking room, an armory, each empty as the tomb, wasting away from neglect, more monuments to past glories than havens for recreation or repose—spiders, moths, and mice the only guests partaking of the home's hospitality anymore.

In the foyer, a great serpentine staircase ascended the full three-story height of the house, forming an atrium from which hung a tremendous gold-and-crystal chandelier wrapped haphazardly in a linen sheet. One could only imagine the glorious light once given off by such an opulent piece, but devoid of its power in the darkened hall, it looked more a giant insect egg sack dangling precariously by a heavy chain.

Cautiously, he proceeded to the main dining room. This, too, had been styled after the Victorian era, with table and chairs to sit a small army. But no places had been set and no trace of the feast could be seen.

Another hall extended toward the western wing of the house where Al came upon a magnificent ballroom done in a garish Louis XVI style. Ivory walls, gilded columns, and high, arched windows supported an ovular ceiling fresco running the entire length of the room. It depicted a Roman bacchanal, complete with piles of food on golden platters and figures in various stages of undress engaging in lewd revelry atop tables, behind columns, even on horseback. Here, too, the mirrored walls that once reflected the glory of the dance stood smashed to bits in their frames. The remains of hundreds of candles dotted the floor with hard, shiny pools of dried red and white wax.

At the far corner of the room stood an old writing desk, looking as out of place in a ballroom as might an elephant in a flower shop. Atop the desk, piles of handwritten pages spilled onto the floor. Peeking out from underneath these was the corner of a leather-bound book. Taking it in hand, he remarked its striking resemblance to Etienne's diary. The same diary he had brought with him, tucked into the pocket of his overcoat.

A tortured cry, like the bawl of a dying animal, rang out. Al recognized it as the voice of the Frenchman and hurried back to the foyer, following the wails of lament like a trail of audible breadcrumbs. At the foot of the stairs, he paused to listen for further signs of life. He called out another hello but, again, was met with only dumb silence.

A hallway extended past the first landing, at the end of which stood an open doorway where Al could just make out the muffled mumbling of a conversation emanating from within, a conversation of one.

Peering inside, a sickly gray light illuminated the shelves of a considerable library. Books lay everywhere—torn from their shelves, some stripped of their covers, many with spines wrought to shreds, others smoldering in the fireplace. The room reeked of burnt ink and alcohol. Amid the ruins sat the Frenchman, slumped in the shadow of a great wingback chair.

"Why do you invade my home?" he said, his voice small and distant. His face drawn and unshaven, he'd again reverted to the marooned man. Al recalled the character of the troubled Dr. Jekyll from Stevenson's tale of horror and drew upon a great swell of pity for his tormented soul.

"It's Al," he said. "Al Valentine. You remember me, don't you?"

"I remember," Etienne said, though, to Al's mind, he spoke not to him but rather the specter of Al he believed standing before him. The memory of the memory of Al. His body remained inert. "I remember everything."

Al took the journal from his pocket, offering it like a piece of raw meat to a crouched lion. "I came to return your book."

"My book?"

"Your diary. I read it. I know everything."

"You know nothing," Etienne spat. "You haven't the faintest inkling of my pain."

"You're right. I have many questions."

"I have no answers."

Amid the ruin of the room, Etienne looked more feral animal than man. Even the leaden hatching on the windows described bars on a cage. Al recalled the devil's words, mumbling to himself.

"The only cells you will find yourself in will be those of your own making."

"What did you say?" Etienne growled from the corner, resembling even more the caged beast, his fingernails, like claws, digging into the arms of the chair.

"We should leave this place," Al said imploringly. "Come away with me. There is only sadness here. Let me take you outside. You need fresh air. Come back to my home."

"This *is* home," Etienne said. "I cannot leave. Don't you see? Sadness *here*? There is only sadness for me."

Al righted a chair and sat.

"You don't believe my story, do you?" Etienne said.

"I do believe it."

"Then you believe I am damned."

"I believe that it is not God's way to let a man cast himself into such despair if He does not intend to show him a way out of it. He won't pull him out Himself, but He will always provide a path."

"Dogmatic rubbish," Etienne said. "I've heard this talk before. What more can you tell me than a cardinal or even the Pope? Lose your own soul, then speak to me of hope."

"Your mother thought differently."

"My mother was a whore. I thought you read that already."

The words stung Al into silence. He knew better than to press the point.

"You are looking for something?" he said, lifting a book from the floor. "Like that man Albin?"

"He didn't find what he was looking for either." Then, with undisguised annoyance: "In the end, that is our fate. All men are looking for something, but, in truth, they only find death."

"Has there never been anything more for you? Have you found nothing in all this time?"

A rapid change overcame Etienne's features. For a fleeting moment, something seemed to push aside the haggard tension gripping his face. But just as quickly as relief came, his jaw hardened with renewed resolve.

"Tell me what happened," Al said.

But the moment had passed, and Etienne spoke no more. He rose and went to the window, pausing briefly to contemplate the decrepit gardens extending in a wide arc around the rear of the house, an arc terminating against a curved line of a dark, foreboding wood.

"'I will not be afraid of death and bane, till Birnam forest come to Dunsinane.'"

"What?"

"*Macbeth*," Etienne said. "The king who possessed all at the expense of happiness, the one thing he desired most. He sacrificed everything to appease dumb ambition."

"And, in the end, was consumed by madness," Al said. "I know the story. It is an old one, told by many men."

It was easy to forget the youthful face gazing out the window, handsome, even, in its dishevelment, was merely a mask concealing the withering spirit of an aged libertine. Al could not help but look upon it and believe he might be talking to his own grown son, this fatherly affection sprouting from the undeniable pathos exuded by the doomed Frenchman.

"It is strange," Al started. "I had come here wanting to listen, thinking that maybe if I could understand better, I might be able to help in some way. I felt like I owed you something."

"You don't owe me anything. No one does. I've done nothing to warrant anyone's love."

"But you have. That day in the temple, you saved me then, didn't you? You saved me from him."

"Identifying a man's sins is a unique gift," Etienne said. "Faltering in one's faith inevitably leads to vengeance against God. Is that not the very definition of wrath? It was not hard to see it building within you. I have encountered it so very many times before. Men's fortunes turn, they lose their faith. Fortunes turn again, and they regain it. You could indeed set your watch to the oscillations of a man's faith."

Al leant down and lifted another book from the floor, one not rent completely asunder. He opened to its title page. *Malleus Maleficarum, Maleficas Et Earum.* He recognized the language as Latin but could in no way understand it.

"You did not answer my question," he said. "You are looking for something. What is it?"

"I'm tired now," Etienne said, turning away from the window. "You're welcome to stay, if you like, but now leave me to my rest."

A vacancy had returned to his gaze, a disaffection in his voice again placing his mind some distance from Al, the library, the house, everything; the man had vanished, usurped once more by the ghost. The house had become an asylum of one.

※

The old man's heart met with the terrible burden of lonesomeness instilled upon it by the dour surroundings. No expense had been spared designing an arena providing for every temptation of the sensual, but now, all those pleasures sat withering away under the weight of their own unviewed splendor. For a long time, Al sat in the dreadful silence of a disused drawing room listening to the creaking in the ceiling over his head, hearing the padded footsteps of Etienne wildly pacing the rooms above.

Eventually, his nomadic route brought him full circle, and he found himself once again at the desk in the ballroom. Among the scattered pages lying across its surface, he picked up a letter, started but never finished. It was written in a hurried, uneven hand.

M.,

Voltaire wrote the wicked only have accomplices while the voluptuous have companions. Were you ever more so the former than the latter, I wonder?

What you gave me, I cannot repay you for, and what you took from me, I no longer wish to possess. Fatuous desire makes for a jealous deity. And how I worshipped at the altar with my one true brother in devotion by my side.

But where I was more the supplicant, you were ever more the philosopher. And while one drinks heartily from the cup of faith, the other has the wisdom to question the doctrine. Ever the fanatic, I could no more comprehend your turn from the dogma than grasp the infinite mysteries of the human heart. Such is the error of the libertine. He who cannot know pure love is doomed to know only the fleeting illusion of ersatz ardors.

I ask you, the philosopher, is there redemption to be found in looking upon the gloom of the past with the light of remorse? How shameful my behavior. How misguided my vengeance. There is no excuse in heaven or on earth for what I have done. Can my actions—

But here, the letter cut off and Al could find nothing more.

His heart sickened at the thought of the poor man trapped alone in this house. How long had he roamed these empty rooms with only his memories of past horrors as his company? It immediately put Al in a frame of mind of escape. He had to leave this place, for fear of becoming trapped as well. He wanted to help, but how does one break the grip of the devil himself?

He took Etienne's journal from his coat pocket and set it on the desk. There, under the mess of loose papers, lay the other book he'd seen earlier. A suffocating fear pressed upon his chest when he looked at it. He could neither ignore it nor pick it up. If he could just get out of the house, he felt all would be right again.

Outside, the mist had lifted, and the milky-gray sky of the morning yielded to blue. Silence reigned across the house. Above, Etienne no longer stirred. Al rushed out of the place, back to the conservatory, to the open door, to freedom.

The fresh air revived him. The oppressive loneliness of the house gave way to the pleasant sensation that he'd somehow broken free of a sort of bondage. He let the cool air fill his lungs as he walked out into the sprawling grounds. Behind him, the manor stood a prison to the past. Out here, it was the present. Life bloomed, even in among the dead hedgerows and perished flowerbeds, new sprouts, tufts of fresh greenery, struggled from deep within the earth to break free to the light of day.

Al suddenly became aware of something in his hand— it was the second book. It weighed heavy in his grip, like a chunk of limestone. He hadn't even realized he'd been carrying it.

It was nearing midday. He found an iron bench beneath a stone trellis covered in creeping vines and lay the book beside him. He glanced sidelong at it with muted disdain. The worn leather cover, like its counterpart, was a dullish shade of cedar. And like its predecessor, it, too, had pages missing; a thick layer of pages torn out from the beginning.

He knew he was going to read it. He didn't want to, but he knew he had to. He also knew Zofia would be starting to worry. He'd been gone for hours, and though he'd reassured her there was no danger to be had, she would worry all the same.

Chapter XIII

"...and your *Polski* has been improving every day," he said.

Even in my weakened state, I could admit that acquiring new languages was a skill I'd been honing these past ten years, though he spoke to me in German most of the time, making things easier for the both of us.

"You received a compliment from Sister Ojeda, I understand," he observed. "That's quite a feat indeed. Though abundant with compassion, she's not one who shows it easily."

"A poor quality in a nun," I said.

"A cross to bear, you might even say," he joked.

Father Englot's spartan cell recalled Sidonie's wretched basement hovel. Save for the crucifix hung over the bedhead and the odor of manure wafting in through the open window, the resemblance was remarkable.

"You seem in better spirits," he said. "I assume now you're well enough that you'll be wanting to get on your way. A boat stops here every few weeks before heading downriver. I'm sure you can catch a ride back to civilization, but you'd do well to remain here awhile longer, get your full strength back."

I accepted the priest's offer to enjoy the hospitality of his small mission. To my suggestion that I be allowed to leave my bed after so many weeks invalid, he welcomed it, but cautioned me not to stray too far for fear my condition would relapse without warning.

"You're not exactly out of the jungle yet," he jested. "But some exercise might do you good, perhaps jog some memories. I'll come dine with you again this evening, if you don't object to the company? We can talk more then."

An oppressive heat lay heavy across the land. At this bend in the river, the ground rises, and thick jungle gives way to a sloping plateau a few hundred yards wide. Here, the tiny village of Biri springs. And here, Father Englot, heeding the call to mission, had set up rugged shop.

Taking a walk for the first time since being dragged unconscious from the swirling waters, I had the opportunity to take in the whole scene with a clearer head.

Dried mud and thatch huts dotted the clearing. Englot and the nuns slept in these, while the village residents lived down along the banks of the river in dwellings built on stilts over the turbid waters. At the top of the hill stood the church: an old Jesuit construction forgotten by Rome. The chapel proper, a one-room mud-brick edifice crowned with a chipped stone cross, was all that remained of a much larger structure long since collapsed.

Encroached on three sides by the jungle and the river on its fourth, Biri was hardly a speck on a map, if it were even noted on one at all. As I stood at the top of the dusty slope leading down to the river, surveying the village below, I struggled to remember just how it was I had come to be there.

❦

"You were, I think, telling me about America," Father Englot said, leaning over his stew that evening at supper. "I assume it's where you acquired this?"

He produced from his pocket the watch I'd purchased in Hamburg, the one I'd intended to present to Dumont but never did. I can't say why I'd kept it. It was the sole item I'd retained from my Parisian days, something not even the gluttonous Kazakov could possess. Seeing it again lifted my spirits.

"I thought it was lost," I said. "Gone down with the boat."

"I'm afraid its mechanism has stopped," he said.

"It hasn't been the first time," I said. "It's funny, in a way. Two years ago, I was in the city of Philadelphia, in America. I was having a home built there, and I wandered into a shop to have it repaired. It was the oddest thing."

"Oh?"

"The shop was this little out-of-the-way place, with a funny sign hanging in its window. The owner took one look at the thing and nearly fainted. Started going on and on about how it was a piece he knew well. Turns out I'd bought it from the man's very uncle in Hamburg. He recognized his family's work instantly."

"*Die welt ist kleiner als wir denken*," Englot said. "Maybe it was Providence brought you together in this small world."

We dined by the light of a dented oil lamp, a rough tuber stew and a few crusts of bread washed down with bitter coffee.

"A man who can afford a watch like this has surely known better tables," he said, laughing.

"But not much better company."

"So, your memories have mostly returned, then? That's good. But what about how you ended up in the river?"

Nothing much had come back to me. Maybe it was the fever, something I was sure I'd contracted on the voyage before the sinking. But of the event itself, I had only fleeting images. A fire, screams, an explosion, then the water. How far I'd drifted downstream, or for how long, I could not say. Nor could I recall being pulled from the river or carried to the mission.

"It's truly a miracle you survived such an ordeal," he said. "Your companions were apparently not so blessed."

"It wasn't God who saved me," I said.

"Oh?" Father Englot raised his old round face from over his bowl. "I don't think the devil is in the business of saving lives."

A sudden terror seized me.

"Still, whether God or just damned blind luck, you should be grateful for your life," he continued. "Knocked unconscious and drowned at the bottom of a river isn't much of an epithet."

"I admit it lacks romanticism," I conceded. "I sincerely hope I've not said too much to offend your sensibilities."

"Offended? You weren't speaking coherently enough to be much understood. It was mostly fragments and bits of memory. But I've heard enough confessions in my time to know when a man is troubled by his past."

After dinner, Father Englot puffed gently from an old briar pipe. Wisps of milky smoke smelling faintly of walnut languished in the thick jungle air while the erratic chirps and hums of insect life stirred outside the window.

"Tomorrow is Sunday," Englot said. "Will you join us for service?"

"Father, I—"

"I'm not asking you to participate," he interrupted. "Just join us. Joseph Magaz comes with his family. He brought you here, you know. If you don't wish to thank God for your life, you could do worse than to thank Joseph."

Reluctantly, I accepted his invitation, knowing the discomfort it would bring. The truth was, whenever I set foot in a church or other sanctuary, I became rocked by a most crippling paroxysm—a freezing of my spirit made manifest by an unspeakable terror I can only describe as akin to the panic of suffocating, or perhaps drowning in darkness. I feel as though I am crushed by an invisible weight. This lack of light, like a lack of air, leaves me stricken with a dread I cannot escape until I am free of the place altogether.

The first manifestation of this spiritual apoplexy occurred several years before, in a village in Lombardy. I'd successfully seduced the impressionable Sister Marguerite, a charming specimen of everything wrong with the ridiculous notion of celibacy. Taking her into my bed proved no small challenge, but one I greatly relished in undertaking. Once the bonds of chastity are rent, guilt can be a most piquant aphrodisiac. Time and again, hers nearly drove her mad with anguish, but the waves of her shame broke their backs crashing against the jagged cliffs of her lust. After every rendezvous, she would flee from me, but always returned—the fire in her loins burning hotter than the flaming sword guarding the gates of Paradise.

When I suggested the fervor of our clandestine amours could be taken to their pinnacle by consummating them at the very feet of the savior to whom she'd committed her soul, she demurred. Until then, our trysts were restricted solely to my rooms. And while tasting the forbidden fruits of God's servant indeed brought pleasures rich and new to my damaged spirit, the thought of committing an act of defilement upon the altar itself, in His own house, became an all-consuming quest.

The siege lasted but briefly, and in the end, her lusts outweighed her shame. We met in the shadow of the church wall as the town slept. But, to my horror, a panic seized me in my tracks upon crossing the threshold of the chancel, an agonizing anguish that gave me over to a fit of convulsions so violent, I fell to my knees and cried out a terrible howl, like the bray of a gazelle snatched by the jaws of a lion. It felt as though my very soul were being rent from my body and gave Sister Marguerite such a fright she thought me possessed. She ran screaming to the image of the Christ hung before the altar and prostrate herself in anguish, begging forgiveness for her weakness. Our cries raised such a ruckus as to awaken the whole town. It took all my strength to drag myself away.

I'd since learned to avoid entering houses of worship, though I break my own rule from time to time, just to test my endurance. It requires the greatest fortitude, but admittedly, there is a most exhilarating arousal to be found just this side of complete suffocation one can only experience if one is willing to endure great pain and fear.

"I hope you don't accept just to humor an old priest," Father Englot said.

"Not at all," I said. "It's been a while since I took the time. I admit my last few visits have been... stimulative."

"Do you remember when you last took confession?"

"I prefer to keep my sins to myself."

Father Englot sucked his pipe, stoking the bowl with two fingers, studying me. Fresh smoke billowed up before his narrowed eyes.

"That is not good," he began. "But I understand. I once knew a man like you. This was many years ago. I was still living in Gliwice. Like you, he was one to move about. Found the settled life unsuitable to his character. His father was a merchant, dealt in hides, followed the old ways. He never thought much of going to church, though he did so to honor his father, of course. But when he reached manhood, he left it all behind to make his own fortunes.

"He wandered a bit, here and there. Stopped going to church. Started paying more attention to women and drink. Then that damned war came, and he found himself helplessly caught up, a rifle in his hand fighting alongside the Prussians. He killed many men. Your countrymen. Too many to count."

He paused, a reflective melancholy cast a shadow over his old, lined face, as if the thunder of cannon fire and the screams of the dying still rung fresh in his ears.

"That's why you went back," I said. "To the church."

He smiled, returning from his memories.

"There is only so much burden a man's soul can bear. No amount of drink can drown it, and no amount of distraction can put enough distance between you and it."

"I'll not be running off to the seminary anytime soon, Father," I said. "Nor to the confessional. I'm quite at home with my soul and plan to share a long life with it."

"And what about after that life has ended? Hasn't your recent brush with death given you the slightest pause? I'm not suggesting you join the church. Heaven forbid! But you are clearly troubled by something."

"I hate to disappoint you, but I've no need to unburden myself at the moment," I said.

"Not even about Herr Vallaton?"

The sound of his name gave me uneasy pause. I'd not thought of Matthieu in years.

"He must have meant a good deal to you. That's the face of a man remembering much but wishing to forget more. You uttered his name many times while in the throes of your fever."

"Vallaton was a friend," I said after a moment. "And then he wasn't. A falling-out. There really isn't much to tell."

Father Englot nodded in silence, taking slow, deliberate puffs from his pipe.

"You said... *you* killed him."

"I was merely being poetic. His death was the result of his own misadventure."

"You *said* you betrayed him."

"Did I? If that is so, it was only because he betrayed me first."

He trained his blue eyes on me, waiting patient as Job, for me to unburden myself of some great weight.

"A man lives his life by certain standards," I said, Englot's indomitable silence unnerving me. "And he expects the same of his teachers. To raise such a person to a position of esteem is to place them beyond reproach. That is the foundation of what you'd call faith, isn't it? That is what God is for men like you."

"Faith is the rock upon which some choose to chain themselves," he said. "Others may take a different view. He is both father and teacher, and yes, His ways are not for men to question nor fully understand. Some see God's works as fluid, the manifestations of Him appearing one day as this, the next as that. But that He *is*, is the bedrock upon which all faith is built."

"I say faith is trust," I said. "Trust that a man's core beliefs are unwavering. What would it do to your faith if you found one day God had simply changed his mind—that what was virtue was now vice, or even the other way around? Would you not feel betrayed? Would you not believe the one in whom you'd laid those foundations had abandoned you? Vallaton surrendered his convictions. He turned his back on everything, on me. And for what?"

"You felt alone," he said, "on this new path."

"I felt like he lacked faith," I said. "Yes, I may have felt alone, but I was more angry than afraid. He drew me to a place, showed me what type of man I should become, and I loved him for it. And I loved being who I'd become. I still do."

"Then what difference whether he came with you or not? A man has to choose his own destiny. You thought you'd reach the end together. You're not the first to think this way, and you won't be the last."

"He betrayed his own values," I said. "They were mine as much as his. There is no room for doubt in the heart of a libertine."

"You're too young a man to have such strong convictions," he said. "It's in people's nature to change. Look at me. When I was your age, I was a soldier with blood on my hands. Today, I teach turning the other cheek."

"I may look young, but I've an old soul," I said. "Loyalty is important. That shouldn't change. Loyalty to oneself, to one's friends, is paramount."

"An odd conviction for a man with no friends," he said. "In your delirium, you spoke of Vienna."

"That is where he went," I said. "After."

"And found comfort in the arms of a woman? It doesn't take much to divine the reason for your parting. Love is a powerful emotion. Strong enough to break the bonds of love that bound you together."

"'Love has no place in the life of a libertine.' It's what he always said. And he was right. He only thought he was in love with that girl. But I knew better. It was a passing fancy, nothing more, and only a matter of time before he came to see the error of his ways."

"But he didn't see them?"

"No, he didn't."

"You had to show him?"

I said nothing.

"Wasn't he happy? What right does anyone have to impugn the happiness of another?"

I had no answer and remained stubbornly silent.

"So, you went to Vienna?"

"I did."

"And stole this girl from him."

"I stole nothing," I said with rancor, leaping to my feet. Then, restraining myself, I sat down again. "I showed him what he thought was love wasn't real at all. Loyalty, Father, loyalty above all. What good was a wife to him who couldn't be loyal?"

"She was loyal. But for your actions, she would have made for him a fine wife."

"If it weren't me, it would have been someone else. She fell for his charms, and mine. It isn't too much to believe there could have been others."

"And then he took his own life," he said solemnly.

"He should have taken hers," I said. "That's what I thought he'd do, the damned fool."

Father Englot casually tamped his pipe, leaving me to my memories. It had grown late. A steady rain had begun to fall.

I thought of Vallaton. I thought of the beautiful Anja tearing at her hair with her bare hands when they pulled his cold body from the Danube. I thought of the tears streaming down her cheeks, falling into the sunken eyes of the lifeless husband she clung to her breast by the shore of the river. It was my vision of vengeance, only cruelly reversed.

I don't know if he ever deduced it was I who'd seduced her away from him. He just knew he'd lost her somehow, that the love he felt and believed to be real was nothing but illusion. He'd taught me a woman's destiny is to be wanton. Hadn't I shown him as much? What more was there to believe in?

"I can take your confession, if you ask me to," Father Englot said.

"I don't need confession," I said defiantly. "I've committed no sin."

※

Footfalls outside the door of Father Englot's hut woke me at sunrise. Ragged bands of sunbaked villagers—men, women, and children all barefoot and robed in flimsy linens—filed solemnly up the slope toward the mission. Below, long dugouts crowded the riverbank as more flooded down from upstream. By the time I'd dressed, a small crowd was huddled by the chapel entrance.

The people settled, their simple nature befitting their simple surroundings. An old table clothed in a white bedsheet served as altar beneath a wood cross hung on the wall of the narrow chancel.

I remained just outside the threshold. Father Englot waited before the altar, dressed in full cassock and collar greeting his congregation. He acknowledged me with a smile, but wisely did not bid me sit. I was grateful.

There was no procession, and Father Englot blessed his sacraments alone. A tame Gloria was sung, and recitations given I'd not heard since my childhood, but his service fell far from traditional given the rough circumstances.

"'But I say unto you, that whosoever is angry with his brother without a cause shall be in danger of the judgment: and whosoever shall say to his brother, Ra'ca, shall be in danger of the council: but whosoever shall say, Thou fool, shall be in danger of hell fire.'"

"Jesus speaks these words on the mount," he said. "Addressing his followers, he recalls the Old Testament commandment given unto Moses by God on Sinai: 'Thou shall not kill,' for surely, one who breaks this commandment will suffer punishment and damnation. But Jesus goes further, stating it is not only murder that offends God but also the anger stirring in the heart bringing forth the act. Hatred toward one's brother, *that* is the sin from which we must turn aside.

"Jesus is telling us, though we feel victimized, that it is we who are the aggressors when we let anger into our hearts. Recall his words later when rebuking the Pharisees:

"'But those things which proceed out of the mouth come forth from the heart; and they defile the man. For out of the heart proceed evil thoughts, murders, adulteries, fornications, thefts, false witness, blasphemies: These are the things which defile a man.'"

"From the heart springs the anger which proceeds the act. Dispel your hearts of your evil thoughts, your anger, and you shall find peace with your brother and your enemy, and your reticence will be rewarded. Do not seek to place blame; do not think others foolish for their practices or the choices they make. To each man, his own path. Let yours be one of forgiveness, for forgiveness is the path to peace, the path opposed to anger, and the only one leading to salvation through the Lord."

The service drew to its conclusion, and observing these simple people rise and limp forward dully to receive their drop of wine and bit of dry wafer, I felt a great swell of pity for them, and a sudden urge to speak drew me forward. Momentarily forgetting myself and crossing the threshold, I was overcome by a terrific heaviness in my chest as if my heart had become a ball of molten lead drawing to the earth like a falling meteor. I felt my brain swelling and pressing against the insides of my skull with such force, I thought it should explode. Father Englot, seeing my anguish, bade me come in, but I could only turn and flee.

A few days later, a bustle arose in the village. The body of a white man had washed up along the banks of the river a few miles downstream. Some of the men found it and had brought it to the mission. Father Englot came to fetch me.

"He's been shot," he said. "Once through the heart."

I followed him to the riverbank. A group of villagers accompanied us, and a few curious children as well, giggling as they ran along the tree line. At the foot of the slope lay a bloated, purple carcass. Dressed in the remnants of a cream-colored suit, the man's shoes were missing and one of his arms had been chewed off at the shoulder by some river beast. A thick red mustache hung over his upper lip, and a distinctive pear-shaped mole behind his left ear left no doubt in my mind, though I'd known immediately when Father Englot had said he'd been shot. It was Maier.

"Someone from your group?" he said as we stood over the body.

I nodded. "A German. From Leipzig, I think."

"Herr Allard, I believe we should talk."

In his rooms, Father Englot paced slowly, his normally sober air betrayed by wrinkles of distress crossing his forehead.

"How did that man die? You know, don't you?"

I admitted I did. He paused before the crucifix hanging over the bed.

"Did you kill him?"

"I shot him, yes," I said. "But whether or not that is what ultimately killed him, I cannot say. You saw yourself, something tried to make a meal of him."

"You are playing me for a fool," he said. "You say you have no clear memory of the events of the past few weeks, but I think you do. I think you remember much more than you say. What else have you not told me?"

"Affairs of the past are best left to the past, Father. Confessing them does not change what has already been done. It certainly won't bring that man back, nor well should it."

"You speak as if your heart were made of stone," he said, confounded by my apathy. "Have you no remorse?"

"I do not," I said. "And if I betrayed your confidences by misleading you before, then know it was not my intention to offend you. Some things are better left unmentioned, and even more left forgotten."

"But murder!" he shouted, breaking from form, losing all sense of himself.

"I'd have preferred things resolved themselves in another way," I said. "I didn't have much choice. Maier was liar, a thief, and a rapist."

"Then he should have been given over to the authorities. What right do you have to kill him?"

"None at all," I said. "But it wasn't me who brought about his fate. His greed defeated him."

"Nonsense!" Englot shouted, his fury redoubled. "Greed didn't put a bullet through his heart. And it is not for any man to punish another man's sins. That right is reserved for God alone."

"'Therefore to him that knoweth to do good, and doeth it not, to him it is sin.'" I quoted James 4:17. "I can volley with you all day if you wish, Father, but I fear we'd not make any headway. Only if you desire to take such a narrow view of the matter could you choose to accuse me of wrongdoing, and frankly, that view doesn't become you. Was I the tool of his destruction? In the narrow view, yes. Was I acting as an instrument of God's justice? In the narrow view, no. I killed Maier for purely selfish reasons, but it doesn't make it any less right that such man should have been blighted from the earth. Ernst Maier was a slaver, Father. Had his greed restricted itself to the acquisition of material things, we would have thought him foolish, perhaps even covetous. He was a thief, as I have said, and his methods effective. But his avarice knew no boundaries.

"When I first met him in Brazzaville, I thought him just another opportunist, and he thought me an easy mark for the taking. When you've money like I do, such men are in no short supply, and often, I have no need to search them out, for they always find me. At first, I played along as he told me of his prospects: a gold mining operation in the Kilo-Moto region. He was looking for investors, of course, and I obliged him. It's when he told me how my investment would help to secure 'labor' I knew him for the type he truly was. Stealing men's possessions is a crime, but stealing men altogether is a sin, wouldn't you agree?"

"I'm well aware such practices still go on in parts," Englot said, calming down some. "It's been going on for decades from Kinshasa to Dar es Salaam. It's part of the reason I came here in the first place, to help push for the freedom of these people. But for as bad as what Maier was doing, what you have done is unforgivable. You've taken a life and, in your error to punish Maier's sins, have committed the most heinous one of all."

"I make no apologies," I said. "And you've no right to judge me. If you understood more than this narrow view, you might see that. But as it is, I don't believe you ever will. I've a secret for you, Father, one you might not like. God doesn't punish sin; he allows it. Maier wasn't the first man whose sins killed him, and he won't be the last either."

Possibly it was the heat weighing down his will, or perhaps it was a holdover from his soldiering days, but his desire to fight had been sapped. For a time, neither of us spoke. The crowd by the river dispersed, and Maier's body was carried up to the mission. The indecipherable murmur of the native tongue could be heard through the open window.

In the end, he could not look at me. He just stood in the doorway and spoke over his shoulder.

"A boat will be arriving this afternoon," he said. "It can take you back to Brazzaville."

❧

Through both experience and experiment my infernal agreement, then approaching the dawn of its third decade, had brought no end of entertainment and no small amount of riches. Though hell's coffers lay open to me, I found significantly more joy in obtaining those treasures that far surpassed mere monetary value.

There is the petite jeweled necklace of Lady Edwina Scott, a brilliant-blue sapphire butterfly wing set in sterling silver the old slut wore when I'd take her to bed. She loved nothing more than to chase me around the bedroom wearing nothing but it slung from her porcelain neck. She was quite spry for a woman of sixty-three.

In my hacienda in Recoleta, I keep the dagger Phillipe Gardel sought to use to bring about my end in 1907 for reasons still unclear to me. A scar beneath my ribs and the stains of his vengeful blood upon the blade stand testament to some unfortunate folly. A man relieved of consequence is oft to forget indiscretions that lead to such violent ends.

One of my favorite memories is of a party I threw in Chicago in the fall of 1899. I remember it well because I'd just acquired a magnificent specimen, a heretofore unknown and unseen self-portrait of Raphael undoubtedly completed in his late period. Its provenance assured, I sought to display the unique work of beauty before a rapt crowd when I was overcome with a sudden, inimitable, and wholly overpowering desire to see the thing destroyed so I might know the sensation of having blotted out of existence something priceless, desired, and one of a kind that I would be the last person on earth to possess. I recall the gasps of horror and the invectives hurled at me as I set the piece ablaze before a flabbergasted crowd of one hundred of the city's most revered citizens, artists, and collectors. A mason jar still houses the ashes of the work somewhere, but where, I've forgotten.

And then, of course, there is my dacha outside Saint Petersburg, which displays an artifact of singular interest: the white meerschaum *porte-cigarette,* once the favored accessory of the slothful Mikhail Alexandrovich Polachev, whose sin had been brought to light by the reckless Kazakov, a casual misstep that unwittingly signed a friend's death warrant and consigned his soul to eternal darkness.

These items, and thousands more, adorn my collection, trophies of innumerable conquests of the human spirit. Some bring joy; others, pain. Some still retain the lingering odor of romantic ardor; others the reek of crushed dreams, ruined families, hatred, suicide, and murder. But all have a single inescapable consequence as well, one playing all too well into the curiosity that draws the wandering eye of my fellow men. For while one so outwardly young as myself should be perfectly able to possess great wealth, circumstance dictates this wealth be spread far and wide so the name Etienne Allard might remain disconnected from affairs that might draw unwanted suspicion. As I no longer physically age, I must move frequently, often visiting a place only once in many years. I keep no close friends, never rekindle the same affairs twice. If I do return, it is in secret, under an assumed name, acquiring new residences, retaining new staff and servants. I have traveled under many such names: Etienne Allard, Robert Drake, Alonzo Monçada, Russell Nash, Veem Verbeer, and Sébastien Chollet, to cite but a few.

It was in the guise of this last name I found myself in Paris once again, on the eve of humanity's greatest trial.

I had not been back since the accursed night when that grotesque merchant of souls paid call. My old home in the Faubourg Saint-Germain, lost long ago to that crooked Russian, was now government offices. It gave me sad pause to know its former glories were lost to time, but also satisfaction knowing it had not been held long by Kazakov or passed on to his kin.

I took rooms near the Arc de Triomphe and eagerly sought to reacquaint myself with the city I had once so loved. It was already late June, and I longed to stroll the boulevards, to hear the intoxicating giggles of girls, and to inhale the odor of the chestnut trees. I would find a café on the Champs-Élysées and sit all day drinking the city in.

But I found the Place de l'Étoile teeming with automobiles, the once quaint sound of horse hooves and carriage wheels all but drowned out by the offensive burping and coughing of the internal combustion engine. The normally heady florals of the Jardin des Tuileries wafting up the avenues for many blocks now competed with the stench of oil and gasoline exhaust.

Seeking relief, I passed into an open café on rue de Rivoli. Near the back, standing about a tall marble top table, a group of gentlemen huddled over the evening edition of *Le Figaro* discussing the report from Sarajevo blazed across the top of the page. In all my years of travel, all the countries I have visited, all of the men I have known, loved, and despised, none in this world can debate like a Frenchman. It's in our blood.

The archduke was dead, his wife too. Their bodies not yet cold, there was already talk of war. With mustaches bristling and fists shaking, they pronounced apocalyptic prognostications.

"There will most certainly be consequences," said one fat fellow.

"You don't know that for sure," said another, but then, with reserved curiosity: "What kind of consequences?"

"Such a lovely woman," said a third, an old, withered man whose entire focus was upon the picture of the dead duchess. "A pity to leave three children without parents. Even if they are royalty."

"There will be consequences," said the fat man again, pounding the table with a fleshy fist. "How should I know what kind? But a thing like this cannot go unanswered."

"Poincaré is going to Russia in a few weeks. Are we really going to ally ourselves with those barbarians?"

"Who cares about this, really? What is an archduke anyway? It's not like they shot the emperor. *That* would be cause for concern."

"High cheekbones. That's what makes a woman regal."

"There is no way I'm going to fight the fucking Prussians again."

"Don't be ridiculous, you fool. You're too old to fight anymore. Its fellows like me they'll send to the meat grinder. And like that poor gent there."

This last speaker, a youth of perhaps twenty, indicated me with a nod.

"What do you think, then," he said addressing me directly. "Think they'll send us to war?"

"Who, him?" the fat one interjected before I could answer. "You've got a lot to learn. Fellows like him don't go to war, boy. Money makes sure of that. And if they do, you can bet it'll be on an officer's commission, sitting nice and comfortable far away from the battle. You should worry about yourself."

The group returned to their discussion, the young fellow especially glancing sharply at me, as if I alone was the author of his unfortunate fate.

"A terrible crime to snuff out such beauty."

I first saw her in the Luxembourg Gardens.

She sat beneath a shade tree beside the Fontaine Medicis reading to a group of three small children, two boys and a girl, picnicked on a blanket at her feet. Words drifted from her lips like dandelion florets carried on the breeze. In a hypnotic voice, alternately soft and coarse, she brought the story to life, and I drifted closer like a sailor helplessly drawn to her siren song.

"Cri-cri-cri!"

"Who is calling me?" asked Pinocchio, greatly frightened.

"I am!"

Pinocchio turned and saw a large cricket crawling slowly up the wall.

"Tell me, Cricket, who are you?"

"I am the Talking Cricket, and I have been living in this room for more than one hundred years."

"Today, however, this room is mine," said the Marionette, "and if you wish to do me a favor, get out now, and don't turn around even once."

"I refuse to leave this spot," answered the Cricket, "until I have told you a great truth."

"Tell it, then, and hurry."

"Woe to boys who refuse to obey their parents and run away from home," I said, my thundering voice bringing the children a delightful shock, setting their hearts aflutter. *"They will*

never be happy in this world, and when they are older, they will be sorry for it."

Surprised by my sudden entrance upon the scene, the girl looked up at me from her pages with the bewilderment of one viewing an unusually large bird, an emu or a cassowary, for the very first time—a countenance that spoke to both curiosity and caution.

"Forgive my intrusion," I said. "I couldn't help but overhear your lively recitation. I know the story well. I remember reading it in the *Giornale per i bambini* when it was first published."

"What's a bambi?" one of the children said. He was a lean blond-haired boy of five or six in a smart sailor suit. Beside him on the blanket lay a model of a sailing schooner.

"A *bambini* is Italian," I said. "It means a small child."

"You speak Italian?" the other boy said. He resembled the first, though clearly older by a few years. I took them to be brothers and the girl, the youngest child, for their sister.

"I speak many languages."

"You must have been quite an intelligent child," their teacher said, "to be able not only to read, but in the original Italian at, what, two, three, years old?

Confused, I'd suddenly forgotten the paradox of my face and age. I had read the story when it was first released, but *that* was 1891, and I'd already turned eleven.

"What I mean to say is, I remember reading it, or rather *it* being read to *me*, when I was a boy, of course," I fumbled like a buffoon. "I reread it much later when I was older. But still a young boy, of course. That is to say..."

"He's a little strange," said the older blond boy.

"Maurice!" she scolded quietly. "Manners."

"*Je suis désolé,* Mademoiselle Elena."

Elena. Her name resonated softly like a distant bell echoing over the hills.

"It's all right," I said. "I didn't mean to give you all a fright."

"Well, you certainly brought the cricket to life better than I," Elena said.

"Would you read us more please?" the little girl said.

"Yes, more," her brothers chimed in.

"It seems you've attracted an audience. Perhaps you'll help me finish this chapter?" she said. Happily, I doffed my hat and seated myself beside this wonderful girl as we commenced with the recitation, she speaking in the easy foolish tones of the wooden boy and I in the throaty rasp of the wise yet doomed cricket. The children grinned with glee, as all young children are wont to do at the spectacle of adults playing at silly voices for their pleasure. When it came time for cricket to die at the hands of Pinocchio, I took pains to pantomime an overly dramatic demise, giving them over to great peals of laughter. When it was over, we received an enthusiastic round of applause for our mutual effort, to which I presented a humble bow.

"They are quite taken with you," Elena said.

"I've always had a love of the theater," I said. "Though, admittedly, this is my first time appearing on the stage."

"Well, you did very well, Mr. Cricket."

"Sébastien," I replied. She smiled a light smile with soft, reserved lips, like the enigmatic grin playing upon the lips of the *Mona Lisa*. It set my heart ablaze. "But I've interrupted your afternoon."

"Not at all," she said. "We were taking a break from our lesson. But we'll have to be getting back soon."

"But, my boat," the older boy, Maurice, said. "We are going to the *basin*, aren't we?"

"Of course," Elena said. "A promise is a promise."

"May I walk with you?"

"You may," she obliged, granting me a second petite smile.

Rousing the children to their feet, I offered to carry their blanket and basket, and we set off through the garden. At the grand pool before the Palais, Maurice unfurled the bright-white sails of his model schooner and set it in the water. Elena and I stood apart, looking on from nearby.

"Maurice is the oldest," she said. "He's bold, like his father. Camille is headstrong too, but more thoughtful, and follows him everywhere. Then there is the petite one, Madeline. *Le trésor de sa mère.*"

"How long have you been with them?"

"About six years. The family has been very good to me. Maurice will be eight next year and off to school. But Madeline is only four, so hopefully I will be with her many more years. She's a joy."

"They seem to love you as well," I said.

"Because I spoil them too much. It was history all morning. I thought a break might be in order."

"It's not a bad thing," I said. "I wish my tutors had felt the same way. It's good for children to be distracted from their studies from time to time."

"Well, we're not doing anything so rigorous as Greek tragedy," she said. "Exactly how many languages do you speak?"

"Four or five," I lied. In truth, I could converse with fluency in virtually every dialect on the continent, and my Arabic and Hindi were coming along nicely.

"It embarrasses me to say I only know French and English."

"My father was a merchant," I said. "He always told me how important it was I be able to speak to a man in his own tongue. Said it would help me read them better."

It struck me then that that had been the first time I'd even thought about my father in more than twenty years. But something in this girl's manner disarmed me. The deep pools of her eyes held a curious brightness. When she looked at me, it felt they unlocked something I'd not known to be there before. I was charmed by her natural, unpretentious way, and we conversed as two people seeking nothing from the other besides the passage of a pleasant afternoon. I spoke little of myself, or rather of the gentleman Sébastien Chollet. Instead, I inquired of her employer, a man named Romilly, and she reveled in telling me stories about her time as governess to his children. She was at her happiest when focused on them and smiled an infectious smile, one that I determined to see every day lest I never be happy again.

"It's getting on," she said. We'd talked for nearly an hour. "I must take the children home."

I walked with them to the boulevard Saint-Michel and reluctantly bid her goodbye. At the gate, Madeline asked with charming politeness if I might join them again to continue the story of the marionette. I said I could hardly decline the petite mademoiselle's request, but only, of course, if her governess would but permit me the pleasure. Again, Elena graced me with her smile and consented. We arranged to meet again three days hence, beside the Fontaine Medicis.

Can words be the only meager method to convey the state of complete bliss I felt after that first encounter? The desire to be near her again filled my soul as I wandered aimlessly after our parting at the garden gate. While all around Paris sank in the mire of the thought of war, enchantment and the rising swell of ardor it imbued in my heart propelled my thoughts above, to heights fantastic and terrifying. I spent those three days waiting in dumb distraction, filling the time listlessly touring galleries and watching inane theater, counting the hours until our next meeting. Usual pleasures, once so fulfilling, now gave me over to feelings of loneliness.

On the third day, I set out for the gardens at noon. I'd had a new suit made for the occasion and paid handsomely to have it ready in time for our reunion, but when I came to the Fontaine Medicis at the appointed hour, neither Elena nor the children were anywhere to be found. Seating myself on a bench, I waited, hoping to see her graceful figure coming up the path. Hours passed. The crowds thinned at the approach of the dinner hour. Evening came on. Disconsolate, I wandered back to my rooms.

For the next two weeks, I returned to the gardens at midday, rain or shine. Each day, I waited for hours, and each day, I left disappointed. Nearing the end of my rope, I recalled the innocuous detail of the name Romilly, and decided to seek the family home. It was a fool's errand. But while lust may make a man foolish, it is only love that truly makes a man a fool. And a fool I'd become, for I could not deny being stricken to my heart with that most deadly of diseases to befall the libertine, love.

❧

I made inquiries and discovered Auguste Romilly had made a name for himself in textiles at a young age and his son Edouard now controlled the family business, living with his wife and children near the Parc Monceau, a mere stone's throw from my rooms. Imagine my astonishment when I'd learned the object of my desire during this cruel and agonizing separation was hiding in plain sight the whole time no more than a dozen streets away! I set out at once, determined to charm my way into an introduction with M. Romilly and subsequentially a reunion with Elena.

But my hopes were dashed before my eyes. At the Romilly door, a manservant curtly told me Edouard had taken his family, Elena included, south for an undisclosed period. The chatter of impending war had clearly become all too loud to too many concerned ears. Out of propriety, he would tell me nothing more.

Dejected, I returned to my solitude to contemplate the loss of this lovely soul from my life. But there would be little time for reflection. The specter of death loomed on the horizon. In a week's time, Germany would close her borders. The day following the announcement, August 2, crowds gathered at the Place de la Concorde to review the posters hung in the early-morning hours. *Mobilisation Générale.* The call to arms had been sounded. France was going to war.

Despite all the reassurances and propaganda promising the war would be short, that the Germans would crumble before the Allies' might and France would know swift victory over her enemies, by late 1914, it was clear the fighting would be both protracted and gruesome.

Still acting under the guise of my assumed name, rather than flee, I joined the fighting as a volunteer attached to a division riding east to Alsace to retake Vieil Armand from the Hun. On Christmas Day, when the world should have been at peace celebrating the birth of their false savior, feasting on fattened goose and puddings, I was knee deep in freezing snow pushing up the Vosges slopes amid the buzz of bullets and the thunder of German Minenwerfer. The irony of being surrounded by death, yet secure in the knowledge it would not come for me, protected as I was by hell's own enfolding embrace, gave me courage. War is a treasure trove of experiences for the libertine not to be replicated, not the least of which is the sensation of mortal terror. However, the constant fear of death does not break a man's will. Loneliness does that.

Not a day passed I did not think of Elena.

The fighting raged for months. One frigid evening, when the guns fell silent and death took a brief respite before resuming his grim work, I heard the name Chollet, called out by a soldier clomping up the duckboards. I'd seen him many times walking the trenches, muddied, bloodied, and exhausted, calling out names, handing out crumpled letters and small parcels in these times of brief quiet. But never had he called out mine. I crawled out of my hole, and he shoved an envelope into my hand before traipsing on, swallowed by the mass of men crowding the trench.

Holding the paper to the flickering light of a dim oil lamp slung from a beam above my dugout, my heart leapt with incomparable joy.

Dear Sébastien,

It's my hope this letter finds you well and in good spirits.

You are probably surprised to be receiving something from me. Truth be told, I was not sure you would even remember our encounter. When Edouard brought us back to Paris a few months ago, I knew you'd most likely been sent off to fight, and so I imagined we would never speak again. I can only hope that Providence has brought us back together.

I am now what is becoming known around the city as a *marraine*, having answered an advertisement in *L'Écho de Paris* asking for volunteers to write letters to our men at the front and in the hospitals. They said there were so many who did not have family to write to, and I knew this was the case for you. I made an inquiry and they found your name on a list. I volunteered to write in the hopes you are indeed the Sébastien Chollet I remember. There are thousands of us godmothers of war now, writing nearly every day. They frame our work as a patriotic duty, that we are serving the country, but I don't think of it this way.

I am told only which army and regiment you are serving in, not where you are, so I can only hope you are safe and somewhere the fighting is not. I wish a swift end to the conflict and your safe return, and the safe return of all the others with you.

Life in Paris is returned to some normalcy. Edouard's factory is turning out uniforms by the hundreds every day. Madame Romilly has taken up the cause as well, in her own way. She volunteers with the La Croix-Rouge, visiting the injured and reading to the convalescing.

The children are well. Maurice, always the headstrong one, has started his own family newspaper *L'Echo de Romilly*, his contribution to the war effort, and he enlisted his brother as correspondent. Together they report on the state of the pantry, the weather, how many times the dog has run up and down the stairs. Madeline tries to participate, of course, but they won't allow her. She takes it in stride, though. She's a strong little one.

The efforts of everyone pulling together is inspiring and brings me hope. It is a ray of sunshine in an otherwise gray world lately so full of reports of death and ruin. I long for days when people didn't speak of such things. I know it's selfish of me to think this way, especially with you and others like you facing horror every day. I'm supposed to focus on the positive, so that I will do.

I will write to you again soon, but I hope you are able to write to me too. I would like it very much to know you are safe and what things you have been doing and the places you have been. And the children would like to know how their favorite Mr. Cricket has been getting on too.

God protect you.

Sincerely,

Elena

I could but press the letter to my breast so I might feel the ghost of her pen pressing against the paper that composed this miraculous missive. I held it to my nostrils and inhaled deeply of its fibers, wishing to catch a fleeting whiff of her perfumed hand as it glided across the pages. I thought I detected the pleasing aroma of the white rose or the lily of the valley, though it was only my mind playing tricks on me. Not even those lovely scents could penetrate the acrid bite of cordite and the stench of rotting flesh. But for a brief second, I was transported back to elegant parlors and roaring fireplaces, and to music rooms where girls like Elena, dressed in their finest, played piano for the family and outside there was only sunshine and no war.

I read the letter again, and then a third time, listening for her euphonious voice speak from my memory over the incessant chatter of the men. I studied her handwriting, absorbed in the slant of the letters, the graceful curve she applied to the *o*'s and *u*'s and *p*'s, noting the evenness of her hand. I knew it to be winter across the continent, but there, in the springtime of my dreams, I imagined her seated at a walnut writing desk before an open window overlooking a garden, her face caressed by a warm passing breeze just as her mind was caressed by a warm passing thought of me.

At the bottom of the last page, below her name, she'd written the address of the Romilly house in Paris and her full name: Elena Jubert. I sought out pencil and paper at once.

Thinking it rash to pour out my heart, I demurred, composing a thoughtful letter reassuring her I was safe but that the fighting had been fierce at times and I had already lost several comrades in arms. This was all true. There was Gaëtan, a boy of just eighteen, the son of a cheesemaker from Champagnole, who'd been shot through the eye as he fought beside me, and Henri, a career soldier at thirty-six, tough and wise, who might have risen to the rank of colonel or even *général de brigade* but for a foul temper and habit of mouthing off.

He'd been brought down at Mulhouse, smashed to pieces by a mortar shell.

I was happy to learn the children were doing well, and if she could, it might raise the spirits of the men to receive a copy of little Maurice's family publication. I spoke of the loneliness of the trenches and being surrounded by so much pain and death, and yet finding a single spark of beauty and compassion in her letter and how her words lit a welcome light in the darkness.

I told her, perhaps foolishly, about my vision of her, like a girl in one of de la Brély's or Gilbert's paintings, quietly composing yet resplendent in her task. Then I apologized for my boldness, but thoughts such as these brought a measure of comfort; recalling the beauty in so many compositions reminded me of happier times.

I ended by imploring her to write again soon. More than a week later, my wish was granted.

> Dear Sébastien,
>
> I received your letter today and was so happy to learn you were alive and well, I sat down almost immediately to write you again. In fact, I'd barely finished reading what you'd written before picking up my pen.
>
> The horrors you describe are almost too terrible to bear, and I can't think what it must be like to have friends taken from you like that. I can only pray you remain safe and that God protects you.
>
> I should like to tell you how you flatter me with the picture you've composed of me, but I'm afraid I am quite ignorant when it comes to the world of art, and I don't know the men of whom you speak. But I assume they are pleasant images, so I'll just say thank

you, and hope one day I might see these pictures in person.

I'm told I should write to you of happy things and tell you stories to lift your spirits, but I'm afraid the life of a *gouvernante* is not very interesting, and anything I could tell you about my day-to-day activities would pale in comparison to what you are facing. I don't wish to bore you, only to let you know I am thinking of you and I do pray every day for you to return safe.

Perhaps in your next letter, you can tell me more about art? It seems to bring you peace, and it is my great hope to bring you some comfort in that terrible place.

She closed the letter encouraging me to remain strong and quoted Paul in his discourse to the Corinthians, from which she said she sometimes derived strength:

"We are troubled on every side, yet not distressed; we are perplexed, but not in despair; persecuted, but not forsaken; cast down, but not destroyed."

I wanted to write back immediately, but time and tide (and war) wait for no man. The next days saw brutality immeasurable in scale—for all the fighting, a gain of fewer than one hundred yards. We held our position for only a day before being driven back by a punishing artillery barrage, finding ourselves right back where we'd started.

Dear Elena,

There are many things I would like to tell you about, but much more I should like to show you. I often find words a poor substitute for experience, and art, like food or music or the theater, is best experienced rather than spoken of. Little in this world is comparable to the feeling of being surrounded by beauty, being immersed in it, as I have been. Fortune has been kind to me and granted me opportunities few others shall ever be given.

I could describe to you Lagrenée's *Mars and Venus*, the nude lovers captured in all their voluptuous romantic bliss, but you would never feel the softness of the bed curtains, green as Japanese moss, or know the gentle cooing of the doves nesting at their bedside, unless you were standing before it in all its majesty. I could tell you about walking the shores of the sea in Patagonia, but you would never know the exquisite silence of that place at the bottom of the world were you not standing there with me. You may marvel at the ornaments of Mdm. Romilly's home, trinkets found in the antique shops of the rue Saint-Honoré, but I tell you they are mere baubles when compared to the treasures found among the palaces of the ancient Rajput, whose halls I have tread and whose pagan secrets I have been privy to discover. There is even beauty to be found here among the dead and dying, if you know but where to seek it out. I wish I were back in Paris so I might show you firsthand. Perhaps when this blasted conflict is at an end, you would do me the honor of accompanying me on a tour of some galleries?

It would not bore me at all to hear of your life and the work you do. You are of a kind soul, and I should like to hear more. Tell me. Reading your words and hearing your voice ring in my memory makes my time here more bearable.

Yours,
Sébastien

The words flew from my pen. Breaking convention, I felt myself overcome with a desire to do nothing more than experience another walk with her and show her the world as I knew it to be. I had traversed the globe, sailed upon every one of its seas, tread ground not known to man's footsteps in centuries, seen the sunrise over the broad horizon of the desolate Saharan expanse, only to see it set once again over the golden mountains of the Hindu Kush at the top of the world. But now, these experiences felt devoid of substance because she had not been there, as if without her, they'd never happened at all.

I suddenly wished to know everything about her, her life, where she'd been, and how she'd come to be where she was. Never had I taken such interest in anyone, and it both frightened and excited me all the more.

Soon, her reply came, and I found myself over the moon once again.

Dear Sébastien,

You asked I tell you about myself, but I fear there is not so much to tell. My mother died when I was just a child. I was raised only by my father. He was a good man, but sad. He did his best for the two of us. We were forced to leave our home when I was four or five and moved often in those early years. I remember him being cross much of the time, mostly at being unable to provide me with the things he thought all little girls should have. He worked as a gardener, and I believe he was ashamed of his low status compared to those in whose employ he found himself. He took to drink often and would complain openly about the whimsy of the well-to-do. But he never raised a hand to me, not once, and his bouts of sadness never lasted too long. Work was scarce, and what little he made always went first to my education. He loved me dearly, that much I know, and wanted much more for me than he thought he could provide. I think it's why he felt he had to send me away.

School was difficult at times, the sisters were more stern than fair, but I suppose I shouldn't have wished for anything more. So many do not even get the chance to be educated. I did, of course, wish for more, I mean, but more often than not, I was grateful for what I had. They taught me well, though apparently not enough about art, a shortcoming you've inspired me to correct. Sadly, many of the galleries have been emptied and walled up to protect against the shelling, so my only recourse is to images in the few books I can acquire on the subject.

The way you describe your travels, I can't even begin to imagine the places you've seen. I read *Cinq semaines en ballon* once, but that is the closest I've come to visiting any far-off places. The life of a *gouvernante* is not an exciting or exotic one. The most I've traveled was from Marseille to Paris, and even then, I was too young to appreciate it. I don't believe in fate. If I'm not meant to have more than I do, then I'm willing to accept it and take comfort. Father died some years ago, but the Romillys treat me well. I have a small room of my own, and they pay me decently enough. But it doesn't mean I don't dream sometimes. Perhaps one day I'll get to see some of the things you've told me about, and it would be nice if you were there to show them to me. You're right about experience. It is something best shared.

I don't worry for the future, because what will come will come, and I don't dwell on the past, because what has been cannot be changed. For me, there is only ever today. When the children grow up, I will leave this house and find other employ. I'm young and still have many more years of work ahead of me, and that brings me comfort too.

Sincerely,

Elena

P.S. I wonder about how you said there is even beauty to be found among the dead and dying. How is this so?

I was struck with pity for the hardship a delicate creature such as she should have had to endure at the hands of an unkind world. Quietly, I railed against dumb fate, denouncing God as an unjust and cruel arbiter of destiny. Had I had the opportunity to know Elena sooner, mightn't I have been able to ease her suffering? Conversely, I felt pride for her fortitude. Her remarkable evenness of spirit displayed a feminine bravery both charming and inspiring.

Then sinking into a depressive state and reflecting on my own weakness of character, at what I had been given and what I had squandered, I began to question what I had to offer this girl except a history of greed and incontinence. I saw in her cleanliness and purity and felt so ashamed of my own filthiness.

Dearest Elena,

I wish there were a better way to express the happiness I am filled with each time I receive your letters. Merely telling you in this crude form of missive does not do it justice.

Though what you've told me of your childhood causes me great pain (it is not fair misfortune should befall someone as kind as you), I am thankful to learn of it, for it gives me the canvas upon which I can sketch the background for the portrait of grace I paint in my mind when I think of you. Your nobility of spirit is heartening and evokes images of gentleness among all this brutality. It puts to shame men who would use fire and steel to destroy each other, while I know a single smile from you could cause them to lay down their arms and cry out in unison: "What fools we are! Look there, are we so blind as to have forgotten such beauty exists in the world?"

I fear I am one of those men. The mercy of your words and affections shines a light upon my own stain. I wonder would you recoil if I were to tell you my own history is filled not with misfortune and perseverance as yours is, but is instead tarnished with remorse and ignominy? Dearest Elena, would your amiable heart show such warmth were you to know all my faults?

I speak of the veneer of the world, but you are its substance. I apologize if my boldness offends you. If I am being rash, it is only because I feel the pressing need to unburden myself before you, that you of all people would allow me to do so willingly and without judgment. Maybe it's this war and the constant presence of fear on the battlefield. But I don't fear death, I never have. There is a reason for that, and perhaps one day I'll tell you why.

Yours,

Sébastien

P.S. You asked where there can be beauty here. They read the Bible in the trenches, many men carry one in their kit, and when there is respite from the bullets and cannon, they hold a simple Mass. These I do not attend, though others find solace in them. To each man his own pain, and so to each his own balm.

But once there was a soldier here, I did not know his name, who chose to read not from that book but rather from his memory a poem he'd stored away. It was a verse I knew well. He would sit in his hole, and while the others prayed, he would recite it.

Dans une terre grasse et pleine d'escargots
Je veux creuser moi-même une fosse profonde,
Où je puisse à loisir étaler mes vieux os
Et dormir dans l'oubli comme un requin
dans l'onde.

Je hais les testaments et je hais les tombeaux;
Plutôt que d'implorer une larme du monde,
Vivant, j'aimerais mieux inviter les corbeaux
A saigner tous les bouts de ma carcasse immonde.

Ô vers! Noirs compagnons sans oreille et sans yeux,
Voyez venir à vous un mort libre et joyeux;
Philosophes viveurs, fils de la pourriture,

A travers ma ruine allez donc sans remords,
Et dites-moi s'il est encore quelque torture
Pour ce vieux corps sans âme et mort parmi

les morts!

There, I say, is beauty.

Many weeks passed after this letter had been sent. Elena was quiet, and with each new day, her silence felt an eternity. I feared terribly I had crossed a boundary. Me, a man who lived his life without limits, trembled like a scolded child at the thought I had overstepped a line between us—that my prophecy was self-fulfilling, and she did recoil in disgust and horror at my audacious impudence. What right did I have to declare myself to her in that manner? What must she have thought of my words?

I despaired to think of the costly error of my foolhardy indiscretion and for many days could not sleep.

On the morning of April 4, my division along with the 152nd pressed the attack on the summit of the Vieil-Armand in an attempt to retake the position and drive the Hun once and for all back down the slopes. After hours of artillery bombardment from our mighty 370 Filloux guns the call came to advance, and every man being for himself, we stormed out and broke for the enemy trenches. The pitiful wails of the wounded sounded up and down the slopes as shells crashed all around us. I pressed uphill against a hail of gunfire and twice felt the sudden tug on my greatcoat as a bullet passed through, mercifully missing the flesh. Undeterred, I plowed on until a third round—this one possibly sent as a message by the devil himself, a reminder of our agreement—struck me at the throat just below my left ear, the impact, like the sharp wrap from a bamboo switch against my neck, stopping me cold. The ferrous taste of blood filled my mouth. I dropped my rifle and fell where I stood.

I'd once shared the last of my wine ration with a frowsy fellow *poilu* named Jean-Martin, and as a result of that generosity, he'd taken to never being far from my side. I believe it was he who'd dragged me from the field, swearing all the way, back to the relative safety of the trenches. I recall the peaceful sensation of my life slipping away, my body feeling lighter and lighter, as if I were not being pulled across the rocky ground but floating atop calm, cool waters. The feeling ended abruptly as Jean-Martin dropped me four feet onto the duckboards, the shock knocking me into oblivion.

Sometime later, I awoke in a cot surrounded by men who themselves were waking in a cot to discover themselves surrounded by men waking in cots. More a horse stable than a hospital, beds of the sick, dying, and the dead lined the walls while nurses in casquette and white aprons spattered with blood flitted about like butterflies. The reek of iodine perforated the air, and the pitiful groans of the wounded invaded the ears.

"Eh, so you made it?" a voice from the bed beside mine said as I opened my bleary eyes. "I thought for sure the devil had your number."

It was Jean-Martin. He'd taken a round in the leg for his troubles but was happy to be safely away from the Vieil-Armand. I opened my mouth to express my thanks but could only bring forth a feeble gurgle. Tremendous pain wracked my neck, almost sending me to faint.

"No use trying to speak with a hole like that in you, friend," he said, indicating the mound of bandage wrapped around my neck and head. "Don't worry, though. I heard them talking before. They say you're incredibly lucky. Another inch to the right and I'd be talking to some other poor sot in that bed. Christ, what I wouldn't give for a smoke."

I felt for the wrapping at my throat, but a passing nurse quickly seized my hand.

"That would be unwise," she said. "Best to leave it be for now."

I tried to speak again. Again, nothing.

"The bullet didn't hit your throat, thank God. But there's a lot of swelling. You won't be talking for some time. Best not to even try. Best to just rest."

Her voice was peaceful and reassuring. She smiled and squeezed my hand warmly before disappearing to attend to the others.

"Been hearing that a lot lately," Jean-Martin said, lying back down. "'Best to just rest.' Sure, rest up, boy. We need you rested up so you can get back to being cannon fodder. Need lots and lots of cannon fodder, we do."

I longed to know how long I'd been lying there, and where exactly there was, when exhaustion once again overtook me, and I passed back into the black void of sleep.

When I awoke the second time, Jean-Martin was gone. A mess of swollen, bloodied flesh lay in his place.

My body felt noticeably heavier. Much like the sensation of exiting a body of water, the feeling of weightlessness had left me. The bandage about my head had been removed, but my neck was still wrapped tight and ached with a terrible strain. A nurse approached to inspect my dressing, and venturing to speak, I was relieved to hear the familiar sound of my own voice, albeit with painful consequences.

"Where am I?" I said.

"Bazoilles-sur-Meuse," she said.

"How long have I been here?"

"Twelve days," she said. "When you did not wake after the surgery, we took you for dead. But somehow you have managed to pull through. When you fell asleep the second time and did not wake, we took you for dead again. That was three days ago."

"Where is Jean-Martin?"

But a doctor down the line called for the nurse's help, and she rushed off without another word.

Later, I was brought a bowl of broth, my first real meal in days. I'd lost nearly seven kilograms in my stupor, and this reflected in my appetite as I greedily sipped the tepid liquid like an unpolished brute, raising the bowl to my lips to see the last gritty drop downed. Many more days would pass before I regained my strength.

And always, my thoughts returned to Elena.

I felt the reckless haste with which I'd bared my feelings in my last missive must have surely driven her away, for if it hadn't, why had no reply come?

I thought to write her once more, and even got so far as to request pen and paper, but a perplexing sort of paralysis stymied my efforts. My thoughts came jumbled, hurried, and despite a great effort, I could find no words sufficient to describe what my heart wished to say, which left me to despair. Thankfully, when I believed all to be lost, fortune intervened and reunited us once more.

Two letters from Elena! They'd been delivered to my position at the front but failed to reach me before my evacuation, only now arriving. I tore open the first with all the hope of a drowning man reaching for a lifeline.

Dear Sébastien,

Though I admit I do not have such a great understanding of the nuances of artistic works that you do, I cannot say I find those lines to be filled with anything but horror. They seed within me with a hopeless dread the men who have been sent to fight will lose themselves, lose their very souls in the mire of war. Your friend is one such man if he chooses to wish for death in such a manner, for I find no sophistication in the creatures of decay, nor do I believe anyone should surrender themselves to ruin out of dumb ennui. I hope against hope you do not feel as he does, and that you see only beauty in the reading of the lines, not in their substance.

Your words flatter me. The misfortunes that we each endure are placed before us, and how we choose to overcome them speaks not of our nobility but only of our faith. I carry that faith in my heart, nothing more. It has taken me some time to reflect on your words. I admit your last letter gave me pause, and for many days, I've been discoursing with myself over my own feelings. That you feel the way you do serves to strengthen them, and I am grateful to you, though I fear you are placing me upon a pedestal I am undeserving of.

My heart has known happiness and sorrow and hatred and love in its turn. I have wished for the opportunity to right the wrongs that have been done to me and my family in the past, and so, in a way, I don't think myself very different from most anyone else.

You say your history is sullied by grief. I have known grief. You say your past is filled with disgrace. I say the shame would be in not facing it.

    Sincerely,

    Elena

The date of this letter read April 4, the day I fell. The date of my most recent letter to her had been nearly a full month before. I read the second, brief message dated some two weeks later.

Dear Sébastien,

    It has been so long since I last heard from you, longer than has ever been before, I find myself despairing this letter is being written for naught and my worst fears have been realized.

    I implored Edouard to make inquiries on my behalf, but still, we receive no word. No one is able to say whether you are alive or dead. Casualty reports are often incomplete, inaccurate, or nonexistent. My heart struggles to find hope you have not fallen, but with each passing day and no word coming of your whereabouts or well-being, this shadow of grief draws ever closer. Like the sun slowly setting over a distant horizon, I feel the light and warmth of your soul gently fading.

    I know if this letter returns to me unopened, then you are dead, and I shall never unseal the envelope that contains these final words of parting. They shall be forever entombed in my spirit, alongside my faith, that perhaps one day you and I shall be reunited.

    Yours,

Elena

Tears filled my eyes anew as I read and reread the lines, resolving at once to write her, if only to tell her I lived. But then I thought it a ridiculous idea. My wound was healing remarkably fast, and I was well enough to travel. I would seek a *permissionnaire* and go to Paris directly, find my love, and grab hold of her forever.

"'Love' is not a word in the libertine's lexicon," Vallaton once said. "To affix oneself to a singular emotion such as love, or hate, for that matter, is to chain oneself for eternity to an illusion without form or substance. Love requires faith, and that is not a word in the libertine's dictionary either."

How wrong he was, and I to believe him. Only, he understood the error of our ways long before I. Could I have been so blind so as not to see a truth laid so bare? To feel love meant to abandon all I had known or ever believed in. What is truth but the sum of our experiences? I did not know love, and so I was libertine. Now that I knew love, I was no longer. It was a revelation.

For the first time, I grieved for my lost friend and the shamelessness of my treachery. I had become as Frankenstein's monster and turned on my creator only when he recognized too late the error of his ways. I had become a grotesque, vile creature of ignoble vainglory. Examining my whole life in those few moments, I found it diseased, worthless, and wanting. I loathed myself then, as I still do today.

I inquired after how I might obtain a leave but was informed a *permissionnaire* would not be issued. I was instead given my medical discharge. A week later, I was ferried by truck with other wounded back to Paris.

☙

The ambulance deposited us beneath the vaulted glass and iron atrium of the Grand Palais—the once joyful space filled with endless rows of the wounded laid out on the floor like so many fish at a monger. The silence was deafening as nurses moved from body to body, changing bandages, bracing broken bones, checking for signs of life in this man, confirming they'd gone in the next.

I tarried not in that morbid house of death and made straight for a taxi, ordering the driver to take me directly to the address of the Romilly house on Parc Monceau.

As the cab puttered up the avenue Matignon, the driver jabbered on about butter shortages and how his wife could no longer make a decent *sole meunière* while I watched absently out the window thinking of what I would say when I stood before Elena. A whirlwind of emotions whipped through my heart. What would she say when she saw me? Would she run into my waiting arms and shower me with tears and kisses at my resurrection, or would she receive me coldly, repelled by my impertinent presumptions of love? Outside the cab window, few if any people walked the streets.

"Where is everyone?" I said.

"Many have left the city," the driver said, interrupting himself midgripe. "The government has only just returned these few months ago."

"Where did they go?"

"Who knows? To Bordeaux, to Limoges, to Toulouse. They feared the guns."

He dropped me on the boulevard de Courcelles, before the doors of number 68. I boldly knocked, hoping it would be she who answered. I imagined her face beaming with wondrous awe at the sight of my return and she would throw herself weeping into my arms. We would embrace, and the others would come running to see the happy commotion.

But instead, a funereal manservant greeted me indifferently. Monsieur Romilly and his entire family were no longer home and had not been so for some weeks.

"They have arranged for a temporary stay at the family estate of Madame Romilly," he said. "For the children, you understand." This estate sat some ten miles from Toulouse.

Exhausted but undeterred, I thanked him for the information and raced to the Gare d'Orsay to purchase a rail ticket south. Two days later, after stops in Orléans and Bordeaux, I disembarked in Toulouse.

The familial home of Brigitte Romilly sat on a low hill overlooking a small lake just east of the city proper. A quaint country estate surrounded by plane trees, it looked a suitably quiet refuge from the war.

Another servant there informed me the family had traveled into the city, to the Musée des Augustins. I was invited to wait but declined. I would go myself to the museum and took my leave, but seeing the still tender scar on my throat, Romilly's man adamantly refused to let me walk.

"You've done enough marching," he said. "I will have Victor bring a car to take you."

The galleries of the Musée des Augustins swarmed with people all looking for a brief escape from the specter of the war. Navigating the crowd as I once navigated the narrow confines of the trenches, I wove my way to and fro, a falling leaf floating through rigid branches, making my way from room to room, upstairs and down, until, at last, like spotting the beacon of a distant lighthouse in a hurricane, I found her.

As lovely as I remembered and twice as radiant, Elena stood with the Romillys and the children, before Delacroix's massive *Death of Sardanapalus*, a work of unspeakable beauty and horror I knew only too well.

The drifting mass of the leisure crowd flowed between us like a river. She bowed to listen as Maurice pointed at the figure of the brutal Moorish slave slaying his horse amid the chaos, the ferocity of the mameluke's black stare matched only by the wide-eyed terror in the animal. They spoke in hushed tones. Edouard Romilly, a man of maybe fifty, graying gracefully at the temples, stood close by his children, his wife, Brigitte, by his side listening as Elena explained the decadence on display before them.

"But why would they kill themselves?" Maurice questioned. "And why kill the animals?"

"So as not to fall into the hands of the enemy," Elena said. "It was common practice in ancient times for kings to destroy their belongings so they wouldn't be taken."

"That's how most kings got their wealth in the first place," Edouard said. "By taking it from other kings. And in those times, horses, sheep, and cattle were as valuable as gold."

"His indifference to it all is utterly horrifying," Brigitte said, noting the weary face of the sultan Sardanapalus overseeing the destruction. A stately woman, younger than her husband by some years, yet still with a motherly bent, she kept a wary distance from the painting, as if to be close to it would somehow ensnare her in the carnage playing out within its gilded frame.

Her words drew my gaze to the languid face of the defeated sultan. A slain concubine sprawled at his bejeweled feet, he remains casually aloof to the carnage; his disinterested head, propped by a crooked arm, weighs heavy on his shoulders, laden further by bags sagging beneath listless eyes. Enrobed in white silks, his body lies in almost insouciant repose, while behind him, the walls of Nineveh prepare to burn beneath the scorching arrows of the invading Bactrians.

Though I'd seen the picture numerous times before, it was only then I saw myself in that spectacle of the failed king lying amid his own ruination. As if she were narrating my past, Elena's soft words shone a harsh light upon the miscarriages of dignity and perfidious corruptions of the soul I'd enacted.

"See all of the women slaves he possessed, all slaughtered just like the animals? See how little human lives were worth to such a tyrant?"

My thoughts drifted back to the whores of Montmartre whose bodies I'd sullied with lecherous abandon, to Eugénie Janvier and the novice Marguerite and countless others with and without names across the globe who I'd used for my own hollow pleasures and then discarded. Some were like me, ruled by their vices and sought only the sensual finding in me an outlet for their scurrilous pursuits. But there were those like the Hindu girl Kaija, whose family shunned her for loving me. When I revealed how she'd given herself to me, they cast her out. My selfishness dissolved many families in its day. There is still a price on my head in that village.

"And those men doing the killing? They're not safe from the sword either. Soon, it will be their turn, betrayed just as much by their king as the others."

How many had I put to the sword of my own pride?

"He lies on a bed of red silks, but see how they flow like blood? It's everywhere: on the bed, on the floor, they wear it on their heads and on their clothes. He fairly floats on it."

I could bear to listen no more, her words like daggers, tearing open the skin of my soul like a vivisected animal put on gruesome display. A whole kingdom built on blood; a whole life built on a lie.

"I'm told that's symbolism," Brigitte said.

"Indeed," Edouard said. "But it's not too difficult to see. When you spend your life chasing money like this fellow did, you're bound to come to a bad end. That's why you should always temper wealth with wisdom."

"'Thinkest thou there is no tyranny but that of blood and chains?'" I said, the words calmly escaping my lips without thought or care, my gaze locked on the grim face of the tired king. "'The despotism of vice—the weakness and the wickedness of luxury—the negligence—the apathy—the evils of sensual sloth—produces ten thousand tyrants, whose delegated cruelty surpasses the worst acts of one energetic master, however harsh and hard in his own bearing.'"

Once again, my sudden appearance proved bewildering. Elena's watery eyes bore a gaze of curious joy and muted fear.

"Lord Byron," I said meekly, bringing their attentions back to the painting. "Actually, Sardanapalus is really just a representation of man's enslavement to sin. He didn't really exist, at least, not as we see him here. You see all his gold, his jewels, all his slaves and chattel, all destroyed, and yet he remains almost indifferent, as you, madame, have said. This is because the real slave in the picture is the sultan himself. It's not his money that has corrupted his soul; it's his sin, in this case, his sloth. He's surrendered himself to his vices and material wealth, abdicating his responsibilities to his kingdom and to God. A man enslaved to another man can eventually be made free. But a man enslaved to his sin is forever chained to it. His look is one of resignation. Everything around him has become a reminder of inescapable sin, and so he is compelled to destroy it. It's a last try at redemption. But it wouldn't work."

"It's you!" Madeline exclaimed, her cheeks beaming. "He's the man from the park. He reads the cricket in the funniest voice."

"So, you are the one our Elena's been corresponding with," Edouard said, extending a hand.

"But you've been injured?" Brigitte observed. "My God, that looks awful."

"I was lucky."

"Not lucky enough," Edouard said. "It would have been better had you not been there at all. This war is a terrible business."

"Did it hurt?" Elena said, the rims of her eyes damp with tears held back. She raised her hand slightly, wanting to touch the wound, but drew it back.

"Honestly, I can't remember," I said. "One minute, we were charging up a hill, and the next, I woke in a hospital bed. A soldier from my division saved my life. I never got to thank him."

"Well, you're here now," Brigitte said. "You're alive and well, and that's all that matters. Have you a place to stay?"

"I've only just arrived this afternoon," I said.

"Then you will stay with us."

"You are very kind, madame," I said. "But I am a stranger and wouldn't presume to burden you."

"Nonsense, it's no burden at all," Brigitte said. "You're no stranger to our Elena. And if she vouches for you, then you must be a good egg. Besides, a young man fresh from the front, wounded, no less, sleeping in some shabby hotel? What kind of barbarians would we be if we allowed that?

It won't do. You'll dine with us this evening *and* stay as our guest. I insist."

"Yes, you must stay with us, at least this evening," Edouard concurred.

I could do no more than happily accept their invitation. Madeline was most excited of all and cheerfully requested I read to her that very night. She chattered on gaily as Brigitte and Edouard moved on, leaving the two of us to our privacy. When they'd gone, Elena seated herself on a nearby bench, her head bent low, a damp handkerchief twisting in her fingers. Suddenly, the gallery seemed devoid of the people and we found ourselves all but alone.

"I thought..." she said.

"I know," I said. "They brought me your letters in the hospital. I lay there, trying to find some eloquent words to say, when all I should have been doing was just writing I was all right. You must think me quite selfish."

"I didn't want to believe it. I wanted to believe you were alive, that, somehow, because of me, you would be seen through it all. I thought, if I just kept sending you letters, you would keep sending them to me, and before either of us knew it, the war would be over. It didn't matter what we wrote, just that we maintained our connection. You said my letters gave you hope. Yours did the same for me."

"But then that connection was broken," I said.

"And I felt powerless. It was like I was the loose end of a ribbon thrashing about in the wind. Suddenly, I had no grounding. I fairly hated you for leaving me alone. My God, I feel so ashamed."

"I find it hard to believe someone like you could feel hatred for anything or anyone," I said. "You're guilty of nothing. I'm the one who should be ashamed. If you forgive me, I promise never to do it again."

I took her hand in mine. She allowed me this small gesture for only a moment before she withdrew it.

"We should rejoin the others," she said, composing herself.

I agreed but suggested we take our time, that she permit me the pleasure of fulfilling my promise. We were, after all, in a gallery. Happily, she acceded, and we ambled on, wandering at a lazy pace, talking the pleasant nonsense two lovers do on their first rendezvous until we came before Caravaggio's *La Mort de la Vierge*, where Elena stopped to scrutinize with profound compassion the cold gray body of Mary.

"She does not look to be at peace at all," she said.

"Nor should she be," I said. "Here she is at her most human. But still, her divinity is overshadowed by the frailty of her mortality. Not even the mother of God is saved from the grip of death."

"Again, the red, flowing like blood," Elena said. "But even in death, there is still light shining upon her. Everyone else remains in shadow, but see how she glows? That's to indicate her passage to heaven is assured, isn't it?"

"I suppose that is one way to take it," I said.

"They shouldn't weep at her passing," she said. "They have reason to rejoice. She's to be reunited with her son."

I looked upon the limp body of the virgin, the disheveled hair, the swollen bare feet, and only for the first time noticed the glow of which she spoke. So focused was I on the humiliation of the divine matriarch brought low, the detail had escaped me. The weeping of the apostles, first losing their God, and now His mother, excited the libertine passions for suffering I'd always sought in those who believed. But in the face of Elena's motherly affection for the fallen woman, I felt humbled by the tenderness in her contemplation.

Walking on, we passed de Roucy's *The Entombment of Atala*, the picture of the suicide clutched by her forlorn savage lover.

"Chactas loved Atala, and she him. But her vow of chastity prevented them from being together. In the end, she took her own life because she could not reconcile the two."

"But she did choose love," Elena said. "Only, not the kind you'd expect."

"How so?" I said.

"She was a woman torn between two different forms of love. The physical one, the one she felt for the Indian, would have brought her happiness, but it would have been fleeting. The spiritual love, the one she felt chained to by her modesty, that was the greater of the two. That is the one she died for. To have broken it and succumb to her purely physical desires would have ensured her betrayal of her higher nature. That's why she appears almost Christlike in this image."

"Insightful and beautiful," I said, thoroughly astonished. "I thought you said you knew little of painting. It seems to me you know more than you think."

"You inspired me to study a bit." She smiled. "What is it you see in this?"

"I see only the suffering of Chactas. How he cradles her in his anguish, his sorrow at her loss matched only by his love for her. See how he sits, with his feet already in the grave before she is even lowered in? He's ready to join her in death. He chooses to go first, a choice he no doubt would have made had Atala not beat him to it."

"A choice few men would make, I think," she said.

A few feet away hung Girodet's enormous *Une Scène de Déluge*.

"What horrors," Elena exclaimed. "A man torn between greed and lust."

"We are all lashed in some way as this poor fellow is, are we not?" I said. "A man torn between his past and his future. And like many others before him, his decision comes too late. The branch he clings to is already snapped, so they are all for the drowning."

"That is a gloomy view of it," she said. "Perhaps if they fall, they can survive by floating on the branch."

"Your capacity for hope inspires," I said. "It's a quality I freely admit I am lacking in. I should like to learn, if you'll teach me?"

Now it was Elena's turn to take my hand in hers. The caress of her fingers against mine, I felt I might be dreaming as she squeezed emphatically, passionately, almost.

"I wish to show you one of my favorites," she said, playfully gliding us toward the next room. We stopped before the intense scene of Jacques-Louis David's *Les Sabines*.

"It is beauty come between two armies," she said quietly. "Beauty in all its forms. There, the old woman bares her breast to the warrior as if to say, *Sacrifice me if you must, but spare the children*. And there, another holds up her child to the line of soldiers, and their commander gives the order to hold. The anguish on their faces speaks volumes about their crimes."

"It's the triumph of innocence over evil," I said.

❧

That evening at the Romilly house, Elena, who normally took her meals in her own rooms, as was customary for someone in her position, sat to dine with the rest of the family. Sitting across the table from her, I fought to keep my attentions focused on my hosts, making my conversation light and polite, questioning little, answering vaguely, and affecting an air of humble gratefulness for Romilly's hospitality while he discussed everything from the ongoing situation on the front to the skyrocketing prices of all common goods.

"Elena told us you are a great lover of art," Brigitte said, seeing my eyes repeatedly drift back to my love. "But I must admit, to recite poetry from memory as you did today is quite a feat. I don't believe I've ever heard anyone do it so eloquently who wasn't a professional on the stage."

"It's something I've always had a talent for," I said. "I forget little, if anything at all. Once I've read some lines of prose or poetry, or viewed an image in a gallery, it's captured permanently. I can recall it to perfection at my own command."

"That's a gift I should like to have myself," Edouard said.

"I would argue it is both a gift and a curse," I said. "There are some things I would just as soon expel from memory."

"But it's not just the words," Brigitte continued apropos of my comment. "The way you read them; you imbue them with such emotion. You are quite well spoken, and I find that unusual for young men today. They resonate with feeling as if coming from the voice of a man twice your age. One who has seen something of the world, of its sadness and its joys. It's a feeling I can't quite place."

"You flatter me," I said. "Perhaps I should have chosen a career in the theater?"

"They echo with tragedy," Elena said quietly, giving everyone pause.

"They do," I agreed. "But from tragedy strength is derived. And good is almost always born of it. After all, it was tragedy that brought me to this good table tonight, to sit among you good people."

"Well spoken yet again," Edouard said, saluting me with his glass.

"What will you do now the war is over for you?" Brigitte said.

"I haven't quite decided. I still receive a modest income from some business dealings I had a few years ago. I think I'll be all right."

"And will you stay in Toulouse long?" Elena asked, almost hopeful.

"I'd like to, though if I must speak the truth, Paris has always been my favorite city. It holds a special place in my heart."

"Why is that?" she said.

"Because there is a beauty there not found anywhere else on earth."

"You've the soul of a poet," Brigitte said.

"I suppose if one must have a soul, a poet's is as good as any," I joked. "But Paris's beauty isn't found in its architecture or its gardens or its cathedrals. It's in the people. It's in the bellow of the fruit sellers in Les Halles at four a.m. and in the soot-stained faces of children playing escargot in the streets of Le Maquis. It's in the smile of a pretty girl under a shade tree in the gardens on a sunny afternoon. French girls, you see, they smile like no other girl in the world."

Elena quickly averted her gaze, a gesture not unnoticed by Edouard.

"Well, I, for one, cannot understand what they were thinking making you a soldier," Brigitte said. "There's no place on a battlefield for a man like you. You should be in the Salon, if they ever brought it back to its glory days. You would have fit in marvelously with the Bourbons."

"Oh, I used to attend from time to time," I said, then, catching myself, I joked: "In my mind, I mean. My dreams. Sometimes I think I might have been born in the wrong decade."

❧

After the meal, Elena and the children retired to the drawing room, while Edouard and I adjourned to the study.

"It must have been hell out there," he said, handing me a snifter of cognac. He leaned casually against his desk, studying me while I reviewed the small collection of books displayed on his shelves, noting nothing remarkable among them.

"I've seen hell," I said casually. "It didn't look like that."

"Poetic to the last," he said. "Elena said you were well read, but she didn't say anything about your wit."

"We never got the chance to speak of it. Humor is a gem rarely unearthed in the trench. There's little room for it, or anything else besides bullets and bandages. What else did she tell you?"

"Only good things, I assure you. Though I'm certain she's kept the best bits for herself. Whenever one of your letters arrived, she could hardly contain her joy. Oh, she hid it well, affecting a demure reserve, almost indifferent, really, but it wasn't hard to tell she was hopping like a frog inside. I see Maurice and Camille do the same thing all the time. A father can easily see through his children's façades."

"But Elena is not your daughter," I said.

"She's been with us for almost six years. I think I know her well enough. She wears her heart on her sleeve, though she'd fight you on that. And the children think the world of her."

"They're right to. She is quite special."

"I know," he said, setting his glass aside. "Which is why it would be a shame to lose her to some unfortunate folly. They'd be devastated."

"Monsieur Romilly—"

"Elena is an intelligent, caring, and respectable young woman," he said, cutting me short, though I detected no malice in his voice. Indeed, he spoke with a fatherly affection I found to be admirable. "A rare pearl. She's not my own daughter, but she may as well be. Her father died years ago, so it's fallen on me to see her through as best I can."

"She spoke only highly of you in her letters," I said.

"Then you understand my apprehension. Holding someone in high regard is one thing. But a man is not defined by the thoughts or opinions of others. He's defined by his own actions and how he acquits himself in deed."

"You're afraid my intentions are less than pure," I said. "And you're right to be. It's a father's duty to protect his daughter. But I assure you I have no other designs upon Elena than to love her as she deserves to be loved and make her my wife if she would have me."

"A noble aim," he said. "If not a bit premature. Apart from a few letters, you hardly know each other."

I sipped the last of my cognac, placing the empty glass on the desk.

"I know I love her," I said. "And I believe she feels the same way. What more need there be? My father did not love my mother. I have known what it is to lust after someone, but I never had someone to show me what it is to feel genuine love. It's our right to explore what we feel, to know if it's right and true. The unfortunate folly would be to deny her the opportunity to decide for herself whether we belong together, would it not?"

Romilly solemnly weighed my worth in the scales of his mind. His decision mattered not, for my own mind was set on making Elena mine with or without his blessings. In the end, the logic of my argument prevailed. Refilling both our glasses, he sighed with not unpleasant resignation.

"I'll be heading back to Paris soon," he said. "Work demands it. Tomorrow afternoon, we're taking the children to Castres to visit cousins. Elena will be coming with us. We'll be back on Thursday, but on Fridays, she does not tutor the children and the day is hers to do with as she pleases. You'll be able to visit again then," he said, adding with fatherly emphasis, "but only if she wishes you to. In the meantime, you are welcome to stay here as our guest."

I thanked him for his kindness but said I would make efforts to locate rooms for myself within the city. I was left to embrace the faith that love is a test of both virtue and patience.

Though far from the front, the war's effect was as palpable in Toulouse as everywhere else in the Republic. A somberness had settled over the city. It could be seen on the faces of the people and read on the walls of the storefronts. One merchant, proprietor of a dry-good establishment, scrawled in white chalk across the door panel of his closed shop, *Pray for our family, both sons serving at the front. Vive la France!* Ambulances ferrying the freshly wounded to hospital were a common sight, as were trainloads of newly enlisted men from the provinces—as well as Algerian goumiers—making ready for deployment.

The Beautiful Era had come to an end not with a balletic ascension into a setting sun but with the ugly blast of a cannon shattering its crystalline elegance. The great lady France, with her stately grace and feminine mystique, would be scarred for years to come. It was against this grim backdrop that the happiest days of my life began.

The following morning, I took rooms at L'Hotel de France near the Place du Capitole and immediately brought in tailors from three different houses to furnish me a new wardrobe tout de suite. I ordered fresh flowers delivered to my rooms every day and paid handsomely for a private car and driver. To prepare for our reunion, I reserved a table for dinner and purchased tickets for the Théâtre du Capitole.

Then I waited for Friday and my Elena to return, cursing the cruel twist of fate that I should be reunited with her only to be separated again so quickly. When your heart brims with amorous delectations to excite the soul, a minute apart from the one you cherish is like an hour, an hour a whole day, and four days nearly a decade.

At long last, Friday arrived, a pleasant spring day augured by a clear sky of crisp blue. A boy brought a breakfast of brioche with coffee. A full-length mirror in a silver frame hung beside the window, and I stood before it admiring my new clothes just arrived from the tailors. My mood could not have been gayer knowing in but a few short hours I would be in Elena's presence once again. But as I sat to eat, a sudden and most unpleasant chill rose through my spine, spreading like icy fingers gripping my torso, enrobing me in a cold I had known only once before but at once recognized with utter contempt and horror.

"Why have you returned?" I spat, dropping my food, my buoyant mood irrevocably darkened.

He would not show himself, choosing instead to remain a silent, frigid presence like an invisible fog.

"I will hold no discourse with the thin air," I said. "Make yourself seen or get away from here. We've nothing to discuss."

"On the contrary," he said, his voice so close over my shoulder, I thought I even felt his infernal breath on my neck. "I come bearing valuable advice."

His voice came from the mirror in which he stood, a disgusting reflection of my own presence. Where there should have been my image was instead his revolting form.

"Will this do?" he said.

"Hardly," I said. "Is this another attempt to mock me? Do you try to show me how similar we are? If so, you fail poorly."

"I wouldn't dream of it," he said, affecting an innocent air. Then, casually, as one might pass unencumbered through an open doorway, he stepped through the surface of the glass into the room.

"Marvelous things," he said, admiring the intricate scrollwork framing the mirror. "Did you know that man made these before he made the wheel? Millennia have been consumed by your vanity, but not without some benefit. We used to just peer through them at your kind. But now, your industrious natures always thinking of the grander scale, they make excellent facilitators of travel."

"There are no mirrors in hell?"

"Of course, there are," he said. "Sin is but a reflection of the soul. *Thinkest thou* that pride dies with the body? You've not forgotten your Byron. Have you already forgotten our last visit?"

"Scoundrel! What are you here for?"

"You've been a busy little bee, Etienne," he said. "Or is it Sébastien now? Should have considered staying Etienne. *He* never would have sent himself to get shot. Tell me, what was it like? Was the sensation of your life draining away everything you'd hoped it would be?"

"You'd have sooner seen me die than see our agreement through?"

"Perish the thought," he said. "Besides, you were never in any real danger. Our arrangement remains intact. In fact, it is that which brings me here."

"You've come too early. I've still nine years before the odious task needs completing again," I said.

"Ah yes, the indolent Polachev. I'd nearly forgotten. Such an easy target, though, I really should cry foul. His conversion cost you practically no effort at all."

"Your reason for being here already," I said, losing the last of my patience. "If you come in the form of a messenger, then deliver the message and enough with your witless banter. If you come in the form of my *humble servant*, then you've nothing I want, so I dismiss you. Either way, state your business and be on your way."

"I come in the form of counselor," he said, casually taking the chair opposite mine. "Your actions of late arouse my curiosity, nothing more. I simply wish to remind you of your obligations, so as not to cause a premature termination of our contract."

"And how would that be?"

"Tell me, this lovely creature Elena you pursue—"

"Do not speak her name!" I shouted, nearly upending the table in my rage.

"What do you possibly hope to gain by this endeavor?" he went on, unperturbed. "Love is a dangerous emotion best left to the more experienced. It is quite inharmonious with someone in your situation. Frankly, I fail to see what makes this girl different than any other of your previous conquests."

"It's of no concern to you," I said. "My reasons and motives are my own. What does the devil care?"

"I care for the preservation of our agreement," he said. "Tell me, how do you intend to explain your unchanging nature to her? Financial wealth comes and goes; it can be easily explained away. But what about in ten years, or twenty, when you've not aged a day and her youth fades before her own eyes? How will you reconcile that, under an oath of secrecy? Breach the oath, and you forfeit your happiness and your soul."

"I know full well my obligations, you need not remind me."

"Then you see my cause for concern. It is in our interests the agreement reaches its natural conclusion, and we receive our seven agreed-upon souls. Renege, and there can only be the steepest of consequences. Commitment to any one soul, especially one no doubt bound for heaven, is antithetical to these ends."

"Perhaps I am only exploring love as yet another sensual experience. Have you considered that? To obtain from it the pleasure it excites and nothing more?"

"We both know it not the case," he said.

"You have said your piece," I said. "And if you've aimed to darken my day, then you've succeeded beyond measure. If there's nothing more, be off, and never return. Leave me to my own affairs."

"You are dismissing me, then?" he said. "Consider your words carefully, for as a humble servant, I am bound to obey the one to whom I am indentured. Send me away now, and I vow to never return until our business is concluded."

"If you wish to serve, then you best serve by vanishing from my sight. I will see you no more."

Acknowledging my desires this time not with a bow but a shrug, the demon quietly rose and, stepping back again through the mirror from whence he'd come, faded into nothingness, the violent chill of damnation vanishing with him.

The vile specter's visit after so many years indelibly fouled my mood. I looked upon my uneaten breakfast with disgust. Even my appetite had been repulsed by his presence.

Instead of pangs of hunger, I felt the hot swell of indignation filling me as I paced about the room quietly seething. Idle hands are the devil's workshop. I absently picked up a coffee cup from the table and carried it about, turning it over in my palm. When again in my ranging I happened before the mirror, a horrendous sight met my eye and fixed me to the spot; I saw not my normal reflection but rather a mere shadow of it, as if where I stood in that opposite room there were not me but the absence of me, a shade with definition and boundary, but wholly without substance, without depth, without life. I gasped in horror and shut my eyes tight against the sight of this hideous *not* me, doomed to roam hell's barren wastes for all eternity. Paralyzed with dread, I hurled the cup at the damnable thing, shattering both with a tremendous crash and raising an alarm throughout the hotel. A moment later, a porter burst through the door.

"Are you all right, sir?" he said, seeing the ruin of glass strewn about the floor. "What has happened?"

Behind the empty frame, there remained only bare wall. Relief overtook me. The apparition had been eradicated.

"I'm fine," I said, collecting myself. "It was an accident."

❧

My foul mood only abated upon my arrival at the Romilly home later that evening where the sight of Elena banished all memory of the miserable morning's affairs.

Wearing a dress of ivory chiffon and lace printed with flowers in Prussian blue, she looked the pure vision of tender modesty sitting patiently on the velvet cushions of the sofa, like a pearl nestled in a great jewelry box. Edouard and Brigitte waited with her listening to Caruso sing sweetly from the brass horn of a Victor phonograph.

"Are you unwell?" Elena said, the remnants of the morning's disconcerting events still lingering about my face. "You look troubled."

I dismissed her concerns pleasantly, assuring her all was fine.

"Where are you off to?" Edouard said.

"I thought perhaps dinner and the theater? They're putting on *Horace*."

"I've not been before," she said.

"Then it should make for a splendid evening," Edouard said.

"But perhaps I should change, then? If I had known, I would have worn something more appropriate, though I'm afraid I really don't have anything so formal as for the theater."

"I think I might have something lying about to suit you," Brigitte said. "If the gentleman wouldn't mind waiting?"

"Not at all."

"It's really not necessary, madame," Elena said, a blush filling her cheeks and the opalescent skin of her throat. But it was too late. With motherly bearing, Brigitte had already taken Elena under the arm.

"Nonsense," she said, guiding her out of the room. "Edouard and I may not be much for the theater these days, but I'm sure I've just the thing for an evening in the box. Oh, you should have a marvelous time. Once, before Maurice was born, I attended a performance of..."

Their conversation drifted off as they passed up the stairs. Romilly poured me a drink and recounted the evening he took his wife to see *Cyrano de Bergerac*. I listened attentively, the dutiful suitor, all the while impatiently stirring for my beloved's return. Ten minutes later, she descended the stairs in a gown of dark-mauve silk tulle with creamy chiffon and lace sleeves set off with glistening pearl sequins. The striking contrast of her auburn hair, dark brows, and ivory skin against the purple fabric immediately suggested to me the beauty of Godward's *Tambourine Girl*. Standing there, bashful in her resplendence, she was nothing short of pure art come to life, the synthesis of imagination and inspiration made flesh.

❧

At dinner, I spoke like a man who'd only just then discovered the sound of his own voice and found it ringing with a tone insincerity. I talked of elegance and beauty, but it all felt so unnatural, pompous, and artificial. I felt myself a fraud. Elena listened attentively, rapt, even, her face curious at times, pleasantly amused at others.

I chattered on, trying to pour out what few details of my life I safely could to her over that one meal, struggling for the right word, sounding foolish most of the time. It was hard to speak truthfully about anything. I couldn't tell of my time at university, or of seeing the opening of Eiffel's magnificent tower. I wanted to tell her of the singular wonder of being the first to view *Le Voyage dans la Lune* or of standing among thousands to witness the first descent of the great ball of electric light over New York's Times Square usher in the year of our Lord 1908. I'd seen the *Maine* burn in Havana harbor and heard the shots that felled McKinley. But these would be for my memories alone. The more I spoke, the more I realized I'd been living a life heretofore bereft of meaning or purpose, one built on cheap illusions and hollow premises.

"I'm sorry," I said after a time. "I feel a bit doltish, nattering on like an imbecile, trying to find the right words. It was much easier to write them than it is to speak them."

She looked slightly bemused.

"It's important for you, isn't it?" she said. "To always know what to say."

"I suppose it is."

"And when you don't?"

I paused to consider.

"When I don't, it's as if something has been stolen from me. I've used words my whole life like other people use money. They're my currency. When they don't come, I feel as though I've been robbed."

"When I was a little girl, my father used to tell me knowing the right thing to say and saying the right thing make for very different men."

"Those were wise words," I said. "He must have been a philosopher."

"A gardener. Which is a philosopher in a way, I suppose."

"How so?"

"Tending to a garden requires patience," she said. "It takes years to cultivate. Just as it does to establish a philosophy. You have to wait and let the flowers, like thoughts, bloom in their own time."

"When I was growing up," I said, "my family had a coach driver like that. I remember him saying once the space separating a truth from a lie is only as wide as the space between your tongue and your teeth."

"He must have been a bit of scoundrel to hold such a view," she said with a laugh that instantly refreshed the air.

"He was," I said. "Unconventional too. But he did teach me a great deal about people. Maybe even more than my father did. He used to take me with him on little gambling jaunts. I think he thought me a good-luck piece.

"You know, your father was quite right. I have spent a great deal of my life talking, and saying the right things has gotten me far, farther than I ever could have thought possible. But sitting here with you, I feel like it's all just been dumb luck, that I've known all along the right thing to say should have been no when instead I said yes, that things I should have accepted with grace I instead impetuously refused with vigor. I regret many of the decisions I've made."

She furrowed her brow. I feared I'd irrevocably darkened the mood.

"I think regret is a sort of lantern in the dark," she said after a moment. "It's best used to illuminate the way forward. It sheds a brief light on our past errors, but by letting us see them more clearly, it prevents us from making those same mistakes twice."

"An optimistic view," I said. "Sadly, my light has never been bright enough. I've never been very good at learning from my missteps."

"The past can't change," she said. "For better or worse, it has made us who we are. We can only work to change who we will become tomorrow. There is always time to learn."

The night was warm, and the square of the Place du Capitole filled with amblers taking the air. Waiting among the crowd in the foyer of the Théâtre du Capitole, I elaborated on the plot of *Horace* for Elena when a second unwelcome specter of my past threatened to destroy the gay mood of the evening.

A gentleman of about fifty, tall, ruddy cheeked, and heavily mustached abruptly approached, a look of pure astonishment on his face.

"*Mon Dieu*!" he exclaimed loudly, drawing many eyes. "It is you! But how is this possible?"

"*Je vous demande pardon*," I said. "Do I know you?"

"L'Hérétique!" he said. "You are l'Hérétique!"

Gripped with terror, my body became as rigid as a stone. Hearing that name once again struck me in the chest like an icy fist, forcing the breath from my lungs.

"How dare you!" Elena said quickly, rising to my defense with a vigor I did not think her capable of possessing.

"I beg a thousand pardons, mademoiselle," he said. "I could not help but forget myself." Then, turning back to me: "But you do not remember me? Le Banquet des Châtaignes? The most exquisite fête Paris has ever seen. It is I, Sextus Tarquinius!"

"Monsieur, I have no idea what you are talking about," I said, turning about, frantically seeking a means of escape. "You must have me mistaken for someone else."

"But how is it you are still so young?" he continued, insinuating himself before me like a great oak barring the path forward. "Certainly, it is you, though. A man does not forget such a night, nor its host."

"Sir, I tell you, you are mistaken," I said, the sudden rancor in my voice taking him aback, the tenor of which drew more unwelcome eyes. I thought for certain I heard the unfortunate name whispered on the fringes of the crowd. Seizing the opportunity to flee, I led Elena past everyone and into the theater to our seats.

"What a foul oaf of a man," she said as we settled into our box. "To call you such a vulgar term. He must be mad. And what was he talking about? Chestnuts?"

"Quite mad," I said, my nerves shattered. Everywhere, I felt the eyes of strangers upon me. Like a nightmare, I was sure everyone at the theater knew me by my former sobriquet. All around I swore I heard their whispers, their quiet murmurs behind finely gloved hands, hands concealing viperous tongues.

They say he's as mad as the March Hare. I heard he kept a cross of Saint Andrew in his boudoir he lashed his women to. But look how young he has remained. Could that really be the Heretic? Who is she, though? I thought he was dead. Surely, a man as reckless as he should have met a bad end by now. So young still. I don't recall a scar, though. She's quite beautiful, even for a harlot. I once saw him cane the flesh off a girl's backside in full view of a hundred people just because she asked him to. Like he's not aged a day. Must be in league with dark powers. Poor girl.

Seeing my discomfiture, Elena placed her hand over mine. Through her soft caress, the tension gripping my brain, squeezing it like an apple in a cider press, relented. In the dim light of the theater box, her face glowed amber, bearing an expression of motherly tenderness. I placed my hand over hers, the creamy suppleness of her skin yielding to the press of my palm. The voices vanished. I felt as if to cry.

"I have so much I want to tell you," I said. "But I don't know where to begin."

"There will be plenty of time for that," she said.

By midsummer, with the western front stagnant and the Schlieffen Plan failed, Romilly moved the family back to Paris once again to resume overseeing his factory. I followed not far behind.

I resolved to see Elena every day, paying regular call to the home to pass a pleasant afternoon. Often we would meet in a café or walk the boulevards lining the Seine. When her duties to the children occupied her and kept me away, I sat in my rooms scrawling long letters of devotion by the window, sometimes posting two a day. When next we met, she would tell me how receiving them pleased her so.

Sometimes we spoke of passion, of sadness, of strength, and of faith. Other times, we spoke of trivial things. Sometimes we laughed at the absurdity of the world, and sometimes we marveled at its beauty and wondrousness.

I listened while she told me stories from her days at school: what she'd hoped to become, where she'd hoped to someday go. The idea of leisure travel was foreign to her, but she'd dreamed of one day visiting the far-off exotic climes she read about in the works of Verne and Kipling. We'd walk amid flowers in the Parc de Bagatelle, and I'd tell her about seeing entire hillsides in the south of India awash in purple kurinji, the flower that blooms only once every twelve years. I told her we would have to wait another seven years to witness its reappearance, but I would happily roam those valleys again, hand in hand with her, so she might see for herself the majesty of a sunrise over amethyst slopes covered in so many blooms it looks as if the whole world were covered in a fresh coating of fluffy violet snow. She made me promise then and there to take her.

Months passed in such days of happiness as these. Each time we parted, my heart died but a little, only to be revived again at our next encounter. To the east, the damnable war dragged on in the countryside, in the communes and hamlets, but there, in Paris, the fighting seemed farther and farther away. With the means at my disposal, I endeavored to never let it touch our lives again. Instead of mud and bandages and smoke and flames, our days were filled with the light of friendship and laughter. My love for Elena grew deeper with each passing day.

We celebrated her twenty-fifth birthday, and at the Romilly home, I surprised one and all by presenting her with a gift, a simple diamond set in a band of gold. There before Edouard and Brigitte, I declared my love and asked she be my wife.

It was December 1915.

❧

"Tell me a secret," Elena said playfully.

The wedding was only a few weeks away. We strolled the avenue near the Place des Vosges talking of silly things. The patrol planes had taken a brief respite, and the crisp April air felt cleaner for their absence.

"What kind of secret?"

"Tell me something you've not told me before. Something you've not told anyone."

I thought for a moment, making a great show of concentration.

"I'm absolutely terrified of lions," I said.

"I'm being serious." Elena laughed, nudging me with her shoulder.

"What's not to believe about that?"

"I know you, Sébastien Chollet," she said. "And I know you're lying. You're not afraid of anything. So, come on, then, tell me a secret. A real secret."

I puzzled briefly, then looked at the gold ring on her finger, the band symbolizing the link that would bind us together forever.

"I never believed I would find someone to love," I said, "or who would love me."

"Why should you think that?"

"For a long time, I didn't even think about it—love, I mean. For a long time, I just accepted my life would necessarily be a solitary one. I was not particularly looking for love."

"What was it you were looking for?"

"Meaning, I suppose," I said. "Or maybe freedom *from* meaning. I always thought it necessary to abandon conventions like love, commitment, dedication. It's like this ring," I said, fingering the small diamond. "Taken as a whole, it is a thing of marvel and beauty, and for most, that is sufficient. But look closer and you can see all the individual faces, each reflecting separate and distinct. That is how I've always looked at life. Each face must be seen, felt, and explored in order to appreciate the whole. But somewhere I lost sight of the diamond and became hopelessly lost in the prism of those reflections. I had a friend once who tried to explain this to me. He said it would be impossible for me to be loved by anyone because I remained too focused on myself and refused to have faith in anything or anyone else."

"But you do believe?" she said. "Don't you?"

"He wasn't speaking of religious faith," I said. "Though he himself had it. No, I think he meant faith of any kind. Faith that life was more than just the sum of experience, that I could and should put my trust in someone other than myself. I admit, at the time, I did not. I trusted only in myself and my perceptions."

"And now?"

"Now I see he was more right than I could have possibly imagined. He was a true friend, but I was too blinded by my own vanity to see. I only wish I were able to tell him. If he saw me here now, with you, it would please him so."

"What's stopping you?"

"I was wretched to him. We haven't spoken in many years. I'm not even sure he's still in Paris. I wouldn't know where to begin looking for him."

"Perhaps one day Providence will reunite you," she said. "I do believe people rarely meet if not for a reason, even if they themselves don't know what the reason is."

"If that's so, then what reason brought you and me together?"

"You needed rescuing." She smiled. "Everyone does from time to time."

We crossed the Seine, sauntering lazily arm in arm until we made our way to the Quai Voltaire lined with the stalls of the *bouquinistes* selling their stacks of used magazines, worn-through maps, and tomes of a bygone era.

An old hawker sat upon a rickety wooden folding chair before his box of books. A ragged top hat rested back on his balding head, and between thick purple lips, hiding in the forest of a great gray beard, he puffed a large, curved pipe. Through beady, wizened eyes, he observed us walking past and called out in a singsong voice.

"Mon coeur a-t-il aimé jusqu'à ce moment? Protestez du contraire, mes yeux, car jusqu'à cette nuit je n'avais jamais vu la veritable beauté."

"Cet homme doit être un Montaigu!" I called back. The old colporteur chuckled and tipped his worn hat.

"Perhaps a book for the beautiful mademoiselle?" he persisted. "I have here a volume of Desbordes-Valmore, for you, monsieur, that you might recite from on your wedding night."

"I prefer *Les Fleur du mal*," I said.

"Ah, what pleasure it must be to a woman to suffer for the one she loves!" he said, quoting Balzac, feigning an attack of the heart. "Do not let him treat you so, mademoiselle. Do not let him subject you to such rank offense as Baudelaire. Demand better."

"Perhaps this, then," I said, turning to Elena, staring deeply into her eyes. *"Dans sa beauté reposent à la fois ma mort et ma vie."*

"Ah, a Frenchman through and through," he said. "Handsome, educated, and sad. Sad beyond all measure. Marry him, girl. Marry this one today, for you will never find another like a true son of tragedy. Eat of his poetry and drink of his eyes. *Parce que demain, demain nous mourrons."*

"Mightn't there be any time for us to be merry first?" Elena said as we walked on, leaving the odd little Senex to tend to his books.

We crossed the Pont Neuf and walked the stairs down to the Square du Vert-Galant to admire the early sunset.

"It's your turn," I said as we seated ourselves on a bench.

"My turn?" Elena said.

"To tell me a secret."

"A woman should always be allowed to keep a few," Elena said. "Lest the allure of our mystique be diminished."

"I'm not asking for all, just one."

She looked off into the middle distance, her eyes squinted against the orange light of the setting sun. She started to speak, then hesitated, then finally started again.

"Once, I fell in love with a boy from the village where we were living. He was twelve, a schoolboy. Auguste Fournier."

"And you?"

"I was eight years old," she said, the memory evoking a smile. "It was a childish obsession. Papa had found work at a chateau near Blois. We moved often in those days, so it was nice to settle in one place for a little while. Auguste was the cook's son. He was a handsome boy, with bright-blond hair and wonderfully blue eyes, but sickly. He suffered from an ailment that kept him inside almost all the time. I'd usually see him seated in the kitchen helping his mother. But sometimes, when the sickness that always seemed to have its hands wrapped around him would mysteriously release its grip for a brief time, I saw him at play with the other boys from his school. Then they'd run off on adventures, chasing through the streets of the village after some imaginary treasure or pretending to be knights-errant battling each other for the king's favor. Sometimes I would trail behind. He was smaller than the other boys, but twice as brave, and to my eight-year-old eyes, he looked a hundred feet tall. When he'd mount a bench or barrel pretending to be astride his mighty steed, I used to imagine it was my rescue he was riding to."

"And what became of this childish obsession," I said.

"He died," she said. "I cried for days, in secret. It was my first real exposure to death. My mother died when I was too young to really know what had happened. But with Auguste, it was different."

"Eight is too young to face death," I said.

"I could not understand why he should have died. Yes, he was ill, but there were so many times I would see him full of life and vigor, as if there were nothing in the world wrong with him. It didn't make any sense. My father tried to console me. I think he suspected my affections for him. He said Auguste had a *brittle* soul, strong but fragile."

Like a note played just half a beat too slow, one perhaps inaudible to any but the most highly trained ear, one that destroys the melody of the whole symphony, so did that word strike such an odd chord in me as to throw the entire harmony of my thoughts out of balance.

"Someone once said that very thing about my mother when she died," I said absently.

"My father said it was something my mother used to say often," Elena said. "But he said she had an unusual way of describing people."

Slowly, as if viewed through the light of a solitary candle expelling its last breath of flame before extinguishing in a pool of milky melted wax, disjointed thoughts and voices and memories began assembling themselves like puzzle pieces in my mind. I saw the muddied envelopes containing the letters she'd sent to the trenches, the elegant curve of the script describing her name Elena Jubert scrawled across their faces. I saw a mysterious figure with sunbaked leathery skin, graying stubble sprouting from sunken cheeks, and dirt-smeared chin beneath a straw hat. Her father, the itinerant gardener, widowed and cast out of his home with his only child by his side. I saw Lipa weeping at my mother Aline's own *brittle* soul. And I saw the letter, received so many years ago begging for aid and dismissed with disgust, written in the simple hand of the uneducated provincial, the letter signed with a name bearing no meaning for me. Hugo Jubert!

My thoughts raced back, returning to my old family home, fresh from my first year of study in Paris. The stink of the ocean and unwelcome harbinger of the unpleasant meeting soon to be had with my father. Lipa greeting me at the door, welcoming me home like my mother should have done but was incapable of doing. Remarking on how much she changed in my youthful eyes, she fairly beamed with delight as she presented me with her new treasure: a cherubic infant swaddled in yellow linen, an infant with bright-brown eyes and the promise of future beauty.

"My Yelena," she'd said. "I called her after Madame, your mother."

I leapt to my feet, my mind reeling.

"What's wrong?" she said as I leaned on the balustrade at the edge of the water. I became dizzy, the world about me spinning like a top. I pressed my hands to the stone. Elena rushed to my side, placing a soothing hand on my shoulder, bringing the spinning to a halt.

Looking down, I caught sight of my reflection in the murky waters, so still by the stone abutment, I thought of Narcissus, who loved only himself and through his contempt of the love of others so ruined the nymph Echo.

"I've another secret to tell you," I said. "But it isn't one so easily bared."

She said nothing, only lay her hand gently over mine.

"You said once your father was a kind man, but sad. I believe I know why."

"What do you mean?" she said.

"I was because of me. I was the cause of his unhappiness. Yours as well."

"Sébastien, that doesn't make any sense," she said. "I don't understand. We should sit—"

"My name isn't Sébastien," I said. "It's Etienne. Etienne Allard. I knew your father many years ago."

"What are you talking about," she said, her face overcome with concern. She placed a hand on my cheek as the blood rushed from my face. "Are you feeling well? You're not making any sense."

"Listen to me," I said, seizing her hand with a brusqueness that took her by surprise. "He asked me for money, after your mother died, and I refused. I refused, and he was driven out of my family home. It was my fault. I sold it. I shouldn't have, but I hated it. I hated *him*."

"You hated my father?"

"*My* father," I said. "Don't you see? It was because of me. It was all because of me. Didn't he ever tell you?"

Words fell fast from my lips, a jumble of fragments of the past only coherent to me. She did not understand. I could not make her understand. The more I spoke, the more her face paled, the more she must have thought me a madman.

I told her everything. I spoke of my childhood and how her mother raised me. I spoke of holding her as an infant in my arms. I told her of my mother and my father, how I grew to despise them. I spoke of Dumont, and Vallaton, and of years lived under the shadow of an all-consuming pride. I told her about her father's letter and the callousness with which I'd dismissed it, that I, and I alone, was the cause of all her troubles. And I told her of Kazakov and of my infernal bargain.

But I didn't stop there. I couldn't stop. Something within me would not allow it. I told her everything. I spoke of revenge, of breaking the will of men, of betrayal, of murder. All of it, all the evils I had wrought in the name of my own pride, all flowed from me like so much water from a burst dam.

When it was done, when the truth lay bare like a cold corpse between us, Elena said nothing. The sun had set on Paris, and despite the mild day, night brought an unwelcome chill. She'd gradually recoiled during my tale and stood apart from me. It was only then I'd noticed, so lost was I in the telling.

I looked at my beloved, so small and innocent, the gulf between us grown insurmountably wide, her face awash in dread. I stepped toward her, but quickly, she stepped back.

I wanted to call to her, but overhead, the leaves of the walnut trees shifted in the night breeze. Their rustle masking a terrible sound, one I knew too well, though its hideous shrill had rung in my ear but only once before. Searching the branches, I chased around, furiously seeking the source, only too late sighting the icy blue-gray stare of the accursed daw.

"*Tchyak, tchyak!*"

I looked back, but Elena had already retreated up the stone stairs. She ran down the Pont Neuf toward the Right Bank. I gave chase, calling her name, my heart struck with terror at the sight of the bird wheeling overhead. She stopped at the Quai du Louvre and tried to hail a passing taxi when, from out of the night sky, the infernal thing swooped down in a great arc at remarkable speed, beating its wing against her ear and sending her reeling into the avenue, into the path of the passing traffic. It all happened so fast, there was no time to stop. A woman screamed. Men ran to help, but there was nothing to be done. I raced to catch up but could only bear helpless witness to the terrible aftermath. My Elena, my beloved, lay dead in the street.

Chapter XIV

A droplet of water patted softly upon the open pages on Al's lap, then another, and another. The sporadic first taps of an approaching rain drew his eyes to the skies. Once clear midday had given way to an encroaching twilight, bringing with it an unwelcome chill and the threat of a storm. He didn't know how long he'd been at reading, but the sudden realization that it had been several hours drew him to his feet with urgency. Zofia would be furious at his absence, but even more so to be feared was the possibility of being trapped in the shadow of that gloomy place of desolation and death once the final rays of sun dissipated. With haste, Al snatched up the book, pulled his coat tight to his chest, and made for the main road.

Night had long fallen when he finally crept up the steps to the apartment, and in his heart of hearts, he'd hoped to find Zofia already in bed fast asleep, that he could avoid the unpleasantness of her castigations. But opening the door, he found her not in bed but waiting for him with damp eyes and ready persecutions.

"Where have you been, Albie?" she said, the breadth of her exasperation belying her small stature. "What is becoming of you? You leave work in the middle of the day? You don't tell Ollie where you are going? You don't tell me where you are going? For hours, you have been gone, and now you sneak back into your own home like some kind of *zlodziej*."

Al lay his coat over the back of his chair and sat down. He tossed his hat on the table. Zofia stood over him waiting for his response. She did not wish to be angry with him, couldn't remember the last time she even might have been. But now, her husband's silence drove her former worry toward vexation.

"This is not how you behave," she said. "It is this wretched man who makes you do these things."

But in his mind, Al was already far away from his apartment, from his shop, from his wife. Since he'd left the manor, he could find no focus other than upon the last words he'd read. Along the path back to the road, in the taxi, aboard the train, even up the stairs to his home, in his thoughts, he'd drifted over the vast expanse of the great, wide ocean, over landscapes unfamiliar yet somehow not unknown, past villages tucked between rolling hills, over fields still scarred by the fires of war and death, to a city bathed in the glimmer of streetlamps and abuzz with the footfalls of pedestrians rushing to a scene of despair. He felt himself push through this crowd of onlookers, all huddled about and murmuring, jostling for a better view of the macabre tableau playing out before them.

He could not help but feel he were looking at a painting hanging in a gallery done by an old master. Before him, the broken body of a most delicate girl hung limp in the arms of his friend kneeling in a frozen agony among the shocked and grim spectators come to witness the death of beauty and light. While up above, a palpable presence—not unlike that which threatened to consume him while he sat praying over his own love that once so recently lay withering away— pressed upon him.

He dare not look at its face to feel the icy stare boring into him. No effort was necessary. It sought him out among the crowd, lording over its cruel victory of the soul. That accursed bird, with oily wings spread like open arms, laughed, actually laughed, at the misery it had wrought, its bony beak parted wide to loose a sinister cackle into the night air, announcing the death of love and the birth of madness.

"Will you say nothing to me?" Zofia said, drawing Al back from this nightmarish vision.

"*Calamitous ruin,*" he muttered, letting the words die as a whisper on his lips.

"What?"

For some seconds, he did not reply, a vacant vagueness plaguing his eyes as they sought their focus on the middle distance.

"When you were asleep," he finally began. "In the hospital, I mean. When you were asleep, what was it like?"

"What do you mean?"

"Did you feel anything? See anything? Could you hear me talking to you?"

"I don't remember," Zofia said.

"Try," Al pressed, taking her hands in his. "Try to remember. Did you know I was beside you? Could you feel me when I took your hand in mine?"

"Why are you asking me this?"

He gently pressed her hands in his, then let them drop to her sides.

"I could feel nothing then," he said. "I tried, but it was as if you had already gone. I did not think I could feel more alone. And then, in the shul..."

"What?" Zofia asked, lowering herself beside him, concern usurping her former disquiet.

He struggled to find the words to bring form to his thoughts.

"It is easy to believe," he started, "that the evil men do is so much of their own making. That God puts a path in front of each of us, and all we must do is follow it and we will be happy and healthy. To turn from this path would be foolish. There are things put in our way, some say to test us, maybe, but this, I do not know for sure. Are these things put here by God? This also, I am now not so sure of.

"When our Henry died, I did not think about such things. There was no time. What was done was done. He had not even known what it was to live, and somehow this made it easier. But it was not easy at all. It was not for a long time that I was able to forgive God for taking our son from us. For many years, I cried. You did not know this, because I did not want you to see. I kept this from you because, as your husband, I am not supposed to let you see this pain. I am supposed to be the strong one, the one who leads us on the way set before us by God. So even through my sadness, I did not turn from this path."

"Now you are being the foolish one," Zofia said. "To think that this is your responsibility alone. I am your wife, Albie."

"And I am supposed to keep you safe," Al continued. "I could not do that for Henry. I did not have the chance. So, when I thought God was going to take you from me too, I grew angry with him, thought to fight him. This path we have walked for so long, and now he would have me go on without my son, without you? It was not fair. So, in the shul, I thought to ask for a chance to save you. That you should go on living, no matter what the price. And that is when I felt it."

"What did you feel?"

Al took his wife's hands again suddenly, almost frightening her with the swiftness of his movement, the fear in his eyes setting her atremble.

"I did not know what it was then, but I do now," he said. "And it is only because of that man that I, too, did not fall under its trap. Don't you see? He saved me. I do not know why he did it. I don't think he knows himself why, but he did. And for this, I am indebted to him. He is owed my help."

"This does not make any sense," Zofia said. "Saved you from what? What are you talking of?"

"It is enough only that you should know I owe him a debt," Al said. "I don't expect you to understand this, but I do expect that you trust me when I tell you I cannot leave him alone when he is surrounded by so much grief. You do trust me, don't you?"

She could see there was little she could do to argue. Al's sincerity, while earnest, did little to dispel her concerns, but she knew as well he would never willingly place himself or her in danger. For more than forty years, she knew that once he'd set himself upon a task, he would see it through no matter how much work it required. In the end, she could only relent.

❧

That night, Zofia lay a weary head on her pillow, a head swirling with unanswered questions and dancing with fantastic visions of the Frenchman's wild face, twisted and grotesque as it had been on the night he'd stormed into their lives. She thought Al bewitched, caught under the spell of a dybbuk, like her great-uncle Olek once was. And with Olek, it had taken two rabbis four days and nearly an entire barrel of doppelbock to bring him back to himself.

These phantasms, and other memories, plagued her restless sleep, while out in the sitting room, beneath the glow of a table lamp, Al, who himself could find no peace, reopened the tale of Etienne's trials, and began once again to read.

Chapter XV

If it is possible that a soul should weep, then mine wept. And if there should be left an indelible mark upon it, then it was the vision of her virtuous face, an expression of serene calm amid the chaos of her earthly death that had burned itself onto mine. I carry it with me always.

I clutched that angelic face to my breast in the green turbid waters of the gutter and cried out in anguish a cry so great and horrendous hell should tremble and heaven take heed. Hot tears seared my cheeks, and I bit my lips so as to tear them from my face.

There were the whispers of the crowd and the whistle of the approaching police.

And there was the revolting bird.

It perched upon a nearby light post, like a great clown of hell, laughing at me, mocking me, standing proud over the terrible vengeance it had wrought.

In that hideous laugh, I saw it had lied. There would be no end to the contract, my soul would not be forfeit. That was its plan all along, that Elena should die and I, I should remain to suffer endless years tormented by the memory of what I had done and what would never be.

Two gendarmes pushed their way forward through the crowd. With my eye still fixed on the daggerlike stare of the daw, I leapt to my feet and seized one of their sidearms from its holster, racing past everyone to launch a volley of fire upon it. A woman screamed; men shielded their wives. In an instant, the soldiers were upon me, wrenching the gun from my grip. They wrestled me to the ground, but I would not be stopped, so filled was I with rage. Seeing no other means, one struck me hard against the side of the head with the butt of his rifle. What came next was enveloping blackness and the fading *tchyak* of my enemy as it flew unscathed into the starless night.

They laid her to rest in the Cimetière Saint-Vincent. I was not there, nor have I ever since visited her tomb. I left Paris, swearing never to return to the city I so loved for fear I might go completely mad. So stricken by my anguish, I let cowardice reign, and where a braver man might have faced his pain, I fled from it as a horse bolts from a barn fire.

For two years, I wandered in mourning, passing through cities and towns, from country to country, directionless, without purpose or feeling. Each new dawn brought a fresh reminder of my sentence. My suffering continued unabated.

In Madrid, I tried to murder myself, the first of many attempts that only ended in humiliation. For months after her death, I barely ate or drank, discovering even hunger and thirst would not kill me, trapped as I was in bondage to the devil. My body withered, but its strength always returned. I tore out my hair, it grew back as black and soft as new. In agonizing fits of rage, I broke all the teeth out of my head only to find them grow back as white as when I was a child. I took blades to my skin, etching my body like a stone to bury the pain of loss beneath the superficial suffering of mere physical torture. The wounds healed, leaving my body a living road-map of torment. I cut deeper, but they healed all the same. And still, I did not die. Each time I awoke to the unrelenting nightmare that even if I could, I should never be reunited with my Elena, not in this life or the next. For as surely as I was damned, she surely resided within the empyrean, a place forever unattainable to my fracture soul.

There, in the depths of my gloom, when the emptiness of my soul rang at its most hollow, I swore vengeance upon the devil.

❦

As the war sputtered to its end, I found myself in Constantinople on the eve of the French and British arrival. They would come on foot, on horseback, and in great metallic beasts upon the sand and the water, in the uniform of the conqueror bearing the flag of victory at its vanguard.

I would enter the city as a beggar in the company of thieves traveling in a small caravan I met along the road from Edirne—Bulgar gypsies chased down from their homes in the hills, forced to drift aimlessly on the tides of time like myself. Unwashed and unshaven, I described a man long on the road, no closer to his destination and no further from the nightmare he was running from.

Sleeping in doorways at night and passing the days on my knees, eating scraps from the gutter like a dog, I remained for days with neither thought nor desire to move. Finding refuge in the shade near the Sahaflar Kapısı, the secondhand bookseller's gate on the northern edge of the Grand Bazaar, I watched passersby in fez and colorful dimiye shuffle about the place when my ear caught the sound of a familiar dialect rising above the general noise.

Its owner, a middle-aged Russian, dressed finely and speaking with the haughty eloquence of a well-paid servant in a foreign land deigning to converse with the local rabble, loudly questioned one of the booksellers, an old, leathery-skinned, walleyed Arab. Condescension hung heavy from his every word.

"But you said three days, and it has been three days," the little Muscovite said. "Where is the book?"

"Beyefendi," the old merchant began. "I said it *might* take three days. Might is not will. Perhaps with some more money, it might come faster. You come back tomorrow?"

"Bah!" the Russian said, throwing his hands up in disgust. "Damned *krest'yanskiy.* Here, here is money! Twice as much. Get the book, damn you."

"I have many others. You are interested in these perhaps? Look, here is work of Pushkin, and here is Al-Jahiz."

"No, you Ottoman *musor!*" he spat back. "Spanish, it must be in Spanish, understand? I don't care how you get it. Just get it."

The Arab smiled greasily as the other handed over a purse of coins. Their curt exchange concluded; the angry butler pottered off in a huff while the old bookseller greedily counted his fee with relish. Intrigued by this scene, I set off to follow the Russian, carried by an uneasy feeling.

His path led him away from the stalls of the bazaar and across the Galata Bridge through a maze of alleys and covered lanes until he emerged on a wide cobbled boulevard leading toward Taksim Square. Turning off the avenue, he entered a large, well-appointed home, clearly fallen into some disre-pair, that overlooked the waters of the Bosporus. I followed close behind.

"*Prostite,*" I called after him.

He wheeled around, barring my entry. I was surprised he didn't slam the door on my face given I looked a man newly risen from the grave, but my Russian must have given him pause.

"Whose house is this?" I said.

"Away with you," he said curtly.

"I must know."

"What business is that of yours?"

"Grisha!" a loud voice boomed from deep within the house. I recognized the stentorian tenor instantly. "Grisha! You useless *nedoumok*, have you got it or not?"

Shoving this Grisha aside, I pushed past through the doorway into the house. He gave chase, shouting all manner of Russian invective as I ran from room to room hunting for the source of the voice. The place was enormous and garishly decorated, filled with trinkets and baubles of an ostentatious flavor all too familiar. Racing upstairs with the butler hot on my heels yelling bloody murder, I burst through a set of heavy doors at the end of a long hall. There on a great bed of white linen positioned before an open sun-drenched terrace overlooking the straight lay the corpulent Kazakov.

He wore a plain tunic of ivory white, splotched yellow with age, over his great bulk, undiminished with the passing of the years. A thick black beard still concealed his pudgy wet lips, and a full mat of coal-black hair still hung over his head in broad, wavy locks. His ruddy skin pulsed with the rosy flow of hot Georgian blood. He looked as healthy as a great Russian bear. He'd not aged a single day.

Even more curious was the room: full of books, dozens upon dozens of books, maybe hundreds, stacked in corners, piled high on tables, strewn about the floor like leaves fallen from a dying oak tree. I thought of Dumont's letter describing his astonishment upon seeing Albin's garret all those years ago. I could only assume this was much the same scene that had greeted him.

Kazakov was reading when I entered. He looked up from the text grasped in his meaty hands. The fiery stare from former days, the look of intensity that once bore into me like an augur tearing into the cold earth, had vanished from his eyes, replaced by but a dim flicker. Where all his power once lay, there remained beneath a withered brow only two simple dark eyes, exhausted and weary, the eyes of a man who had lost all hope.

"If you've come looking for revenge, you are too late," he said by way of greeting. "Grisha, bring my guest a drink."

The little butler stood frozen and shrunken in the doorway, daring not to enter for fear his second failure of the day would certainly bring the full wrath of his master upon him. Quietly, he slunk away.

"Come, sit," Kazakov said, his normally orotund manner mercifully quieted. "So, he got you too, after all, eh?"

A chair stood near the terrace doors stacked with papers. I set these aside and sat.

"What do you mean?"

"What do I mean?" He laughed. "He asks me what do I mean? Your face, lad. It's not been some ten-dollar bottle of snake oil that's been keeping your face so fresh and young all these years."

"Then, you know? You've met him too?"

"Did you really think you were the only one? He's been at this for centuries, probably longer."

"When did you—"

"Too long ago to remember," he said with a great sigh.

"Then I didn't lose everything because you beat me?" I said. "You never beat me at all."

"You could not have won," he said. "Your fate was already decided before you ever arrived at my door."

The shock of the revelation struck me dumb.

"But why me?"

"Why not?" he said with a shrug of his heavy shoulders. "Did you think very hard when you chose your own prey? No, you just looked at the man and decided he was ripe for the picking. A certain desperation in the eye? Your reputation preceded you. The great Yeretik. What, did you think yourself a God among men just because you had some talent at the gaming tables? You parlayed it into some very profitable encounters, of varied sorts too. One could hardly pass an evening without someone mentioning your name. Paris, Berlin, Vienna. You were inescapable. It was only natural for me, once I'd heard of you. I knew it would be me who would bring you low. Everyone said you were unbeatable at the tables. But with the scale of your pride, and the devil on my side, your fall was all but assured."

"Then he *is* the devil?" I said. Kazakov paused and reflected.

"*The* devil? No. But a devil."

"There's a difference?"

"The king of hell holds court with many apostates. He is but one, but together, they are many."

"Legion," I said quietly. Kazakov nodded and cast a quizzical eye at me.

"How did he appear to you?"

Just then Grisha reappeared with a tray and two cups of tea. When he'd gone and shut the doors behind him, I related to Kazakov the events of the night in my bedroom just as I have related them within the confines of these pages.

"When he came to me, it was in the same form," he said. "That disgusting bird!"

"He claims he can come in any form he chooses."

"So I have been reading," he said, gesturing to the piles of books surrounding us. "He travels in many guises, but always with an open hand and a carriage load of promises."

"How many others have there been?"

"Four that I have found," he said. "You and I make five and six. But there have been countless more, of this, I've no doubt."

"I believe I may have known one," I said, recalling Albin.

"I met a fellow in Baghdad once," he said. "Might have been, but I couldn't say for certain. All I know is, the arrangement is always the same. Seventy years for seven souls."

I considered this for a brief moment, then realized a terrible truth.

"Was I to be one of yours?" I said.

"Indeed," he said. "And yet here you remain. He must have taken a liking to you for you to have survived. I thought for sure I'd sent you to a swift death by your own hand that night. Sorry for that, by the way."

I dismissed his tepid apology with a wave of my hand.

"Does he have a name?"

Kazakov inhaled slowly through his two great wide nostrils, breathing volumes of the stale sea air for several moments. His mind seemed to drift elsewhere, and when it returned, he looked out over the water, exhausted.

"He sometimes calls himself Arman Sur."

"What does he—" I started.

"No more questions," Kazakov said, turning his weary head back to me, the energy within him perceptibly dimmed. "There will be time for them later. There is still some time left. Now I need sleep. You are welcome to stay in the house as long as you like. Grisha will arrange everything."

And with these words, he closed his eyes and drifted quickly off to sleep.

That night, I slept an uneasy sleep in a bed of luxury I'd been denying myself since the night of Elena's death. It felt a betrayal of the vow I'd taken to turn my back on the devil's gifts, and visions of suffering and pain plagued my dreams.

I was at home, my halls once again filled with revelry of old. But what I thought the shrieks of laughter were only the cries of the tortured, as each punished the other according to his sin.

A row of women lay bare on a table, a human buffet, devoured by men with dripping mouths and venomous teeth. Others, coveting clothes, jewels, even the skin off their neighbor's back, clawed at each other with bloodied fingernails. Lustful lovers—turned into hideous animallike creatures half human, half beast—copulated endlessly with both the living and the dead, their spasms uncontrollable, violent, and agonizing.

I sought to escape the turmoil of the infernal bacchanal but could find no egress. Fleeing from room to room, fresh tortures met my eyes at every turn until sights atrocious and screams of despair filled my head and I felt I might be swallowed whole in that pit of unceasing woe.

It was only when Grisha thrust aside the curtains, flooding the room with sunlight, that those horrid visions fled. I welcomed the new day with relief.

* * *

Grisha arranged for new clothes to be brought for me. I cleaned myself up and bathed for the first time in weeks. Returning to my room, I found him laying out a simple breakfast. I expressed my desire to see Kazakov, but he informed me that I would only be permitted an audience after lunch.

"The *gospòdin*'s illness keeps him bedridden these days," he said, slightly perturbed. "He always sleeps through the morning. I will be going out shortly. The house is at your disposal, but under no circumstances is he to be disturbed. I will take you to see him when I return."

"What is the book you were trying to obtain yesterday?" I said as he made to leave.

"The master collects many books," he said. "It is not mine to either know their contents or to care what they may be. He requests them, I obtain them."

"How long have you been in his employ?"

"Long enough to know it is not permitted for me to fail in my duties. If you'll excuse me."

With Grisha gone, no doubt on a return visit to the booksellers, I took the opportunity to explore the house.

A magnificent palatial estate, the place recalled for me my homes of the past, with each room like the gallery of a great museum, cold and impersonal.

At the center of the house stood a bright, wide atrium, open to the sky three floors above, which allow in a pillar of natural light. This illuminated a massive wall fountain tiled white and indigo in the Moorish style. A stream of clear water poured from an ornate copper spout nearly twenty feet in the air and terminated in a great half-moon basin made of solid gold.

Everything radiated away from this glorious spine of the house. I walked from room to room, passing under archways and great columns of carved limestone, a curious mix of Ottoman and Gothic architecture no doubt a result of the eternal crossings of histories through this narrow pathway between the ancient and modern worlds. Colorful lamps of stained glass hung from the pinnacles of vaulted ceilings, and massive Anatolian rugs carpeted the floor beneath my feet.

There were no cooks tending the kitchen, no footmen standing sentinel at the doors. No battery of maids bustled about dusting and polishing. There was no need. None of the chairs or sofas had been sat in, none of the glasses had been drunk from. Every room like a sepulcher, exquisitely appointed and lavishly arranged, but still just a tomb for various pieces of furniture, books, and baubles. Layers of dust had settled everywhere, and cobwebs encroached from the shadows of every corner.

Eventually, I found myself standing before the double doors leading to the main bed chamber. Despite Grisha's warning, I went inside.

Kazakov lay asleep. A gentle sea breeze blew in through the open terrace doors. I stepped out into a bright Anatolian sun that instantly warmed my face. Placing my hands on the stone balustrade and gazing down into the waters, I was struck by the memory of the Square du Vert-Galant, standing as I had been in the same manner when my love was taken from me. I could but turn aside, my throat choked with remorse.

"You look sicker than I do," Kazakov said. He'd woken and was watching me from the bed.

"I thought we couldn't get sick," I said, knowing this to be false. My body had been ravaged by all manner of disease. Yet I recovered all the same.

"This isn't a mortal illness," he said. "My soul is dying. What's left of it anyway."

"You're nearing the end?"

"Nearing? I'd say I'm practically upon it. A few days, maybe more."

"I'm sorry," I said.

Kazakov sighed, his great bulk swelling beneath the linen sheets.

"Tell me, what were you thinking just then?"

I told him of Elena, of our first meeting and of the war. I described to him her beauty, her innocent yet masterful insight. Bathing in the memory of our love, I almost forgot all that had transpired. Speaking of it for the first time in two years, it felt as if she were not dead, that I were not damned, and tomorrow I would return to Paris as if from a long journey. We would once again stroll the promenades of the Seine, tour the galleries and gardens in a perpetual springtime paradise, and embrace as only two souls in love could.

When I'd finished, the sober face of the Russian held a far-off look, as if he, too, were trapped in his own reverie of lost happiness.

"To hear you speak of love in this way," he said. "It is almost too much to bear."

"Then you, too, have known this same pain?"

"A man does not live as long as I have and not loved. It's a story much older than the two of us. There, on the table."

Kazakov indicated a bureau atop which lay scattered books and scraps of hand-scrawled notes. Among these was a roll of canvas tied with a tattered silk ribbon. I brought it to the beside and undid the ribbon, unfurling the image of the peasant girl I'd seen hanging over the fire in his house in Meudon. It had been hastily cut from its frame.

"Gohar," I said quietly.

"Do you know," he said, his gaze lost in the face held in my hands, "that night was the first time I'd uttered her name in nearly fifty years. I hated you for making me say it. Everyone else knew never to ask. But you? I knew then I would have your ruin, if for no other reason."

A red shawl tied beneath her chin framed her face and covered her hair. Her clothes, a simple black tunic tied about her below her breasts, showed the wear of fieldwork and stopped halfway down her calves, exposing a pair of muddy bare feet. She was beautiful, but her pale-blue eyes, faded blue like the petals of an iris, held within them a profound and immeasurable sadness.

"Her father was a vintner, of sorts," Kazakov said. "A boorish man named Bessarion. I bought wine from him. Well, I took it, if I'm to be honest. What was fair was fair, though. I owned the land he grew his grapes on. My father was a *zemlevladelets*, and he controlled the land surrounding the village. I was still a young man when he died, and I inherited all his holdings. They were substantial. But he was not a well-liked man. And as the son of a wealthy, hated man, it was easy for me to be despised as well."

"I find that not terribly difficult to believe," I said.

"Gohar was a beautiful child," he said, ignoring my comment. "From the day she was born, she was the envy of the village. *Bessarion,* they would say to her father, *how could a brute like you produce such a delicate flower?* And they would all laugh and drink his wine deep into the night.

"I cared not for the child of peasants. Why should I? Over the years, I took what I liked from their stores, threatening eviction if my demands weren't met. I feasted while they and their children toiled on the edge of starvation. The Bible says to put a knife to your throat if you are given over to gluttony. I put it to theirs instead, took what I pleased, and the devil take the rest!"

His bile rising, a violent fit of coughing seized him and only subsided after several minutes, during which a profuse sweat broke out across his brow. When it was over, it seemed his very essence had been drained by the ordeal.

"*Gula* is a terrible sin," he said dabbing spittle from his mouth.

"Aren't they all?" I said.

"Why couldn't I have been given over to lust? At least then I'd still want to fuck!"

"They are all the same," I said. "That's the rub. They may be called by different names, but at its heart, a sin is a sin. Lust is just gluttony for physical pleasure, no different from greed. Focusing all your attentions on one desire to the detriment of all others is only another form of sloth."

"And what of your pride?" he said.

"A mechanism for my avarice, nothing more."

"The devil would disagree," he said. "And he has."

"What of Gohar?" I said, trying to redirect the interrogatory light shining on my own failures.

"She grew from a beautiful child into a beautiful woman before everyone's eyes. She sparkled like a gemstone in the craggy rock face of her wretched village. There were suitors, peasants all of them, and all of them turned away by Bessarion. But I fell in love with her from afar. I sent gifts, trinkets mostly, signed with no name, to win her favor. I commissioned her picture and had it sent to her. That was my downfall."

"How so?" I said.

"It was obvious. I was the only one in the whole of the valley who could possibly have afforded such a ridiculous thing. Who else but I could have sent it?"

"What made you fall in love with her?"

"Who is to know why such things happen? They just do. What brought you to your Elena? Why did she, out of all the other girls in the world, take your heart? Was she more beautiful than the others, or was it not beauty but something else entirely that drew you to her? It's not for anyone to know why. It just is. I loved Gohar and did not question why. Watching her tend the vines with her family, seeing her dance at the Rtveli celebrations under the mid-autumn sky, a man could get lost in such reverie. And I did.

"But it didn't matter. When she discovered it was me who was showering her with gifts, she became furious. Said I was a terrible man, greedy and incontinent. Called me fat. Told me it was because of my gluttony everyone on my lands was poor and suffering. I became enraged."

"What did you do?"

"Drove her and her father off my land. Drove them all off my land, the entire village—well, practically all of them. Cast them out of the valley and into the hills or God knows where. It was foolish. In short time, with no one working the fields and vineyards, my finances dried up. Then it was me who was starving."

"And that's when he came," I said.

"And brought with him a tale so bright, it might have been spun from pure gold," Kazakov said. "Sins for years, and all the food and drink and money and power I could ever want or need. But no amount of any of it can wash away the stain of love she put on my heart."

"You could not have known," I said. "Nor could I."

"And therein lies the truth of the curse," he said, turning grim as death. "You will ask for death, even beg for it, but it won't come. I've tried, as I'm sure you have. But that's the *real* rub. Hell is not some other place for us, my friend. It is right and truly here, and we are already in it. Death is only an escape from this hell into another. There is no difference. *That* is the devil's greatest achievement. He figured out how to make fools like us extend our eternity of suffering and damnation by bridging the void between this world and the next. Don't you see? He's cheated God himself and prolonged the infinite by using against Him the very sins *He* created."

With each passing day, Kazakov's spirit gradually weakened, until the afternoon of the fourth day, when his health took its worst turn.

On that morning, he dismissed Grisha, sending the callous man off with a large satchel of money, more than he'd probably seen in his lifetime, and instructions to take whatever he liked from the house, save the books.

"The books stay," Kazakov boomed. He lay in bed propped up on a mountain of pillows, but his dark and weary eyes still yet glowed with determination. "They belong to Monsieur Allard. All of them. He may do with them as he wishes."

Outside, Constantinople hummed with activity. The first French brigades had arrived to occupy the city. The British would arrive the very next day, and soon, the straight below the terrace would play host to warships bearing the Union Jack. The streets swarmed with Ottomans lining up to view their conquerors with loathing and mistrust, while the Greeks were throwing parties, celebrating the defeat of the Turk at the hands of the Allies.

But that excitement did not penetrate the confines of the house. Late in the day, Kazakov called for me. Grisha, his trunks loaded with valuable loot plundered from nearly every room, stopped by to tell me my presence was, at last, requested.

"The miserable *sukinsyn* wants to see you," he said on his way out. The last servile act he'd ever perform complete, he left the house at the wheel of Kazakov's Rolls-Royce Silver Ghost.

❧

I stayed away until evening time. The eastern sky had grown a dark bluish purple, and already across the water, the streets of Üsküdar shimmered with yellow lights all the way up to Çamlıca Hill. The first stars penetrated the growing twilight. Soon, the vault of the heavens would be aglow with them, while the house was as dark and empty and quiet as ever. Sitting vigil at Kazakov's bedside, I made for an odd father confessor.

"Do you know why you are damned?" he said. Beads of sweat dotted his brow, and he labored over every breath. The last of his strength was slipping away.

"I think that decision may have been made before I was even born," I said.

"Bah!" he said, brushing aside my words with a limp wave of his hand. "I am damned because I chose to be so. Because I did not want to ally myself with a God who showed so little regard for *His* children. Because I did not want to live by His rules. I sought to be free of the shackles of faith and to have the world on my own terms. Your reasons were no different, your choice just the same as mine."

"Maybe so," I said.

"And I think, like me, you have regretted your decision from the moment you made it."

"At the time, I was too blinded by arrogance to regret. It took half a lifetime to see my error. Elena once said regret was like a light in the dark, shining down on our mistakes, but also illuminating the way forward."

"But there is no way forward." He coughed. "Only damnation lay ahead for me. I have failed to find the path back to redemption. It is up to you now to save me. It is why you've come."

I thought him raving, the ravages of his inner illness playing havoc with his mind. I tamped his sweaty brow.

"Drink," he said. "I must have a drink!"

Kazakov reached a pale, trembling hand toward the sideboard. A glass of wine stood already poured among the piles of books and manuscripts. I brought it to him, and he drank it down greedily in large gulps.

"The *gula* grips me to the last," he said, regarding the glass. Then he fixed his stare on me. "I am one hundred and eighty-four years old this very day, and still, my desires remain unsated."

The incredulity of his words astonished me.

"You look as though you've seen a ghost," he said. "But it isn't so hard to deduce, is it? The devil, too, has his own sin. He takes great pride in flaunting his defiance of God. My unending gluttony fed his ego. When my seventy years were up, I simply desired seventy more. These he granted without reserve. I asked for more, but even the devil has his limits."

A sudden paroxysm shook him. His breathing became shallow and rapid. Despite the warm air, Kazakov's skin was cool and clammy to the touch. Death was quickening.

"These books," he said, regaining his wind, his eyes shaded by heavy lids. "Take them. Learn what you can. The answer is not here, but the way, the way to the answer must be."

"What answer?" I said perplexed. "What way?"

"You must find the way. It was found once before. It can be found again. I learned of it, and for twenty years, I have been searching. I've found nothing, but I know it is there. You must find it to save me, to save yourself. Together we can cheat him as he cheated us, as he cheated God! Avenge God, and we will surely be admitted into heaven."

"You need sleep," I said.

"No!" he said fiercely, drawing forth the strength to oppose the shroud of darkness encroaching on his soul. His eyes flashed wildly as his vision left him. He reached forth and seized my arm in a viselike grip. "No sleep. You must listen. You must hear me. It is the only way. There was one who learned the secret. Harrowed hell like Christ himself and freed his soul from eternal damnation. A Spaniard. Wrote it down. You must find his book and learn the secret. Make your soul whole, take back what you surrendered to him. It's the only way you might see your Elena again. The devil thinks he's won, but you can make him pay for what he has stolen."

A violent spasm jolted up his spine. His body stiffened beneath the covers, an expression of agonizing pain tearing across his face. In a moment, it passed, and he fell limp against the mattress, his once booming voice become but a faint whisper.

"The wine," he said, indicating the empty glass. "Cyanide. I give my gluttonous soul to you for the devil's due. Ten more years. Find the book. Succeed where I have failed. Learn the secret. Save..."

The words choked in his throat as the muscles of his face slackened and the last breath of life pushed forth from his lips. The grip of his great hand loosened. His cold, glassy eyes fixed their stare in the middle distance and moved no more, their light forever extinguished.

The substance of my terminal conversation with Kazakov dispelled any lingering doubt Albin, the hermit secreted away all those years in Madame Crespi's garret, had himself been obsessed with finding the means of extricating his soul from its infernal bondage. He'd been on the same trail as Kazakov, but his death would suggest he, too, had failed to locate the secret to undoing his bargain.

Kazakov's theory, that recovering the lost piece of my soul was the key to salvation and a return to Elena gave me a new sense of hope and purpose. As determined as I once was to formulate every action with the aim of achieving the greatest pleasure, so did I set about this new mission—to reunite my soul with hers—with infinitely more verve and passion.

I had his body burned and buried the ashes in the small garden overlooking the straight. Then, collecting every book from the bedroom, library, and everywhere else I could find within the house, I began combing through each text page by page in order to learn everything Kazakov had about the devil's dealings.

For weeks, I stayed locked in the house poring over books, manuscripts, and scrolls day and night with a mania I had not known before. Kazakov's archive, amassed over the course of twenty years or more, included texts from virtually every country on earth. There were treatises on pacts with the devil; volumes written in Latin, Greek, Spanish, Italian, German, and dozens of other languages; trial records from Salem, Toulouse, and Fulda; codex on papyrus and vellum; accounts of the Inquisition from various eras, including the texts I had gleaned in his collection in Meudon; transcriptions of interviews with Navajo and Comanche tribesmen; illuminated manuscripts of incalculable value; quartos from the Mughal Empire; even some works by Aleister Crowley.

From this study, using texts dating back as early as 435 AD, I pieced together, as Kazakov had, the tales of at least four individuals, three men and a woman, whose stories, at least on their face, mirrored my own. But vague as these accounts read, I gleaned little hint or clue that their lives ended in any way other than expected. They committed their souls to eternal damnation in defiance of God, with no recourse to reversing their histories. None had any mention of an encounter with a Spaniard or his journal, either directly or obliquely.

By the end of February, it was clear the answers I sought would not be found within these texts, nor did they suggest a future course of search. I resolved to return to Paris, to seek out my one-time friend Dumont in the hopes he had not parted with any or all of Albin's archive. Hoping the balm of time had sweetened the bitterness of our parting, I still wished to forestall this reunion as long as I could for fear of opening old wounds and showing myself a mercenary at his gates.

I'd given no thought as to how I would explain my unchanged nature, but this consideration was secondary to my getting my hands on Albin's library. Already seized by a singular monomania, I was convinced the answers I sought would be found therein, I would have those books by persuasion or, if necessary, by force. I made arrangements to return to Paris on the Express d'Orient as soon as possible. Three days later, my train pulled into the Gare de l'Est.

I wasted no time making inquiries at several hospitals across the city as well as the medical school at the Sorbonne. It appeared a certain Dr. Paul Dumont had made somewhat of a name for himself in the field of virology over the previous two decades. His name drew praise and esteem wherever I uttered it, and many former colleagues enjoyed telling me of his exploits. I learned he'd served several years at the Salpêtrière and most recently offered his service to the Republic treating casualties as they poured off the line. Before the war ended, he moved south and took up a residency as chief physician of a clinic outside Chamonix to carry on his work in virus research. A sanitarium mainly for the wealthy, the Quinault Clinic, as it was called, provided ample facilities and funding for the good doctor, and his career would have progressed marvelously on its illustrious path, but alas, he'd died the year before after succumbing to a brief illness.

It hardly bears saying that Paul's death landed a devastating blow. The hope of any reconciliation between us dissipated before my eyes at hearing the news, and the likelihood of his library, meaning that of Albin's, remaining intact seemed highly improbable. Nevertheless, I endeavored to travel on to Chamonix, to his clinic in the shadow of Mont Blanc, to learn of the fate of my friend, the collection, and to pick up the thread of its trail.

You wonder if while in my brief interval in Paris I paid visit to the Cimetière Saint-Vincent, to the tomb of my dear Elena? I did not. I ask you: How could I dare approach that hallowed place? I who had murdered my love with the shame of my sin just as surely as if I had plunged a dagger into her very heart? I had already disgraced her in life, I would not let my wretchedness sully her repose in death.

The Quinault Clinic, so named after its founder and chief patron Rene Quinault, a wealthy mountaineer and adventurer from Bern, perched on a rocky outcropping seven hundred feet above the river Arve between the towns of Les Houches and Saint-Gervais-les-Bains, a sort of mountain fortress when viewed from the valley below, imposing and impenetrable.

The car carrying me up to these formidable heights wound a circuitous route through rich green mountain forests and along sheer rocky cliff faces to deposit me at the doors of the main admissions hall and hospital, a building more closely resembling a medieval keep than a house of healing. Immense, gray, and cold, it loomed foreboding and grim in the alpine mist, the atmosphere casting a decidedly sullen gloom over the place, belying its altruistic purpose.

Waiting to greet me in a pristine white coat was the clinic's chief physician and Dumont's successor, the silver-bearded Dr. Reverdin. I'd sent word ahead I would be coming and wished to make inquiries, claiming to be an admirer of the late doctor and his work. The clinic was only too happy to oblige.

"Monsieur l'Docteur Dumont was the youngest to occupy the position of chief physician here at the Quinault Clinic," this Reverdin said as we toured the austere halls. Pausing frequently to point out some obscure piece of medical equipment, he expounded on the legacy of my old friend. "But his contributions to the science of healing were always of the highest quality. He specialized in viruses, you know. Developed rather an affinity for them, you might say. Was working on a theory they contributed to addiction to narcotics like opium. But I don't think he'd made it very far."

"He always did have a passion for study," I said. We'd stopped before a hall lined with portraits, each painting depicting a previous chief physician of the clinic dating back to 1873. On the end hung Dumont's.

The likeness to the image of my old friend was remarkable. The artist, no doubt a seasoned master, had captured all the humble grace of his character. His glassy eyes rimmed by those familiar gold pince-nez retained their deep gaze as he stared off boldly into the distance while his smooth face, still youthful but slightly pale, held an expression of proud yet kind stoicism. The thin lines of time framed his lips and eyes, and the creases of a critical thinker traced faintly across his forehead, but beyond those nuances, and a slight graying of the hair at his temples, he was represented in the dignified manner of a man befitting his respected position.

"He was just forty-five when he died," Reverdin said, remarking on the portrait. "Had only held the position for a little over a year."

"How did it happen?" I said, feeling a tear form at the corner of my eye, a most unexpected thing.

"Peacefully," Reverdin said. "A condition he'd had since childhood, I believe. Chronic."

"I didn't know," I lied.

"How could you?" he said. "A man of science, such as he was, would have known his time was limited. I believe he immersed himself in his work so vigorously because of this, and we are all better for his efforts. But I only knew him in a professional capacity. If you really want insight into the type of man he was, you should speak to his wife. She lives here on the grounds with her son in the residence normally reserved for the chief physician. But I don't need such a place. I keep a small apartment adjoining my office here in the clinic facilities. It's quite suitable for me. And Madame Dumont works to curate the clinic's library and records, so the arrangement is amenable to everyone."

"A son?"

"Yes. Martin. A good lad. Already showing the bent of a scientific mind like his father."

I left Dr. Reverdin at the admissions hall and followed his directions toward the west end of the clinic grounds to find the small chalet of the chief physician situated among a grove at the base of a hillside leading farther up the mountain. The crunching of gravel underfoot preceded my approach, and as I rounded a bend, I was greeted by the curious glance of a blond-haired youth of five examining the decomposing carcass of an adolescent sparrow on the path with a magnifying glass. He regarded me casually, but ultimately uninterested in my presence, he returned his attentions to the bird.

"You must be Martin," I said, crouching beside him over the body. He did not answer.

"What have you got there?" I said.

"It fell," he said. "Yesterday. Would you like to see?" He offered me the glass. It had a handle made of walnut inlaid with strips of mother-of-pearl. I recognized it as his father's. He'd purchased it in a shop in the rue Erasme not long after we'd met.

"Thank you," I said, warmed by the kindly gesture. He possessed his father's eyes, and the same slight downturned curl at the corners of his mouth, giving him a perpetual yet endearing pout. His bright, rosy face bore none of the signs of the anemia that had plagued Dumont.

"I'm told you like science," I said. "Dr. Reverdin said so. Your father liked it too."

"You knew him?"

"Briefly," I said. "Many years ago."

"Father was a doctor," he said with a proud smile that slowly waned. "But then he died."

"I know," I said, handing him back the glass.

"I want to be a doctor too," he said, turning back to the bird.

"I think he would like that very much."

"*Maman* says doctors help sick people. She said my father helped lots of people."

"I'm sure he did."

"Did he help you?"

"He tried to once," I said. "But I didn't listen to his instructions."

"Are you still sick?"

"I'm afraid so. But that's why I'm here. So, in a way, you could say he's still trying to help me."

Just then, the front door to the chalet opened and Madame Dumont came forward to greet me.

I had expected to meet the face of Caroline, who I'd so offended all those years ago, but, instead, the youthful, vibrant face of a wholly different woman greeted me. This girl was of rugged alpine stock, moon faced, but comely after the provincial way. A woman of maybe thirty years, with blonde hair the same shining tint as her son's, she shook my hand with a forwardness that took me aback and introduced herself as Hanna.

We left the child to his investigations. Inside, I wandered about the living room, noting two framed photographs atop the mantle. The first was a wedding photo, taken before a cloth backdrop depicting a forest glade: Dumont standing rigid and stone-faced beside his seated bride. The second was of the two of them standing before the garden gate of the chalet. Linked arm in arm and squinting their eyes against a bright alpine sun, they were all the more the happy couple because of the bright-faced handsome little boy nestled between them.

"He didn't put you off, I hope?" Hanna said, bringing coffee. "Martin always gets excited when he gets to use his father's old pieces."

"He's a charming boy," I said, observing the child through the window. "I'm sure he'll make a fine doctor someday."

I could not fail to see in his movements and expressions the shadow of his father behind each one. My mind conjured the memory of happening upon him at his studies, his serious eyes fixed on some intractable question or bit of medical tedium pulled from his lecture notes. Gazing upon my old friend's issue, I felt an unusual swell of happiness for him that he should have known, however briefly, his legacy would survive beyond his years. Simultaneously, I felt a great swell of sadness my own would not.

"Dr. Reverdin said you'd be coming. When he received your letter about Paul, he thought it best to tell me to expect you."

"I am sorry to have heard about his passing," I said.

"How exactly did you know my husband?"

"Indirectly, I'm afraid," I said. "He'd contacted me a few years ago regarding some medical texts. I deal in rare books, you see. He'd mentioned a desire to locate a few volumes, and I offered my services. Unfortunately, I was unable to find them until recently."

"He never mentioned anything to me about it," she said.

"From the few communications we'd had, I'd gotten the distinct impression Dr. Dumont wasn't exactly given over to prolixity. It's a pity. I would like to have gotten to know him a bit more. He seemed an interesting fellow, and quite intelligent. I found his theories on addiction fascinating."

"He was dedicated to his work," she said with pride. "And his family."

She looked to the photos on the mantle.

"How long were you married?" I said. "If I may ask?"

"Almost seven years. We met in Geneva. His first wife died some years ago."

"I didn't know."

"Caroline," she said. "Paul spoke of her often. They couldn't have children. That kind of a thing would have destroyed most marriages. But Paul was a kind soul. They were together a long time."

"Then Martin is your son?" I said. "I understand from Dr. Reverdin he's following in his father's footsteps."

"My budding scientist," she said. "Always investigating the mysteries of the little worlds of the insects or collecting unusual stones. He's got a studious mind. It does his father's memory proud. It's a good thing for a good man to have a legacy, don't you think?"

I agreed it probably was.

"Are you married?" she said. "Do you have children of your own?"

"I was almost married once, but sadly, it wasn't meant to be."

"Pity. But it is never too late. Paul was living proof. But I'm sorry, I shouldn't have asked such a question. It's clearly upset you."

Without realizing it, I'd begun to tear up.

"Forgive me, madame," I said, discarding my melancholic expression. "It's no fault of yours. It was I who started our conversation down this rather unprofessional path. Allow me to get back to the matter at hand."

"Which is?"

"The books," I said. "As I said, I was able to locate the texts your late husband was seeking out. I understand he kept quite an extensive library."

"He did," she said. "But I'm afraid they wouldn't be of much use to me."

"Perhaps they may be of benefit to the clinic, then?"

"That is another matter," she said happily. "If Paul saw value in having them, then I'm sure Dr. Reverdin would be happy to review them."

"Excellent!" I said. "I understand Dr. Dumont also kept an extensive private library as well."

"He did. Would you like to see?"

"I would consider it a privilege and honor. I might be able to provide you some history and perhaps some values for your future considerations," I said, adding as an enticement to my sincerity: "Services to be provided free of charge, of course."

Madame Dumont led me upstairs to my old friend's study. Exceptionally organized and quintessentially Dumont, the place held the same professional, almost museum-like quality I instantly recognized as the style my father once employed. Everything, from the desk to the specimen cabinet to the worn leather chair where the doctor sat reviewing records, charts, and case histories, was pristine and arranged such that it would be prepared to accept him warmly upon his return at any moment. But he would not be returning, and the task of maintaining the room in this ready state fell to his wife, who accepted the responsibility gladly as a way to honor her late husband and show reverence for his works.

Along the wall stood a low bookshelf, the entirety of the doctor's library in little more than two dozen volumes.

"But," I said, regarding the paltry case, "surely, there must be more than these?"

"He kept all of his medical texts at the clinic library," Madame Dumont said. "These were the only personal books he kept."

Glancing at the spines in the case, my heart sank. Some volumes of poetry, the works of Balzac, Dumas, and some others. Nothing unusual, foreign, or remotely rare.

"I'm not sure why he would have told you he had an extensive book collection," she said. "Unless..."

"Yes?" I said hopefully.

"My husband kept an old portmanteau. Ugly, hulking thing. I keep it upstairs in the garret. I know there were some in there. He showed them to me once. Old, dusty things. Quite smelly too."

I followed Madame Dumont up to a low attic beneath the sloping beams of the chalet roof. A few wooden boxes collected dust, and a disused child's bed lay pushed to one side, upon which were piled several neatly folded blankets. A squat alcove beneath a small window contained a writing desk and chair. Beside this lay an old trunk.

"I know he came up here from time to time if he wanted to be away from his work for a little while," she said. "He'd occasionally write letters under the window."

The portmanteau was not very big, but I recognized it immediately as one Dumont kept in his room during our school days. Not much bigger than the standard sea trunk of the day, perhaps made to hold a few suits and maybe a week's worth of essentials, it couldn't possibly hold all the works of Albin's library.

"May I?" I said.

Madame Dumont stood aside as I undid the leather clasps and lifted the lid. A musty odor rising from within transported me back to the rue du Cardinal Lemoine, to Dumont's old room and long nights, working by candlelight, as he catalogued the vast assortment of the old hermit's collection.

I identified a text in German bound in cracked red leather, and then another, a small black book, Venetian in origin, branded with the figure of a hippogriff. These lay atop the pile, while, beneath, my eyes met more familiar sights. Carefully stacked and slid together to maximize space, the trunk contained maybe seventy of Albin's books in all, a paltry portion of the once tremendous collection.

I begged for privacy to conduct my assessment. Hanna said I might stay for as long as I thought necessary and left me in peace. I waited a few moments after she'd gone until I could see her again outside below the window busying herself with her son before returning to the trunk.

I dove headlong into Albin's books, scrutinizing each carefully in turn, sifting through page after page, line after line of text, until all of the words, regardless of their language, began flowing together in an endless stream of letters, symbols, and sounds, none making any sense, so jumbled were they in Greek, Chinese, Russian, English, Spanish, and any number of other languages, some old, some ancient, and some long dead. But, just as before, I found no answer among them.

By evening, I'd given up hope. Nearing the bottom of the trunk and the last of the texts, my eyes alighted on an unusual piece of paper jutting out from a very old, very worn volume bound in pale leather that nearly fell apart when I tried to lift it.

Sliding out the folded paper stuck in its pages, I discovered it a short, handwritten note, from the late Madame Crespi. Addressed to Dumont, it read simply:

> M. Dumont,
> This was found wedged beneath a loose board under the wood stove in the late M. Albin's rooms. Rather than discard it, I thought you would like to have it, as you have chosen to care for his others.
> Angelique

Beneath this, Dumont had hastily scrawled an additional note. Certainly made at a later date, it read: *late Spanish Renaissance, unknown origin, missing last third of text, binding not original, further investigation needed?*

But it appeared he'd forgotten about it, since there was no evidence any further investigation had been done. The note looked as though it were stuffed haphazardly inside, and the book itself subsequently stored and forgotten some time ago.

Carefully leafing through the pages, my curiosity only increased, for the "late Spanish Renaissance" text was written in German rather than Iberian. Indeed, the binding was not original, since the pages barely held together, while the covers held the most interest: wood planks bound in stitched leather, the front cover of which bulged in a most unusual fashion. Running my hands over the inside face of the plank, I felt the distinct outline of an irregular packet sewn inside between the hide and the inner board.

Rifling the drawers of the desk, I found a small penknife and delicately prized the seams of the cover apart. A shallow, rectangular hollow had been carved in the wooden cover-board concealing a packet of maybe two dozen or so folded, yellowed pages, written in a cramped yet patient hand. These themselves were but a fraction of pages torn from yet another larger volume.

Unfolding the pages, my heart leapt. A cursory glance of a few lines showed I may have held in my hands the answer I had been seeking, the missing piece of a puzzle Kazakov, Albin, and countless others had been searching out, the document that would be my savior and hold the key to reuniting with my beloved Elena!

Written in Castilian dialect with dates and place identifiers, it presented as a section of a traveler's journal, at least the first few pages. There were several gaps in time, pages lost, dates missing. It took some time just to arrange the sheets into some semblance of order. About a third of the way through, where the dating ceased, a much longer, more personal narrative began.

Leaning greedily over the desk in the alcove beneath the window, the alpine light dimming with each passing moment, I read.

- PART II -

Chapter XVI

Another sleepless night. Restlessness has fast become an unwelcome habit with Al, whose mind could neither stop turning over the events of the past, nor ignore the horrors of the present. But whose past and present was it that troubled him more, his own or those of the Frenchman?

He lay awake for hours reflecting on all he'd read. It seemed to him a man is not unlike a watch. Both are merely vehicles for containing the mechanism that gives them their purpose. With a watch, the case holds the movement, which measures time everlasting. In the case of a man, it is his will that contains his soul everlasting. But break the movement of a watch, and time proceeds ever forward apropos of the mechanism, whereas when a man's will is broken, does his soul not remain, stagnating and withering, as well?

To be left in such a state, Al reckoned, could not be permitted to be the fate of any man.

Etienne's thoughts had ended abruptly. Whatever story the Spaniard had to tell remained a mystery not contained within the pages of the diary. The answers could only be found within the tortured mind of that man and the house of woe in which he dwelt.

He worked in silence all the next day, more automaton than man, drifting from task to task without thought or passion. Oliver asked a question; he provided an answer. A customer needed tending; he smiled politely, showing this piece or that. But in his mind, he was already roaming empty rooms and darkened passageways. Al knew he had to go back.

At three o'clock, Zofia left to visit Maja. Al took the opportunity to dismiss Oliver and close shop. Despite Zofia's protestations from the night before, heard but unheeded all the same, he made his way to the station, where some time later, a taxi once again deposited him at the gates of that gloomy edifice.

Approaching the entranceway, a fresh cacophony of cries assailed Al's ears. Etienne yet haunted his own halls, Stevenson's monstrous Hyde still in clear possession of the man, as it were. He found him in an upstairs bedroom.

Blind rage had riven the man from his senses again. The room, like the library, lay in ruin. Paper hung in shreds from the walls, torn apart by bloodied fingertips. A grand bed in carved walnut dominated the center of the room, its posts a series of intricately sculpted caryatids resting on feet of lascivious satyrs with furry legs and sizable members. One post had broken away. The heavy canopy frame sagged unevenly under its own great weight. Light came from a set of bow windows overlooking the gardens. Before them stood the cherrywood framework of an ovular cheval mirror, its glass knocked out.

Etienne lay upon the bed panting like a dog, his face drenched in sticky sweat. He cupped the crown of his head in his hands in a vain effort to quiet the storm in his mind.

"Is there any water?" Al said timidly as he approached. "You look as if you haven't eaten or drank in days."

"There is wine there," Etienne said, indicating a dusty decanter filled with a sickly brownish-red liquid standing on a sideboard. Al wanted to ask how he'd acquired alcohol in these prohibitive times, but then realized the point moot. Etienne downed the glass in one gulp but obtained no relief.

"My every desire met. My every whim sated. But what good is any of it anymore? It is nothing but a curse to have anything I wish but still not have the one thing I wish for most. The only thing that matters."

"But still, you must eat."

"I don't require food. Or drink."

"But the pain?"

"What do I care of pain? I feel nothing anymore. My body is numb to the ravages of the sensual world. Oh, the memories remain vivid. That, too, is part of this prison. I forget nothing. Memories, I can tell you, make for jealous cellmates, always vying for my attentions, always struggling to tempt me. They disguise themselves as prisoners, but I know them to be my jailers."

"Maybe those memories remain not to remind you of your sins but to remind of what you no longer are. What you no longer want to be."

"You are forever the optimist."

"Shouldn't I be? I choose to believe you are not the man I have read about in this book." Al tossed the journal on the bed. "*That* man lived only for himself. But you, I think, have been struggling to break free of the memory of that man ever since you lost your love. The struggle gives you meaning. It gives you strength and relieves your pain. It brings you closer to the man you were when you were together."

"That man is long dead," Etienne said. "He died when she did."

"I don't believe that. Otherwise, you would have killed yourself long ago."

"You forget, I cannot die. I can only wait. My time here will go on. I will go on. And so will my pain. This has always been *his* plan."

Etienne mustered his strength and shuffled to the sideboard. Taking the decanter, he poured another portion of the turbid wine but did not drink.

"You know, it's the nature of most pleasures to be forbidden," he said, turning the glass in his hand. "It's why they are so appealing. To know you are in some way violating a rule or moral code by partaking. But when the rules no longer apply to you, the forbidden quickly becomes the banal. That, too, is something he does not tell you. Nor damned well should he."

Al thought the talking to be doing some good. He'd been alone in this place, this walking hell for so long, without companion or a sympathetic ear. He watched from the bedside as Etienne drifted about the room, lost in his thoughts, his hands trailing over the surfaces of the furniture, the carved cheek of one of the caryatid bedposts. He ran a fingertip over the rim of the wineglass, making it ring a single note. He pressed his palm flat against the wall and closed his eyes; in his head, the faint echoes of laughter and the hum of long-silenced music filled his ears. Each action a key to another memory he wished nothing more than to forget. Eventually, he stood before the broken frame of the cheval mirror, an expression of cold disdain tensing his face.

"Tell me about him," Al said, indicating the mirror with a nod.

"There is nothing to tell," Etienne said. "You already know all there is to know."

"But you must have learned something more in all this time?"

"Speculations. Hearsay. Much is written by those with little true knowledge. I have found no other tales like my own."

"Except for the Spaniard's."

"There was nothing to be learned there either," he said, defeated.

"But the Russian said he'd found a way."

"He did," Etienne said, his spirits sinking ever lower. "But that road, too, is closed to me."

"Why?"

Standing before the windows, silhouetted against the setting sun low in the western sky, Etienne's body had darkened into little more than a shadow.

"He had in his possession a talisman of some sort, a relic since lost to history. I have searched the globe these last six years looking for it, but to no avail. Without it, there is no hope."

"I should like to read his story for myself," Al said.

"And you will learn nothing more than I did. I even translated his diary into every language I knew, hoping perhaps hidden in the translation there might be some key, a linguistic turn, some clue escaping my grasp. But there is nothing."

"All the same, I would like to see."

Etienne returned to the bed and sat, but his eyes drifted to the mirror frame standing like an open doorway in the middle of the room. Al circled it, observing it as one might a taxidermized heron in an antique shop, a sort of morbid curiosity mixed with revulsion.

"And this is how he travels? I cannot believe it."

"I have seen it done. It is but one method at his disposal. I am sure there are others."

"They are his eyes and ears. By breaking all of them, you hope to blind him and make him deaf to your cries. Did it work?"

Etienne drifted into bitter reflection.

"He did appear to me once more, despite my command never to return. Though not physically in my presence, he remained to me only an image within the glass. It was in Samarkand, two, maybe three, years ago."

"What did he say?"

"He said nothing. Those horrid avian eyes flashed through mine, and I watched my reflection contort hideously as if torn asunder by the current of violent waters until it was his repugnant rictus I saw staring back at me. He remained only until I could bear his sight no more and shut my eyes tight to the apparition. When I opened them again, only my own terror remained. That was when I knew he could see me whenever he wished. I would be forever under his prying eyes so long as the doorways stood open."

Al nudged a shard of broken glass lying at his feet.

"I've broken them all," Etienne said. "Every one in every one of the places I have dwelt. But it does no good. I can still feel his gaze upon me. He watches me always. The light of my sin draws his eyes. It is how he found me the first time, how he still finds me today."

A rueful pensiveness seized him. Every avenue detoured, every doorway locked. Misery and resignation hemmed him in on all sides. Al, too, felt brought low by the crushing weight of his inadequacy in the face of such an insurmountable task.

"I once took Elena to the Montparnasse Cemetery, to the grave of Baudelaire," Etienne reflected. "She thought it beastly, at first, to spend an afternoon in a place surrounded by death. But I told her, as I always believed, beauty could be found in anything, if you knew where to look for it. She asked me to recite something for her. I chose 'The Death of Lovers.' I'd been thinking of that poem for some time. Even then, I think I knew our love would be fleeting."

Al wanted to say something more, but words failed him. In the fading light of late day, the room took on more sullenness than was bearable. He felt once again the house tightening its grip like a giant hand closing its fist around the two of them. He could see no way to fight against the encroaching darkness.

"Let me take you away from here," he said. "Zofia will make you a proper meal, and you can sleep among friends. This place is cursed. You cannot stay."

Etienne put up no fight.

They made their way quietly into the shop under cover of darkness, speaking low to conceal their voices. Despite his promise of a warm meal and bed, believing Zofia would not protest had certainly been an overreach. All the same, he was prepared to face the consequences.

They entered through the alley door. Though the lights were off and the door at the top of the stairs closed, a thin band of white shone through under its bottom edge. Al stopped to listen for footsteps overhead padding softly up the stairs like a burglar in his own home. He'd been gone nearly the full day and expected Zofia to have long gone to sleep by now. To his dismay, he found her waiting at their kitchen table, a cup of tea gone cold for her worry.

"So, you brought the dybbuk back into our home?"

"Quiet," he whispered, shutting the door behind him. "He might hear you."

"I should care?"

Al shuffled past her to the pantry and began scanning the shelves.

"He is a man possessed, yes," he said. "But not in the way you think. To leave him to his fate would be cruel."

"What fate?" she whispered back. "Albie, what are you talking about? If he is a sick man, then take him to a hospital."

"He doesn't need medicine."

"Then what does he need?"

"I don't know. I do know he thinks God has turned his back on him. Maybe it is true. But I will not. He has nowhere left to go."

Al grabbed olives, carrots, and potatoes from the pantry and cold roast beef from the refrigerator and placed them on the counter. Zofia watched all this from her seat, affecting a disinterested air.

"What are you doing?"

"Making soup."

"That is not how you make soup."

"I promised him food."

"Get away," she said, shooing Al from the stove. "How is it you can make such perfect little movements dance under your fingers, but you can't ever make a simple *polewka*? I will do this. Hand me the stewpot. You go down and make sure he is not conjuring *diabły* from the thin air."

"*Er ist kein zauberer*," he dismissed.

"You don't know what he is, or what he could do to us."

"I know if he meant to do harm, he would have done so already. But I think he is alone and has lost his way. It would be an *aveira* to turn a blind eye to his suffering. You know this."

"I know you think it is," she said. "I just worry you are bringing trouble onto yourself. There is something very wrong with that man. I don't know what it is, but I know sickness when I see it. By what reason have you decided to take on this burden? What are you not telling me?"

Al took the two volumes of Etienne's journal and placed them on the table.

"Read these, and perhaps, maybe, you will begin to understand."

⚜

Etienne had already fallen asleep in the folds of the cot when Al returned. He'd not removed his clothing, only lay his greatcoat over himself as a blanket. Even his shoes were still on his feet.

Beside him, on the chair, lay a stack of unbound pages, a translation of the Spaniard's text. Etienne had secreted them away before they'd left the house. Al collected the pages and brought them under the light. He'd just settled into his chair to begin reading when he caught a glimpse of his own reflection staring back at him from the small mirror hung over his workbench. It had been there for years—how many, he couldn't remember. It was just something that had always been there. Maybe Jacob Hart had hung it there, maybe Zofia? Its shiny silvered face looked innocent enough, but in the light of what he'd come to learn, it suddenly seemed a sinister thing, and he quickly yanked it from the wall and lay it facedown on the table. Then he opened the top drawer of the bench and tossed it inside and slammed it tight. Then he opened the bottommost drawer, pulled the mirror out again, and threw it down there, covering it with a pile of oily rags, slamming the drawer shut and holding it fast with the side of his foot.

Satisfied, at last, he'd secured his privacy, he read.

Chapter XVII

. . . of the hills. This charming countryside has put me in a mood of peace I have not known in some time.

Bartolomé pines for home every day, accustomed as he is to the comforts of my father's hacienda. The road does not suit him. He is a loyal servant and a good friend, but I fear he does not appreciate the joy of travel as I do. Perhaps it would have been best had he stayed in Zaragoza, but my father would hear nothing of it.

All the same, this journey has been the better for his companionship.

14 Mayo 1510

Today we crossed the river Elbe at a little village with no name. To call it a village is to be generous, as it was nothing more than a cluster of two or three small farms and a disused fishing hut whose roof had been knocked in some time ago. Still, the people living in this hamlet were kind to travelers and offered a comfortable table to sit at while our horses were watered and rested. Perhaps they are used to seeing men on the road, though I doubt many foreigners venture through these regions who aren't attached to a military regiment come to invade. The sight of three mounted Castilians, their baggage and servants trailing behind, must have given them pause.

Gonçalo wasted no time and immediately set about searching out the prettiest girl in the village to take into his bed. His need for such distractions inspires awe in me and no little disgust in Bartolomé. He sees the local *campesina* as uncivilized, even more so than our own. They generally lack the beauty of our native girls. Their skin is often pale and sickly. At home, you are much more likely to come across a rose among the weeds when traveling the countryside. Here, roses are very rare. But Gonçalo always has a way of finding one. I have no doubt tonight while we are sleeping, he will be laboring his leather with the pick of the village down by the riverbank.

17 Julio 1510

We will be arriving in Brandenburg in a few days, where it is my hope I may be welcomed at court as a guest of the realm. I am taking language practice nearly every day, sometimes on horseback as we travel, which is no easy feat, and the interminable Herr Lewtz, whom I engaged some time ago to assist me in my lessons, gives me no end of criticism. He's constantly drawing attention to my "lazy Spanish tongue" and its filthy Moorish heritage. Bartolomé rages at his impudence, but I just laugh. I am entertained by the old clown; I do not know why. It is for this reason alone I allow him his little liberties.

19 Julio 1510

This day, we were greeted by a horrific yet not unfamiliar scene. Approaching the town of Brandenburg from the western road, clear pillars of acrid gray smoke could be seen climbing high over the walls from near the city center. The few people we'd passed along the route to the gate were themselves hurrying toward town to view the same spectacle.

Bartolomé urged we not enter the city, that we already knew the danger and the gruesome display awaiting us, but still, I wished to see for myself and rode steadily on. He had no choice but to follow.

We dismounted and stabled the horses, proceeding on foot with the rest of the crowd. The market square was already choked with onlookers by the time we arrived. Hundreds had come out to witness the burning of nearly three dozen that day. Bartolomé refused to accompany me, and I gave him his leave to remain at an inn with the rest of the group while I went on with Herr Lewtz.

At the center of the crowd stood four great wooden poles, each with three or four men lashed to them back to back. A *sacerdote* stood before them reciting liturgy, but I was too far away to hear, and the noise of the crowd drowned out his words.

I asked the man standing beside me why these men were being executed. He said they'd been convicted of *profanación*, that they had sullied the most holy and sacred, the host of our Lord Jesus Christ. They were filthy Jews and so they would burn in the righteous fires of God's judgment. I turned away from this man as the city guards set the pyres alight.

I do not know how long I stood there watching those men burn. Their cries, at first, came clear and distinct over the din of the mob come out to view their deaths, but soon, even these were muted by the roar of the flames become great whirling columns of orange fire. Embers from this spectacle drifted overhead and settled everywhere; a rain of human ashes fell across the town.

I am told forty men in total are to be put to the fire for their crimes, all of them Jews. There is word the rest, maybe four or five hundred men, women, and children in total, are to be expelled from the city. It is as it was in Barcelona, Valencia, Seville, and all the others. There is no place for these people, no home for them they cannot be forced from at the point of a sword or the flame of a torch.

I find myself suddenly missing my home in Zaragoza, my father and my mother. But most of all, I am longing to be again with Constanza. Ah, Constanza! I can close my eyes and see her, kneeling before the image of Santa María in the cathedral, her hands pressed reverently together before her pale-blue veil. She always wears blue when she goes to pray.

Our parting was not on good terms, for she still believes me responsible for the death of Raoul. But a brother's love for his only sister runs deeper than the petty amorous promises of a known rake and *sinvergüenza*. Father may have been fooled by his trappings of finery and the words of praise from the *condes*, but I ask, what good are their words if the man is nothing but a rank blackguard, scheming, distrustful, and evil? What kind of brother would I be if I allowed such a man to bring infamy upon our house and sully the purity of my sister?

If I had told her what I knew of the man, she would not have believed me, blinded as she was by love. But his treachery ran deep, and their union would have surely ended in her shame and the ruin of the Moreno name. But it was not I who—

4 Agosto 1510

This morning, we came upon a family—a man, his wife, and three children—on the roadside. These, too, were Jews banished after the burnings, much like we'd been seeing regularly along our journey after leaving that place God had clearly abandoned. Like the others, their goods had been confiscated and the family cast out, without food or home or destination. The starved children gave rise within me a heartfelt sorrow for their woeful state, and I ordered Bartolomé to give them some of our stores and a small purse. This, he did, but with noticeable contempt. I scolded him for his gall, to which he replied were I to give away all our food and money to every Jew we found, it would be us who certainly would starve.

He has clearly forgotten his own history, and mine. For if he remembered the sacrifice of his ancestors, he would not seat himself upon such a lofty pedestal.

***Agosto 1510*

I am told we are nearing the town of Nürnberg. This news excites me, as I have heard tale of a man there who has created a new and unique type of *almohadilla perfumada*, one that does not hold perfumes but rather encases a mechanism for keeping the time of day. Bartolomé reminds me if I continue to give my money to the Jews, there will be none left to purchase such a treasure. I remind him if he insists on chastising my charity, it will be his money I will use to buy it. Gonçalo thought this a clever plan. But I do not covet this treasure for my own desires. I intend to commission one so I may present it as a gift to my father upon my return to Zaragoza.

Despite my best efforts, I cannot but still dwell unhappily upon Constanza's anger toward me, and the unpleasant words shared at our parting. I regret none of what I spoke about the knave who'd stolen her heart, but I know some of what I said hurt her deeply.

This journey is, in part, an act of apology to her. I pray the distance and time I place between us will serve to heal the wound. For I know it is an offense to God to bring dishonor and discord to one's family. I fear my wrathful indiscretion, an overreaction perhaps, has done irreparable damage to my soul. I have asked for God's forgiveness, but in this country, on this road, I wonder if he can hear my pleas.

23 Agosto 1510

Today I paid visit to Herr Henlein to see for myself these amazing timepieces that have brought him such renown.

He was in his workshop toiling away, as I am told he does every day. I was expecting to find him hunched over a table in a cramped hovel working by the light of a dying candle. But the truth was far from this image.

Herr Henlein's workshop was bright, flooded with natural sunlight pouring in through a large arched window overlooking the street. There were several men at work when we arrived. One tended a large open furnace, while two others sat side by side at a long table working with small hammers and pincers to bend and shape warm metal into rings, curves, and fine strips. These were undoubtedly *aprendices* studying the craft. On a wooden shelf beside the furnace, a fat gray cat lounged peacefully, his curled tail swinging back and forth like a pendulum. This was most certainly the foreman of the shop.

The maestro himself was seated close to the window. I was surprised to see he was a man no older than myself, maybe only twenty-five. I did not expect the maker of such finery would be quite so young. He held in his left hand a hemisphere of copper plated with gold, the inside of which contained an intricate mechanism of infinite delicacy and complexity. In his right hand, he held what looked to my eyes nothing more than an ordinary needle but was indeed a tiny tool used to tune the miniscule gearworks to a perfect harmony of movement.

Herr Henlein welcomed me warmly and was most pleased to show me his workshop. An unusual man, he spoke little of where or how he'd learned his craft. Instead, he chose to give praise to the Franciscans as possessors of great knowledge and technique. He took pride in explaining details of his trade and showed me several works in progress destined for the nobles of court.

When it was over, I humbly requested he build one of his remarkable creations for me as a gift for my father. I told him to spare no expense, use only the finest metals available, asking it be plated in gold and embellished with a floral pattern. As a final touch, I asked his name, Don Julio Cristóbal Moreno de Zaragoza, be etched into the underside of the lid.

To my joy, the maestro has agreed to my commission. It is my hope that when—

Here the travelogue ceased abruptly. A note scrawled by Etienne in the margins indicated the next pages, though still written in the Spaniard's hand, were probably written at a much later date. A variation in ink and a change in the quality of the paper evidenced as much.

. . . By the middle of *Noviembre,* we were just two days' sail from Barcelona, where fresh horses would be waiting to take me on to Zaragoza and into the embrace of my family once again. I had been gone nearly a year and longed to see my father and mother. But more than this, I longed to see Constanza and, with God's help, make peace with her. Gonçalo had left Bartolomé and I in Venecia three months beforehand, word having reached him of his father's sudden death. I looked forward to seeing my friend again, as well as to paying my respects at the tomb of Don Fernandez. Our voyage had been a pleasant one, with calm seas and favorable winds following us since leaving Cagliari. I took the time to compose a letter to my family announcing my return I would have sent on ahead upon our arrival, and settled in for the remainder of the journey.

At port, tension filled the air. A crowd had formed near the Basilica de Santa Maria del Pi where three *conversos* were being burned in effigy. Two others, I was told by a fellow in the crowd, had been executed the day before when it was revealed they were involved in a plot to assassinate the inquisitor Jorge de Huesca while he was in pursuit of the duties of his most holy office.

"Those three," the man said, pointing to the inferno raging around the straw likenesses, "it's said they are involved as well. Juan Nelleda and two of his cousins. But they fled some time ago. Marrano dogs."

The inquisitor himself was seated on a raised platform so he could oversee the proceedings and, more importantly, so others present could see him at his task. A foul-looking man, his bald head ringed in a halo of short white hairs like a laurel wreath, he looked on with fiery, terrifying black eyes that reflected the dancing flames like a mirror. The pleasure the spectacle brought him was evident; he'd been filled with a holy power that had descended into lust. It was the same with them all. The inquisitors had come to Aragon with wrath in their hearts and hatred in their souls only eclipsed by their unquenchable desire to become as gods among men. They betrayed their Christ for it, even going so far as to proclaim their sin in his name. They carry him like a banner before them so he might not look back at the ruin they wrought in his wake.

Bartolomé suggested quietly we leave the place immediately, and for once, I agreed with his counsel.

Several days later, we reached the banks of the river Ebro south of Quinto. The fortresslike walls of the Iglesia de la Asunción loomed high atop the rise overlooking the village below. Home was no more than a day's ride. We rested about an hour north of the town, assured that, by nightfall the following day, we would be sleeping in our own beds once again.

Rising early, we saddled the horses, and by late midday, the silhouettes of the rooftops of Zaragoza appeared to us on the distant horizon. At their sight, Bartolomé paused to say a blessing and prayer to San Cristóbal for seeing our safe return.

But as we approached the city, a strange sense of unease overcame me. Those we passed on the road moved quickly by. I offered pleasant greetings to several riders, only to be ignored. To those whom I had even presented myself formally by name, I was outright shunned. This odd behavior went on for several hours, and soon, we found ourselves alone on a road normally filled with travelers.

Then, of a sudden, my eyes caught sight of a rider on horseback approaching at full tilt. He whipped his horse mercilessly, an enormous cloud of grayish-red dust rising up behind him as he coursed straight for us. Instinctively, Bartolomé panicked and began another prayer for our protection, but I put no such stock in the intervention of hapless martyrs and drew my sword. Surveying the terrain about me, I positioned myself on high ground, but this maneuver did not deter my opponent, and he came on all the same.

It was only when he was much closer, perhaps a hundred yards away, that he began calling out to us, and I recognized the voice of Gonçalo. Overcome with joy at seeing him again, I sheathed my sword and dismounted, only to have my old friend jump down from his saddle and hastily usher me back to my horse.

"You must leave," he said, to my astonishment. "There is little time. You must go, my friend."

"What in the name..." I stammered as he shoved me toward a clump of scrub by the roadside.

"If they find you, they will surely kill you," he said. "It's not safe here."

"What are you talking about?" I said. "Have you gone mad? Who is going to kill me?"

"Francisco Luengo."

"But I know no one by that name."

"It matters not. He knows you," he said. There was a terror in my friend's eyes I'd not seen before. Gonçalo was by nature a strong and confident man. But merely uttering this man Luengo's name brought him great fear.

"I cannot understand you," I said. "My father would not—"

"Your father is dead," he said.

I felt as if my legs had been cut out from under me by the swipe of an invisible sword. I swooned and stumbled back against my horse. Bartolomé quickly dismounted and rushed to my aid. Together, he and Gonçalo helped me to sit on a low boulder.

"How?" I began. "How has this happened?"

"It was murder," Gonçalo said. "By the order of Jorge de Huerca. But it was the doing of Francisco Luengo. Of that, I am sure. He was… put to the flame after Luengo accused him before La Inquisición of practicing the rituals of the Jews."

"But that is not true," I said, knowing what I said to be a lie. "Who is this Luengo?"

"A *capitán* in de Huerca's detail," he said. "He remains in the city still. If he learns you have returned, you will suffer your father's fate."

"But why would he accuse Don Moreno?" Bartolomé said.

"Luengo is a filthy man," Gonçalo spat with disgust. "Full of evil and lust. His impure gaze fell upon your sister and would not be turned from her."

"Constanza?" I said. "Where is she? And what of my mother?"

Gonçalo's eyes could not meet mine. I implored him to answer me. He cast a somber glance at my feet, his cheeks streamed wet with tears.

"I'm sorry," was all he could say.

I swooned again as a great cry burst from my lips. A feeling that I was falling, propelling down into a bottomless abyss, overcame me. The last thing I remember was the sight of my two compatriots rushing to me as I tumbled from the rock.

❧

I don't know how long I lay in my stupor, but when I finally awoke, night had fallen, and a cold wind swept the plains.

We were camped in an enclosure, a cavity high in the rocks making a long, narrow chamber. It was a perfect location where bandits or highwaymen might have taken refuge from pursuit. Bartolomé crouched in the center of the cave tending a small fire, while Gonçalo stared at the flames pensively. I was brought wine, which helped rejuvenate my spirit. My stomach burned with hunger, but all my thoughts were fixed on Constanza and the terrible fate that had befallen her.

"You will tell me what happened to my family," I said to Gonçalo. "And spare me no detail, or, by God, I will murder you here and now."

"I am sorry, my friend," Gonçalo began. "It was necessary to get you away from Zaragoza as soon as possible. It was only by God's grace I learned you had returned. You passed a servant of mine on the road who recognized you. Immediately, he ran to me so that I might stop you from entering the city and being arrested on sight. The Moreno name is a curse in Zaragoza. I have saved you from the flames, my dear Juan Cristóbal. We are safe here tonight, but tomorrow, you must ride far from here. You can never return, or you will most certainly be put to death."

I thanked my friend for rescuing me from a fate I could know nothing about and apologized for my outburst. But I begged him once more to tell me what had happened in my absence. With a heavy heart, he acquiesced.

"Francisco Luengo rode in at the head of a detachment of two dozen *soldado* commissioned to accompany the inquisitor de Huerca to Zaragoza," he said. "A new inquisitorial court was to be established. There were rumors of a conspiracy. Enemies of the church, *conversos*, were plotting to assassinate de Huerca himself."

"We saw effigies burning in Barcelona," Bartolomé said.

"Then you saw de Huerca in the flesh."

"But Don Moreno was no *converso*," Bartolomé protested.

"One does not have to be. To be accused is sufficient to be suspect and put on trial," I said.

"Precisely," Gonçalo agreed. "And Luengo knows as much. He has de Huerca's ear. The old man uses all manner of spies, none more ruthless and efficient than the captain. After he arrived in the city, he saw your sister at la Nuestra Señora del Pilar. Her beauty unwittingly ensnared him, and he became obsessed with making her his own.

"Constanza would never have such a man," I said. "Her heart was as pure as a mountain flower. A villain such as this Luengo would never draw her eye."

"Her eyes were drawn by Raoul de Anda," Bartolomé said. "And his trade was lies and deceit as well."

"Say his name again, and I will cut out your tongue," I said, my ire rising by the second as I saw the innocence of my beloved sister being assailed on all sides by these two agents of base infamy. I cursed myself for ever having been absent during her time of greatest need.

"Naturally, she rebuffed his advances," Gonçalo continued. "She did not play the *coqueta* like some other girls might have. But this did not stop him from trying and trying again to win her heart. He came to her with gifts, with promises of riches for your father, but to no avail. She was as a boulder in a raging river, unmoved by the torrent of his dubious affections."

"Dubious?" I said.

"The man's reputation precedes him," Gonçalo said. "There are stories of other women, other towns."

"No doubt the good Constanza had heard them herself," Bartolomé said. "Clever girl."

"Not clever enough," Gonçalo said. "Her resistance only served to inflame Luengo's passions and enrage him all the more that he could not have her. So he turned his anger to vengeful purposes."

"De Huerca," I said.

"Perhaps he thought that by turning the courts on your father and mother, Constanza would relent. Many in her position would. But Don Moreno was not a man easily intimidated."

"My grandfather was born in Teruel," I said. "Opposing La Inquisición is almost a family business."

"Nevertheless, charges were brought, witnesses produced. All claimed your family practiced the rituals of the *judío* in secret."

"No doubt spouting such lies to save their own skins," Bartolomé said. "But why weren't they just expelled?"

"Because Luengo's rage knew no bounds," Gonçalo said. "Documents were produced, all false, of course, but taken as truth, nonetheless. They were tied to the Nelleda plot. It sealed their fates. That is the power this man wields."

I could listen to no more, so great was the pain in my heart. At first, I thought to beg for death, that my suffering would be brought to an end and I be reunited with Constanza and my parents in the next life, wherever that may be.

But quickly, these thoughts were usurped by a desire for vengeance. The injustice done to my family and my family name called out to be righted.

"Do not seek to revenge yourself, I beg you," Bartolomé said. "Vengeance is for God alone. If you pursue this Luengo, you will only hasten your own undoing. It would be better to leave Aragon."

"Do not speak to me of God," I spat. "Is it not he who gives his blessing to the infernal undertakings of men like de Huerca? Where is God in the *mazmorra*? Where is he in the trials? Where was he when they put the torch to my sister's feet? My sister!"

I wailed in sorrow once again as the horrific vision of Constanza's body tormented by flames passed before my eyes. I heard her cries, her cries to me to rescue her, but remained paralyzed to help.

"To the devil with your God," I cried and swooned once more, collapsing to the dirt unconscious.

My vision darkened, and the figure of Constanza suddenly vanished. I was no longer in the place of execution. I was instead on a low hilltop overlooking a vast and desolate plain that stretched to the horizon. Everywhere about me, ruined structures dotted the landscape, and overhead, an endless black vault, the starless heavens. Yet in this darkness, I could see shapes, forms, movement—lines of shadows drifting in and out of the ruins, organized like crowds of people milling about. One of these ruins I thought, for only a moment, to recognize. It was but a strange shadow of itself, but, yes, I had seen those lines and towering crenellations before. They were a familiar sight. It was the apse of the Catedral del Salvador, a place I knew well.

Though this vision felt to last only a moment, when again my eyes opened, I found myself alone in the rocky cavern. Both Bartolomé and Gonçalo, along with their horses, had vanished.

❧

Daylight threatened to break. Already a reddish glow rose on the eastern horizon. The stars began to dim, their light giving way to the rising sun.

I stood at the mouth of the chamber. There was no sign of my friends. I did not recognize the terrain either. How far had Gonçalo brought me? A terrible chill filled the air, freezing me to the marrow.

"Your friends did not desert you," a voice called from behind. "But neither will they return."

I spun on my heels and snatched my sword from its sheath, my eyes searching the dim glow around the dying fire. Just beyond the flames, deep within the shadows, I could make out only the faintest of movements. A chip of rock tumbled from the wall beyond my sight. A sudden flapping of wings stirred the dust, and with frenzied speed, a greasy black bird swooped down from above, its hooked talons fairly parting the hair on my head. I swiped at it with my sword, missing by inches, but when it wheeled around again for a second pass, I felt the tip of my blade catch a glancing blow. The bird cried out with a hideous cackle and fled back into the shadows.

My muscles tensed. At any moment, I expected the thing to dive at me from the darkness. Minutes passed, but it made no sign of returning. Taking a rag from my satchel, I cleaned the vile thing's sticky blood from the point of my rapier and absently tucked it back into my bag. It was only when I had let my guard down that I was taken unawares yet again. But it was not the bird that reemerged from the confines of the shadows this time but rather the incredible figure of a man.

He stepped forward to warm his hands by the dying fire as if it were his own. He seemed to take no notice of me at all. I stepped forward and offered his chin the point of my blade.

"How do you come to be here?" I demanded. "Where are my compatriots? Speak, bandit!"

"Odd that one who secrets himself in such a place as this would accuse others of banditry," he offered in reply. "But I am no more brigand than you. Admittedly, neither of us is dressed for such low pursuits, wouldn't you agree?"

He spoke with a tongue both fluent and natural, though he was clearly a Moor. Clad in fine silken robes of red and yellow under a hooded *albornoz* threaded in gold, he carried himself with a noble air. His feet, shod in exquisite goat leather, showed no signs of the mud of the road, but unlike other Moors, he bore his bald head to the elements, and beneath dark eyebrows, he gazed at the world through two sickly milky-blue eyes.

"Sheath your blade, good sir," he said. "Men cannot freely converse if there is the threat of violence. As you can see, I am without weapon myself."

"It is foolish of you to travel the roads at night without arms," I said.

"I've never had need for them," the Moor said. "I much prefer to settle disputes by more peaceful means."

"How can I be assured you don't have compatriots waiting for me to drop guard so you can rob and murder me?"

"I travel alone," was his reply. "Always alone. And why would I wish to murder you? I come to you as your humble servant, dear sir."

"I have a servant," I said.

"Yes, but he is not here, is he? A proper servant should be present if he is to serve, whereas a servant who flees at the first sign of danger is clearly serving only himself as master. You would do better to let poor Bartolomé be on his way. He can no longer serve you as you require."

"How do you know his name?" I demanded, suddenly feeling the icy chill of the morning air press against the back of my neck. "What did you do with him?"

"A man's name is no mystery," he said. "Simply ask him for it, and he will tell you. This may be well for a common servant, but for Juan Cristóbal Moreno de Zaragoza, the matter has become a little more complicated, has it not?"

I stepped back, keeping my eye fixed on the Moor as he crouched by the fire. Instinctively, I made to raise my sword again.

"What kind of servant would I be if I did not already know my master?" he said with a smile. "Don't worry, I do not represent that strange institution from which you draw your fears. Stay your blade. Neither pope nor king has the reach to extend to us here. Come, sit by the fire. The nip in the air is as sharp as a serpent's tongue."

I stood my ground, refusing to move.

"As you wish," was his casual reply. "But this fire is dying, and soon, we will both be freezing."

"If you are my servant," I said, "then fetch some wood and revive it."

"That is a task better suited to a valet," he replied indignantly. "Much below my talents. But if you insist."

The Moor rose and begrudgingly shuffled off into the shadows, only to emerge a moment later with an armload of branches. These he put to use, and soon, the flames of a large fire illuminated the walls of the cavern. Yet still, the chill remained.

"And now you should like me to fetch some food to break your fast?" he said, returning to his place beside the fire. "A dish of fine *arroz con cerdo*, perhaps? Surely, you sully your lips with the flesh of swine like some other *conversos* who have surrendered their faith in the name of saving their own skins?"

"I am not *converso*," I said indignantly.

"Do not fear," he said. "Your secret is safe with me. Truth be told, I find it most honorable your father and mother were willing to go to the stake to protect their faith."

"They ate pork openly," I said. "And worshipped at the cross openly."

"And asked forgiveness in secret," he said. "And held secret Seder. And sought their atonement in secret on the day appointed by Him for such purposes. Just as your father's father did, and his father before him. I must agree, it is better to partake of a little bacon than to become some for the amusement of the Inquisition."

"Your tone of mockery enrages me," I shouted. "You jest about their fate like some fool at court."

"But all their concealing did nothing in the end," he said without pause. "They were found out all the same. Now you should feel you can order off the menu as you please, without fear of anyone questioning your aversion to a decently prepared chop."

"Do not joke again!" I roared, drawing my sword. "Or I will cut your head from your shoulders as I would cut... would cut..."

But words failed me. White froth boiling on my lips, it was not the Moor's neck I wished to draw my blade against but the one whose jealousy and lustful abandon took my dearest Constanza from me.

"I promise to jest no more," he said. "We have come to the heart of the matter. Your heart and your mind are as one against a common foe. The hour of parlay draws near. I, your humble servant, seek only to grant you that which your soul most cries out for."

"What I want you cannot possibly grant me," I said. "And besides this..."

I let my words trail off into dumb silence.

"What? Contemplating Bartolomé's words? Think you God will avenge your dear departed family? Rot! God is not in the habit of retribution. Once, perhaps, now too long ago to remember. But treat with me and you will see the deed done. With me at your side, God himself will not quench the fire of your wrath."

I gazed into the Moor's bilious eyes. They fixed their stare on me, his cold, glassy black irises aflame with the reflection of the fire dancing before them. A sudden terror overcame me. I raised my sword to him once again and slowly backed away.

"If you're thinking to order me behind you, you'll do me the kindness to step away from the ledge?"

"You," I stammered. "You're..."

"I am merely an emissary," he said. "Like any ambassador, I have it within my means to offer contract on behalf of my Lord. And you are a man seeking revenge. It is not the first time your wrath has gotten the better of you. A certain Raoul de Anda, was it? Another who sought to wrong your family and violate the sanctity of your good sister. Someone should have taught her better. Protecting her integrity is a full-time business for you—well, at least it was."

His mockery drew my ire, and I made to strike him, but the indifferent stare of his ugly eyes kept me rooted to the spot.

"Nothing stayed your blade with him, so why should Luengo be any different?" he continued. "I tell you again, stay your blade and lend your ear. After I have said my piece, if you wish me gone, I shall take my leave and never return."

It shames me to admit, but weakness of spirit and mortal sorrow caused me to listen to everything. He spoke with eloquence, almost with kindness, as he put forth the means for my revenge. Luengo would fall at my hand, de Huerca too, and no ills would befall me, no threat of the dungeon, no trials. My fate would be my own to decide, no one else's. There would be—

But Juan Cristóbal's thoughts would remain incomplete. There were no more pages to this part of the manuscript.

The rest of the translation began with another marginal note made by Etienne. These pages had been found hidden in the same volume as the first—only, these had been secreted under the leather of the book's rear cover. Still in the Spaniard's hand, the make of the paper was again distinctly different from the previous group. No date of origin could be determined, but it was clearly some years after the events of his meeting in the cave.

. . . it could only lead to disaster. Time proves the only true enemy. All else is folly. My course is set.

Sixty-one years have I wandered doing the devil's bidding. How many souls have I committed to damnation in payment of my debt? Luengo, de Huerca, Franchetti, Mac Quane, Horvantinčić, the names go on and on. All dead by my hand. Yet still, I live.

Is there no end to this wandering? My wrath sated so long ago, I live only as a hollow shell of a man, bereft of passion and spirit, only too aware of my destiny. What was so distant and blurry in the fog of my rage now looms close on my heels like my shadow. I cannot escape it. My soul is bound for darkness, forfeit by my own dumb fury. In desperation, I commit myself to the endeavor and these words to page so others might learn from my folly and flee from the devil and his promises.

Some time ago, in Andalusia, I met a hermit, a holy man who'd taken to calling himself Agustín after the bishop of Hippo. This old anchorite had secreted himself in an abandoned monastery nestled deep in the Sierra Norte hills, and it was only by God's good grace he was set in my path.

At first, he welcomed me as a weary traveler, providing me a table of simple yet rough fare. Sharing what little wine he had, I listened as he told me of his life, one of devotion and piety, but also one of study. His travels had taken him to the distant shores of Arabia and Ceylon, and to the great kingdoms of Africa and Persia. He'd wandered as far north as Hadrian's Wall and endured the harsh Muscovite winters, all in what he called his personal Via Dolorosa, his own path of sorrow.

He possessed knowledge unsurpassed by the holy texts of ancient Christendom and Islam, in the form of a trove of scrolls, books, and parchments collected on his travels, which he kept secreted in a reading room. His own faith remained a mystery, but a reverence for the holy in all its forms was his portion. He professed allegiance to no one but God, in whatever form He should take, and in this way, he revealed himself more sorcerer than priest. He spoke of the wisdom of the Kabbala and at length about the gods of the Greeks and the ancient peoples of the Shaivite faith and could read several long dead or dying languages including Mysian and Amorite.

His tale at an end, he bid me relate to him the travails of my own sorrows, which I reluctantly did. Through it all, he listened with growing unease, his wizened eyes casting disdain at my shame and frailty of spirit so that I felt as a scolded child standing before the judgment of his father.

"And have you renounced your allegiance to this enemy of God?" he said when I had finished my story.

"How can I?" I replied. "My soul was pledged for vengeance. God can only reject me. My fate is already sealed."

"Then be gone from this place, agent of evil!" he commanded and shut his door to me.

For three days and three nights, I remained outside his door, begging his forgiveness and pleading for guidance for my lost soul. I neither slept nor ate, but still, he would not grant me entry. Steeled against my entreaties by his mortal misgivings, he remained cloistered in his rooms, but on the morning of the fourth day, his more holy nature softened his resolve, and he opened his door to me again.

I would remain under the tutelage and protection of Agustín for the next three years. In that time, the increasing fervor of the outside world would not penetrate our meditations, nor would the shadow of the Inquisition cast its gloom over the secluded valley where my new home lay. This, I attributed to the promises made to me all those years ago by the fiend that my life's thread would not be threatened or cut by any mortal man. Ironic that it was the very caveat he imposed for his own benefit that should ultimately aid me in his undoing. For his part, Agustín attributed it to diligent prayer and the placement of various relics of strange origins about the place of which he claimed served to both enlighten and protect. Could it have been these same artifacts that kept the devil at bay as well and preserved the life of my teacher after hearing my tale?

Our days were filled with reflection, prayer, and study as we worked tirelessly to break the curse I had brought upon myself. We consulted holy books from many lands collected over the years of his travels, paid call on seers and mystics high in the hills, scoured endless rolls of scroll and parchments looking for some hint, some clue. The days were long, the nights endless. Despite the hardship and rough living of the abbey, Agustín forbade me from using the influence of my contract to improve our lot.

"What God does not provide is the feast of the devil," he would often say as we sat down to a paltry meal of olives, bread crusts, and bitter wine. "Let the ones who follow the path of evil glut themselves on ill-gotten spoils. For us, let knowledge and wisdom be our meat."

❧

Autumns bled into winters. Winters gave way to vibrant springs and humid summers, which, in turn, ceded their warmth to the cool breezes of new autumns and then the frigid darkness of the mountain winter nights once again.

On one of those nights, by the flickering light of a tallow taper, our revelation finally came.

"It is here!" he declared joyously through happy tears welling in the corners of his wrinkled eyes. "Here!"

He'd been reading a text that recounted an oral history of a people long since vanished. Scant were the details, but clearly, there existed a cult of sorts who'd worshipped a demon in the form of a bird. These people predated the Amorites.

"He demanded sacrifices of gold," Agustín noted.

"So did many other gods and devils," I said.

"But he was one of the earliest," he said. "If not the first. It is written the bird could bring about an endless harvest and cause illnesses to be cured in exchange for simple tokens of gold. These he coveted above all else and took with him back to the dwelling place of the demons."

"I do not understand how this is helpful," I said. "It proves only that I am not the only one to have encountered him."

"It's more than that," Agustín said. "Much more. This cult worshipped in only one place and built their temple to the demon there. The Moors claim it as Damascus today. You spoke to me of a vision you had just before the demon appeared, did you not? Of a barren place where the souls of the dead dwell. It was there you saw the ruined apse of the Catedral del Salvador?"

"Yes?"

"Then if the vision you described to me is to be believed, where his temple once stood in this earthly plane, its foundations must still stand in the infernal one."

"Still, I do not understand," I said hopelessly.

"If the demon who visited you is indeed this demon whom they revered at Dammeśeq, then perhaps it is there where he makes his home and has brought the token of your father with which you sealed your agreement."

"But how can you be sure?" I said.

"I cannot," he replied. "But every bird has its nest. It is written the bird's eye is drawn to that which glistens like gold or gleams like a precious stone to adorn its home. These were its sacrifices. This prideful weakness of the rook and the daw has been known for a long time. They are thieving, covetous creatures. When man makes a sacrifice to God, it is in praise of Him, not for His material gain. What use does God have for the slaughtered calf or the fumes of incense? He doesn't take through deceit what is freely given. The items themselves are of no value, if only as vessels that are imbued with the spirit of charity. And what is charity but a gift of the soul? So it was with you when you offered the token to that fiend. You must retrieve your sacrifice, the gift you made of your soul, if it is to ever be made whole again. What he took from you then holds what is missing from you now. Without it, you can never fully cleanse the sin from your spirit."

"This is an impossible task," I said, overcome with despair. "How can I retrieve what no longer exists? What path can bring me to such a place? The devil appears and disappears at his will. There is no power that can give a man such ability."

Agustín rubbed the white stubble upon his pitted chin and lost himself in reflection. At length, he questioned me about my encounter with the daw and the Moor. I recounted again all I could from that horrible night.

"And you say he has visited you twice since then," he said.

"He has," I replied. "Once in Lyon and then again in Naples."

"In what manner did he manifest his presence?"

I said in both instances he came first as my reflection in a mirror, then, as if crossing a threshold, he used the thing as a door to bring himself forward into my sphere. This revelation sparked a curious expression on Agustín's face, and quickly, he rose, his mind suddenly occupied with a new thought.

"I must make preparations," he said, gathering himself up. "Tomorrow I will make for Córdoba. There is a certain prior there with whom I must make inquiries."

"I will accompany you," I said.

"No," he said. "You must remain here under the protection of the abbey. If the devil learns of what we have discussed here tonight, all may be lost. Stay here and keep to our work. I will return in one week. If there is to be—"

Al paused, shuffling through the remaining pages. Only a disjointed series of random thoughts followed, snippets of confused ravings, incoherent plans, and a most curious resolution.

...reappeared four days ago under the crumbling eaves of the ruined castle turret. I can make no start until he leaves. The halls echo night and day with his incessant, mocking cries. They fill my waking dreams and pursue me into the depths of my slumber. I know not if I've the strength of fortitude to complete the task. Agustín's words ring in my memory, yet I waver still. There can be no...

... from his blood was derived the portal. Such a gruesome relic...

... that which was stolen. It must be retrieved. The hour is close at hand. Fled Valladolid under cover of darkness with horses and...

... entry at Genoa, at the Catedral de San Lorenzo. Enduring the tremendous pain can only serve to prepare my living soul for the agony that awaits. But endure I must, as Agustín had instructed. Passage through a holy place, where evil's wicked talons dare not step, behind whose walls evil's pale stare cannot penetrate. The arrangements have been ordered. The mirror I shall install at the...

... falling through water, the air parts for me as the waves of the Red Sea before the might of Moses. Sins only memories floating among shadows so cold... lonely in darkness, blackest night, empty hope so full of hope unrequited... empty vessels overflowing, cascades of sorrow, sorrow's river flows from within its own heart, bleeding bloody woe to sing a hymn of unending plea... from place to place to place to place to place... *pulvis et umbra sumus...*

... to have emerged from the depths of the horrid hole into the glory and the light of the living once again! Can it be a full five years? My friend, my master, had perished. Sorrow filled my heart, but entrusted the relic was to another who only through the grace of all-mighty God set me free of the prison. I inquired this mullah on my flight from the city, who gave his name as Abd Al-Samad, who declared it the twenty-fifth of Jumada Al-Thani in the year of the prophet 987. This I reckoned to be the nineteenth of August 1579, exactly five years to the day. Apart from the sands of the time of kings and men, what seemed perhaps a journey of only days recorded my living history not in hours but in years. But I've no time to reflect, for one journey is at an end and the next is just yet begun. Embraced against my chest, my father's token reclaimed, I hold its sorrowful history closest to my heart so I may never again repeat my folly. *La mancha del mal,* which marked my soul and which I have retained all these long years as a reminder sealed within to be carried the remainder of my living days. My soul reunited I take the—

Here ended Juan Cristóbal's story. On the reverse of the last page, written not by the Spaniard but by Etienne, a final notation on the text:

These last six years I have spent in constant contemplation of the record left by Juan Cristóbal and in an unceasing search for the token of his father, in the ever-fading hope that perhaps within there remains a detail yet uncovered that will unlock the secret of how he completed his passage into that horrid place of "hope unrequited" and the means used to extricate himself back to the domain of the living body—an incantation noted, a ritual practiced, some manner of dark art invoked that granted him such a gift. But all attempts to locate such a clue have borne no fruit. I fear the means to my salvation has been lost to history and will forever elude me.

There remains no record of the life of Juan Cristóbal Moreno of Zaragoza beyond what he himself documented within the pages of his own journal. Upon his emergence in Damascus, he made every effort to conceal himself from the prying eyes of the devil. But even a man so bent on making himself invisible, especially one with such a remarkable history, cannot truly vanish.

In Madrid, I learned of an abbey high in the Galician hills, a cloister known to the Cistercians to contain a library documenting the history of their order. It was there I read among the rosters of the monks the name of one Christoforo Moreno who'd entered the monastery in 1582 and remained there until his death in 1619, but no record of his burial could be found, and the prior himself admitted to me original abbey, located some distance away, had burned in 1793 and been rebuilt on the new spot where it still stands today. It was only by the grace of God, he said, most of the oldest records had survived the inferno.

My search goes on.

The bird does not return. The wicked servant obeyed my final command and has fallen silent. If it is his blood I require, he will not give it freely. So, it is upon Juan Cristóbal's timepiece my eyes have been set, and my days and nights since filled in this mad endeavor. I know in my heart I shall never locate the object of my desire, but still, I press on. My suffering extends even further beyond his reach, extended by my own hands. It is as Kazakov once said. My eternity is that much longer for my knowledge and my damnable pride.

Elena, my beloved, my light, my unending divine, is lost to me forever. Her soul is surely warmed by an eternal love and reposes in a bliss I shall never know, whereas mine is bound for that eternal night of unending sorrow.

My life endures, but my journey is come to its end. There is no hope of salvation, no hope of ever finding my Elena again. Time without her, unending time, is all that remains for me.

My hell has only just begun.

Chapter XVIII

The door groaned unexpectedly as she opened it. Zofia peered warily down the steps into the dark of the storeroom. The sun had yet to come up.

Standing with one hand grasping the jamb, she leaned forward as far as she could to see what she could, which was little. The light from the kitchen shone down the stairs, illuminating a small trapezoid of floor at the bottom, but nothing more. In her other hand, she brandished her weapon: a long-handled wooden spoon. She remained there, rigid as a statue, hoping she'd not been heard. Almost a full minute had passed, and still, she hadn't moved.

"I know you are there, *Babcia*," Etienne said from the shadows below. "You can come down if you like. I'm not going to bite."

"Is Albie down there with you?"

"No."

"Then I will stay here."

Etienne appeared at the foot of the stairs. He'd smoothed his greasy hair and scraggly beard into a semblance of order and straightened his wrinkled clothes with the flats of his palms. Rest had restored him some. To Zofia's eyes, he looked just an ordinary young fellow perhaps a bit down on his luck. Pathetic, really.

"Your husband has gone," he said. "I'm afraid I don't know where. He left while I was still asleep."

Zofia made no reply but kept a distrustful eye fixed on him from behind the round lenses of her glasses.

"I know I already thanked him for his kindness, but I believe I have not done you the same turn. It's not easy for me. Sometimes I find it terribly difficult to talk. I am sorry about that. I'm sorry for a lot of things. But thank you for the bed, and the soup. It was delicious. The last time I had such a hearty *polewka* was in Górny Śląsk, near a little village called Wisła Wielka on the Vistula. A lovely place. Perhaps you know it?"

Again, Etienne was met with a leery glare.

"No, I imagine you don't," he said, trying to fill the uneasy silence.

"My family comes from Katowice," she said. "I know the village you speak of."

Etienne smiled a charming boyish smile, not unlike Oliver's. Calm and reserved, she thought he looked little more than a boy himself.

"I passed through there once on my way to Saint Petersburg..." he started to say, but then trailed off. He could see no point in telling her anything more.

Zofia released her grip on the doorjamb but still clutched the wooden spoon before her like a dagger. Her diminutive figure barely filled half the doorframe.

"Well," Etienne said, turning back to the darkened room, "I'll just wait here, then."

"Is it true what Albie told me?" she said. "In the temple. What you said to him?"

"I don't believe I told him anything he did not already know himself. Perhaps I only just reminded him of it. He loves you dearly, you know."

"I know."

"Then you know the lengths a man will go to preserve that love. We do horrible things, but glorious things too. It's only when we are separated from our love we are at our weakest. Women can bear that separation with dignity and restraint, but men, I fear, lack grace. We act rashly, without reason, to move heaven and earth just to have one more moment with the one we cherish. We curse God, but more so, we castigate our own selves. What we would not risk in such times."

Etienne glowered at the darkness, his pain written clearly upon his face.

"She was special to you," she said, lowering the spoon. "This one you lost."

"You know of it?"

"No," she said. "But it is not hard to read the look in your eyes."

"She made me more of a man than I could ever have dreamed possible. To be without her forevermore is..." His thoughts trailed off. "I'm sorry."

Zofia took one careful step, then another, and another, and three more, stopping just before the bottom of the stairs, making sure to keep a safe distance. She could still not muster the belief that, despite his youthful appearance, he was not as harmless as Al would like her to think. A dybbuk he might not be, but still, she chose to reserve final judgment as to the ultimate nature of his character. Etienne sensed her fears, giving her a wide berth.

"I like to think what I was told as a child is not so," she said, "and when this life is done, there will be a time with the ones we love. I will be with Albie, and with my Henry. He will grow up there and become the man he was not allowed to be. And you will find this one who your heart is in such pain for. I think everyone needs to believe there is something beyond this. It is not wrong to hope for more time."

Etienne sat on the cot, leaving room for Zofia, but she chose to remain apart.

"I have done terrible things," he said. "Even if I were to see her again, how could she possibly accept me?"

"If she loves you, she will forgive you. But you must forgive yourself. To do that, you have to begin forgetting the past. Whatever bad things you did cannot be undone. But what you do from today forward is what will bring you closer to her. I realized this when I lost my son. I could not grow with all the sadness holding me down. It was like a big *otoczak*, a stone pressing on my heart. Some days, I could not breathe. Some days, I did not even want to. But this anger, it does not bring him back to me. He cannot come back to me. I must go to him. One day, I know this will be so. It is the same for you. And you have already begun a new life. You say you did many bad things in the past. OK. But you also helped my Albie, even if you think you did not. And that is something good. If all you know is the bad, then it should be easy for you to see it in others. Then you can show them the good, and this will help them too. In this way, your life can go on. You can become this good man she believed you to be again."

❧

They talked in this fashion for some time, losing track of it themselves. Only when Al came hurriedly through the front door of the shop did they realize the sun had risen and the day had begun anew. He locked the door fast behind him, stopping to watch the empty street with a conspiratorial air, then came to them with a look of nervous but vibrant excitement in his wizened eyes.

"Where did you go off to?" Zofia said, helping him out of his coat and hat. Al could barely stand still for all his agitation. His behavior was baffling. Etienne looked upon his rattled friend with the same confused awe Al had on the night of their first meeting.

"The bank," he said. "I wanted to get there early. I had to."

"So, you left before light? They did not open until maybe an hour ago. What was so important you should go out in the dark?"

"I waited outside. I couldn't wait here." He hurried to Etienne, took him under the arm, and led him to his bench, chattering wildly all the way. "I read it. I read it, and I knew. I mean, I do not know for certain, but I think it must be. It has to be. It cannot be any other. If it is, all may be lost, but if it is not, and it is here, then there is still hope. But I remembered his words, how it had to be kept safe. And I thought if there are only three or four, then maybe this is the one, and if it is, I had to bring it to you."

"Whose words?" Zofia said, exacerbated. She'd not seen her husband in such a frantic state of excitement before. "This is the one what?"

Al shifted on his feet like an eager schoolboy waiting to receive a piece of candy and placed on the table a small wooden box. The anticlimax of the moment gave Zofia and

Etienne curious, almost apprehensive pause. But Al beamed with joy, a great grin lighting up his tired old face. He lifted the lid using both hands and gently extracted the bundle of folded cotton cloth inside. It looked nothing more than an old rag, but peeling back the layers revealed the treasure within in all its gleaming splendor: Gerhort's little egg.

Etienne's breath caught in his throat. He could neither speak nor move. He could only stare. It was smaller than he'd ever imagined it to be. The craftsmanship was extraordinary. For a moment, the three of them stood in dumb silence. Even the clocks seemed to fall mute, captivated by the sight of their curious ancestor.

"How came you by this?" Etienne said, his voice but a whisper, the pits of his deep-blue-green eyes opened wide as saucers.

Al lifted it to the light. Though more than four hundred years old, its smooth golden surface still beamed with the reddish fire of a fine-cut ruby.

Etienne hesitated. He could no more bring himself to reach out to touch it than he could have willed himself to levitate.

"Take it," Al said.

It was remarkably light. In all the years of searching, he'd never considered that it would have weight, or dimension or color, or its surface would be cold to the touch. He held it in his trembling hand as one might a seedling or the wing of a dragonfly, cupped to shield it from a sudden breeze blowing it away forever. With the tip of his finger, he nudged open the clasp holding the two hemispheres together and lifted the lid. The iron hour hand secured on its central spindle by a tiny pin of gold indicated just a few minutes past eleven o'clock, as it had for untold years. There were scratches on the underside of the lid, obliterating what was once the owner's inscription.

"But," he said, "how can you know? Is it really his? Is it the one?"

Al opened his toolbox. Zofia had not seen such import in her husband's actions before. His movements were like those of a surgeon preparing the theater for a great operation. He cleared away the box and the cotton cloth and set out his screwdrivers, his awl, his tweezers, and pincers with measured precision.

He placed the egg on the table, his hands steady as iron beams. Peering through the spectacles perched at the end of his nose, he gently freed the hinge pin and separated the two hemispheres. This gave him freer access to a seam no thicker than a human hair running around the circumference joining the face and movement to the lower half of the orb. He used the flat of a knife and the fine hooked end of a Swiss lever to lightly, almost tenderly, prize apart this seam, separating the internal workings from their case. A pungent, musty smell filled their nostrils as air hundreds of years old trapped within escaped from its prison. At last, the movement was free.

Both men leaned over the now empty lower half of the case. There, resting in the well of the orb, a folded scrap of grayish-blue fabric no bigger than a fingernail—at its center, like a droplet of merlot, a dried streak of crimson blood.

"*La mancha del mal*," Etienne whispered. "Evil's stain."

- PART III -

Chapter XIX

"That there should be joy in life and in all things a man does with his time on earth, that is the main thing," Arthur said. "Does she make you happy?"

"She brings me more happiness in one day than the Phillies have in the last three years."

"This is clearly a man with his priorities in order," Nathan said. "Marriage is about more than happiness. It's about commitment. It's about honor and sacrifice. Without those things, there can never be lasting happiness between you."

"Doing right by Ruth by being the stand-up guy we all know you are," Arthur added. "Working hard, providing for your house, having kids."

"I know," Oliver said.

Al and his nephews had gathered for dinner at an eatery off Broad Street, in the shadow of city hall, just the men, at a quiet table near the back. It wasn't rare, them all getting together to share a meal, but the absence of the wives and children made this an occasion more special than usual. As it was, the subject of Oliver's impending nuptials occupied much of the dinner conversation. The wedding was only a few weeks away.

"Your brothers have much experience in these things," Al said. "You would do well to listen to them. But most importantly, listen to yourself, and listen to your wife. The heart is the greatest guide. Happiness in marriage comes from the partnership. The man and the woman, they are like two halves of this table. Apart, they would teeter and fall over. But bring them together, lean them on each other, and they will stand strong and bear weight."

Oliver and his brothers agreed. When their uncle spoke, they listened to his words as if spoken by their own father. For his part, Al was the only father Oliver had ever really known, and Oliver being the closest thing Al had to his own son, he took it upon himself to measure his words carefully when speaking to the young man, especially in matters of the heart.

"There can be no deception between them, no lies," he went on. "A man must be prepared to bare his virtues and his faults to the woman he loves. Only then, after she has seen his real self, will she decide if she can accept him for the man he is. It is always the woman's decision to accept, not the man's to force upon her."

"Is that how it has always been with you and Aunt Zofia?" Arthur said. "You must keep some secrets from each other from time to time."

"Secrets and deception are different things," Al said. "Secrets can be kept to protect someone you love. Lying can only bring trouble. If there is something you know that your wife cannot, tell her this. But do not try to conceal the truth from her. This can only lead to disaster. I have seen it for myself.

When you carry a burden, do not let your pride blind you into believing you should bear it alone."

"So, you do keep secrets from each other?" Oliver said. "I thought you were against that?"

"I said I did not approve of it. But, when you have lived as long as I have, you learn sometimes it is best to keep some things hidden until the time is right."

"Why all the sudden interest in secrets?" Nathan asked Arthur good-naturedly. "What are you keeping from your wife this time?"

They laughed heartily. It was a time for celebration. Al was in an exceptionally good mood. The wedding loomed bright on the horizon. The shadow of Zofia's illness had lifted. When she'd grown well enough, it was decided Oliver would receive a minority stake in the business after the wedding. In due time, when he'd demonstrated he could manage balancing the shop and his marriage on his own, the enterprise would become his alone. Al had chosen this evening's dinner to let his nephews in on the happy plans.

❧

Later that night, Al returned home to find Zofia waiting in the sitting room knitting, listening to the delicate notes of Erik Satie playing quietly from the phonograph. He hung his hat and coat and sat beside her. For a long time, neither spoke. Both found contentment in the simple act of being in each other's presence.

"How are the boys?" she said, her eyes lowered to her knitting.

"They give their love, as always," he said. "Ollie is nervous. It is not hard to see."

"He will make a fine husband. Don't worry. He's young, but love can make a man do great things."

Al agreed. Again, they fell quiet. On the phonograph, Satie played silence as if it were another key on his piano.

"Will you be going back?"

"I don't think so," Al said. "Much is up to him now. He's gone away, but he will be back. And then…"

"You've done all that you can," she said.

"There is still more to be done. I will have to leave. I don't know when."

"I know."

"You've finished it, then?"

"I did."

"Then you know why I have to do this thing?"

"I know you believe you have to," she said. "That is enough for me. But I'm not sure he is deserving of it. I don't know if he has learned anything."

"But to do nothing," Al said. "To just condemn him…"

"Would be a sin," Zofia said. "Greater than his own. This I know."

Chapter XX

Al would have preferred the ceremony take place in the shul, as his had, and his parents' had before him. But the ever-forward sweep of time meant as people changed, and so did their traditions. The conventions of old are forgotten, replaced by the glamour of the new. Mythologies become outmoded; rituals once solemn and revered are usurped by popular fads and youthful delectations.

The chuppah, draped in white linen, Al happily noted, evoked tradition, even if nothing else about the ceremony bore any semblance to familiar customs. It stood in the shade of a line of plane trees at the edge of the wood, just in the shadow of the great Gladwyne manor.

Oliver and Ruth wished for an outdoor wedding, and the vast green of Fairmount Park was the obvious choice. But when Al informed the Felsheims that he knew of a quite unique home, a little out of the way, but no more perfect place to celebrate the union of two young, loving souls, their curiosity was piqued. Would the owner of the residence object? Of course not, Al reassured them. The man was a loyal customer and trusted friend. But could they not see the home for themselves to ensure it would be the proper venue?

"I have the complete assurance of the owner. Everything will be magnificent and as perfect as can be by the day of the ceremony," he told them. "And as his gift, he wants nothing more than to prepare all the arrangements free of charge." In the face of such generosity, the Felsheims could do nothing but happily agree.

The overwhelming beauty of the setting put any lingering doubt at ease the instant all arrived the morning of the festivities. Absolutely no expense had been spared, and by the end of the day, not one guest could remember having themselves ever attended an estate of such remarkable prestige.

Every room of the grand mansion, restored to their Renaissance-inspired glories, recalled the elegance, refinement, and luxury of another time. Rich oak, walnut, and mahogany paneling and parquetry, all polished to a deep shine, lined the walls and floors of the halls and antechambers. Ambling guests were treated to sights and aromas to arouse only the most tasteful pleasures of the senses. Gilded cornices, rococo ceilings, and towering arches put one in the frame of mind of Versailles or the Winter Palace, while bright floral and greenery arrangements recalled the images of springtime captured in the paintings of Fragonard and Winterhalter. Indeed, works by Boucher, Gainsborough, Lemoyne, and countless others hung throughout the house in all their colorful splendor. The walls of the gallery itself had been dedicated solely to images of pure love and devotion. Stollers could feast their eyes on the swinging lovers in Pierre-Auguste Cot's *Spring* or contemplate the melodious notes of Watteau's *The Love Song* while reflecting on the joyous occasion they'd come to witness.

Tall, clear windows let the brilliant light of midsummer flood through each and every room. (Glaziers brought in at tremendous expense worked tirelessly round the clock for days repairing each broken pane.) A battery of attendants ferried trays of delicacies and sumptuous morsels to delight the palate. A magnificent meal awaited the reception dinner in the main dining room, the table piled high end to end with platters of fruit, hot and cold beef, and pastries inciting whimsical fancies, while the ballroom, restored to its mirrored grandeur once again, rang with the melody of music and the grace of the dance.

The gardens, too, presented a most astounding picture of effulgence and plenty. Barren flower beds had been filled with all manner of the exotic, the rare, and the splendiferous, while the many fountains dotting the grounds flowed and bubbled with life once again. Electric lights strung through the treetops and hedgerows ensured the festivities would carry on uninterrupted well after dark.

In all, the house and gardens stood a monument to joy and life and love; a new temple erected upon the ruins of the old. A veritable snub at the face of the devil.

Al reflected on this happy juxtaposition as he stood overlooking the gardens. A festive, carnival-like atmosphere reigned. Family, friends, and no short number of complete strangers all turned out to participate in the union of Oliver and Ruth, to celebrate a most happy occasion, and to partake in their host's most gracious hospitality. Indeed, the doors of the manor had been thrown open to one and all. Along the gravel pathways snaking through the garden, children chased about in between the bushes, their shrieks of gay laughter filling the air, while the ballroom hummed with the melody of a Strauss waltz. In the central round of the gardens, young

Oliver and his new bride danced among an encircling crowd of well-wishers, while Fat Maja sat looking on, white flecks of crumble cake dusting the front of her blouse. And seated beside her, his Zofia, her bright, smiling eyes, indeed her whole body, aglow with joy.

He thought to go down to her, but then caught sight of a familiar figure seated alone on a stone bench beneath the line of trees marking the far boundary of the grounds. Leaving the din of the festivities behind, Al went to join him.

"It is many weeks since I have seen you," Al said, quietly ambling up to his friend. Even here, at the farthest end of the gardens, the faint notes of the orchestra floated like butterflies about their ears.

"There was much to be done," Etienne said and looked upon the imposing house, its high walls brought to vivid life by the sun. There was peace in his voice. "This place had never known such happiness."

"It was you who brought it here."

"I saw the ceremony," Etienne said. "It was beautiful."

"I had hoped you might. I hear many people asking after the host. They want to tell him how much they have enjoyed his home. They ask if he will be making an appearance."

"Well, it is enough to know they are pleased, I think. You'll make my excuses, won't you? It is better this way. There would be questions; always, there are questions."

For a time, they sat side by side, enjoying the serene setting, neither electing to speak. What can be said between two friends when they know their time is short?

"I've made all the arrangements," Etienne said. "You and Zofia will want for nothing."

"We have no need."

"It will be at your disposal all the same. I can think of nothing else to give."

"You have nothing to give but your reassurance that you will come back to us when this thing is done."

"That is something I cannot give," Etienne said thoughtfully. "There is little more I can do but see it through as we've planned and keep to my task."

Al nodded in agreement. They were men standing upon the precipice of a murky endeavor, their futures shrouded in a fog of calamitous ruin.

"How long do you think it will be?"

"Ten years."

"Ten years?" Al said, his heart sinking. "You are certain?"

"I am sorry. It is as near as I can place it. God willing, it will be enough time."

Chapter XXI

It is perhaps fitting that after what has been an all-too-brief interlude, I should once again put pen to paper and document the events of what I now consider to be the starting point of my life begun anew. For as surely as damnation follows sin, so does hope follow redemption, and while my past stands as a confession of my former inequities, let my future stand as a testament to the virtue of my fealty to my one true and only love.

My dearest Elena, shall I ever be truly forgiven and feel the warmth of your love and compassion once again, or is it the pride that once brought me so low the same now making me believe I should find a home by your side for all eternity? Perhaps only time will truly tell, and I press forward all the same, but renewed with hope. Not the unquenchable hope, the unrequited faith once darkening my horizons, but the hope that, though the ears of God may indeed be too big to hear the voice of just one man, His heart may yet find forgiveness for that man's transgressions and grant him safe and welcome passage back to you.

We'd set upon our task with the resolve of men borne aloft on the belief that the triumph of evil must be thwarted at every turn—that a man's failings of spirit need not spell his doom, but rather they become as the stones he builds the foundation upon which rests his own salvation.

Zofia warned us of the sure folly of our endeavor. But Albert's mind was at peace with his duty, and he would not be turned from it. The Spaniard's token had been found; the swatch of that vile bird's blood contained safe within, hidden, perhaps by the sheer grace of God alone, for centuries. My journey seemed willed to be undertaken by the fortune of its discovery. But folly indeed, for the testament of Juan Cristóbal Moreno de Zaragoza left much to be desired, and even less to be taken as gospel.

Questions remained, their answers lost to the abyss of time. Why had he chosen Genoa as his point of departure? He hadn't taken the cloth containing the droplet of blood with him through the gate, that much could be guessed. But his thoughts concealed why he'd made this decision.

"He said he was 'set free of the prison,'" Albert said. "In that case, this would suggest a door that can only be opened from the *outside*."

"Perhaps it is why he did not take it with him," I replied. "He couldn't for some reason. He was prevented?"

"The key would have done him no good once he'd left," Albert said of the bloodied swatch. "This we may never know for certain. All we do know is the devil can pass back and forth through a mirror at will. You have seen this done."

"Once. But I have also seen him pass through fire as easily as you or I might pass through water. This assures us of nothing."

"But you went with him, didn't you? He brought you with him on the night you met?"

"Only faint impressions remain with me of that time," I said. "Disjointed images. I passed through with him, but there was no art in the feat whatsoever. I observed no ritual. There was no incantation or infernal blessing. We simply walked through as one would step through an open door. After that, I remember virtually nothing."

"You wrote it down," he said. "Those pages were missing from your diary."

"Destroyed years ago," I said flatly. "Committed to fire in a fit of rage, and along with them, any memory I had of that horrid place we went to." What I could recall was useless anyway. Every time I attempted to bring those visions to mind, I became engulfed in horror. My hands would not put to paper what my brain commanded, just streams of meaningless gibberish. Perhaps that, too, was part of his plan.

"Can you remember nothing at all?"

"Only that when we returned, some time had passed. Nearly a month. I don't know how long I was there, but it is as Juan Cristóbal wrote. What felt like only minutes to me had been days, if not more."

My mentor reflected on this for some time, our joint consternation giving us over to hours of pensive meditations. If the rule of time, something Albert himself had been a student of nearly all his days, ceased to be in that infernal district, then how could Agustín have known exactly when Juan Cristóbal would have reemerged after his departure and been there to open the doorway? The puzzled furrow in his brow told me this question burned as much in his mind as my own.

"They must have conducted a trial somehow," he said after a long interlude working quietly at his desk. "A test to measure this hole in time."

❧

If I were to follow in the footsteps of Juan Cristóbal, then a test would need to be performed—an experiment to ascertain the method of entry as well as to determine with as much precision as mortal men could the structure of time in a place where it does not exist.

The Sunday next was the evening appointed for this trial. "Passage through a holy place, where evil's wicked talons dare not step, behind whose walls evil's pale stare cannot penetrate." Albert made the arrangements. He sought and received permission from the leader of his small congregation, a certain Rabbi Schulman, to have access to the temple after the conclusion of the services. Unassuming and inconspicuous, this temple, a small sanctuary located in a narrow row home, would be private and hopefully obscure our scheme. At first, the rabbi demurred, but his reluctance to appease such an unusual request dissolved with the assurance of a substantial donation offered freely and without reservation from an unknown yet thankful patron.

I sourced a mirror for our purpose from my former boudoir, a brash example of rococo extravagance, but one best suited to our needs, and paid handsomely to have it brought to the temple discreetly under cover of darkness.

Albert alone oversaw the arrival of the glass and its establishment within the sanctuary. Despite my increased tolerance to the pain, I remained outside the threshold and observed from afar. With all the art of a man orchestrating the positioning of a great masterpiece for public display, he conducted the work crew of four past the benches and around the bimah to stand the mirror along the east-facing wall.

"Why the east wall?" I said.

"I am told east is the traditional direction of prayer," he said. "I myself do not place such stock in these things, but better safe than sorry, I think."

The work complete, the workers departed, leaving only Albert and myself.

"Are you ready to begin?" he said.

I hesitated at the doorway of the temple, knowing the anguish awaiting me. But like passing through a cleansing fire, I endured the agony of my broken spirit and stepped through. The torment was almost too much to bear, but I forced myself with stoic resolve to see the thing done. Albert observed the discomfort running across my face and sought to ease my suffering.

"Think of Elena," he said. "What is this pain compared to the joy you will feel when you are with her once again? She would see you do this thing to prove yourself to her once and for all. She watches you. Stand strong, with hope in your heart. Take it with you, and you will succeed."

He pulled from his vest pocket two watches, his own and Dumont's. He'd repaired the broken chain and tuned the mechanism to perfection. Placing the faces side by side, he set them to synchroneity, kept his own, and handed me the other.

"Nine fifty-three p.m. Keep this close with you," he said, then joked dryly: "And please bring it back undamaged. It holds some sentimental value."

I could not help but chuckle, a singularly odd sensation that instantly, if only for a fraction of a second, cut through the terrible anguish oppressing my heart. We embraced, and for a moment, I felt a strange closeness to him—a closeness to humanity I had not felt in ages, separated as I was from the general light of the human soul.

The hour had arrived. I produced the egg, secreted in my pocket, and from within extracted the nefarious piece of cloth bearing the mark of evil upon it. In the upturned palm of my hand, it was such a small thing, unassuming and harmless. That it should be the key to unlocking the door to man's most mortal fears was incomprehensible.

We knew not how to unlock that door. Guided by sheer instinct, an intuition led me to believe there be only one course before us, and I raised the swatch to the glass and touched the spot to the surface. Thereupon a ripple, like that of a stone breaking the surface of a still mountain pond, spread across the face of our reflections, twisting and contorting our separate forms into one hideous mass, which then reconstituted its diverse parts, namely Albert and I, into their respective forms. However, where my mentor's reflection stood apart and whole, mine own had degenerated into that hideous absence I had once observed all those years ago, a form at once of substance yet filled with the nameless, shapeless, depthless void—the reflection of the *not* me.

"*Mein Gott,*" Albert exclaimed, stumbling over his own feet as he recoiled from the terrible vision.

"Strength, my friend," I said, catching hold of him. I pressed the swatch of cloth into his hand. "I am the only one to fear anything here." Approaching the glass, I observed my absent reflection do the same, mirroring, as it were, my own tenuous steps, a freakish mimic, curious and mocking. It might have been fascinating had not a freezing terror rising within me threatened to force the very marrow from my bones.

I looked back at Albert, whose old eyes had become wide with awe and sorrow, for only then it was, I believe, he truly comprehended the depth of my suffering. I glanced at Gerhort's watch still clutched in the palm of my hand and observed as it struck precisely ten p.m. Then turning once again to the face of my damned soul, I stepped through the portal.

Like the crushing seal of water as it flows together over the head of the drowning man, down, down, he is pulled farther from any light into the depths of cold and bitter darkness. So felt I when fully through the portal I came. The warmth of life rushed from my lungs, lungs no longer, but the absence of lungs, the absence of heart, of bone, of blood. The absence of being. The *not* being, existing forever in a place absent of all substance. The not temple, its crumbling walls, its broken benches, its shattered sanctuary lay around me. Its ceiling cracked open to the infinite blackness of a starless heaven, the barren hall once filled with song now filled only with the baleful wails and sickening cries of countless unceasing pleas. Millions of individual sobs rising as one monstrous howl into the void. I clasped my hands to my ears, but in the absence of either ears or hands, the moans of the damned poured through the emptiness of my soul and filled it with their own sorrows till it flowed over in a cascade of immortal woe.

I had to flee. I turned about, but to my terrible alarm, the portal from whence I'd come had closed and stood nothing more than a dark mirror reflecting the devastation around me. I knew not where to go. The sea of those shadows flowed before me like a mighty river, and I feared as though I would be swept away in the current and lost forever. I looked about for some other sign of another portal but found none. Only the surging, roiling mass of shades moving from place to place to place to place in a sorrowful parade, beginning nowhere, leading nowhere. And beyond the ruined walls of the temple, my eyes beheld the horrific sight of the wastes stretching out in all directions, the march of the lost and the damned progressing uninterrupted, blind, and unceasing. All around stood the ruins of man's temples, his holy houses, his mosques and synagogues, all monuments of his broken faith, like scars upon the landscape, in that reflected hell.

Had I knees to fall to, I would have collapsed in a heap before the utter horror of such a sight. I felt the last of my hope, the hope I'd brought with me through the gateway, evaporate from my spirit like the last droplet of rain on a sunbaked rock. Though I wished to resist, I felt myself surrendering to the hopelessness of those wandering souls about me when, of a sudden, a light from the portal materialized before me.

Like seeing sunlight breaking through the surface of water from its dreary depths, a brighter world shimmered into focus. I saw the interior of the sanctuary restored to its living glory, and therein, Albert, the cloth containing the devil's blood still clutched in his fingers. I wasted no time and stepped back through the door.

"*Mein Gott!*" he exclaimed upon seeing me reappear, my corporeal self miraculously restored. Tears streamed down his cheeks. His lips trembled beneath the white bristles of his mustache. He raced to me, and I opened my arms to embrace him. But, to my shock, he pushed past me and with great force tipped the mirror to the floor, shattering it to bits, sealing the unholy doorway. It was only then I noticed his haggard face and exhausted eyes.

"How is it you are so tired?" I said. "This trial has worn on you almost as much as it has worn on me. I must sit down. Why did you close the portal behind me? No matter, we can discuss it later. My God, what my eyes have beheld you cannot possibly imagine. But what we have gained cannot possibly be measured. Our endeavor was a success. Look, it has been three minutes, no more."

I showed him the face of Gerhort's watch. Its hands read 10:03 p.m. exactly.

"My friend," Albert said, shaking with disbelief. "This is not possible. You have been gone fully three whole days!"

❧

Seventy-two hours to the second, to be more precise. I begged him for details. What had happened in those three days?

"As God as my witness, I did not close the door," he said. "Once you were fully though, the dark shade of your reflection vanished with you. I could then only see my own. I touched the surface with my fingertips, expecting to pass through as you did, but it remained solid. I panicked and pressed the stain to the glass, as you had done, but nothing changed. The glass remained solid as ice. The door had been shut."

"Something we have overlooked, then?" I said.

"I tried and I tried, every few minutes, but nothing," Al said, tears coursing from his old eyes. "I thought you lost forever. Rabbi Schulman came. He was furious and demanded to be let back in. He said we had taken the shul hostage and threatened to get the police. I pleaded with him for more time, told him there would be more money. He said he would back in the morning to evict us from the temple. I didn't know what to do. I kept trying and trying. I pressed this damned cloth everywhere, the back, the corners, the frame, everywhere, but nothing worked. I'd all but given up hope. I thought to try one last time; I pressed it to the glass, and like a miracle, the door opened as it had before. I cannot explain this."

We left the temple behind and returned to the shop. Zofia looked positively horrified when she saw her husband's state: unwashed, unshaven, and ambling about as if in a fog. Her chastisements came fast and furious, nor was I spared censure. In the end, she left the two of us to our work, wringing her hands in dismay and muttering to herself in her native tongue words I dare not repeat here.

"Perhaps it's to do with me," I said.

"In what way?"

"It's difficult to put into words. But the more time I spent there, the less I felt myself and the more I felt the seep of their sorrow filling me. When I found the doorway gone, I did not panic but rather sensed a sort of slipping. It was as if all feelings of hope and success of the endeavor had faded from me. Only when I felt all hope was lost, then doorway reappeared to me."

Albert considered this.

"Then maybe this answers the question of why Juan Cristóbal did not take the blood with him when he went through," he said. "If things are as you say, and that place is merely a reflection of this one, then the hope we have here is what makes the door open. If, on that side, there is no hope, then the blood would be useless. There must be someone here to hold on to that hope you lose when you leave it behind. For the Spaniard, it was Agustín. For you, it will be me."

"I cannot ask you to take on such a task," I said, my heart overburdened with guilt. "You don't know what you are saying. I don't know how long it will take to complete the journey. It may be years before I return. If I am even able to."

"You are not asking anything of me. I do this because I wish to."

※

What words could convey to him all the emotions filling my heart? How can a man whose very soul, blackened and besmirched by decades of despair, now finally come to feel once again the warmth of human love, give thanks for so selfless a promise? I think it impossible, and I fail at the task.

Arrangements needed to be made for my departure. Exiling myself in order that I might prepare for the arduous journey ahead, I determined a suitable window of opportunity based on my and Albert's findings of our trial. Ten years of mortal time to cleanse the stain from my soul and recover what was taken from me. But what will feel like only days for me will take years off my mentor's life. I cannot hope to repay in gratitude the burden he takes upon himself, nor is there any gift I could give to compare to his sacrifice.

To rebuke the vanity so saturating my soul, making it drunk with excess, let the coffers of hell be thrown open to those wiser and more deserving. Divesting myself of my fortunes, I established accounts for Albert and his family in perpetuity so they may never be in want for anything. And I sent on a sizeable contribution to the Quinualt Clinic, that it might continue the good works of my old friend Dumont. I also arranged an anonymous gift for Hanna and Martin, to ensure her and the boy's futures. This was the only thing I could think to do to repay my friend for his wisdom and his compassion.

When I learned of the planned nuptials of Albert's nephew, I felt it only proper to offer my home as the place of his union. What more fortifying sight to behold on the eve of my perilous journey than the union of two souls in love, as mine and Elena's once were and, God willing, will be again.

I watched that union this day, looking on from afar. The committing of those young souls to each other, binding them for all eternity, I could yet still see the glow of their spirits and the warmth of their passion for each other, and it brought a joy to my heart it had not felt in ages. I thought of Elena and recalled the lines of the poem I'd recited to her that happy day in the Montparnasse Cemetery, when we, too, were so alive with love and life. These words I recall again to give me strength as I prepare to pass into that place of eternal woe.

There shall be couches whence faint odors rise,
Divans like sepulchers, deep and profound;
Strange flowers that bloomed beneath diviner skies,
The deathbed of our love shall breathe around.

And guarding their last embers till the end,
Our hearts shall be the torches of the shrine.
And their two leaping flames shall fade and blend,
In the twin mirrors of your soul and mine.

And through the eve of rose and mystic blue
A beam of love shall pass from me to you,
Like a long sigh charged with a last farewell;

And later still an angel, flinging wide
The gates, shall bring to life with joyful spell
The tarnished mirrors and the flames that died.

Chapter XXII

5:04 a.m.

"Allahu 'akbar, Allahu 'akbar. Ashhadu an la ilaha illa-Allah."

The first rays of sun warmed the back of Al's neck as they cascaded over him, around him, glistening against the face of the mirror like the flashes of a thousand cameras all going off at once: each capturing the look of wonder and awe gracing the old man's face.

It was as if Nature herself had reversed her flow. Whereas a man walking from the dark recesses of a cave might become more recognizable as he emerges into the light of day, so did this form seem to do the very opposite. Emerging from the light, its shape grew darker and darker still, until standing beside Al's own reflection, it materialized in the shape of a man—a man without features or substance, what might rightly be called the absence of a man, merely the shade of a man, a hole in space where a man might be, but distinctly was not. Beside Al in the courtyard, not a soul could be found save his own.

Then, like a bubble gradually rising up from the darkest depths of the deep, this absence of a person took a step forward, then another, silently approaching the face of the mirror from within until, with a final, almost measured stride, he stepped over the lower half of the gilded frame like a threshold and broke through its surface into true light of day.

Before Al stood the Frenchman.

The old watchmaker stumbled back, speechless with joy and disbelief, his eyes welling with tears, his promise finally fulfilled. The two embraced. Al patted his back, his arms, his chest, to make sure he was truly real. Etienne could only smile. But this smile waned as he observed the weathered face that greeted him.

"So old, my friend," he said. "The years have been unkind to you."

"It was a long time to wait," Al said, touching Etienne's cheek. "But you? So young yet. It is as if you never left at all."

It was true. Etienne still bore the youthful look of a man no more than twenty-five; the travails of his soul's journey had left no scars upon his corporeal self. His intense blue-green eyes still shone with the fiery intensity Al remembered, though he knew him to be only a mere ten years his junior.

"Have you got it?" Al said. Etienne smiled again, reaching two fingers into his vest pocket and procuring from it the object of all his misery, and now the sole key to his salvation, a single French centime. Al quietly marveled at the brilliant yet wholly ordinary-looking coin as if he were viewing the most valuable object in all the universe. His eyes welled up anew at the sight of it.

"Zofia?" Etienne asked, scanning the courtyard for any sight of her. Al closed his teary eyes, lowering his head in quiet reverence.

"I am so sorry, my friend."

"It is all right," Al said, shaking off his momentary melancholy.

"When?"

"Two years ago. But she never gave up hope that we would succeed."

"I asked too much of you," Etienne said ruefully, his own eyes grown damp. "From both of you."

Al shook his head, taking his friend's hand in his own.

"It was her time," he said. "She understood. In the end, she understood everything. You were always in her thoughts these past years."

The two paused, their gazes falling to the coin lying in Etienne's palm, each silently wishing there could be more time, each knowing there was none left.

"I must go," Etienne said.

They worked quickly now, with purpose and frightful determination. Time, unstoppable time, inescapable time, marched on. The two men approached the great mirror, that freakish doorway, and, each taking a side, with tremendous effort, tilted it forward till it fell to the stone with a colossal crash, disintegrating into thousands of shimmering shards. They gazed upon the shattered ruins of the looking glass—its once marvelous, gilded frame now cracked like the hull of a ship cast upon the rocks.

"He will come looking for me," Etienne said. "He may even come find you."

"What can he do?" Al joked. "I am just an old tinker. Remember, time has always been on my side."

Etienne smiled and laid a hand on Al's shoulder.

"All I have given you remains yours to do with as you wish. Use it well."

Al held up the little yellowed swatch of cloth still clutched in his fingertips and placed it back into its brass coffin. Then Etienne nestled his centime in beside it. These treasures secured, together they sealed the box with a click. Al handed it to his friend, along with the key.

"This that I have made, I return to you. You know the combination to unlock it, don't you?"

"I have already forgotten, my friend. And I hope to never remember."

Their task complete, they again embraced for a final goodbye.

"Where will you go?" Al said, but Etienne gave no reply. Al knew he couldn't. He only smiled one last time, and Al witnessed within his companion's deep, serious eyes a calm he had not seen before. Though this look lasted only a moment, therein passed between them the knowledge of two entire lifetimes, one of great joy and peace, the other of great horror and hope.

Then, with all their words spent, and time drawing to its close, the Frenchman turned and fled the courtyard of the great Umayyad Mosque through the western gate, into the shadows of the city, and out of Al's sight forever.

Epilogue

Philadelphia, 1937

"This is a shop most charming," he said as he looked about the little showroom. "And what a fine bon mot with which to adorn your window."

The gentleman had sauntered casually into the shop with all the pride of the peacock. A finely tailored suit clothed him in opulence. In one gloved hand, he bore a crooked ebony cane.

"I wonder if perhaps you haven't got a touch of the poet in you?"

"An appreciation my uncle helped me to develop," Oliver said from behind the display counter. "How may I help you?"

"Is the owner here? Might I speak with him?"

"You are speaking with him. This is my shop."

The gentleman cocked his head slightly and cast an inquisitive glance through sickly blue eyes.

"Then Mr. Valentine is deceased?"

"This past winter, yes."

"A dreadful pity," the odd man said. "But perhaps you can assist me. It has come to my attention that an item once in my possession, misplaced some time ago, passed through this shop recently. Mr. Valentine, in turn, passed the item on to another individual who now possesses it. It brings me no small amount of dismay to learn of his passing, but perhaps he told you something of this item? It was quite a rare and beautiful heirloom—a timepiece encased in a golden orb."

Oliver smiled, and bid the man wait. A moment later, he reappeared with a small wooden box. Placing it on the display counter, he opened it and unwrapped Gerhort's egg.

"He told me you might come for it one day, and that I should keep it safe for you," Oliver said.

The strange gentleman's eyes lit like fires, and his bony fingers twitched anxiously. Fairly chirping with glee, he opened the lid and stared into the empty well of the sphere. Instantly, the brightness in his evil eyes dimmed and flickered out into a dull blankness when he beheld its contents: a solitary copper penny.

www.ingramcontent.com/pod-product-compliance
Lightning Source LLC
Chambersburg PA
CBHW070305310726
48976CB00005B/1574